SNOWY DAY AND OTHER STORIES

ALSO BY LEE CHANG-DONG

소지(燒 紙)

Burning Paper

(Munhakgwajiseongsa, 1987)

녹천에는 똥이 많다

There's a Lot of Shit in Nokcheon

(Munhakgwajiseongsa, 1992)

SNOWY DAY AND OTHER STORIES

Lee Chang-dong

Translated by Heinz Insu Fenkl
and Yoosup Chang

PENGUIN PRESS

NEW YORK

2025

PENGUIN PRESS
An imprint of Penguin Random House LLC
1745 Broadway, New York, NY 10019
penguinrandomhouse.com

PP colophon is a registered trademark of Penguin Random House LLC.

Book design by Daniel Lagin

LIBRARY OF CONGRESS CATALOGING-IN-PUBLICATION DATA
Names: Yi, Ch'ang-dong, author. | Fenkl, Heinz Insu, 1960– translator. |
Chang, Yoosup, translator.
Title: Snowy day and other stories / Lee Chang-dong ;
Heinz Insu Fenkl and Yoosup Chang, transl.
Description: New York : Penguin Press, 2025. | Identifiers: LCCN 2024019945 |
ISBN 9780593657256 (hardcover) | ISBN 9780593657263 (ebook)
Subjects: LCSH: Yi, Ch'ang-dong—Translations into English. | LCGFT: Short stories.
Classification: LCC PL992.9.C3335 S66 2025 | DDC 895.73/4—dc23/eng/20240801
LC record available at https://lccn.loc.gov/2024019945

"Snowy Day" previously appeared in *The New Yorker*.

Printed in the United States of America
1st Printing

The authorized representative in the EU for product safety and compliance is
Penguin Random House Ireland, Morrison Chambers, 32 Nassau Street,
Dublin D02 YH68, Ireland, https://eu-contact.penguin.ie.

CONTENTS

AUTHOR'S NOTE

Rereading these stories for the first time in a very long time, my heart ached as if I were reading an old diary. It's because the short stories I wrote in this collection are based on my actual experiences in those days, or they're about my family, friends, or people close to me—and some were even written just as they happened, with very little fictionalizing.

Three years before I published my first short story, "War Trophy," many hundreds of citizens resisting a military coup were massacred in Korea. That national crime was kept secret for years under strict media control. *To write poetry after Auschwitz is barbaric.* I had just begun my life as a writer, but those words of Theodor Adorno's became a proposition that I could not deny. And yet I still had to write. What role can a line of writing play in changing reality? Even as I asked myself such questions, I had to write my stories as a way to avoid escaping reality. And now that I'm rereading these words, it seems I can feel the air of the streets of those days mixed with the exhaust fumes and tear gas that stung my eyes; and the damp smell around Nokcheon Station, which was under construction then, seems to come back to me with the chronic pain–like anger that weighed on my young heart and a burning thirst whose object I did not know.

It's been nearly forty years since then. Korean society has changed profoundly, and the world itself has also changed. At the time, I could not have imagined the world as it is now, or even that I would be making movies the way I am today. But even now, as I am making films, I am still questioning the meaning of what I do and how my films relate to reality. How much distance is there between movies and reality? When people are angry and despairing over the pain of reality, what can movies do for them? In that respect, I could say that who I am today is not much different from the person I was when I wrote these stories.

Now the stories in this volume have reached new readers across a long span of time and a vast distance, and they are coming to life again in the present. I am truly grateful to everyone who created such an opportunity. First of all, I would like to thank John Burnham Schwartz and Helen Rouner of Penguin Random House. I would also like to thank Jin Auh of The Wylie Agency. And I would like to express my heartfelt gratitude to Heinz Insu Fenkl and Yoosup Chang, the two translators of this collection. Heinz Insu, who is an excellent novelist himself, played a decisive role in bringing this volume together. Finally, more than anyone else, I would like to express my sincere gratitude to the readers who will read this book with an open mind.

Lee Chang-dong

TRANSLATOR'S NOTE

I first started translating Lee Chang-dong late in the summer of 1984, a few days after I arrived in Seoul to begin my Fulbright fellowship at a time when terms like "Hallyu" and "K-Wave" didn't yet exist. I had read a short story by Lee the previous year in a literary journal that came free of charge with the Korean women's magazine my mother often bought at the local Korean market in Marina, California. I still have those first several pages of translation notes neatly printed in technical pen, dated September 3.

What struck me about the story—and I remember this very clearly—was how its imagery seemed to transcend the words that conveyed it. There was a visceral quality to the scenes that outlasted my memory of the words. I held the images of that story in my mind permanently—like the memory of a good film.

When I first saw the film *Oasis* in 2004, I felt an immediate familiarity. It was as if the camera were my own consciousness playing memories back at me. In the opening scenes, when Jong-du, freezing in his Hawaiian shirt, does something as simple as eat the brick of tofu (a traditional ritual after release from prison), I felt tears well up in my eyes. He was just like a cousin of mine. The particulars of the world he lived in—down to specific camera angles—were those I remembered from my own life, and the use of illumination—from the mundane scenes to the fantasy sequences—also felt oddly familiar to me. I did not realize that Lee Chang-dong was the director until I watched the DVD for the second time.

Even as it generated a great deal of controversy after its release in 2002, *Oasis* won numerous international awards. Lee had established himself as a significant force in the world of film, a director whom many now consider Korea's best. I think that for Koreans, *Oasis* was, in an ironic way, too familiar, too close to home. It was a brutally realistic depiction of a part of Korean society that many found embarrassing and dissonant. But for those who stayed with it, *Oasis* also offered a kind of transcendent release by its conclusion. This was not only due to the power of its characterizations and the underlying moral consciousness; much of the film's force came from the technique behind its cinematography, which I found to be already present back in the early 1980s in the language of Lee's short stories.

Recently, I dug up my old translation notes and the original text once again. The magazine itself was badly yellowed, the cheap paper having decomposed and gone brittle in the intervening forty years. I found the story and the author interview, and there he was, Lee Chang-dong, looking oddly feral in his puffy coat, posed in front of a painting of tigers, looking more like a future political prisoner than a future auteur. I remembered that when I went to my first meeting with an official at the Korean Culture and Arts Foundation, ready with the list of writers I wanted to translate during my Fulbright, he had crossed out most of them with a terse remark that my fellowship would be rescinded if I worked on any of them. (One of the writers on that list would later be imprisoned.) I thought it better not to show that official my initial attempt at translating a story by Lee.

I grew up in Korea in the 1960s and early 1970s under the regime of the dictator Park Chung Hee, and I lived there once again for a year in the mid-1980s during the volatile period that followed the Gwangju massacre, while another military dictator, Chun Doo-Hwan, was still very much in power. Now, as a professor who teaches both literature and creative writing, I find myself having to remind my students that in many places, literary writing is still an endeavor with potentially life-threatening consequences. Until very recently, that was the case for serious writers in Korea, who risked prison sentences for themselves, their relatives, their editors, and their publishers. The stories in this volume come from experiences that most Americans will neither have to endure, see, nor hear about in our new bubble of digital isolation-ism. They are masterful, deeply felt, and come to us when we are ex-periencing our own volatile times.

If Hallyu is the Korean Wave, then the stories in this collection are the ocean from which that wave emerges. It is the ocean of history, its depths full of tragedy, oppression, hope, and redemption—all the un-comfortable reality that made Korea's current global economic and cultural power possible. To write about it involved great personal risk and vulnerability.

When asked about his short stories, Lee once said, "I always wrote for one person, for this person who thought and felt the same way as I do. It almost felt like I was writing a love letter to this very specific person who would understand what I'm writing and share the same feelings and thoughts." My fellow translator, Yoosup Chang, and I have received that letter in our hearts, and I hope that you will, too.

Heinz Insu Fenkl

SNOWY DAY AND OTHER STORIES

SNOWY DAY

THE GUARD ON DUTY BLOCKED THE WOMAN WITH HIS M16. She was slender, one shoulder slanted down as if the suitcase she carried in her hand were too heavy for her. As she spoke to him, the steam of her breath rose up in the cold air.

The window of the guard post, which stood like a little tower at the entrance to the base, snapped open. "Hey, what's she saying?" a staff sergeant called out. "Send her in."

The staff sergeant wore his winter cap mashed flat on his head. "What brings you here?" he asked when the woman came closer.

"I came to visit Private Kim. Kim Young-min."

"What unit is he with?"

"I'm not sure," she said. "I wouldn't know that sort of thing. I just know he's here." The woman's face was red from walking so far in the cold. She automatically covered her mouth with her white-gloved hand when she spoke.

"Miss, we can't find him with just that. You've got to know exactly what unit he's in." Another man, whose head had been hidden in the

3

opening of the rusty stove he was lighting, stood up, stretching his back. He was a sergeant, but with his long, soot-stained nose he looked so comical the woman had to suppress a laugh.

"Can't you figure it out?" she said. "You're in the same company. He's tall. He's got a slim face, and his eyelids have a double fold."

The sergeant and the staff sergeant looked at each other as if they were holding back their own laughter. "And what's his relationship to you?" the sergeant asked with an amused smile.

The woman didn't answer. Her hand still covering her mouth, she suddenly turned away, her smile gone cold. The parade ground behind the guard post was pure white, blanketed in snow. The whole way up there, she'd worried that she would miss the snow. Sunbeams shone like spikes of ice above the parade ground, and the barracks beyond were buried in the deep shadow of the mountains—the division between light and dark seemed especially sharp. The tops of pine trees pierced the dark silhouette of the mountains in the low sunlight, glinting like bayonets affixed to rifle barrels.

"Well, since you came all this way looking for him I'll make a special effort," the sergeant said.

The woman said thank-you so softly that he could barely hear her.

The sergeant lifted the handset of the field telephone, and while he cranked out a signal the staff sergeant flung open the visitor log.

"What's your name, miss?"

"Lee Young-sook."

"And your address?"

"Seoul."

"Your home is all of Seoul?" the sergeant holding the handset said sarcastically.

"It's Guro-dong, Guro-gu."

"Wow, you're from a nice neighborhood," the sergeant said.

"House number?"

"Twenty-sixth *tong*, fourth *ban*, number 169."

"Your occupation?"

The woman's white-gloved hand went back up to her mouth.

She hesitated with the answer, her lips purple from the cold. The staff sergeant tapped on the window ledge with a ballpoint pen.

"You don't have a job?"

"I'm a factory worker."

"Excuse me?"

"Factory worker. I work in a factory."

The two soldiers exchanged looks again and laughed silently.

"What's with 'factory worker'? How about the more elegant 'office worker'?" It was the sergeant again. The signal must have gone through just then, because he began yelling into the handset, but the reception was bad and he'd purse his lips, whistle a couple of times, and start yelling again.

"I said *Kim. Young. Min! Private!* What?" His expression suddenly hardened. "You're sure the guy's name is Kim Young-min? *Goddammit!*"

The sergeant covered the handset with his palm and glanced toward the staff sergeant. The two huddled in a corner and whispered to each other. Now the staff sergeant took the handset, his expression noticeably tense. The woman watched them nervously, and when her eyes met those of the sergeant, who was staring straight at her, she looked away.

The long military road that had brought her there stretched out between the snow-covered fields, its tail hidden behind the saddle of the mountain. She realized that she hadn't once given a thought to how she would travel back on that road. For now, it seemed too distant to be real.

Beside the guardhouse, with its label designating the post number, stood large signs with slogans like CRUSH THEM FROM THE START! and EXTERMINATE COMMUNISM! She noticed long rolls of barbed wire strung along the perimeter of the base, the distant barracks, the vast, snow-covered parade ground pierced by cold sunbeams. Everything seemed wrapped in a blanket of stillness. But for some reason she felt in danger, as if she were standing on ice that was about to crack, and her entire body shook with this unknowable fear.

Suddenly, he's awake. And once he's awake—though it's obvious—he realizes that he is a soldier, a private in the Army, and that right now he is on night guard duty.

HE MUST HAVE NODDED OFF, STANDING, WITH HIS M16 SLUNG CROOK-edly over his shoulder. He is shivering. His knees and teeth, especially—which have been chattering since the start of his shift—are shaking nonstop.

He opens his eyes wide. Except for the occasional sound of wind, it is dead quiet in all directions. Darkness lies before him, and a few steps into that darkness there is barbed wire, and beyond the barbed wire an even thicker darkness. Though the landscape is never-changing, he senses that there has been a change. Only after something cold and wet hits the tip of his nose does he realize what it is. Snow. Snow is falling, and gradually lighting the darkness.

He looks back at the guard post quite a distance away. His co-worker is in that guardhouse, but there's no indication of whether or not he knows it's snowing. He may have fallen asleep with his butt seated on his steel helmet.

"Hey! Stay alert. If you see the patrol, challenge him. Loudly!" That's what his colleague had said at the start of their shift, before crawling into the guardhouse. When a superior says something like that, it usually means he intends to relax, get some shut-eye. He himself is a private, and his superior is a corporal. Suddenly he wants to get the corporal and shout out to him that it's snowing.

But, immediately, the private regrets it. Because he knows there's no way the corporal will enjoy the snow as much as he does. And now the corporal is coming out of the guardhouse, flustered, as if he'd been asleep on his helmet, just as the private thought.

"What? What's the matter?"

"It's snowing," the private says.

"*What?*"

"Snow. It's the first snow of the season."

"Fucking *idiot*! You scared me! This the first time you seen snow, dumbass?"

It's been six months since the private started his military service, but there's a lot he still cannot understand. For instance, until now he would never, ever have imagined that he'd be treated like an idiot because he was happy to see snow falling.

"How long's it been?" the corporal asks. "The time, I mean."

The private digs out his wristwatch from inside his thick, Arctic uniform sleeve and holds it right up to his eyes.

"Thirty . . . No, forty minutes."

"*Shee-it.* Every minute feels like a fucking year."

The corporal spits through his teeth. It's rare that every other word out of his mouth isn't an obscenity. But through his unique use of tone and inflection he has a way of making it sound like he isn't swearing at all. There's a tradition of cursing in the military, and the corporal has a mastery of military conventions beyond his years. The private knows that the corporal is actually four years younger than he is—the corporal started his military service early because of a government registration error. His eyes are prematurely old, but apart from that the corporal still has the face of a kid.

Compared with the corporal, the private is utterly inept at picking up military traditions. For a while, after he was called up and his head was buzzed, he couldn't even state his name and rank properly. Whenever the drill instructor jabbed him in the belly at roll call and said, "*You!*" he knew he was supposed to yell at the top of his lungs: "*Yes, sir! Trainee! Kim! Yo-ung! Mee-in!*" But he couldn't. It all felt like a ridiculous play to him and, like a self-conscious actor with no talent, he just could not perform his role convincingly. He had even tried to duck his military service. But no one gave a damn about something as trivial as his self-consciousness. He was punished—his toes braced on his bed and his melon head pushed against the cement floor of the barracks—until he could properly state his name and rank.

"*Motherf—!*" the corporal says, his head thrown back to watch the thickening snowflakes. "Looks like we gonna be stuck on snow removal all morning tomorrow."

Tomorrow is Sunday. How sad, the private thinks, to be concerned only about tomorrow, having to be on snow detail, when he could be appreciating the snow falling right now. But the private envies the corporal, who knows how to think and feel like a soldier, and sometimes he feels inferior.

"Corporal Choi . . ." he says. Better to talk than to just let his jaw tremble in the cold. "What did you do back home? If I may inquire."

"If you *may inquire?* You sure like using those pretty words. You think I don't know you went to college?" The corporal shoves his face close and, in a soft and intimate voice, he says, "I guess the Army *does* have its perks, huh? I mean, out in the world, how could you be acting like this in front of someone like me?"

The corporal is smiling, his teeth bared, but the private doesn't dare smile along. If there's one thing he's learned thus far, it's that he has to be cautious when a superior behaves erratically like this.

"The Army is truly fair, if you think about it," the corporal says. "See, in the Army, how many mess-hall trays you rack up tells you everything you need to know. What could be fairer, see? I just can't understand assholes who say Army life is hard. When I was a civilian I never got more than four hours of sleep a night. But here—not even counting when I'm on duty—I get at least six. And, even if the sky were to split in two, have you ever not had three squares a day?" He pauses for a moment, and when he continues it sounds like he's spitting. "You *really* want to know? I worked in a *bathhouse*."

"A *bathhouse*? What kind of work do you do in a bathhouse?"

"Fucking moron, you think you wear a necktie and do office work in a bathhouse?"

The corporal is silent after that, and for a short while all that can be heard is the sound of their footsteps in the snow. He must be angry, the private thinks. Maybe he regrets flapping his jaw a bit too much in front of a newbie.

"Hey, how long's it been?" the corporal asks after a while, his voice hoarse.

The private looks at his watch. Everything seems noticeably brighter now because of the snow.

"It's been thirty minutes."

"Fucking *son*ofabitch!"

It takes the private a moment to realize what's wrong.

"Didn't you say *forty* minutes before?"

"I'm sorry. It's just so dark. . . ."

"Get over here, you little shit."

He steps forward, approaching the corporal, whose eyes are shining in the dark like those of some animal.

"Are you making fun of a superior, punk? If forty minutes went by just a little while ago, and now it's only thirty, how many minutes did I just lose because of you?"

"I'm not—I just . . . read the watch wrong because it's dark."

"No excuses! In the Army, ten minutes is enough to have a quick fuck and still have time left over to eat a bowl of ramen. You understand?"

The corporal looks barely old enough to have finished high school, so it's doubtful that he's ever even had a "quick fuck." But he continues, in a commanding tone: "You will now commence taking responsibility for the ten minutes that Army Corporal Choi has unjustly lost. Is that clear?"

When the private is silent, the corporal's voice grows louder.

"Why aren't you answering? Did you just laugh at me?"

"How am I supposed to take responsibility?"

"Tell me a good story. So good we don't even notice the time going by."

"But . . . I don't know how to tell stories."

"What are you talking about, punk? You had a taste of college, so you must know lots of stuff. Talk about your love life out in the world."

"I never dated."

"Would you look at this punk? No fighting spirit. Assume the position, you little shit."

Still wearing his helmet, the private crouches, bends over, and plants his head on the ground, the cold snow digging into the nape of his neck. There's a thought he has whenever something like this happens: This is just a play. That bastard is playing the role of a corporal, and he himself is playing a private. But he has absolutely no aptitude for playacting.

He thinks about how puny and foolish a being he is. If there's anything he's learned by coming to the military, it is that. It's as if the enormous machine called the military existed to teach precisely this lesson, and men like his commanding officer—and even his peers, like Corporal Choi—are conspirators faithfully executing their mission to that end.

During basic training, he often suffered because he had to pee at night. Maybe it was because he was tense. He had to wake up five, six times a night to pee, but, according to regulations, you couldn't just run to the latrine whenever you had to go. Trainees were required to leave their quarters in groups of three. Once, he'd awakened before dawn with an unbearable urge to pee, but he could not bring himself to wake the guys who were fast asleep at his side. The night watch would not let him go to the latrine alone, and after a long ordeal, clutching his swollen balloon of a bladder, he had no choice but to rouse his neighbors. But they got angry and refused to get up. When it got to the point where the urine was about to dribble out, he crawled back onto the sleeping platform. He took out his canteen, covered up with a blanket, lay down. And, in the darkness under the blanket, he pissed into the canteen, grinding his teeth in agony. Feeling the weight and heat of the canteen in his hands, he realized that he no longer had anything left into which he could relieve himself. At roll call that night, the officer on duty inspected their canteens, of all things. While his was being opened, he prayed that the duty officer's nose was stuffed up, but the officer was not congested, and when he flipped the canteen upside down and poured out its contents, anyone would have realized that what fell to the floor of the barracks was not water but urine. He wasn't able to come up with a plausible explanation for why his canteen was filled with piss. That was when they started treating him— almost officially—like an idiot.

....

"HEY, PUNK! ON YOUR FEET!"

Suddenly, the corporal pulls him by the arm, whispering sharply. Then, still bent at the waist, he skitters like a squirrel to hide behind a boulder. The private awkwardly follows behind the corporal, peering into the darkness, where he's already in a perfect sitting position, ready to open fire.

"Hands up!"

"Hey, it's just me," a voice says.

A dark human silhouette is visible among the bushes on the hill that rises up from the barracks. From the sound of the voice, it's probably the staff sergeant on patrol. But the corporal doesn't care and yells loudly once again.

"Hands up!"

"Damn it! I said it's *me*. Patrol."

Because of the snow and the cold, the patrol probably just wants to do a quick lap and go crawl back under his blanket again. But the sharp and rather unpleasant sound of metal scraping metal that follows stops him in his tracks. The corporal has worked the charging handle on his M16, chambering a round. The patrol abruptly raises his arms.

"About face."

The corporal's voice isn't very loud, but it has authority behind it. Even as he grumbles, the patrol, arms half-raised, can only meekly obey.

"Hotel."

"Pillow."

"Who are you?"

"Patrol."

"Your business?"

"*Patro-ol.*"

The corporal asks the questions one after another, according to regulations, his tone very serious. He seems like a kid carried away with playing war, and the private shudders with trepidation.

"About face! Three steps forward toward the sentry."

The patrol steps closer, and the corporal finally lowers his rifle and salutes smartly.

"*Loyal-ty!* All quiet during duty."

"Good, good. Very sharp. Who's the other guy?"

The private steps forward, answering with a barely audible mumble.

"It's the college boy! Did you remember to bring your weapon today?" the patrol asks with a sideways glance.

The private feels the familiar humiliation but remains silent. He knows full well that when people call him "college boy" they mean the opposite.

On his first day of guard duty as a private, he'd come out to the post and left his rifle behind in the barracks. What made it worse was that he hadn't even realized he'd done so until he was caught by the patrol. It was his first time on guard duty and he was terribly nervous, but how he could forget the all-important rifle even he could not comprehend. After that, they all called him "college boy" instead of "dimwit," and he guessed that between the two labels there was a hierarchy more complicated than a simple degree of humiliation.

The patrol looks around the guard post once. With nothing else to do, he tosses out a few words, as if he feels guilty having to go back without accomplishing anything. "Do a good job," he says. "Who knows, maybe you'll even make the papers and they'll reward you with a leave."

"Damn—what are you gonna find? It's not like we're gonna catch a seal up here in the mountains."

"What's with a seal? If you're lucky, maybe some bug-eyed mutt will come by—in a *low crawl*." The staff sergeant snickers as he walks back down the hill.

Not long ago, there had been an incident at a base on the coast. A soldier on night watch discovered a mysterious form crawling up the beach. He gave the command to halt, but the dark shape continued to advance, so he opened fire. It turned out that the creature was just a seal. The story was that the lucky soldier who shot it was granted a leave in recognition of his exemplary night tactics and "one shot, one kill" marksmanship. They'd read that story in a newsletter and—just last night—had had to listen to the unit commander lecture them on the need to be especially alert on nighttime guard duty. He'd used that lucky soldier as a motivational example.

"Do you know what it feels like when someone holds his hands up in front of my sights?" the corporal blurts after the staff sergeant has disappeared into the darkness. With a flourish, he pops the magazine out, unchambers the seated cartridge, and slaps the magazine back in. "I just wanna waste him."

The private is instantly chilled—he knows that the corporal isn't joking. He shoulders his rifle more tightly and its hard stock digs into his side.

The trigger—as the marksmanship instructor always said in basic training—needs to be squeezed gently, like your girlfriend's tit. But the private never understood the comparison between the particular coldness of a metal trigger and a girl's breast. . . . It's like that with everything for him, but he's especially bad at marksmanship, so bad that he hasn't qualified on the range even once since he began his military service.

Which is why, to this day, he has never been allowed to go on leave. Every time his turn came around, his name was left off the roster. After three or four such occurrences, he went to see the company commander.

The CO was the sort of man who never took off his hat and sat ramrod straight at his desk, as if he were under inspection. When the private told the CO that he wanted to know why his name was left off the order logs for leave, the reply was "That's obvious. You can't go out on leave."

The CO did not open his mouth again. He just glared up from under the low bill of his cap, his eyes slits.

After a long moment, the private asked, "Sir, may I know the reason?"

"You failed to qualify in marksmanship. You fail marksmanship, you can't leave the base. That's my policy."

He had no choice but to retreat then. But he could never qualify in marksmanship, so, as expected, he was left off the next list as well. Once again, he went to see the company commander, but this time—because the CO was extremely annoyed—he was literally kicked out, his shins left black and blue. And yet he still tirelessly went back to the CO every time a new list was posted.

"I just cannot qualify in marksmanship, sir. My eyes are terrible."

"Then why don't you get glasses?"

"Sir, to get fitted for glasses I need to leave the base."

"Then qualify in marksmanship!"

He knew it was reckless, perhaps laughable, but he could not give up his protest. He himself had no idea why, even as he was engaged in the act. Kicked in the shins, threatened with a stint in the stockade for insubordination, yet still he doggedly sought out the CO

"Are you *protesting* against me?" the CO said at some point, exasperated. "A *demonstration*—is that it? It must be second nature for you."

In the end, the private couldn't tell whether he refused to give up on this reckless and foolish behavior in order to prove that he wasn't an idiot, or because he *was* an idiot. Eventually, he even became afraid that the CO might actually grant him the leave.

"Hey! How many minutes?" the corporal shouts.

Once again, the private makes an effort to look at his watch.

"Now . . . it's been an hour and ten minutes."

"So how many minutes left?"

"Around fifty minutes."

"Ugh, this is unbearable. Un-fucking-bearable," the corporal says in a voice that sounds like chattering teeth. The private looks up at the countless snowflakes disintegrating into the empty air. The sky, the barracks on the far side of the hill, the hills and fields scattered all over the country aren't visible; the only things he can see now are snow and barbed wire. There's nothing left in the world but barbed wire. Funny—that's what they're guarding. The barbed wire.

"Corporal Choi, where is your home?"

"What? *Home?*" The bastard answers in a loud voice, as if he'd never heard that word before.

The two of them are stamping their feet, walking in place without rest. It's partly because their feet are cold, but, also, if they stopped moving even for a moment their ankles would be buried in snow. After a long while, the corporal opens his mouth again.

"Fuck, you're just full of useless questions, aren't you? Our place is on top of the mountain in Sadang-dong, in Seoul. Quite a sight. Couldn't afford shit, but we were a big litter in a house the size of an apple crate. Family of six, crawling all over each other.

"Hey, you know who I hate the most in this world?" the corporal asks suddenly. "It's my old man. Day in, day out, he comes home after getting shit-faced and beats us kids like it was his job. The old lady's a real piece of work, too, calling that man a husband, playing dead like a mouse in front of a cat—not a squeak. Truly pathetic. So, the second person I hate most in the world? None other than her." The corporal forcefully kicks the snow under his feet.

Out of nowhere, the private feels a strange urge to console him. The corporal is glowing, his eyes like a beast's, but his voice is a young child's, starving for something. Under the falling snow, the private feels as if the two of them were the sole survivors of a shipwreck, clinging to a rotten plank in a vast ocean.

"How is it that you've only learned to resent the world?" Those were the words of his adviser in college. Of all the things he'd said, that was what pierced the private's heart and, for some reason, felt more insulting than anything else.

He looks at the corporal and thinks, *How is it that you've only learned to resent the world?*

A MONTH AGO, WHILE WASHING THE DISHES IN AN ICY CREEK FLOWING next to the barracks, the private received a message to come quickly to HQ. He was being ordered to ready himself for leave immediately and to report to the company commander. He ran to his quarters, taking off the rubber gloves that had frozen stiff on his hands, confused about what was going on.

When he stepped into the unit's admin office, the CO handed him a sheet of paper. It was a letter notifying him that his father had passed away. "Three nights, four days special leave," he said. "Starting today."

As the private was about to leave, the CO called out to stop him. "You! You wouldn't be planning on going AWOL, would you?"

He did not answer. He had to change long-distance buses twice and go through four checkpoints to get to Seoul, and by the time he got off the night train, in Busan, it was dawn. When he entered his house for the first time in more than half a year, his brother was wearing a hempen funerary hat, his face blank. He seemed to have aged to the point where you could no longer tell how old he was, and their mother just lay there facing the wall. It all felt surreal to the private. His brother crossed the narrow room to move the folding screen that stood there a bit precariously and told him to look behind it. He lifted the end of the thin shroud and saw the face of the corpse.

"He started drinking a lot after you entered the service," his brother said behind him, his voice hoarse and faltering. "You know he had to avoid alcohol because of his blood pressure. One day, he came home after drinking a ton, and then he just couldn't get up. We didn't even have time to do anything." It sounded like he was making excuses.

His father was an elementary school vice principal put out to pasture in the countryside, waiting for retirement. When the private had come home from university, wanted by the law for avoiding military service, his father had held him by his side and called the police himself. He was handcuffed in front of his father, and fifteen days later he was sent off to basic training.

IT WAS A THREE-DAY FUNERAL, BUT TWO DAYS HAD ALREADY PASSED by the time he arrived. They buried his father the next day on a hillside outside town, among countless other grave mounds that swelled up from the earth like large, scabby boils. The day before returning to the base, he went to Seoul. As always, the air at the entrance to the university campus was filled with tear gas from the riot police quelling the constant student demonstrations. Familiar faces gathered to greet him; their throats were hoarse, and they were enjoying their debates, as usual. And no one got drunk as quickly as he did. Seeing his old friends, he felt a combination of envy and betrayal, the way a child does after experiencing something he shouldn't have. When they sang the familiar songs, he was silent, and when they finished he started singing alone. *The match girl who works in a match factory in Incheon . . .* It was what he'd sung during basic training, a song that taught the soldiers how becoming shameless helps one forget the pain. He raised his voice especially at the part where the girl's pubic hair gets burned off as she tries to smuggle a matchbox under her skirt, but when he came to the end there was no one left beside him. He returned to base a day earlier than the date printed on his pass.

"Want to hear a funny story?" The corporal seems talkative now, for some reason. Thick snowflakes are beginning to pour down. The corporal tilts his head back to look up at the sky.

"I told you before that I worked in a bathhouse, right? I'm at some bathhouse in Miari at ten o'clock at night after we finished all our work, and the owner lady calls me over. She's a widow who lives by herself—doesn't know where to spend her money. When I go in and see her laying there stark naked next to the tub, I can't breathe. She's a real heavyweight, must weigh more than a hundred kilos. Well, the bitch says to me—laying there—'Mister Choi, come here and scrub my back.'" He mimics the woman's nasal tone perfectly.

"You know what I did? As I gently scrubbed her back, I politely told her something: 'Lady, you'd be an eyeful hung up like this at a butcher shop.' Then the bitch starts screaming at me. Her eyes are bugging and she's calling me an idiot that doesn't know his place, and says how I'm talking shit. Before I knew it, I was strangling her. She flailed around at first, then her eyes rolled back in her head. I guess if I'd applied a bit more pressure she woulda been a goner. I packed my bags and left right away. But you know what? After that, that feeling of grabbing her fatty flesh with my hands—it wouldn't go away. Like that unsatisfied feeling you get when you don't finish what you started."

Suddenly, the corporal's voice is oddly somber. He pauses for a moment before he continues. "I mean, after that happened, even when I'm walking down the street, if I see someone with a fat neck I want to grab them and strangle them with my bare hands."

The private laughs, but it sounds too deliberate, and he realizes that it might seem inappropriate or fake.

"I'm not kidding!" the corporal says, his voice harsh. "You stupid fuck." He adds, "What this world needs is a war to kill off about half the population."

"Corporal Choi," the private says, "if a war breaks out, don't you think that you might die first?"

"Why would I die, you moron? I know I'll make it out alive. And, even if I *do* die, it doesn't matter. It's chance, anyway. It's all a matter of who kills who first and survives. That's more than fair."

"That's the wrong way of thinking about it."

"What's wrong about it?"

The private is frustrated and depressed. He wants to say something but can't figure out what. He can't escape the helpless feeling of knowing that words won't change anything. "Whatever the case . . ." he says. "No one should die. That bathhouse lady, your father or mother—even you. No one deserves to die."

"Oh, fuck off! Are you lecturing *me*—your *superior*—because you got some education?" The corporal turns around, his eyes gleaming with hostility in the darkness, and pokes the private with the end of his rifle.

Because his feet are freezing, the private can only march in place. "Corporal Choi," he says, "can I tell you a story, too? Though I don't know if it would be considered a dating story. . . ."

"You shoulda told it in the first place, *dumbass*. Okay. Go on."

But the private briefly tilts his head back and looks up at the sky. Snowflakes are falling, countless, glowing like embers.

"Hey! What are you waiting for?" the corporal yells impatiently. "Don't leave me hanging."

IT WAS A SUNDAY, A FEW WEEKS BACK. A CHOIR FROM SOME CHURCH IN Seoul had come on a morale-boosting mission to the Field Church, the small church on base. The inside of the church was colorfully decorated like an elementary school classroom ready for show-and-tell. The conductor was a man, but the choir was all young women, and most of them seemed to be college students. The whole time they were singing pop songs for the troops, he was looking at one woman in the front row. Why, amid those many faces, did she catch his eye? Was it the out-of-style perm that didn't suit her despite the high hopes that must have taken her to the hair salon? Maybe that's why she looked more awkward, more needlessly nervous, than any of the other women, her face serious like that of a child singing a hymn. She blushed when she noticed his gaze. At first, she avoided eye contact, but then gradually, cautiously, she looked at him until she couldn't take her eyes off him, and her face blushed even redder.

After the singing, the women and the soldiers played a game in which they were paired up as couples, and it was just his luck that she was his partner. When the conductor had them line up in front, holding hands, hers were rough. Her knuckles were larger than his. "What kind of a soldier has such small hands?" she whispered, her voice low, as if she were out of breath. Those were the first words she said to him.

The conductor was a lanky man with a friendly smile pasted onto his face like a Sunday school teacher. A guitar hung around his neck, and he occasionally told a joke, treating both the women and the soldiers like children. Sure enough, every time he said something, the women tittered like well-behaved schoolkids, as if they had rehearsed. The game was a contest to see which couple would be the first to finish the task announced by the conductor. There were challenges like finding Bible verses, or things like "one military sock and one lady's stocking," and the private and his partner always did well, because the woman worked harder than anyone else.

"Now I will pose the final question," the conductor said as the game reached its climax. "It's the thing that is the easiest yet hardest thing to find in the world. What is it? *Love!* Find love and bring it here."

The women and the soldiers, who had been laughing and joking up to that point, all fell silent. But the conductor was making a serious face to show that it was no joke. The soldiers complained. In that moment, the woman whispered to the private, "Let's go up." She ran up to the conductor, pulling him by the arm.

The conductor exaggerated his surprise and asked in a theatrical tone, "Have *you two* found love?"

"Yes!" the woman answered, breathless, ever the model student.

"Then will you *show* us?"

She turned and looked straight at the private, her face, as small as a child's, flushed red. Until then, he had not even been able to guess what the woman was thinking. Everyone was looking at them. She seemed to hesitate for a moment, but then she suddenly lifted her arms and wrapped them around his neck. By the time he felt her face coming closer, her lips had already touched his. The women all sighed, and the soldiers cheered and applauded loudly. But after the woman's lips retreated, after the stolen kiss that had lasted for the blink of an eye, he just stood there like an idiot.

. . . .

"*WHAT? THAT'S IT?*" THE CORPORAL EXCLAIMS WHEN THE PRIVATE
stops talking.

"Yes, that's the end of the story."

"Dumbass. You said you were gonna tell a dating story. Why's it
so dull?"

Now the private regrets telling the story. It feels as if he's been insulted, as if something has been tainted.

"So how did it taste?" the corporal asks, licking his lips, unsatisfied. "Why didn't you just bite 'em off and swallow?" His face says that
he could not be more disappointed that such luck hadn't come to him.
"How much time left now?"

As the private is about to peer at his watch yet again, the two of
them simultaneously sense that something is off, and as they have that
realization they hear a loud noise—the empty cans hanging from the
barbed wire clattering in alarm. In an instant they are on the ground,
flat on their stomachs. A black silhouette, darker than the night, is
caught on the barbed wire, and there is no doubt that it is human. The
private presses himself into the ground. An icy shudder shoots up his
spine and his entire body trembles as if he were having a seizure.

"Who—who is it?" It's the strangled voice of the corporal. But
there's no sound from the darkness.

"Answer! I asked who is it. I'll sh-shoot!"

"D-don't shoot . . ." The voice comes out of the dark after a long
while. "I'm . . . n-not a spy. . . ."

It's the voice of an old man shaking in terror, too drunk to manip-
ulate his tongue. He's hunched over, frozen stiff, unable to say anything more. Only his heavy breathing is audible. He sounds like a sick
animal.

The private feels a strange sense of disappointment along with relief. It is probably a local farmer who got caught in the barbed wire as he was stumbling around drunk. They must not have heard him crossing the field and approaching the barbed wire.

"Let's do him," Corporal Choi says in a hushed voice.

"What do you mean, 'do him'?"

"I mean, shoot him."

"Are you crazy?" the private says. "The man's a *civilian*. Can't you see?"

"Shut up, you stupid fuck."

The corporal jabs the private's side with his elbow and lowers his voice. "I'll take care of it, so you just keep your trap shut. Who's gonna know? The story is an unidentified intruder kept coming closer even when we challenged him and ordered him to stop. In a *low crawl*, I mean. Not a seal but a *real infiltrator.*"

The private gets goose bumps. Not because of the corporal's words but because, in that moment, he understands what he himself is feeling. What he feels is definitely the urge to kill. It is hard for him to believe, but the life of a human being hangs on the tip of his finger. As his heart pounds, he feels a suffocating fear and an urgency, as if he were holding in a necessary bodily function. As that fear and urgency grow more intense, the desire to kill becomes clearer and more real.

The old man is not budging; he's like a target set up on a firing range. The private feels the cold and rigid sensation of the trigger on his finger. If he were to move it, just a little, this silent frozen darkness would be instantly shattered and a human being would die bleeding—perhaps the entire world would shatter.

When the impulse becomes irresistible, the private yells out to the old man, "On your feet!"

A sharp metallic sound cracks the air and echoes in the night. It's a horrifying sound. The corporal has pulled back the bolt and chambered a round.

"What are you doing, you idiot?" The private instinctively grabs the corporal's arm.

"Huh? Are you serious? You insolent grunt!" the corporal yells as he gets up.

But the private does not release his arm and the two tumble to the ground again, grappling. The corporal screams in rage, trapped under him. "Let go, you fuck! Let go! I'm gonna shoot!"

The private suddenly realizes that his ears have stopped working. The strength is draining from his arms. At first, he is disoriented, but then he feels his chest burning and hears the sound of the corporal's terrified voice.

"I *shot* you. I really shot you."

The private sees that his body has crumpled to the ground, and he feels the cold earth against his cheek.

"I didn't mean to," the corporal whimpers. "Private Kim, I really didn't mean to shoot."

The private touches the right side of his chest. There's something sticky and wet on his hand. But, strangely, he feels no pain at all, only that his arms and legs are now unresponsive, as if they belong to someone else. His whole body feels heavy, as though it were sinking into the ground.

"What do I do now?" the corporal says. "Oh, *no*! What am I gonna *do*?"

The phone in the guard post is ringing and ringing, again and again. They are probably checking in with each post to determine the source of the gunshot. But the corporal just sits there, flat on the ground, crying like a child.

The private musters all his remaining strength to lift his leg and kicks him. "Get up! Hurry, get up and do what I tell you!"

He can't tell if the corporal can even hear him. He tries to be as loud as he can. "First, get rid of that guy. Quickly . . ."

There's no need now. Even with his dimming vision he can make out the shape of the old man stumbling over the snow-covered furrows in the field as he runs away.

"Now."

The private suddenly feels a strange euphoria. For the first time since entering the military, he has escaped formation and can be himself. Not a soldier but a human being. He opens his eyes wide, tears them open. The image of the corporal collapsed beside him is receding, blurring into the distance.

"Take out your magazine and replace it with mine. The rifle . . . I'm the one who fired it. *I'm* the one who misfired. Got it?"

But the corporal just looks at him blankly, still sitting there on the ground. The ringing of the telephone sounds ever more urgent. He tries to kick the corporal again, but already his foot does not respond. All he can manage is to draw up a shallow breath from deep within his throat and shout.

"What are you doing, idiot?"

The corporal finally stirs. The private is trembling violently. He watches the corporal's every move.

"Good . . . Now . . . answer the phone. Report . . . there was an accidental weapons discharge."

He suddenly realizes that his plan is laughable. Nothing can change reality, the private thinks. The bastard fired, and I got hit. But I am merely spinning it convincingly, like a scene in a novel. To prove I'm not an idiot? To show that I'm not an impersonal and anonymous soldier but a unique human being?

His throat tightens and crackles with thirst. His parched tongue spasms painfully. Even as his entire body trembles, as if he'd caught a chill, a wave of sleepiness washes over him.

"Private Kim! Please, wake up. . . ."

The sound of the corporal's tear-filled voice is hazy, coming from very far away. There's something he must tell the corporal. He hurriedly gathers his thoughts, panting with effort, but he cannot figure out what it is. He must remember, quickly. There is no time. . . . Suddenly, he recalls the woman's face, flushed as if she were about to burst, looking up as she wrapped her arms around his neck. He vividly recalls the touch of her lips, the feeling it left behind, burning him with fire.

"I'll come visit. On the day of the first snow. You'll wait for me, promise?" That was what she whispered into his ear as she left after the choir's morale-boosting visit. Now—regardless of what happens in the future, whatever his fate—one thing is certain: he will never see the woman again, and that is the cause of his greatest despair. He is completely drained, and yet, still, he has to will himself, with all his might, to fight back the surge of tears, and before he knows it the snow has stopped falling.

"MISS? THIS IS REALLY UNFORTUNATE. . . ." THE STAFF SERGEANT SAID, sticking his head out the window. "Um . . . they say he's been evacuated to the rear."

"What do you mean, 'evacuated'?"

"'Evacuated'? It means he was sick and got sent to the hospital."

With a doubtful expression, the woman shifted her gaze back and forth between the faces of the two soldiers.

"You came here all the way from Seoul. . . . I'm sorry, but you're going to have to give up and go back."

"How sick is he that they needed to send him to the hospital? Which hospital?"

As the staff sergeant began to mumble something, looking panicked, the sergeant quickly butted in. "How should we know? In any case, he's not here, so you can't visit him. Do you understand?"

The woman gave him a puzzled look, as if she had no idea what he was saying, and after a moment she silently picked up her bag. It felt very heavy. She thought of the food inside that would be cooling and hardening.

"It's really too bad. Of all the days you could have come . . . The buses probably stopped running, so you'll have to find a room at an inn in town!" The sergeant called out to her, crinkling his long nose, as she left.

The woman bowed her head toward the guard shack and, covering her face with one hand, walked quickly past the sentry. But just a few short steps later she was walking like someone exhausted, her shoulders drooping, the bag almost dragging on the ground.

"Just can't figure him out," the staff sergeant said. "Of all the things—why would he go and do that the day before a woman comes to see him?"

"Wait a minute. . . ." The sergeant suddenly stood up, putting on his cap. "I'll be back in a couple of hours," he said. "It's not right for a man to just let her go off like that. Least I can do is get her a room."

"Hey, you trying to make trouble in your last year of service?"

"All that Army chow and you still haven't got any sense. Don't worry, I'll watch my mouth."

"Just your mouth? Nothing else?" the staff sergeant called out.

But the door to the guard shack had already closed. The sergeant caught up to the woman in no time. He could be seen busily making conversation and reaching to take the woman's bag. The two argued over the bag between them, but in the end it looked as if the sergeant's stubbornness won. Once the woman had given up the bag, she followed the sergeant obediently, like someone who had lost everything. A flock of birds hiding by the roadside flew up and scattered in front of them.

Translated by Yoosup Chang & Heinz Insu Fenkl

FIRE & DUST

S ATURDAY. THE SKY WAS CLEAR FOR THE FIRST TIME IN A WHILE. The weather was typical for May and tear gas still swirled in the streets. At Jamsil Baseball Stadium the weekend match was on between the Haetae and OB corporate teams and—despite the risk of clashes with the police—it was the day the opposition party had chosen to press on with their constitutional amendment rally in Incheon. It was also the fifth day that two Seoul National University students—who had attempted suicide by self-immolation—were hovering between life and death with burns over their entire bodies. That was the day I finished my morning classes and headed to the market to buy flowers.

When I stepped into the dim and narrow market alley lined with shabby food stalls, my eyes were assaulted by the sight of pigs' feet, neatly arranged and fully extended to show off their toenails; boiled pigs' heads, their pale, skinny faces smiling as if they had just bathed; and dark, glistening intestines. The nauseating smell of boiled pork and the intense odor of frying oil agitated my empty stomach, and I struggled against dry heaves that nearly turned my guts inside out. It was past three and I hadn't had lunch. All I'd had that day was a glass of orange juice I forced myself to gulp down while I was jammed in among the kids at the school cafeteria. For two days, my throat had swollen up for no reason, making me unable to swallow food. And it wasn't just my throat that ailed me—my eyes were bloodshot from some infection, but I was bearing it all without the thought of getting checked out at the hospital, as if the bodily pain was something I was supposed to suffer through like a seasonal allergy.

The flower shop was deep within the market alley, bookended on one side by a shop that sold rice cakes and a side-dish store on the other. Because the natural light was bad, the fluorescents were on even though it was afternoon, and the flowers all seemed to lack vitality, like wreaths that had been laid out for too long at a funeral.

"What did you have in mind?" the shop owner asked.

I looked around at the variety of flowers that filled the cramped store, but I was a bit embarrassed, realizing that I barely knew the names of any. I had never bought flowers myself, let alone learned what they were called. Maybe it was because I was unaware of what use flowers were in people's lives.

I pointed to each kind of flower and asked what it was called.

The owner answered, one by one: baby's breath, China pink, hydrangea, canna, hyacinth. Then she said, apologetically, "Prices have gone up quite a bit these days. It must be because of the fallout."

"Fallout?"

"You know, the radiation that turns to ashes and falls from the sky."

Oh, *fallout*. I looked at the shop owner's face—she seemed sickly behind her thick glasses. In the newspapers and on broadcasts they were continuously going on about the accident at the nuclear power plant in Chernobyl. They said it was possible that the deadly radiation leaking from that place could even reach the skies above the Korean peninsula, but I had a hard time understanding why that would cause flower prices to rise in Korea.

"Prices were already high because of the holidays," the woman added. "Parents' Day is next week, you know."

What jumped out at me in the store were the red carnations. At least I could recognize carnations without asking the owner. I pulled out one red flower from a bundle. The bulb was still closed tightly like a tiny, clenched fist, but a faint fragrance—like a gentle breath—brushed past the tip of my nose, and suddenly I felt a sharp stab of pain in my chest.

It was exactly one year ago, today. . . . The last thing he did was hold a carnation. He held his mother's hand to tag along to the market, and he must have begged her to buy a carnation from a street vendor. And on their way home, until a 2.5-ton Titan truck ran him over in the alley, he held that flower in his tiny hand. When I ran into the emergency room after getting the call, what my wife desperately clung to—like something that could not be lost—was that single flower.

"Would you like the carnations?" the woman said.

I asked her to wrap them up together with a bundle of baby's breath and some China pinks.

"Give me ones in full bloom," I said when I saw her picking out only ones that hadn't opened.

"This is better, if you're going to put them in a vase. Open ones will wilt quickly."

"They aren't going in a vase. It's fine."

I watched the woman's hands—so pale they appeared almost blue—as she meticulously wrapped the flowers in thin, white paper.

"What if all the flowers die from the fallout?" she said as she passed them to me.

"Then I guess you won't be able to sell flowers anymore," I said.

My answer must have sounded rude. Until I settled the bill and left the shop, the owner maintained an expression of betrayal. With the flowers in hand, I waded through the bustling crowd of people and escaped that repulsive smell of fried food and boiled pork.

The woman worried about all the flowers on Earth dying from radioactive fallout, but she didn't know about the cruelty of the single flower that bloomed without fail with the coming of spring. And it wasn't just the flower—all things with life were cruel. That's the thought that had engulfed me for the past year. A child had died and the world no longer showed a trace of him. Seasons changed as usual, and spring returned, and the sun was warm enough to feel like a mild fever. Outside the classroom window, pollen floated pale over the athletic field like dust from a cotton gin; and as I breathed the stinging air that pricked at the eyes—the spicy air mixed with tear gas that made one sneeze uncontrollably—I trembled at the thought of that tiresome season, the return of yet another May.

I walked out to the main road and waited for a taxi, but I saw nothing vacant in the busy stream of cars sweeping by. Even as I stepped one foot off the curb, trying to flag down one of the passing taxis, I debated whether or not I should call home. There wouldn't have been anything to say even if I did. My wife had surely invited church people over for the memorial service, or whatever. They would already be at the house right about now.

"Please come home early today," my wife had said to me as I walked out the apartment door. "The pastor from church said he was coming. The service starts at five, so don't be late." She spoke in a low, parched voice, avoiding my eyes, as usual. I raised my voice. "I told you not to do that." She looked straight at me then, and I saw that her eyes were red.

"Why, exactly?" she said. "I just can't understand why you're so against it."

"Let's just treat it like any other day," I said. "Service or whatever . . . It's all useless and foolish."

"That's not true," she said. "I believe in our child's eternal life and resurrection. As long as we don't forget and keep praying." Her voice was trembling, but my wife was looking at me defiantly.

"Call them," I spat. "And tell them it's been canceled. I won't be home anyway." I heard the heavy door slam behind me as I left. And as I descended the five long flights of stairs, from the very top to very bottom, I despaired, wondering how long these parched and interminable days must go on.

Eternal life. Resurrection. I couldn't control my anger whenever I heard such words. I just could not accept how they tried to explain and console away the death of a two-year-old child. If eternal life and resurrection awaited after his death, how could he have been allowed to die in the first place? How on Earth could any kind of providence or meaning be hidden in the sudden death of an innocent child who had only just begun to see the world and explore it? But my wife persistently clung to those words. She had suddenly started going to church—which she had never attended before—more zealously than any fanatic, trying to overcome her pain through prayer and hymns. As for me, I could not believe that those things could really save my wife. And yet, I did not know of any other way for her to overcome her pain. For the past year, we'd tried hard not to touch each other, even in bed. As if the slightest contact of skin would transmit each other's pain. With her body turned away, my wife often prayed by herself or wept quietly in the dark, and I would pretend not to notice.

"Take me to the Han River," I said.

"Han River. Which part?" the taxi driver asked, looking into the rearview, alternating between my face and the flowers in my hand.

"Would you happen to know where I could rent a boat?"

"You want a boat ride?"

"I was there once, last year. But can't remember where it was. There were boat rides, and it was like a park."

"How do you expect me to find it from that description?" the taxi driver said, turning sideways to look at me. "I need to know the exact name of the place."

Seeing his darkly tanned neck and his frustrated expression, I felt suddenly defeated. I realized then that I had started out without a plan. I tried to conjure up the scenery I had seen on that certain day a year ago, but only the faintest memories remained.

It hadn't been a typical spring day. A nasty rain was falling, and by the old floodgate that led like a tunnel down to the river, the long stretch of embankment was wet. Shabby establishments were lined up all along there—boat rental places and eateries that served liquor and spicy stews. I remembered the view of the wretched little park bereft of visitors because of the rain; the bluish-green weeds covering the riverbank; the strong, murky current; and beyond, on the other side, the shapes of high-rise apartments looking unreal, like a stage set. But I could not tell the driver any of these things. That day, I'd rented a boat with my wife and headed for the middle of the river, where we scattered our child's ashes in the swift current of the Han. But strangely, the memories from that day only remained as scenes from a nightmare or single shots among a few tattered photos that did not fit into any meaningful sequence. On the way back from the crematorium at Byeokjae, after we got out of the hearse and took the taxi, I was choking with pain and despair and did not notice where we were along the Han River or what the place was called. I finally had to get out of the taxi.

I stared blankly at the glare of sunlight overwhelming the street, then set out to find a pay phone. I'd remembered my friend who had accompanied us from the crematorium to that place by the river. I thought he might know where it was.

Luckily, he was at his desk. "Hey, what do want to go there for?" he exclaimed, as if he were rebuking me, when he heard my story.

"Today's the anniversary of his death," I said.

"Has it been that long, already? Then you should be home consoling your wife instead of trying to go out there."

"Just tell me where it is."

"Come over here instead. I need to see your pathetic face before I forget it. I'm not telling you until I see you in person. Come to the coffee shop in the lobby. How long will it take? Half an hour? Twenty minutes? Alright, I'll come down in exactly twenty minutes."

After hanging up, I squinted at my watch. It was almost four o'clock. Four o'clock . . . That's when he'd just been moved to the hospital. As I watched the sunlight clinging to the leaves on the tree by the phone booth, I felt my heart start to pound. I suddenly heard my wife's voice assaulting my ears: "What should we do? Mukwoo was in an accident. He's in the hospital . . . and they say there's no hope. What can we do?" Even much later, I would often hear that unfamiliar, hoarse voice—like an auditory hallucination—so mixed with tears that I couldn't tell if it was really my wife's. And then I'd feel an unbearable pain like a knife slicing my heart.

My only thought as I raced to the hospital was to wish that it was all just a dream, and that I had misunderstood my wife's words. "They say there's no hope. . . ." But the reality was undeniable—it couldn't be turned back. When I opened the hospital door and stepped inside, my wife was in the hallway crying, her forehead against the wall outside the emergency room. "What do we do. . . . What do we do. . . ." She just repeated that phrase over and over, her body writhing, as if she had lost her mind. I pushed open the door to the emergency room, and when I went in, I could see our child, lying unconscious on a cold metal gurney, surrounded by four or five young doctors. It looked to me that, instead of doing anything to help him, they were just waiting for him to stop breathing. Other than a dark bruise around his right temple, he did not seem to have any external injuries. He was clean, and he appeared to be sleeping deeply in a pose so familiar to me.

"Wait outside. You can't just come in here." Someone stuck their head out of the room and shouted, "Hey, nurse! Why did you let this man in?" Then another doctor pushed me out.

"We're doing everything we can," he said. "Try to be calm and wait outside." But I collapsed right there on that spot because, at that moment, I thought I needed to pray. I had never once prayed until then, and I had never believed in things like the power of prayer, but I now resorted to grasping at straws out of desperation. I knelt on the hard floor and clasped my hands together. I begged God to forgive me for not believing in His existence until now. I said that I would repent for all my sins if He would please save my son. Many other things slipped out of my mouth, and the more I prayed, the more the belief grew in me that some being—an all-knowing and all-powerful one that could determine the life or death of the child—existed. Even so, I felt my prayers would be insufficient. I thought I needed to provide some collateral that He could trust, make a promise that would cause Him to take interest in my prayer. So I prayed that I had many sins, and He should let my child live and take me instead. I swore that if I had to die in his place, I would do so willingly. I had no way of knowing how much time had passed while I was kneeling there on the concrete floor absorbed in prayer. Someone tapped my shoulder. One of the young doctors, draped in a white gown, was standing over me. "He's stopped breathing," he said.

My friend was already waiting at the coffee shop in the lobby of the newspaper building.

"What's with the flowers?" he said before I could even take a seat. "Carrying around flowers in these troubled times . . . you writers certainly are different."

He often called me a writer with the affection befitting an old high school classmate, but I hadn't written a single decent story since I'd just barely made the cut in the New Year Literary Contest.

"Don't keep calling me a writer," I said. "It makes me feel like you're mocking me."

"What's wrong with being a writer? It's better than working for a Chinese restaurant delivering *jjajangmyeon*."

"Delivering *jjajangmyeon*? What does that mean?"

"This shitty job—I might as well be delivering black bean noodles," he said, as if he had a bitter taste in his mouth. "I'm gonna quit." He blew a plume of cigarette smoke up into the air.

"Something happened, huh?"

"Get this . . . I had just gotten to the office and sat down, when the phone rang. When I picked up, some guy said he was a reader and had something to say about an article. A piece that went out yesterday, knocking the opposition party a bit. The guy said he wasn't an opposition party member—he just wanted to chime in, purely as a citizen—but why were we insulting the opposition like that? When I told him, 'It must've been meant to encourage them through constructive criticism,' he said, 'Then why're you only criticizing the opposition and not the incumbents? What's so great about the press that makes you guys think you can kick the opposition party around like that?' He was so worked up his voice was shaking. I thought it would just be more trouble if I tried to argue, so I backed off by saying, 'I'm not the reporter who wrote that article.' Then the guy started grilling me. He said, 'Aren't you a reporter, too?' So I told him, 'I'm not a reporter and have no connection to that story.' I don't know why I said such an idiotic thing. You know what he said next? He started screaming at me. 'What *are* you then, huh? Are you just there delivering *jjajangmyeon*? Then why the fuck is a delivery guy like you answering the phone, you piece of shit?'"

He stubbed out his cigarette and bolted up from his seat. "Hey, let's grab a drink."

"It's still midday," I said. "Besides, aren't you busy?"

"I'm done with deliveries for today."

From the way he said it without even cracking a smile, that phone call must have upset him quite a bit. He walked to the door first, and I had no choice but to follow. "What's the matter with your eyes?" he said, peering into my face as we stepped out into the sun.

"Did you get hit with tear gas or something?"

"No. It's an infection. Conjunctivitis maybe. Not sure, since I haven't been to the hospital."

"Eyes as crimson as the carnations clutched to his chest. What do you think? You think I could make it as a writer too?"

"What? You think writing a novel is like talking in your sleep?"

"You're right. It must be hard writing a novel. In the streets and in the newspapers, real stories are being played out every day, so what more can a novelist say?"

We slipped out of the parking lot, which was lined with shining luxury sedans. People were crowding the streets, pollen flying everywhere, and there were riot police buses hooded in wire mesh. As we waited for the crosswalk signal to change, we saw a plain-clothed riot policeman standing guard behind a police bus, holding a shield with the number 88-1 written on it. He looked as young and innocent as most of the eleventh graders I saw every day in my classroom. Next to him, on the crosswalk, was a female college student controlling traffic as a part-time job. She wore a helmet that said ORDER and held a yellow flag with the same ORDER printed on it. She looked as young as the riot policeman.

My friend elbowed my side, pointing ahead with his chin. An American GI in civilian clothes was standing with a young Korean woman by his side. The GI was tall and handsome. He wore a shiny, sky-blue jacket. On the back, embroidered in gold thread, was a map of the Korean peninsula, with the letters DMZ and a thick line that ran across it, cutting it in half. There were place names like SEOUL and BUSAN, and even the YELLOW SEA and EAST SEA were labeled. On the peninsula, the Korean flag and the American Stars and Stripes were placed side by side like brothers on good terms. "Just look at that," my friend said. There was a sentence written in English below the map, embroidered in fat letters: I'M SURELY GOING TO HEAVEN 'CAUSE I SERVED MY TIME IN HELL.

"He's going around advertising the Republic of Korea as Hell," my friend said as we crossed the street. "That should be considered a crime, either way. But is it 'spreading false rumors' or 'leaking state secrets?'"

"It must be about his time in the military," I said. "Everyone thinks of their life in the military as Hell."

My friend led the way through the narrow, cluttered alley of restaurants behind a forest of buildings to a small bar with a sign that read

CAFÉ hanging outside. He pushed open the door and we stepped inside to an unexpectedly splendid interior. The lighting was subtle and elegant, and music was playing.

"Can they openly sell liquor during the day like this?" I asked. "Isn't it illegal?"

"Isn't this the kind of world where all desires are fundamentally tolerated?" my friend asked in response.

A young woman wearing red lipstick brought the beer we ordered and sat down next to my friend. "May I sit here?" she asked.

"You're already sitting," he said.

"Should I get up, then?"

"You say that, but you know you don't want to get up."

"I know how to get up," she said, suddenly annoyed. She got up and left.

My friend poured the drinks himself, mumbling, "Bitch isn't even that pretty."

"Why'd you do that?" I said. "Picking a fight with a blameless woman."

"I know," he said, looking suddenly tired. "It's strange. These days I see these bitches' faces and my hatred just boils over. You think maybe it's because they're easy targets? A few days ago, I got into a lot of trouble for slapping the girl who sat down next to me at a bar."

I tried to superimpose the face of the man sitting across from me, who had just entered his thirties, with the face I remembered from our high school days. He could have been someone else now—a complete stranger. In high school, my friend's nickname was Missy. He was in the school newspaper club and a great singer. I barely managed to suppress a sharp pain that felt like the beer I had swallowed on an empty stomach shooting back up.

"Why do people have to be such cowards?" he asked, staring into his glass as if he were talking to himself.

"What kind of nonsense is that?"

"If each of us only had the guts to give up what we have, we could change the current state of things. But humans aren't like that, are they? Because if that fundamental human weakness didn't exist, then how could domination or submission exist? There's one thing I could never understand whenever I heard about the Nazi concentration camps. It's the fact that so many Jews didn't show any resistance, even when they were facing imminent death. They didn't resist as they marched in line to the gas chambers, as the Nazi officer pointed his finger, as if they were going to a bathhouse. Why do you think that is? Is it because they didn't want to die by their own actions—until the faucets were turned on for them? Humans are basically weak beings like that."

"Is that the life philosophy of a *jjajangmyeon* delivery man?" I said, deliberately joking, but he kept prattling on with the same tired expression on his face.

"But college students still pour paint thinner over themselves and light themselves on fire. Naive optimists who say they believe in humanity and the power of history. Naivete is pretty frightening when you think about it. They used to say the wolves ate the sheep, but now they're calling for the sheep to get together and eat the wolves. They don't want to accept the fact that sheep can never become wolves. No matter how much the sheep join forces, can they ever grow fangs? That's what religion is for: 'The last shall be the first.' 'Blessed are those who are persecuted because of righteousness, for theirs is the Kingdom of Heaven.' Those that are most oppressed today shall be seated in the highest place, but only when they're dead and get to Heaven."

He was mumbling what sounded like a bunch of gibberish, but suddenly my friend lifted his face, his eyes already red-rimmed. "Hey," he said, "drink your drink. You writer, you . . . carrying around flowers in these troubled times. Why do you write novels, anyway?"

It was just a rhetorical question, so I didn't answer. I drank my beer. My swollen throat throbbed like it was burned, and the pain was coming back in my gut. As I suppressed the nausea, I thought about the real reason why I couldn't give up on writing.

For four years after passing through the gate of my so-called "debut," I had barely managed to toss out a few short stories. And then, for the whole year after my son died, I hadn't been able to write a single thing. My precious worldview, broad-minded until then, wasn't just cracked but completely shattered, and I couldn't figure out what stories I could possibly tell about life. Life was like a canvas that had been torn to tatters.

"The truth is, I'm just waiting for those kids to die," my friend said, his tone full of self-loathing now. "Those kids . . . I'm talking about the college students who torched themselves. I have to write their obituaries."

I thought it was about time for me to get up. I needed to get to the Han River before sunset. But when he finally heard my story, my friend said, "Why do you have to go there? Forget it. That's the best medicine."

"He doesn't even have a grave for people to visit," I said. "That's why I want to at least throw him some flowers at the place where his ashes are scattered."

"Man, why are you wearing such a long face—like Orpheus going to the underworld to find his dead wife?"

"You're not wrong there," I said. "I wish I *was* Orpheus. Why can't we call back the dead like they did back then?"

"Are you already drunk? That's a myth, man. There are no gods anymore."

"That's what I mean. . . . Why are there no gods now?"

He laughed. "If there were, would the world be in this sorry state? A world where gods existed must have been a happier place. A world full of criminals and liars—that's the tragedy of a world without gods."

Then he said, more seriously, "Speaking of Orpheus—I read it in high school, so I don't remember it all that well, but isn't there a river of forgetfulness called 'Lethe' or something? Why do you think there's a river of forgetfulness? Don't you think they're telling you to forget? We have to forget the dead."

"Just tell me where the place is," I said.

"Okay, I give up. It was the park at Ttukseom."

Ttukseom? In the taxicab, I tried to reconcile that place name with my memories of that day a year ago and my heart trembled. An unbearable sadness welled up as the vivid pain from that day was resurrected. I wondered if it was futile, as my friend had said. What meaning would there be for me in returning to that place? Maybe he was right—it was like a pitch-black land of forgetfulness to which the living could never go. I thought of my wife, who must be holding the memorial service about now, trying not to forget our child, afraid of losing even the most trivial memory and hanging on for dear life to keep them from getting buried into oblivion, denying our son's death. Sometimes my wife would lay out old photos of him and ask me, "What color shirt was he wearing the last time we visited Deoksugung Palace?" When I would tell her to please try to forget, she would say, "How sad would he be if we forgot him? I can't bear that thought—it feels like we're committing a sin against him." My wife did not want to accept the fact that it was a futile struggle, that our child had slipped through our fingers and disappeared like a handful of dust.

He was gone now. He existed only faintly in our memories, and what was most unbearable for me was the fact that there was no meaning in his death. That child, only two years old—who had just started looking at the world through sun-dazzled eyes, who was learning about the things around him as he pointed to them one by one—had ended up dead by the negligence of an elderly truck driver. A death as meaningless as that of an insect. And if that was the case, then what possible meaning could there be in his short life that would end in such a death? What is the meaning of a human life, anyway? When I first heard on the TV news about the students who had lit themselves on fire, I had felt the usual pain in my chest that had already become a kind of chronic illness. And still, the question that preoccupied me was, *Did they know the meaning of their death?* According to the news, they had poured paint thinner all over their bodies, lit themselves on fire, and then jumped off the roof of a three-story building, shouting something. What went through their minds in those moments? I couldn't sleep that night because of the terrible image of them in flames, falling. Did they truly fall holding on to some value that transcended their own lives? How were their deaths and the death of my child different? I believed that, as they immolated themselves, that act must have been a part of their struggle to find meaning for their lives in history and society. But my body trembled at the undeniable truth that everything they had given their lives for would, in the end, become the inheritance of cowardly survivors; they would be scattered like a fistful of dust and disappear into a pitch-black emptiness.

When we returned home after cremating our child, the rented room that had been our nest was unfamiliar and eerily quiet. And it wasn't only because the child who had completely filled our lives from the time we had gotten married had disappeared. Then, I saw the world through eyes already dead—the world after my death, the world where I did not exist. Then, I would feel unbearable hatred toward a book that stood, unchanging, on a bookshelf, even a small potted flower visible through a window. Life, and every living thing, felt cruel and cowardly to me.

As the taxi turned right, just short of the Seongsu Bridge, onto a narrow road that traced the river, my heart started pounding. What I could see outside the window felt familiar: a little Catholic church topped with a cross; dusty buildings that looked like small factories, barely managing. Even the shops lining the street looked familiar. "You can let me out here," I said to the driver. When he made another turn to let me off, I could see the dike and floodgate in the distance.

The slanted light of the late afternoon illuminated the road, and a breeze blew in from the river. I walked, looking at the distant flood-gate that was open like a tunnel. I felt an ache in my head, and sadness, as if I were finding the way to my son's grave. My wife had been against cremating him. She said that scattering his body without even a grave would be unbearable. "Now we're his grave," I said to her. "Don't they say that when parents die, they're buried on the mountain, and when children die, they're buried in your heart?" But the truth was that my feeble heart couldn't properly fill the role of a child's grave.

When I finally walked through the run-down floodgate cut to the river, I was shocked. I could not believe what I saw. There were no houses along the riverbank, no canopied rental boats, not even a weeping willow with its hair down. The whole area had become a des-olate construction site, the only visible things being mounds of exca-vated dirt and heavy equipment like bulldozers and trucks. Then I remembered what was called "The Comprehensive Han River Devel-opment Plan" that I must have heard about on the radio. This place was probably one of those that had been demolished at that time, and everyone had moved away. Wind-borne dust blew in my face.

I trudged through piles of excavated dirt toward the river. It hadn't changed, flowing on, dragging its massive body. That day, we had launched from here, in a small rowboat, to the middle of the river. An old man rowed for us, and raindrops that found their way through the gaps in the canopy were splashing onto the deck. I opened the envelope that I had held against my chest all the way from the cremation site. The bones barely filled half of the manila envelope. My wife and I each grasped a handful of what remained of our child's body, ground so finely it was like powder, and scattered it onto the water. The dust that left our hands was swallowed up by the current and disappeared instantly into the river.

I had planned to go out on that same boat again and toss the flowers from the spot where we'd scattered his ashes. But that was impossible now. I looked down at the dirty river water under my feet. Fragments of newspaper and plastic were floating about and dark green river weeds that looked like a drowned woman's hair waved this way and that in the current. Standing by a beached rowboat, broken and upside down, I could do nothing but watch the black river flowing silently before my eyes.

When I left the riverbank and slipped out of the floodgate again, I saw an old tented food cart nearby. The dark-faced owner stood watch over a few bottles of soju and some meager snacks, and a gray-haired drunk old man was asleep in front of her with his nose buried in the table. I sat myself down on a corner of the narrow plywood bench by the old man and ordered a drink.

"When did the park disappear?" I asked.

"Last year," the woman said. "They started construction in the fall and completely tore it apart. What would you like to eat?"

Before the food was even ready, I emptied my soju glass again and again. The tent flaps parted at each gust of wind, letting in dust and dirt.

"There's so much dust. . . . It must be all the construction," the woman said apologetically.

"Business must be slow since the park is gone."

"It's not much different," she said. "Any change in business here, it's never more than a couple thousand won. You think people coming for the park would eat at a snack cart like this? There's a lot of factories down this alley, so the factory workers are always stopping by to pick up *tteokbokki* and such."

I watched a few young men at the other end of an alley that connected to the dike. They were energetically kicking a ball around, wearing dirty tank tops stained red with rust, and for some reason that made me think of my wife's pale face. Had the memorial service ended? I wondered what she was doing now, after the church people left. Suddenly my entire body was awash with a terrible fatigue.

"You must've come to enjoy the park and struck out," the woman said.

I emptied the glass again. My body felt heavy, as if I were about to collapse, and the strong soju was stirring up my empty stomach, and yet for some reason I knew I could not leave this place without getting drunk.

"I came here to find someone."

"You're looking for a person?" The woman noticed my bloodshot eyes. "Someone who used to be at the park?"

"That's right, where did all those people go? I mean, the people who used to pilot the boats."

"They're scattered all over. I heard some went to the ferry at Cheonho-dong, but most just split and drifted away, here and there."

I thought he'd been asleep, but just then the old man lifted his disheveled head. "You came looking for someone?" he asked. "Who?" He looked around, sniffing, his nose red with burst blood vessels.

"Oh, you old geezer, please just go home now," the woman said. "How can you get so sloshed this early in the day?"

The old man pretended not to hear. "Give me my bottle," he said, blinking his rheumy eyes.

"What bottle?"

"The one I left with you."

"You didn't leave any bottle with me. You don't even have anything left to drink. Please, just go home. I wouldn't sell you any more liquor even if you offered to pay."

Still, the old man lingered, mumbling something, until the woman shouted, "Go home! Now!" And then he rose unsteadily from the bench.

The woman clicked her tongue and watched him stagger away with his fallen pants exposing his backside. "That old geezer used to be a boatman here. I think he's a local. Born here, used to fish, too. Now that he's got nowhere to go, he's become that old wreck."

I got up from my spot, stomach churning, barely resisting the urge to throw up as my insides twisted into knots of pain. I passed through the floodgate and had to climb over the mound of excavated earth and a willow tree uprooted on its side to get to the river. I threw up then. Since I'd had nothing to eat all day, there was nothing to come up, but I continued to vomit for a long time, as if to purge everything I was holding inside me. Tiny gadflies flew between the poisonous blue weeds. In other spots, nameless wildflowers poked up through the dirty rocks, lifting their heads to the sky.

I watched a lone seagull flapping its tired wings and flying off somewhere toward the red, dipping sun. Suddenly, I recalled an image of my smiling son—he had always loved to laugh—and I felt my throat burn with longing and nostalgia.

I was just about to leave when I saw a young girl in the distance, hunched over and looking into the water. As I approached her, I realized she was struggling to put something into the water. It looked like a plastic bag with something in it.

"What is that?" I asked.

Still hunched over, the girl lifted her face to look up at me. She must have been ten or eleven. "It's my goldfish," she said.

"What are you doing with the bag?"

"I think they're dying. So I wanted to set them free in the river."

"I'll help you."

Because of the high bank, she couldn't reach down to the water. I took the water-filled plastic bag from her hand. Inside were two goldfish, already half dead. I let them loose in the water, into the flow of the murky river, where they showed their pale bellies and then quickly disappeared.

"You know, goldfish aren't supposed to live in the river," I said.

"It's alright. It's still better than dying on land, don't you think?"

"No," I said. "I'm sure they're going to live." I looked at the girl, her face red in the setting sun. "Where do you live?" I asked.

"Nearby." She looked straight at me and spoke with confidence. "Why are *you* here instead of home, mister? Don't you have a home?"

"Of course I do. Why wouldn't I have a home?"

"Are you married?"

"Yes, I'm married."

"Then your wife's waiting for you."

"Wife?" I laughed. "Would you like these flowers?"

The girl looked at the flowers I presented in surprise, not even trying to hide how much she wanted them. "They're carnations," she said in a whisper.

"Take them. You can put them on your desk."

She took the flowers without a word of thanks and, holding them close, smelled their fragrance. She took a few steps, then stopped for some reason and came walking back to me.

"Here," she said. "You take the flowers, mister."

The girl put the flowers in my hands, spun around, and ran off. There was no time even to say anything. Still holding the flowers, I stood there for a long time, overcome with emotion, watching her recede into the distance. *Yes*, I thought, *like she said, I should leave this place and return to where I ought to be.*

I paused before leaving through the floodgate when I saw the glare of the red dusk dyeing the river. The desolately cratered construction site, the silently flowing river, the piers under the long spans of the Seongsu Bridge—even the apartment buildings lined up on the other side—all seemed aflame in red. I remembered the story of Orpheus, who had brought his wife back from the realm of the dead but then looked back before crossing the river of forgetfulness and ended up losing his wife forever. I stared at that place for a very long time.

It was during the taxi ride back that I heard the news that one of the Seoul National University students who had immolated themselves had died. Among other news—the opposition party's constitutional amendment rally being turned into a violent riot by the extreme leftist faction; Olympic Boulevard opening; a worker, who had lost his job and threatened a food manufacturer with poison, being arrested— the radio briefly mentioned the death of the young student. It was at five thirty that afternoon, after five days of hovering between life and death.

"It's only the precious kids who die," the taxi driver said bitterly. "What a wretched world. . . . How many more is it gonna kill?"

I did not say anything. It was while I was wandering the desolate riverside that the student was dying. Maybe I went all the way out there to keep vigil over his death. I looked out the window as the taxi passed between the piers under a subway rail bridge. The streets were winding down the day as usual, subway trains passing noisily overhead, a bus filled with people—their expressions blank, as if made of clay—rushing somewhere. I noticed I was trembling, as if I'd caught a chill. I felt a pain, as if my heart were being torn out, and along with it something unbearably hot—an ecstasy filling up my body. I saw it clearly, just then, through the gigantic piers becoming tinged with darkness: a human figure wrapped in flames, burning. But it was not falling down; it was ascending, breaking upward beyond death.

Translated by Yoosup Chang & Heinz Insu Fenkl

WAR TROPHY

I

I picked up the handset, inserted a coin, and slowly dialed. A long, thin signal wailed for several seconds before the gulp of the coin being swallowed, and then, in a singsong voice bright as day, a woman's voice flowed from the receiver.

"Hello?"

I instantly hung up, as if I'd heard a horrible profanity—or seen something I should not have after accidentally opening the door to the ladies' room.

It was a hot afternoon in August. The entire city was cooking, and the hottest place of all, as far as I was concerned, was the inside of the phone booth in front of the Majang-dong intercity bus terminal, where I was desperately wishing my sweat-soaked underwear would stop sticking to my butt. After I put down the receiver, I stood there like an idiot for a moment, tugging at my underwear. This was really unexpected. I had completely forgotten that the place was a residential area for Americans until after I'd dialed the phone, and only then had I realized that the whole neighborhood around Hannam-dong had become a foreigner's ghetto. I was trying to call a woman who lived there.

I looked down at a business card, soaked from the sweat of my hand, and tried to remember the few English words I knew. I composed a simple sentence in my head and awkwardly tried pronouncing it out loud:

Hello. Please. Give. Me. Number. . . .

No. Instead of *please*, shouldn't I start with *would you?*

In middle school, I'd been in an English class taught by an American woman—a Peace Corps volunteer—and I was always terribly shy in front of her. I still cannot believe how tall she was—like the pines along the hillside behind the school—or how her eyes were blue like the sea, or her sympathetic smile, unbelievably wide and pliable. And I never understood why it was that I could never relax in front of her. I couldn't even answer the simple question, *"What is your name?"* All I could manage, my face bright red and turned downward, was to steal glances, through the corners of my eyes, at her slender white arms covered in golden fuzz. She would wait patiently, then walk away, shaking her head as if to say there was nothing more she could do. All I managed to remember from that English class was the assortment of lewd graffiti, on the dim and musty walls of the school bathrooms, depicting her private parts.

In any event, I had to make the phone call. The more the time passed, the hotter it would get in the booth, and my damned underwear was getting plastered to my butt.

After coming up with the best sentence I could and mumbling it to myself several times, I inserted another coin and turned the dial. The long signal again, then the phone swallowing the coin, and then the cheerful voice of the woman, who didn't seem to have a care in the world.

"Hello?"

My mind went blank and the sentence I had struggled to assemble in English instantly evaporated. Before I knew it, I found myself shouting in Korean, "Can you put me through to number 42? It's exchange 42. Number 42! Do you understand?"

Damn it, I thought. I felt as if my strength was draining from me. I waited for the woman's next response with a sense of desperation. But then, surprisingly, she continued in an even more cheerful and melodic voice, in Korean:

"Yes, wait one moment please."

It was only then that I finally realized the operator was a Korean woman. I let out a long sigh, grateful that the place where I stood was a part of the Korean peninsula and its affiliated islands. The signal stopped, and the sultry voice of another woman came on.

"Hello?"

Why did that word make me jump every time I heard it? At that moment I actually had to restrain myself from flinging the handset with all my might.

"Is Miss Oh Mija there?" I said, silently hoping it was not a breach of courtesy to say "Oh Mija" instead of "Mrs. So-and-so."

"Who is this? This is Oh Mija. . . ." The pitch of her voice rose.

Once again I let out a long sigh, and finally—as if to conserve my native tongue—I calmly pronounced one word at a time. "How are you, Miss Oh? It's Gu Bonsu."

"Wow! Hello, Mr. Gu Bonsu. What's going on? I mean, *really*, what's going on that makes you call me after all this time?"

I hadn't expected her to be so excited to hear the three syllables of my name.

"It's really great to hear from you," she said. "It's been a long time since I heard 'Is Miss Oh Mija there?' over the phone. Where are you?"

"I'm in the Majang-dong intercity bus terminal parking lot."

"Oh my, you must be going somewhere on holiday. Or on your way back? Are you with someone? A friend? Girlfriend? How are you doing?"

Now, I suspected that—of all the numerous and unexpected difficulties I had to go through since picking up the phone to call her—only the final crucial task remained.

I briefly paused. "The truth is," I said, "I'm calling because there's something I need to tell you. Kim Jangsu is dead."

For a moment, there was no sound. In case she hadn't heard, I once again breathed an ominous breath into the tiny holes that perforated the handset. "Are you listening? Kim Jangsu is dead."

Not a peep. I patiently waited for her to say something after the shock wore off, but the truth was that I might have secretly wanted to savor the length of that shock. After a long silence, I could finally hear the kind of pained moans I'd often heard before while watching Hollywood films.

"*Oh, God.*" Her voice was slightly hoarse. "I'm s-sorry, Bonsu," she said. "C-could you call me back in a little bit? Right now, I don't know what's what."

"Alright. I'll hang up and call again."

I put the receiver down. My palm was slick with sweat. I slid my hand into my front pocket to pull at my underwear, and I felt something.

I had completely forgotten it was there. When I'd gotten off the long-distance bus and found my way to the phone booth, that small object must have rubbed continuously, with every step, against my sweaty thigh in my thin summer trousers. But strangely, I had been unaware of it. It was hard and light, like some kind of solid fuel with a bit of warmth left to it.

As I felt its rough texture with the tips of my fingers, I realized that

I had an unanticipated problem. This wasn't something I should be carrying around in my pocket and playing with. It was too hard to keep in my pants pocket and certainly not something I could just carry around in my hand.

Suddenly I felt the subtle signs of movement in my body, something quietly lifting its head from deep within: an unexpected and inappropriate arousal, as if it were from the object in my pocket transmitting warmth, like a person's breath, as it pressed into my thigh.

I frowned, watching the steamy August streets and—like a pauper made uncomfortable by a sudden windfall—struggled with the erection that tented my pants.

And I thought of Oh Mija, the obvious object of that lust. I had sworn that I would meet her. And the truth of it was that I hadn't called her only to tell her the news that Jangsu had died.

He was dead. I still could not actually grasp that fact, and before feeling sorrow or pain, my first reaction to his death had been this preposterous and inexplicable lust for Oh Mija. I scowled. I scowled and scowled, thinking about that night when Jangsu had had his first fit.

AT THE NURSE'S STATION AT TWO IN THE MORNING, THE NURSE ON duty was alone, reading. She took off her glasses and placed them on top of her book, forcefully blinking her tired eyes as if to ask, *What brings you here?*

"He's having a fit," I said.

The nurse looked up at me, her expression saying that there was no point in me trying to frighten her in the middle of the night.

"What room?"

"319."

She flipped slowly through the medical charts, her hands not showing the slightest sign of haste. I felt embarrassed for having run from Jangsu's room down the dim corridor to get there.

"319 . . . Kim Jangsu, cirrhosis of the liver, age twenty-eight. . . . Right?"

"Yes, that's right."

"So, what did you say happened to the patient?"

"He's having some kind of fit. He's talking nonsense and laughing hysterically, like he's lost his mind or something."

I suppressed the urge to imitate the strange stuttering noise—a sound like Jangsu was tapping at the root of his tongue—for the expressionless nurse. The fact that someone would suddenly make such a sound was surely the sign of a fit, but I couldn't find the right words to describe it to the nurse, who was already exhausted from the night shift, at two a.m.

"Wait here a minute," she said. "The doctor on duty should be here soon."

"JUST A MOMENT, PLEASE. I'LL CONNECT YOU NOW."

I almost said thank-you in response to the operator's consistently kind voice. I heard the familiar signal and then the same voice again.

"I just can't believe he's dead. When did it happen?"

"Two days ago at one thirty in the afternoon. I'm on my way back from the funeral, just now." I paused for a second to tug at my underwear. "Can't even call it a funeral, really. Since Jangsu didn't have much in terms of family, a few friends got together and took care of it with a simple ceremony. The person who really should have been there is you, Mija." Now I paused to give her time to respond, but she did not say anything, one way or the other.

"After the cremation, we went all the way out to Hantan River," I said. "Because we thought the water near Seoul might be dirty. We spread his ashes with our own hands. In the blue waters of Hantan River."

As I spoke, I felt like we were in sync. And then, before I had even finished talking, guffaws erupted out of nowhere. Incomprehensible, rapid-fire English, mixed with laughter, continued for a long time.

"Hello. Hello?"

"I'm listening, Bonsu."

"What did you just say?"

"Never mind. Our phone lines must be getting crossed." When she stopped talking, the rapid monotone of foreign speech was audible again. "Was his death peaceful?" she asked.

Her voice was very calm. I guessed she must have wracked her brain while we were disconnected to come up with that one line, and then her voice, too, sounded like it was straight out of a play. As I replied, I felt an extreme animus toward the sweat drenching my palm while I held the phone, the August heat steaming up the phone booth, and even myself—because I couldn't just swear at her and hang up.

"He was twenty-eight," I said. "How would he have to die for it to be 'peaceful' at that age?"

"What was that?" Mija raised her voice over the background noise. "Hello? I can't make out what you're saying."

I enunciated every word clearly—as if I were doing a voice-over—so that she would understand. "It was a very peaceful death. He died painlessly, like he was falling asleep."

THE GLOOM THAT PERMEATED THE THIRD-FLOOR HOSPITAL HALLWAY made it feel like it was suffering some sort of internal injury. The strong smell of ether that emanates every time a surgical patient exhales, the smell of disinfectant, and all sorts of other foul odors were tangled together there amidst the ominous silence in the heat of a late summer night. The faint light from fluorescents, cast here and there on the hallway ceiling, was the only thing eating away at the darkness. At least one of the lamps, with a faulty bulb, just blinked continuously, struggling to light up. All the way at the end of the dim hallway, in room 319, on an old metal bed, lay Kim Jangsu.

When I stepped inside with the doctor on duty, the hospital room was already terribly quiet. The constant random buzzing of a flying bug—trapped by the window screen—only seemed to emphasize that ominous silence.

"Why's he so quiet?" I asked. "He was throwing a fit just a little while ago."

"Let's have a look."

With skilled hands, the doctor opened Jangsu's shroudlike hospital gown and put a stethoscope to his chest. Still, Jangsu—his eyes open vacantly—did not show any reaction.

I could already see that his eyes had lost the ability to focus. They were frozen, unable to move in the slightest, and they had a dull luster as they reflected the fluorescent lights. If it wasn't for his belly, moving quietly up and down under the sheet at regular intervals, I would have thought he was dead. In fact, his belly—though it was swollen like a woman's in her ninth month of pregnancy—looked like a grave mound, evoking not birth, but death.

But the thing that caught my attention was his close-shaved head. It shone blue like a knife blade and, compared to everything else in the hospital room, the color was so pure, almost tragic. A month had passed since his release, but every morning he still painstakingly shaved his head with a razor. Had he decided to be a seeker on some personal path for the remainder of his life? Or was he saying he was still just a prisoner in an enormous prison cell?

The examination dragged on, and during the whole time, the expression on the young doctor's face was grim. It looked as if he were frantically flipping through a thick medical textbook in his head and comparing what he read there to the complex symptoms in front of him. Finally, he spoke decisively, as if he were certain about what he said, but it was so unexpected that I was a little dumbstruck.

"How many do you see?"

He raised two fingers and waved them in front of Jangsu's eyes as if he were playing with a kid. Of course, the patient showed no response. Yet, despite that, the doctor stubbornly continued with the child's play, and with an utterly serious face asked, again and again, "How many is it? How many?"

The doctor's sad efforts were thwarted by a strange sound that leaked from Jangsu's mouth. It was a barely audible laugh. It must have been unexpected for the doctor as well, or maybe he perceived it as his patient mocking him. He glared at Jangsu with a look of betrayal.

"Why is his head shaved like this?" the doctor asked me.

"Don't worry," I said. "He's not an escaped convict."

"What?"

"He was in prison until just recently. . . ." I paused to see the doctor's reaction. "He was released a month ago with a suspended sentence."

The doctor's face, already long, seemed to grow even longer to express his shock. "Is that right?" the doctor said. "He seems . . ." and there was definitely a little fear in that long face ". . . like a nice guy. . . . What was he in for?"

Jangsu's hand went up just then, slowly, and bobbed in the air a couple of times. I assumed it was a signal for me to come closer. His lips bulged slightly as if he were trying to say something. I took his hand and brought my face right up to his. He spoke in a low but clear voice:

"Find Oh Mija."

"What's he saying?" the doctor asked impatiently.

Still holding Jangsu's hand, I gave the doctor an unreadable smile. Jangsu's knuckles were stiff and shockingly cold.

"Don't look for Oh Mija," I told Jangsu. "There's no use, no matter how much you look for her. She's already dead."

I didn't tell Jangsu that for any particular reason except that I thought his story was totally ill-suited for the serious atmosphere in the hospital room at two in the morning. Just to be sure, I hammered it in again. "Do you understand? That woman is dead and gone."

What Jangsu did next was probably enough to wash away any doubts the young doctor might have had. Jangsu suddenly broke out into laughter, as if he had heard something unbearably funny—he was surely having a fit.

That insane, cackling laugh continued without any sign of letting up. Jangsu rolled around in the rickety hospital bed, wrapped in a sheet, the dark pupils disappearing from his clouded eyes, which had rolled back in his head. He was foaming at the mouth.

I couldn't tell if this new attack was from the shock of what I'd said or just a symptom of his physical pain. But, all the same, it appeared there was no way to stop it, regardless of what had caused it. I looked back at the doctor's face, and he was shaking his head as if he were thinking the same thing.

"THANK YOU, BONSU. REALLY. FOR TAKING THE TROUBLE TO CONTACT me." It sounded like she was about to hang up.

"Mija, wait!" I exclaimed. The persistent arousal that had come out of nowhere poked at my thigh. The object was still warm in my pocket, and the heat in the phone booth was becoming unbearable. My voice came crawling back in shame.

"I . . . really need to see you," I said. "I have something to tell you about Jangsu, and I . . ."

There was no response.

"Is that not possible?"

Instead of an answer, I heard a loud guffaw. The American woman, with whom our lines had crossed, was laughing now. The only thing I could understand in her rapid-fire foreign tongue was "*Darling, darling,*" which she repeated in a soft, nasal whisper. I mouthed the refrain, *Fuck, fuck,* at the ends of those words.

"Alright," Mija said. "When should we meet?"

"I'd like to meet now."

She hesitated, and the soft and sweet *darling*s continued. "Do you really need to see me?" she said after a long pause.

"Well . . . so . . . Jangsu . . . like I said . . ."

I wanted to scream into the handset until I was out of breath, right then and there, but barely managed to suppress the urge. Instead, I shoved a hand down into my pocket and tightly clenched the part of me that was hard.

"I really need to see you right now."

"Fine, let's do it, then. Where should I meet you?"

Damn it. . . . I swept my sweaty hand down my sweaty face. No suitable place came to mind as I anxiously searched my memory.

"How about this, Bonsu?" she said. "Let's meet in front of school. I want to visit it again. The Ivory Tower across from the front gate should still be there, right?"

"Alright, I'll wait for you at the Ivory Tower Café."

"Okay."

2

"*Oh!* What are you doing?"

The nurse let out a short yelp and stepped back. Jangsu had pulled up her skirt. She stopped wrapping the blood pressure cuff around his arm and turned toward the doctor with a look on her face that said, *Is this guy crazy?* The doctor's affirming nod and Jangsu's cackling that followed were almost simultaneous.

"Please hold him down," the nurse said to me.

I held on to Jangsu's shoulders. While she inflated the blood pressure cuff, the nurse continued to watch his face, her brows furrowed. Her expression was reminiscent of a shaman's looking down at a malicious spirit possessing a client's body. Jangsu constantly writhed and cackled, spitting out fragments of words in between his laughter, but I couldn't understand any of it.

All the while, the nurse was making cheerful sounds as she chewed her gum with well-practiced movements of her mouth. It almost looked as if she were scorning the patient's crazy behavior with the sound of that gum chewing.

"What about his temperature?" she asked.

"Put a thermometer in his mouth," the doctor said.

The hospital room at two in the morning was not very warm, but the young doctor's face was serious, and he was sweating profusely. He must have been feeling an intense occupational excitement and sense of duty. This time I had to pinion Jangsu's neck with both arms so he wouldn't spit out the thermometer.

"His temperature is normal," the nurse said, sounding disappointed.

The doctor contemplated deeply, with his head down for a long time, then looked up at me as if to say he'd finally come to a conclusion.

"What's happened?" I asked in as polite a tone as possible.

He answered a little hesitantly, "Well . . . not here. . . ."

It seemed to mean that he could not say it in front of the patient.

"It's alright," I said. "It looks to me like nothing's going to get through those ears."

"Still, for some reason I feel sorry to say such a thing in front of the patient."

It seemed the doctor had finally decided to hand down a grim sentence. He stopped talking again and took off his glasses. I was impatient but had to wait a long time until he wiped the sweat from around his eyes and adjusted his glasses.

"That is the final stage," he said. He pointed to Jangsu with the tip of his chin. "It's the final symptom of liver cirrhosis, called hepatic encephalopathy. There are two types: one where the patient throws fits as if they've gone mad, and the other where they fall asleep as if they're dead. There's a chance of both occurring at the same time. But in either case, the fact remains—they will not wake up."

The doctor was laying out his technical knowledge as if he were reciting something from memory. He didn't seem to have any sense that what he had pronounced was a death sentence for Jangsu.

"Is there *no* hope?" I asked.

"The time for intervention on our part has already passed. You shouldn't have left him in that condition until now. Are you a member of the family?" He threw me a quick glance, as if he were rebuking me.

"No," I said. "I was the class after him at university."

"Then you should contact the family. Quickly."

"How much time does he have?"

"Um . . . well . . . that's the rotten part. It could drag out for a long time in this condition. You see, his mind is gone, but because he's young, his heart and lungs are strong. If it's quick, a few hours, and if it's slow . . . it could go on for over a day."

"You're saying there's nothing at all the hospital can do for him? Like, extend his life just a little bit. . . ."

"Well . . . this is just my personal opinion, but in that shape, what would be the point of extending his life? Even for the patient, I mean."

Just then, as if to applaud the doctor's words, Jangsu burst out in laughter, and the nurse jumped back in horror. One of the first symptoms of hepatic encephalopathy—the fits that seemed like insanity—was intensifying by the hour.

"I think you should contact the patient's family and start the discharge process. Wouldn't it be better for him to be with his family than in the hospital?"

". . . Truth is, he doesn't *have* any family to contact." *Damn it.* The last part I added silently in my heart. In my head, what had unfolded was the horrifying scenario of not being able to contact anyone and having to shoulder the burden of Jangsu's death by myself.

"Both his parents passed away," I said. "I think he has relatives back home, but they all seem to have disowned him. Because he went to prison and such. . . ."

"Oh, I meant to ask earlier, but . . ." The doctor surreptitiously lowered his voice. "Who is Oh Mija?"

"What?"

"Wasn't that her name? Who the patient was asking for."

"She was his girlfriend."

"Is she pretty?"

I looked straight into the doctor's long face. When he smiled, he resembled a horse silently baring its teeth. He happened to be smiling now, his expression saying, *I'm just kidding.*

"Yes, she's very pretty," I answered, making a face that said, *I'm in no mood to kid around.*

He instantly wiped the smile from his lips and nodded his head seriously.

"It's really a shame. To leave this world when he's still so young. On top of that, leaving a pretty girl behind."

Raucous cries startled the doctor and drowned out what he was saying. Jangsu was bouncing around like a madman, the worn bedsprings popping with the force, the legs of the bed scraping across the floor with sharp metallic shrieks.

The bug that was trapped in the window screen now started buzzing loudly again, as if it had been waiting for this moment.

To tell the truth, I'd never thought of Mija as being pretty. If you had to describe her, you'd say she was more like a guy than a woman. No—it would be an exaggeration to say she was a guy. But, to be precise, she was like a girl who had been deprived of all sexual charm.

Carelessly cut hair, a loose-fitting shirt with rolled-up sleeves, faded jeans, and a stack of books always held against her chest—that's what typified her appearance. In short, she looked like a female guerrilla from some South American country that you see from time to time in the newspapers, and she was—of course—considered irredeemable among us. And when speaking of Mija, you could not leave out her mother.

It was now demolished to widen the road, but in those days, there was a shantytown clustered against the front of the school. There was an unlicensed restaurant called "Mama's House" among the shacks, where we always sequestered ourselves to get drunk in broad daylight. The proprietor was an old woman who wore a greasy money belt and spouted obscenities from her native Pyeongan-do up north. She was very fat and had such a husky voice that she sounded like a man. We loved the fried bean cakes she made, and we called her "Comrade Mama" because of her Pyeongan-do disposition and her superbly foul language. Calling her that didn't mean we thought she had some sort of suspicious ideology; we were just imitating a corny anti-communist drama we all watched on TV. She had a daughter she cherished—a lone girl among the many boys who frequented her place—and in consideration of that fact, we would sometimes honor her with the title of "Mother-in-law." Her daughter was Mija.

Mija would occasionally shuttle bean cakes and *makgeolli* when it got busy and didn't hesitate to squeeze in between us drunkards to imbibe the cloudy rice wine from the *makgeolli* bowl. The one who used to set the mood at our drinking bouts was Jangsu, and we had no choice but to timidly submit to his drinking prowess and his loud voice making pronouncements on the latest election, or the people, or the current state of the country's division into North and South, and on and on. Jangsu always walked around campus in white rubber shoes that shone brightly like a symbol of protest, and they had become his trademark. He was tacitly stating that he was on the side of the poor masses, since rubber shoes were what poor farmers wore. And Mija was always by his side. I would often see her at a table in Mama's House, mingling with Jangsu and others, participating in those intense debates that revived old political labels, tagging along behind him, calling him *"hyu-eong, hyeong"* in her clipped voice. On such occasions, I wondered if she'd grown up entirely ignorant of appropriate gender roles.

One especially clear fall day, I witnessed a peculiar sight as I walked toward the school rotary between my third and fourth period classes. In the middle of the rotary—which everyone in school had to pass at least once a day—was a white clock tower emblazoned with the logo of a well-known conglomerate. Someone had climbed to the top. Scores of people had gathered around the rotary to look up at the clock tower at the man who was shouting, shaking his clenched fist. As I continued walking, what caught my eye was Mija standing in the crowd, and I realized the man atop the clock tower must be Jangsu. He was wearing a white dress shirt and black pants, but more noticeable were his bare feet, pale and glowing in the bright sun.

He was continuously shouting something, but at that distance I couldn't understand what he was saying—it looked almost as if he were performing some sort of especially complicated pantomime. As I got closer, I could gradually make out what he was shouting:

"Down with the military dictatorship that obliterates democracy!

"Let's topple this autocratic regime and achieve freedom of the press!"

I reached Mija and stood right next to her, but she was looking up at Jangsu through tear-filled eyes, her face flushed. I saw a pair of white rubber shoes neatly placed at the base of the clock tower. Those kinds of shoes were prone to slipping off, and they must have been a hindrance to Jangsu's climbing the tower. They reminded me of the shoes left behind by people who threw themselves off of a bridge over the Han River.

"Guarantee the three basic rights of labor! Stop the oppression!

"Resume South-North talks to achieve peaceful unification!"

Among the scores of students and faculty staring up at the clock tower, there was no one who responded to his cries. His loud, clear voice just scattered, without an echo, into the air.

According to Emergency Measure No. 9, any gathering, protest, or act that denied or opposed the constitution—or advocated for or incited its amendment or abolishment—resulted in a prison sentence of over one year. All of us gathered around the base of that clock tower knew this. At a certain point, the police had started living on the school grounds, and the sight of riot policemen playing hacky sack on campus had become an everyday thing. Anyone who shouted an anti-government slogan anywhere on campus could be gagged and dragged off in an instant.

That was probably why Jangsu had climbed to the top of the clock tower. It would take time to crawl up there to capture him—and he could always threaten to jump.

Out of nowhere, two men, who were obviously plainclothes cops, appeared and started to climb up the clock tower.

Jangsu started singing the national anthem.

'Til the waters of the East Sea run dry and Mount Baekdu is worn away . . .

Someone near me started singing along.

Under God's blessing, long live our country . . .

The source of that tearful voice was Mija, but aside from her, there were no others who had dared to open their mouths.

Jangsu didn't jump from the clock tower as we all expected. He gave himself up, without resistance, to the plainclothes cops.

And the second verse hadn't even ended yet.

"You dogs!"

That's what I remembered as the last thing Mija had said. It was in the school rotary while Jangsu was being dragged away, right before our eyes, and hauled by the plainclothes cops into a black van. She hadn't pointed me out specifically, but she'd cursed all of us who were at the scene. And since I was among them, in her eyes I, too, must have been a dog.

Shortly after that, I enlisted and did not have a chance to see Mija again for a long time. In the military, I occasionally thought of her, and her last words would resurface vividly. When I was alone on guard duty, or at bedtime when I lay under my blanket with my hand in my shorts, I would recall every woman I knew one by one, and Mija was always the last in line.

"Dogs!"

Under the rough wool of my army-issued blanket, the breathless tangle of intimate pink flesh parading through my mind, I could finally hear Mija's cry in my ear, and when that happened, I could not resist the sharp, intense pleasure that stabbed me like the blade of a knife.

After I was discharged, I learned that Mama's House in front of the school had been torn down. No one had any news of Mija, but there was talk about Jangsu. He'd been tagged with additional charges for colluding with a treasonous organization, so he wouldn't be seeing the outside of a prison for several years. I re-registered in school and started drinking at the new draft beer hall across from the front gate. The president had been assassinated while I'd been in the military. A former general had become the new president, and an alarming rumor was circulating about several hundred people being killed by the military in a city in the south. But school was unaffected. It was as if nothing had happened.

If one thing had changed on campus, it was that the clock tower at the rotary had disappeared. Now an impressive fountain stood in its place, shooting up endless streams of water in the sunlight, creating rainbows as solid as steel, putting on a show of peace that only seemed breakable if a bomb were to be chucked at it.

One day, I discovered some graffiti neatly printed on the wall in a corner of the men's room in the Teacher's College:

DRIVE OUT THE YANKEE BASTARDS WHO AIDED
AND ABETTED THE GWANGJU MASSACRE!

The slogan seemed obscene somehow, as much as it was secretive and cowardly, and—out of nowhere—it brought back to mind the scrawled graffiti I had seen in middle school about the blond American woman, the Peace Corps volunteer who had been my English teacher.

The next time I saw Mija, it was by happenstance after I'd graduated. I was walking down to the bus stop just after work when I heard a woman's voice call out, "Gu Bonsu!"

A chocolate-colored luxury sedan pulled up next to me, and I could see the woman's face, in heavy makeup, through the half-open car window. Actually, what I saw first were the aviator shades that covered half her face.

"It's me," she said. "Don't you recognize me?"

"Do I know you?"

"How thoughtless. Not to recognize me."

When she took off the shades, a shockingly familiar face appeared. I could hardly believe she was Oh Mija. And when she said, "Say, hello. This is Emory. *My husband*," and indicated the driver's seat next to her, when a large hand—hairy like a fleshy sea crab—was stuck out in front of me, I couldn't figure out what was heads or tails. I took the hand, and when I bent down to look inside the car, I saw that its owner was a white guy, his face the color of a pale wine you might see in an American film. He clasped my hand tightly and spewed a long series of words I couldn't understand.

Mija laughed uproariously. "He's saying it's nice to meet you. Say something. You know how to say that much in English, don't you?"

Unfortunately, I did not know how to give even such a response. What made me finally open my mouth was seeing the old Korean woman in the back seat.

"Oh," I said. "How are . . . you?" I almost called her "Comrade Mama."

"Do you recognize me?" Comrade Mama was as assertive as ever. "How long has it been, Bonsu?"

"Well, I think this must be the first time since graduating."

"So, two and a half years? Three and a half? What have you been up to?"

"I went into the military and . . ."

"*Oh-ho* . . . that's plenty enough. Serve in the military, get a job, get married . . . that's right. Are you married?"

"Not yet," I said.

"Get in, Bonsu. You're going into the city, aren't you? We'll give you a ride."

I sat in the back seat with Comrade Mama.

When the car started moving, she opened her mouth again. "You must work around here," she said. "Where is it?"

I vaguely gestured toward the rear window. The building, built precariously like a castle on a hillside, seemed to grow taller as the car moved farther away.

"You mean that building? Isn't that a school?" Mija asked, turning her body.

Once again, I gave a vague nod.

"You're a schoolteacher? That must be hard work."

Mija must have been telling her husband what I did, and whatever she'd said, it made the middle-aged American laugh out loud. I stared, stupefied, at the network of fine wrinkles that instantly formed on his face.

"What do you make?" Mija's mother asked.

When I didn't understand what she'd said, she clapped me on the shoulder with her large hand.

"Hey, I mean your pay."

"Oh, yes," I said. "About three hundred thousand won. . . ." *More or less*, I added under my breath.

"That must be tough. Can you live on that?"

"You don't teach for the money." It sounded like a lie, even to me.

"Right," she said. "You must be doing it for the *satisfaction* it gives. You were always on the slow side when it came to money, you know. Always months behind. You could never pay your tab on time."

She laughed vigorously, and I followed with a meek chuckle. Mija and her husband were laughing and giggling continuously up front. The American's arm lay across Mija's shoulders, glistening, covered in golden hairs. His thick hand was fondling her—the edge of her ear, the back of her neck, sliding all the way to her shoulder—and I watched in wonder: this foreign stranger fondling a Korean woman I knew well. Whenever he said something, she answered, *"Yes, darling. Yes, darling."* Mija had been an English lit major in college, but I'd never known that she spoke English so well. I'd never realized that the word *darling* could sound so sweet.

After waiting, and after long deliberation, I finally managed to speak. "Mija," I said. "I heard Jangsu was asking for you. From prison."

3

"A lot has changed," Mija said as she sat down.

I nodded. "Yes. I can see you've changed as much as I have."

"I meant . . ." she smiled briefly, ". . . this café has changed. The Ivory Tower wasn't this noisy back then."

There was something that hadn't changed: the fine wrinkles that formed around her eyes and the bridge of her nose when she laughed. Seeing that, I suddenly felt weak, my entire body overcome by something like vertigo, as if the most vulnerable part of me was slowly being tickled by someone's soft touch. It was a subtle pain alerting me to a chronic ailment lurking deep in my belly.

"You've gotten prettier," I said. "I almost didn't recognize you."

"Oh, my. Thank you."

It was true. She looked so mature that I'd had to do a double take and ask myself if it was really her. How could I put it? She had the voluptuousness of a fruit so ripe it could burst at the slightest touch, and a dizzying fragrance, so much that I simply could not believe she was the woman who, in the old days, used to roam around campus like an urchin.

"Come to think of it, you've changed a lot, too. Knowing how to flatter a woman. How is it—are you satisfied?"

"What do you mean, 'satisfied'?"

"I mean, as a teacher."

Satisfaction . . . I thought as I pulled out a cigarette to put in my mouth. The matches I kept in my shirt pocket were damp from sweat and would not light easily.

"Sure," I said. "Our occupation survives on satisfaction, right?"

I answered that way because I thought the story would get too long if I'd said that I *didn't* feel satisfied. I felt anger slowly rising in me. As I finally lit a match for my cigarette, I recalled the things that had preoccupied me for the past six months: quarterly tuition charts I'd had to draw for each class, self-study initiatives, truancy lists. I wanted to make all those brats just run away from home as I snapped pieces of chalk between my fingers and smacked them over the head with my attendance book.

There was a brief silence between us. She was wearing black as if she were attending a funeral. But the dress had a neckline that plunged far too low and suggestively to be appropriate for that. I stole glances at her taut, bare skin, exposed by that dress, and I started to feel a tension growing from the bottom of my chest. I knew what I had to say now. It seemed that Mija had realized it, too, after listening to the silence for a while.

"Jangsu . . ." I said finally.

"Jangsu . . ."

We both stopped at the same time. Once again, the silence continued. It was a charged silence and—as if to explain its meaning—the lilting voice in the café's mood music was now letting out a series of urgent, breathy moans.

....

"MR. GU, PHONE CALL," WHISPERED MR. YUN, THE BIOLOGY TEACHER who sat in front of me. I frowned and whispered back, "Whoever it is, tell them to call back later." We were in the middle of a meeting, in the middle of the principal's speech. He loved giving speeches and, like anyone who loves giving speeches, hated it most when his passionate oratory was interrupted. But Yun passed me the handset anyway. "Take it," he said. "Whoever it is, he's very insistent."

I put the handset to my mouth and whispered, "Hello?"

"It's me. Your big brother."

"Hello? Who is this?"

"It's *me*, you idiot. Did you already forget my voice?"

A cold shiver ran up my spine. There are things you can forget. But how could I forget that voice?

"Who . . . Who is this?" I asked again in a whisper. I did *not* want it to be Jangsu. No, I refused to believe it was his voice. It sounded like it was coming from the cold and dark land of the dead.

"You idiot," he rumbled. "It's *me. Jangsu*. Why are you so surprised? You sound like you've seen a ghost. Idiot, I didn't break out of jail, so relax. It's been about a week. Here? I'm right under your nose. That's right. I've decided to pay you a visit. What's the starting salary for a second-class schoolteacher, anyway? Come buy a drink for prisoner number 2509. In the middle of what? A meeting? Fine, I'll wait. I waited three years—what's another couple of hours?"

"JANGSU HAD ASPIRATIONS," MIJA SAID.

"Coffee for me. And you, Mija?"

"Me too."

"From what I know," I said when the waitress had left with our order, "you were more ambitious than anyone."

"That's right. And that was also why I liked Jangsu. In that regard, we had something in common. People thought Jangsu's plans were reckless. Some even thought they were dangerous and foolish, but I believed in him. I dreamed the same dream as he did."

When a coil of hair fell on her forehead, she swept it back with her hand. The tops of her breasts were visible in the low-cut one-piece dress she wore.

"After I graduated, I worked at the Korean branch of an American company," she said.

She stirred her coffee as she started telling her story.

"You know that my degree was in English lit, right? I worked as the secretary for Emory, who was in charge of that company. And I learned that he was a divorced single father with two kids. One day, he invited my family out to dinner. As far as family goes, it's just Mom and me, but we met at a hotel restaurant. For my mother, it was the first time in her life at a place like that. Of course, it was her first time dining with an American, too. When the waiter was taking our order, she couldn't recognize anything with all the strange things on the menu. She said, 'I'm just gonna have a *jjajangmyeon*.' I was a little annoyed that she'd order such a low-class dish at a fancy restaurant, but I went ahead and told Emory that what my mother wanted was *jjajangmyeon*—noodles in black bean sauce. He ordered just that, but the waiter said they didn't have that dish. He said, 'If that's what you want, then you'll have to go to a Chinese restaurant.' I translated word for word. Then Emory called the manager. To ask him to order one from a Chinese restaurant. Think about it. The scene it must have made—a Chinese delivery boy, with the eyes of all the other restaurant guests on us, dropping off a bowl of *jjajangmyeon* at our table."

She paused for a moment, as if to give me a chance to picture that scene.

"Is that the reason you married him?" I asked.

"That's when I knew. That Jangsu's ambitions and that bowl of *jjajangmyeon* were the same thing."

"So you abandoned Jangsu and chose the *jjajangmyeon*."

"I didn't abandon Jangsu. I just saw the truth behind the things I'd been dreaming about then. Jangsu had ambition but no power. The American lacked ambition but he had power. That was enough for me. Because *I* had the ambition."

I shoved a hand into my pocket. The thing was still there. A warmth, like the body heat of a living person, was transmitted through my fingers. It was pulsing in my hand like the sweltering heat of the summer evening. I suddenly felt like I had to piss.

"WHAT HAPPENED?" I ASKED JANGSU.

We were sitting down, across from each other at a bar, for the first time in many years. I wasn't asking how he happened to be released from prison with years still left on his sentence. The extent of his illness was obvious from just a glance at his face. His skin was so jaundiced it looked like he'd been dipped in yellow paint. Even the whites of his eyes were yellow, and his close-shaved head made it more noticeable.

Without a word, Jangsu undid his belt and showed it to me. He indicated one end of it with his finger. I saw several newly made holes, besides the original ones, gradually moving closer to the tip. And the last one—showing the white of the inner leather—was precarious, dangling at the very end as if it were about to tear.

"It's a disease that makes it impossible to buckle your belt," Jangsu said, as if he were talking to a stranger. He rubbed his belly, which was swollen like a pregnant woman about to deliver.

"It's full of shitty water," he said. "Apparently, they didn't know what to do, either. So, they let me out. You could say they took my punishment out of the hands of man and passed it on to the hand of God."

He looked up at the empty sky and mimicked the sign of the cross. He had definitely changed—just as garrulous, but his former seriousness had become a kind of brash self-mockery. It was not funny to me as I watched him add the measure of a glass of beer to the already immense volume indicated by the dome of his belly.

"Isn't it bad for you to be drinking?" I asked.

"At least beer helps me piss," he said. "With this damn condition, it's really a bitch. They had to drain me with a rubber hose once. My liver's so swollen it can't even filter out piss anymore. Strange, isn't it? Before I got sick, I didn't even know what the liver did. When the liver stops working, you get to learn of its existence, and when the appendix ruptures, you become aware of its existence—you see? What it comes down to is that existence is pain, and pain is existence. Have you heard any news about Mija?"

I was flustered, and because his question was so sudden, I couldn't hide my embarrassment.

"By the time I visited the school, Mama's House was torn down without a trace," he said. "No one has any news about her."

He shot a look straight at me. His shaved head gleamed like a knife blade in the light. It was like cold air flowing down the walls, and it instantly sent a chill down my spine. I ignored his gaze.

"You little shit. You're hiding something, aren't you?"

....

"I'M LEAVING FOR AMERICA, NEXT MONTH," MIJA SAID. "MY HUSBAND'S hometown is in Tennessee, a place called Memphis. He's always bragging about how that's where Elvis Presley is buried."

She smiled a little, parting her lips and exposing her pink gums. A desperate longing stirred in my heart.

"Dogs," I mumbled to myself.

"What?" she said.

"Don't you remember? What you said to us the day Jangsu was arrested? Under the clock tower?"

There was a light sheen of sweat around her neck. I imagined myself kissing that smooth, white skin, my arms wrapped around her neck. I could taste her fragrant perspiration on my lips and see the vivid marks they left—like tattoos—all over her body. I suddenly, very much, wanted to hear the word *darling* come from Mija's mouth.

"Let's get out of here," she said, getting up. "It's too stuffy."

4

Jangsu's fits were now at their peak. He shouted and contorted his body without rest, bouncing up and down in the bed like a shaman possessed by spirits. But even as he was causing the commotion, his eyes were fixed on a certain spot in the air. Someone invisible to us was beating him, and it looked as if he were trying, with all his might, to resist that unbearable pain.

We watched the fits absentmindedly. We were the ones who used to drain copious amounts of *makgeolli* at the old Mama's House. Now we were an insurance agent, a graduate student, and a magazine reporter, but we were the ones who remembered Jangsu. With time so short, I had hastily summoned them, and they'd made excuses on the phone—too much drinking the previous night, lack of sleep—but they'd eventually shown up, their eyes still puffy.

"As I said before," the doctor said, "I think it's best to take him home now. There's nothing the hospital can do for him. All that's left is the vigil, and that should be at home, don't you think?"

"Isn't there some way to at least calm him down? Like, maybe giving him a shot?"

"I don't know. Wouldn't it be cruel to go so far as to anesthetize a patient in that condition just to stop his fits?"

"Cruel? What about chasing such a patient out of the hospital? That would hardly be a compassionate thing to do."

"The patient's fate would be the same anyway," the doctor said, "whether he's in the hospital or at home. From a medical perspective, we've tried our best and there's nothing else we can do. There's no point in him staying here in the hospital. The hospital might as well be the side of a road."

"How long will those fits last? Until he's dead?"

"Normally, they would have stopped by now, but he's on the stubborn side. These types of patients tend to cause problems later, too. When the fits stop, he'll fall asleep, and he'll slowly pass away in his sleep. Very slowly. The stubborn ones drag it out just hanging on. Watch. It will be exhausting."

"Well, regardless, you'll have to take care of him in the hospital until the end. We have nowhere to go."

"Look, the problem is his shouting. It's bothering the other patients. The patient next door is scheduled for surgery tomorrow, and he's terribly stressed because he can't get any sleep. As you know, peace and quiet are crucial before surgery. . . . Isn't there *some* way you could contact the patient's family?"

"Even if we could reach them, it's too late now. Truth is, we don't know his family situation well, either. About all we know is he's from somewhere in the countryside in Jeolla-do, and he had an elderly mother who passed away recently . . . and he's cut all ties with his hometown."

. . . .

"DO YOU KNOW WHAT THE FOLKS BACK HOME SAY ABOUT ME?" JANGSU said. "They say I'm possessed by a communist ghost. My father died before I was born. Like father like son, they say."

IT WAS TURNING LIGHT OUTSIDE THE WINDOW. BEHIND THE GLOOMY hospital building, the city was stirring, waking from its sleep. The blood-red glow of dawn hung in the distance, foreshadowing the heat of the day to come.

"We've been forced to take on a difficult burden."

The insurance agent clicked his tongue.

"I have to travel all the way to Busan—today."

"What are you talking about?" the graduate student said. "This is called friendship, not a burden."

"I thought that way, too, at first. When we agreed to hospitalize him and split the cost, it was a burden, but I thought our past friendship could handle it. That I'd be able to give up my business trip. If I called in sick, someone else would probably go. But now we're stuck with taking care of his death. I didn't want Jangsu's death to become my responsibility."

Because what he said was true, we didn't have a reply.

Just then, the nurse exclaimed, "Oh, no! What do we do? Come look at this."

She pointed at Jangsu, who was wrapped in a white sheet. The area around his groin was turning dark and wet. He had suddenly become very quiet. We gathered around the bed with bated breath, as if we were viewing some spectacle, and watched the wetness spread across the sheet.

The nurse groaned. "He's peeing," she said in a hushed voice.

"What's the fuss?" the doctor said. "Is this your first time seeing someone piss?" But he, too, couldn't take his eyes off the sheet, which was quickly soaked. "The fits have finally stopped," he explained. "Look—he's quiet, isn't he?

"Usually, liver cirrhosis is a condition that interferes with normal urination. That's why patients suffer so much. But you see how strong the flow is now? That's the last sign. His autonomic nervous system is paralyzed, and it's just leaking out. There are some who cry because they can't urinate, so, in a way, his wish is being fulfilled. He can just let loose like that. It's a shame he can't feel that release, since he's unconscious."

But to us it looked as though Jangsu was enjoying the feeling of release. He was unbelievably calm now, with a satisfied grin on his face. The way he was snoring softly—as if dreaming a sweet dream— could not have seemed more peaceful.

"This is the beginning of his long sleep," the doctor said quietly.

5

"You haven't asked me once how Jangsu died."

I lifted the beer bottle and filled the glass. The dark liquid reached the top and spewed thick foam.

"Aren't you curious? Whether he died from a disease, a car accident, suicide. . . ."

We were at a nightclub now, at the very top of a hotel. Loud disco music played in the dance hall. Red and blue lights flashed convulsively, and a crowd of men and women were tangled together on the dance floor, shaking their bodies.

"That's not important," Mija said as she lifted her glass. I watched her long pale neck as she gulped down the beer and emptied the glass. "You said on the phone that his death was peaceful, didn't you? I don't believe that. His death must have been wretched. That suits him better."

We filled each other's glasses again and emptied them at the same time. A light chill shot up my spine and settled in my head. I knew I was getting drunk. Mija gently licked the beer suds from her lips as she looked straight at me. Then a light tickling sensation made the hairs on my body stand on end like metal shavings being drawn by a magnet. And something started bobbing inside my body like a fishing float, and the line connected to that float grew taut. I knew what it was. It was my desire ambushing me while my guard was down.

"We always thought that Jangsu was so strong he never even caught a cold," I said. "But we never realized what he was hiding. His insides were a wreck. It was liver cirrhosis."

"What kind of disease is that?"

"It hardens your liver like cement, according to the doctor. He said the cause was malnutrition from when Jangsu was an infant."

Mija stared for a long time in the direction of the stage where people were dancing. A woman was moving frantically, as if she had disassembled all her limbs and was now putting them back together. Under the suggestive lights, her expression looked like someone moaning with fever.

"Do you know how he got the name Jangsu?" Mija asked, her eyes still turned away from me.

"I know a lot about his childhood. You know he was born in '53, right? He told me his father died just before the end of the war, accused of being a communist. When his mother saw her husband's bloody corpse, she had a miscarriage and passed out. I'll tell you what Jangsu said: When they picked up that baby's legs to throw it out, it started squirming and crying. That's why they named him Jangsu. *Jang*, meaning long, and *Su*, meaning life, so he might live a long life since it was almost cut short."

We emptied our glasses again. A chill, even faster and more powerful than before, rushed up to the top of my head.

"You said it was malnutrition from infancy? Then it's like his death was preordained from the start. At birth." She stopped.

I grasped the object in my pocket, one of the presents left behind by Jangsu. As we'd returned from the funeral, we divided them up among ourselves and each got a piece. I thought about what I was going to do with it now. As far as I knew, there was no way to take care of it, at least under the skies of this city. I wondered how the others took care of their presents. I watched the people dancing as if they were possessed. I imagined each of them hiding the same thing in their pockets. They just weren't showing it. Something like nausea circulated in my gut and surged upward.

I looked at Mija, who was clearly drunk now, and suddenly couldn't restrain myself from saying something terrible to her.

"Jangsu didn't just die. It was murder. We all killed him."

"Are you saying we're accomplices?" Mija threw her head back and laughed. Something flashed in her eyes—just a tear, tiny, like a drop of rat's piss.

The string that had been pulled deep inside me was now so taut I couldn't tell if what I felt was desire or pain. Every time I moved and the string shifted, pulled tight, and jolted me with an intense, unbearable sensation, I reflexively grasped the object in my pocket.

THE ONLY THING LEFT AT THE BOTTOM OF THE CLOCK TOWER IN THE rotary was the pair of white rubber shoes that had fallen from Jangsu's feet. Mija picked them up and turned toward us.

"You dogs!" she screamed at the students who hadn't yet dispersed. She held the rubber shoes in one hand and pointed the index finger of her other hand at us. Her face was blotchy, flushed red with rage and sadness. We watched the barrel of that gun slowly draw a semicircle as it took aim at us, one by one. We all remained silent until her finger made a full 360-degree circle.

"You dogs!" she screamed again. "You're *all* fucking accomplices."

....

"YOU'RE RIGHT," MIJA SAID WHEN SHE STOPPED LAUGHING. "WE WERE all complicit."

The more I drank, the more parched I became. Mija tilted her head back and drank slowly, as if to say, *Just look how beautiful my neck is.* I could see it clearly, of course, and at the same time I fitfully imagined wrapping my arms around that long neck and kissing it—once, twice, three times.

WE WERE LISTENING TO JANGSU'S BREATHING. IT ALREADY SOUNDED like a worn-out compressor, too rough to be called respiration, and it came in two distinct parts: a sharp metallic noise with the inhale followed by the sound of congestion.

All the parts of his body were now being used for the task of breathing. It sounded like water was being pumped from the soles of his feet to the crown of his head before sinking back down, deep underground. The tense part was that, after taking a breath, he would be entirely silent for a moment, and then we had to wait, intently watching his throat, fearing that the silence might go on forever.

But what followed—as if to mock our concern—was the quiet sound of a phlegmy exhale. It fooled us every time, and yet we couldn't help but tense up each time, only to taste both disappointment and relief whenever his breathing stopped and started again.

The sound of his congestion didn't seem to be coming from his throat but leaking out from somewhere much deeper. Whenever there was a sharp vibration of his larynx, like a scratch on a metal plate, we felt horribly congested, as if that gelatinous yellow phlegm was filling our own mouths.

I bolted up and went to the open window. The backyard of the hospital was visible below. I hawked up my phlegm, as if to wring it out from my whole body, and spat it out. I watched it draw a long arc and fall to the ground far below.

Then one of my friends ran up next to me and spat as well, and before his ball of phlegm even hit the ground, another one was launched. In the end, we were all hanging out of the windows, straining our bodies to spit, each trying to outdo the other to make our wads of phlegm arc wider and land farther away.

"How long has it been?"

"It's been seven hours and twenty minutes."

"Just like him to hold on for such a long time."

"You think maybe we're being fooled?" the insurance agent asked. His eyes were still watery from all the hawking up.

"Jangsu's actually sleeping. Passed out in a very deep sleep. And he's gonna get up any minute and go, 'Hey, what are you guys doing over there?' Just look at that peaceful face." He went on excitedly as if he'd made a great discovery. "Or he might not be sleeping. He's tricking us. He's pretending to sleep and listening to everything we say around him. I'm right, aren't I, Jangsu?"

Then he collapsed into a chair.

"Ahhh, if it would only rain. . . ."

I LOOKED AT MIJA. SHE WAS HOLDING A HALF-FULL GLASS AND HAD HER head down. Each time she took a deep breath, her breasts heaved, and I realized what I had been wanting.

I was going somewhere, supporting her, to a room that was sealed on all four sides. She was completely drunk, almost passed out. I laid her down and took her clothes off. They came away, one layer at a time, like onion peels, and that whole time she mumbled, constantly, "*Darling, darling.*" I imagined the body heat transmitted when my fingers touched her skin. I imagined that elasticity and the softest texture that might rub off like flower pollen against my fingers. . . .

"What time is it?" she asked, instead of looking at the watch on her wrist.

"It's a little past eleven."

She vaguely nodded her head, as if she wasn't much troubled by the late hour. I thought about whether I should call the waiter and order more beer. I knew she could drink, and the amount of alcohol we'd consumed already was surely approaching the limits of safety. But in order to get her drunk enough to lose control, I needed to get more alcohol into her. I knew very well that what I was thinking now was completely inappropriate, and yet I could not let it go. But what if she realized that it was getting late just when I ordered more beer. . . .

"Jangsu isn't dead," she said with her head down.

I picked up the lamp in front of me to call the waiter, hoping she wouldn't notice.

"He's alive," Mija said. "Only him. He won't commit any sins or fall into temptation. He lives forever."

The light of the lamp cast a red glow over her face, and she didn't see the waiter approaching. I held up two fingers, and to make sure he understood that I meant two bottles of beer, I pointed to the empty bottles in front of me. He nodded and went back.

"If he's alive, then *we* must be dead," I replied half-heartedly as I casually put a cigarette in my mouth.

Mija placed her hand on top of mine, and the warmth of her body instantly summoned the heat of desire in me.

"Yes. We're the dead ones," she said, her voice just above a whisper.

Just then, the waiter appeared with the bottles of beer. I stopped him before he could distract us by noisily popping the caps and opened them myself. When I filled Mija's glass halfway, she stood up, staggering a little.

"What's wrong?"

"I should go," she said.

"The beer just got here."

"I need to go, first. The rest . . ." She smiled with just one side of her mouth, and—perhaps it was just my perception—it looked like she was mocking me.

"You can finish it," she said.

"Uh, wait for me. I'll see you out."

I picked up her purse. She was definitely drunk—her neck, exposed by her low-cut dress, confirmed that fact. I stared vacantly at the red patch, mottled into an exotic design, beneath her pale skin. In that moment, I wanted to lie down, spread-eagle on the floor. It seemed the only way to stop her was to have an epileptic seizure.

"Sir."

Someone tapped my shoulder as we were about to leave. It was the waiter, looking at me, smiling. "This is yours, isn't it? It was left on your seat."

He placed something in my hand, and I quickly shoved it in my pocket. Then, as he was about to turn away, I asked, "Do you know what this is?"

"Not really," he said. "I don't know what it is, sir, but it looks very strange."

He was smiling, wearing a slippery expression. I couldn't tell what he was really thinking.

"Please come again," he said, bowing at the waist.

I stepped out of the club.

"Are you alright?" I called out to Mija.

She was standing in front of the elevator waiting for the door to open. She looked at me with indifference, her face seeming to say, *Who is this guy, exactly?* Then she nodded slowly, as if she finally recognized my face. I looked at my watch. It was eleven thirty. I thought to myself how great it would have been if the national curfew was still in force.

"You don't look good," I said.

"You, Bonsu . . ." After studying me carefully, perplexed for some reason, she slurred the end of her sentence. "Look *very* good." Then she quickly turned away and stared at the number display, looking uncomfortably stiff.

The lighted numbers were slowly counting up. I stole a glance at my reflection in the hallway mirror. My face was very red. Not just my face, but every part not covered by clothing was red. As I was about to turn away, I was startled to see that something was bulging from the crotch of my pants. To anyone seeing it—no, even when I saw it—it looked like my pants were tented by a shameless hard-on. But, actually, it was the thing I'd shoved into my pocket earlier.

The elevator opened, and a very fat, old woman staggered out with a very thin man, both of them drunk. We got in, and with the door closed, even when it was just the two of us inside the cramped space, Mija did not say anything. With her back turned to me, she was fixated on the number display.

I suddenly felt laughter welling up. I had just realized why she was suddenly ignoring me and acting so awkward. I looked down at my pants. The bulge was still there, standing tall. I hastily covered my mouth with my hand and suppressed the laughter. Somehow, this was all so terribly funny I could hardly bear it.

"*Taxiii!*" I called out as soon as we exited the hotel. A pair of head-lights was rushing toward us from the other end of the street. I ran out into the middle of the road and waved it down.

"Hannam-dong!"

The taxi slowed momentarily, then drove off.

"It might be tough to catch a cab," I said to Mija, putting on my best worried expression. She was lost in thought over something, not budging from the hotel entrance. A light was approaching slowly in the distance—a taxi, obviously looking for an additional fare, a rideshare customer.

I raised my hand to stop the cab and saw the driver stick his head out the window.

"Hannam-dong," I said.

"Hannam-dong? Good!"

There was a middle-aged man in the back seat. He looked like he could be passed-out drunk, but he shouted as if he were talking in his sleep. "Get in!"

I left the taxi door open and called out, "Mija!"

She approached slowly. But instead of climbing into the cab, she bent over at the waist and spoke to the driver. "Just go," she said.

"What?"

"I'm not getting in, so just go."

"Are you people drunk?" The driver gunned the car forward, as if to say, *Good riddance.*

"I'm not going home tonight," Mija said.

"What are you saying?"

"Don't you know what it means when a woman says she's not going home?"

6

The bellhop flipped the switch on the wall. I blinked at the sudden bright light and stared at the scene it revealed in a daze.

"It's quite a view. You can see all of Seoul's nightscape from up here."

"Thank you." Mija opened her purse to withdraw a single bill and deftly placed it in the bellhop's palm.

He bent down ninety degrees at the waist. "Thank *you*. And . . ." he turned his head toward me and winked. ". . . Have a good night."

I tried to wink back at him but couldn't—I just made an odd grimace. For some reason, I had lost all confidence as soon as I walked back into the hotel, and my body was suddenly overcome by the alcohol. I tried to speak nonchalantly but the sound that came out was so loud that even I was startled.

"Is there a TV? Television?"

"Of course there is," the bellhop replied, as if he'd anticipated the question.

"Color, I mean."

"Of course it's color." He went into the room and turned the TV on. We heard the sound of applause and then the sound of a familiar song.

"That's fine," Mija said. "You can go now."

Before leaving, the bellhop paused in the hall and winked at me again, but I decided not to return the gesture.

"What are you doing out there?" Mija said from inside.

"Uh, I'm coming."

Of course, I should have gone in, but for some reason my feet would not move. I had imagined scenes like this for a long time—thousands of times. And yet, now that I was actually alone with a woman in a hotel room, I could not, for the life of me, remember what to do or how to start a conversation.

Mija sat on the edge of the bed, watching TV. She looked as if she had completely forgotten that she had just now walked into a hotel room with a man who was not her husband. She seemed so oblivious that I considered slipping out the door and running away.

I went over to the window and looked outside. In the distance, light from the banks of the Han River was beginning to surrender to the darkness, and in the streets, the processions of cars were gradually diminishing, making way for the silence and night. I bent my neck and looked down below the window. I could see the hotel entrance fifteen floors below, and a light—spread out like a white handkerchief—on the street. I suddenly felt the urge to jump. My body would descend in a flash and crash into the ground. It would not take long, even from fifteen stories up. There might not even be enough time to scream, and my face would be pulverized, kissing the pavement. The images were vivid—I could even feel the solid, cold touch of the hard asphalt, and it gave me a dull and heavy sensation of pleasure.

I thought of Jangsu's final appearance. He died twenty-eight hours after the onset of his fits, twenty-four hours after falling asleep. And during those final twenty-four hours, he died slowly. His breathing grew more labored, and his body gradually wasted away. It looked as if he had lived his whole life in the span of that time. Finally, his face became just skin and bones and froze into a jester's mask. The next morning, he drew his last breath. I clearly recalled the moment when we were changing him out of his hospital gown and into a shroud. We briefly paused in the middle of taking off his underwear as the first rays of the morning sun serendipitously shone in through the window onto his exposed penis. Surprisingly, though he had been in the military, he was still uncircumcised, and we stared for a long time at the dead man's sex organ as it gleamed like a newborn child's, illuminated by that single ray of sunlight.

"How long are you going to stay like that?" Mija said with her back turned to me.

At that moment, I wanted to run up to her, grab her by the hair, and speak roughly to her, saying, "Now tell me how you want it." But what I barely managed to say, instead, sounded stupid even to me:

"What do we do now?"

She turned around laughing loudly. "Hey, Bonsu," she said, and looking straight at me, she whispered, in a sweet voice, "Do you know why I came here with you?"

She smiled and gave me a wink. It was my second time seeing that kind of smile in this hotel room. But this one was a far better sight than the bellhop's. Her lips were slightly parted, revealing her glistening gums. I stared absently at her gums, shining and livid in the soft light of the hotel room, her teeth oddly distinct and sturdy like tiles. She straightened one of her fingers and pointed at the crotch of my pants.

"I noticed that a while ago. And I figured out what it is you wanted."

I bowed my head to look down at myself. That bulge was still there. But I was sure it was the thing in my pocket, though it was a real mystery to me how it could protrude so obviously all night. I spoke, suppressing the urge to pull the thing out of my pocket and hold it in front of her eyes, to tell her to take a close look.

"Is that how Americans think?" I asked.

"Not at all, it's the opposite," she said. "It's because you're Korean, Bonsu. You see, I've never slept with a Korean man."

It looked like she was coming closer, but then she abruptly stopped. She narrowed her eyes and raised her arms slightly. "Now, let's celebrate our complicity."

I slowly stepped forward to meet her.

Her body was softer and more voluptuous than I'd imagined. It was so unexpected to me that her body would be so receptive, and yet my hands remained on her waist, frozen. If I did as I wanted, I would have known well how to move those hands, but I could not. Some unknowable fear weighed heavily on me—it felt as if I were about to do a terrible and despicable thing.

"NOW IT'S YOUR TURN." THE GRAD STUDENT GAVE ME A NUDGE.

I got up from my seat. The magazine reporter had just finished his turn. He was wet up to his knees, staggering out of the water with a ghastly, pale face like a man who had just done something awful.

"I'm gonna pass," I said, sitting down again.

"What's the matter?"

"My stomach's acting up. I've never touched anything like that with my own hands."

"You dumbass! You think anyone else is used to this sort of thing?"

He shoved me. I staggered into the water and waded out. As the magazine reporter passed me, our palms touched somberly, like players being substituted in a sports arena. The ground under my feet was slippery, and the current was so strong I teetered precariously with every step. I looked ahead, barely keeping my body upright. It was the Hantan River. After finishing the cremation, we'd found our way there, carrying Jangsu's ashes. All we had left to do was wade through the current and spread his ashes in the water, one person at a time.

AS OUR LIPS MET, SHE PUSHED SOMETHING SOFT AND SPONGY INTO my mouth, slick with desire, licking every crevice inside. I felt myself being sucked into some pitch-black wetland, suffocating from lack of oxygen. At the same time, my entire body became so weak that I found it difficult to stand. I could hear the sounds of us moaning as we moved backward, trying to maintain that posture, and I was certain it would probably end on the pink sheets that covered the bed. We both staggered, unable to find our balance, panting as if we were running a three-legged race. When she fumbled around and flipped off the lights, the curtain of darkness engulfed us. We bumped into something and fell over.

THE CURRENT CLUTCHED MY LEGS AND MADE ME SLIP. I RAISED MY body again, catching myself over and over as I moved forward. Jangsu was about halfway into the middle of the river. No, actually, his ashes were in the hands of the insurance salesman, waiting to be scattered by me.

The insurance salesman shook them in front of me. "Welcome. Mr. Kim Jangsu presently awaits your outstretched hand."

I somehow ended up with my face being dunked in the water.

....

THE SOUND OF A FIRE TRUCK SIREN CAME FROM SOMEWHERE. IT started faintly in the distance, then gradually grew louder, vaulting through the window, and after its horrific wailing, which lasted for a while, it diminished in intensity and once again slowly slipped away to some unseen place in the darkness. An ominous silence set in.

My mouth kept going dry. Bit by bit, the scent of Mija's mouth slipped me into vertigo. The dizzying scent of overripe fruit bursting—it was also the smell of worldly things decaying. Something enormous was slowly toppling over into the flames. Embers scattered in the night sky like fireflies. The whole world had burned up and was crumbling at the mere touch of a hand. Her lips were persistent, and they left me breathless.

I BARELY MANAGED TO STAND UP. THAT THING, WRAPPED IN WHITE paper, was suddenly thrust before my eyes.

"Now, grab a handful and scatter it."

Needless to say, they were human bones—pale white, some ground finely and some remaining as large lumps. There were fragments with blood-colored speckles, like rust, but what I felt more than anything, when it was put in front of me, was the intense warmth, like the breath of a living person, coming from the ashes. It was Jangsu's breath.

"YOU'RE DEAD," I PANTED. THEN I SAID TO MIJA, IN A HOARSE VOICE, "Do you know how much Jangsu asked for you? Until the moment he died, he only asked for you. And that's what I told him . . ." Her sweaty face was pressed so close to mine that it felt like I wasn't talking to her but rather to myself. ". . . that you were dead."

But Mija was alive. Her body feverish in the corner room of the kind of hotel you could find anywhere in this city, she was moving against me, her breasts pressing down on me.

"That's right," she said. "I died." Her voice was unexpectedly calm. "All the promises made to our generation are already dead. I just learned that a bit early. Now, let's bury our corpses." Her hand slid down and searched my body. With startling speed, she found my member and grasped it.

"Now raise that tombstone for me," she said. "Hurry."

Her voice had an irresistible power and sounded as if it were coming from that deep, dark place, far away, or from a place so high as to be invisible. Her hand gripped the tombstone and raised it.

"SAY SOMETHING. SAY THAT YOU PRAY HE RESTS IN PEACE," THE SALESman said.

But I couldn't say anything. When the heat shot up—the moment I thought of it as Jangsu's breath—I felt an unbearable queasiness. In a daze, I grabbed the ashes with both hands and scattered them into the air. But Jangsu's breath did not disappear. It clung to my body and persisted, licking at me. Then a gust of wind blew in my direction, and I was enveloped in white, as if I were covered in flour. I dunked myself in the river, vomit shooting up from my throat. While I flailed around in the water to wash away Jangsu's breath, I could not stop the involuntary retching.

YOU HAVE BEEN WATCHING KBS, BROADCASTING FROM SEOUL, REPUBLIC of Korea. . . . The TV station we had left on was ending its broadcast day. The national anthem blared. *'Til the waters of the East Sea run dry and*

Mount Baekdu is worn away . . . That somber and melancholy song—always inadequate and depressing whenever I heard it—now seemed fitting. As the music played, the Korean colors came down the flagpole. It was Mija's black dress, wrapped around her like a flag, and as it came down, it revealed a world, bright and abundant, in the empty space left behind.

I was frantically fumbling with my hands, but things did not go as planned. I'd been through situations like this countless times before in my imagination. But in real life, a woman's clothes are much more complicated and full of booby traps—like buttons and hooks—parts that you can touch but whose use you cannot figure out.

"Don't you want to see what Jangsu looks like now?" I asked. I still can't understand why I said such a stupid thing.

"What do you mean?"

"Jangsu's here with us now. Want to see?"

Still, it seemed that Mija had no idea what I was talking about.

"Touch it," I said.

In the darkness, I guided her hand onto that hard, lumpy object.

"What *is* this?" she whispered, the pitch of her voice rising.

I realized that I was running toward a place from which there would be no returning, a cliff that—if I took one more step—would send me hurtling into the abyss. And yet, at the same time, I could not resist the pleasure that was spreading precariously in my chest. I extended my arm to turn on the nightstand lamp.

"Take a good look."

For a moment, nothing. But in the next moment, there were two short screams, back-to-back. The first came from Mija, and the next from me. Then I realized I'd been shoved—in that brief moment—off the bed, and that I had tumbled head over heels onto the floor, my chin striking so hard I thought it might have broken.

"Get out," she said from above me. "Get out, Bonsu."

I couldn't answer because of the pain in my chin. The only thing I was able to communicate was "Ouch!" And only when she got up and stood on the floor did I barely manage to speak. "Hey, what's going on?"

"Get out of here," she said coldly. "Now!" Then she corrected herself and said, "No, I'll leave."

Clutching my chin with one hand, I watched her quickly getting dressed, arranging her clothes. They seemed surprisingly uncomplicated under the bright light, and I had the absurd thought that if I got the chance to undress her again, I could do it easily.

I could have said something simple like, "I'm sorry, Mija. Please, hear me out," or "I'll go—you sleep here," and so on. But my chin hurt too much. Until she picked up her purse and slammed the door shut behind her, there was not even the sound of a cough between us.

I sat there, still, listening to her rapid footsteps growing distant down the hallway. The terrible pain swam to the top of my head. I got up slowly.

The thing was on the pink sheet. That object, so out of place on a bed for two—it lay there quietly as if it had been there for a long time. I picked it up.

"IT'S NOT OVER, YET!" THE INSURANCE SALESMAN SHOUTED. "THERE'S still the last part of the ceremony."

During the long bus ride back, a strange lively energy was circulating among us. We looked like we had just been through a shamanic ceremony that exorcised bad fortune, and thus had gained a certain optimism and confidence about our lives.

The salesman deliberately craned his neck to look around at those present and spoke in a polished voice. "Um . . . on behalf of the deceased, I would like to offer sincere gratitude for attending despite the extreme heat. To uphold the wishes of the deceased, I would like to pass on a gift to each of you. Now, what could this be?"

He lifted up what he was holding in his hand and waved the object—wrapped in white paper—in front of our eyes.

"Kim Jangsu may have been carried away by the waters of the Hantan River, but we wish for him to remain by our side for all time. The deceased did not ignore our desperate wishes. That is why he left us this gift. What I mean is, we must equally share these in consideration of the last wishes of the deceased."

"Hey, your introduction is too long," the grad student said.

The salesman paused for a moment while he caught his balance in the moving bus. "Let the dead judge the living," he said. "Let the living bear witness for the dead. The condition of life, as a poet once said, is loneliness. . . ." He paused again, but this time it was because of hiccups.

Staggering and hiccupping, and yet still managing to act like a priest on a pulpit, he took the objects wrapped in paper and divided them among us.

"We must engrave on our hearts that the reason for our preserving these relics is to remember him and bear witness on his behalf. Oh, dear departed, may you rest in peace. And may you live with us forever."

"Amen," the grad student added.

The magazine reporter was sitting next to me. "I read somewhere that warriors in this one tribe in Africa wear a very special ornament around their necks," he said. "I saw a picture once. They were wearing war trophies around their necks, from battles they won against other tribes. They say the most prized trophy of all is the bones of a man they killed themselves."

I looked down at the so-called present from Kim Jangsu I held in my hand. That light and solid object lying silent and impassive in my palm—it was a piece of bone.

FROM SOMEWHERE, THE FAINT SOUND OF A SIREN APPROACHED AND then disappeared. I had a terrible headache. I lifted my body and staggered to the window.

The city was smothered in darkness. I looked down into it for a long time. Somewhere, a person will die and something will decay, and as inevitably as a rat will gnaw on old wood, an ember resurrected from a pile of ashes will slowly grow and burn again.

But there was no sound. It was all terribly quiet, and everyone was trapped in a deep sleep from which they could not awake.

Suddenly, I felt I was suffocating from an unbearable shame. I bowed my head and pressed my forehead against the cool glass. A lump of heat rose up from deep within my throat. When it was so large that I could no longer contain it, I finally threw it up. I was crying.

I extended my arm into the darkness like a soldier about to throw a grenade. And I hurled that fragment of Jangsu's bone with all my might. It flew high up into the thin air like a small bird freed from its cage, and then it disappeared, as if it had been sucked into a silent abyss.

But in the next instant, I could hear it clearly—an enormous boom that could, in a single breath, blow away this world's terrible slumber.

Translated by Yoosup Chang & Heinz Insu Fenkl

THE LEPER

... to survive, to hang on,

waiting for the new world to dawn,

what can you do but become a leper

nobody in the world would deign to touch?

—FROM "WINDY EVENING" BY KIM SEONG-DONG

BEFORE I KNOCKED, I TOOK A MOMENT TO CALM MY BREATH-
ing. But even a couple of deep breaths did nothing to lessen
my anxiety, and to the sound of voices on the other side, I
carefully pushed open the thick door.

A female clerk sat at the desk just inside. "How may I help you?"
she asked. The room wasn't as large as I'd imagined. Directly in my
line of sight from the door, I could see a man in his forties sitting with
his back to the window. He seemed to be the boss of this office.

"I'm here to see the prosecutor," I said.

"May I ask your name?"

"Uh . . . my name is Kim Youngjin. I got a phone call yesterday. . . ."

"Ah, please have a seat and wait over there." Instead of the clerk, it
was the man sitting next to her who spoke. He seemed to be the prosecutor's secretary, and perhaps because of that I found him very blunt
and harsh, though I was too preoccupied to take offense at his tone of
voice. I sat myself in the chair facing them.

The prosecutor was talking to someone on the phone. Leaning

back in his seat, swiveling this way and that, he spoke in a soft voice
as if he were chatting with a close friend. "Legal procedure," "execute
the warrant," "keep the case open"—those were some of the phrases
he used as he discussed the relationship between senior and junior
colleagues—interspersed with observations about the quality of service provided by the madam at a certain bar. Other than the prosecutor's voice there was no sound; it was quiet in the office, so quiet the
whole place felt oddly solemn.

"Are you Kim Hakgyu's son?" the prosecutor asked as he stood,
hanging up the phone.

"Yes, sir. How do you do? I'm Kim Youngjin." Bowing much
lower than necessary, I took his outstretched hand. I noticed he had
just used my father's name without prefacing it with the title "Mr."
and that struck me with the terrifying realization that those three
syllables—KIM HAK GYU—were already being treated as the name of
a criminal who did not deserve respect.

"I hear you teach at a school out in the countryside. Sorry to incon-
venience you, having to come all the way up here."

"N-no . . . not at all. I should thank *you* for meeting with me. It's
been frustrating. All this time, wondering what's going on and not
knowing who to ask."

Before I sat down, I politely accepted the business card he
handed me. His hair was neatly combed back and he wore glasses, but
other than that, there was nothing special about the prosecutor's
appearance—at least on the surface. He had an ordinary face, and yet
his plain looks did nothing to mitigate my uneasiness and anxiety.

"So—a family of fighters," he said, looking up from the thick file
he'd been leafing through for some time. "Do you often hear from
your sister?"

"I'm not sure what . . ."

"Your younger sister, Hyoseon. Would you say she's made quite a name for herself in the labor movement? The police are looking for her now and it's been quite a headache."

"Is that so? I live out in the country. . . . I haven't seen her in over a year. I really had no idea she would get caught up in something like that. She couldn't go to school because of the family circumstances, but she was always a kindhearted, good girl."

As the prosecutor listened to my awkward response, a mysterious smile appeared on his lips. "That's all fine and good," he said. "But I didn't ask you to come in to talk about Hyoseon."

He looked back down at the file and said, "Mr. Kim, it says here that you have two names. Is that correct? In addition to Youngjin, you have another name, Maksu."

"It's not another name. That was the name I had when I was a kid. I changed it later."

"Why did you change it?"

"It was . . . 'Maksu' just isn't a good name to call someone, is it? My friends would make fun of me because of it when I was young."

As I made that poor excuse, I had the helpless feeling that this was what everything had inevitably come to. I had tried, all that time, to distance myself from my old name, Maksu, but now I realized that it was ultimately no more erasable than the problems of my father's past—I couldn't distance myself from it one inch.

I HAD FIRST HEARD ABOUT WHAT HAPPENED TO MY FATHER TWO weeks ago when my aunt, his sister, had called the school where I worked. "Kim . . . *who?* There's nobody by that name here. It's not just one or two Kims here, you know. Ah, Mr. Kim Youngjin? Why didn't you say so the first time? Just a minute."

It seemed that my aunt had asked for me using my old name, Maksu, and it had taken the vice principal, who answered the call, several tries before finally getting my proper name out of her.

Even after I was handed the phone, the voice on the other end was still urgently shouting in a thick Gyeongsang accent.

"Hello? May I speak to Mr. Kim, please? I mean Mr. Kim *Youngjin*. . . ."

"Kim Youngjin speaking. Who is this?"

"*Aigo*, Youngjin . . . no, Maksu. Is that really you, Maksu?"

It was only then that I recognized the old woman's familiar, heavily accented voice.

"Auntie? What's the matter? Where are you?"

"Where am I? In Seoul, of course! But what are we gonna do, Maksu? Your father . . . they came and took him away."

"What? What are you saying?"

"They came and took him away. *Aigo*, what are we gonna do? What in the world . . . it's been more than thirty years . . . it's like a bolt out of the blue. . . ."

"Calm down and just tell me what happened. My father went away . . . where to?"

Even in the excitement, I managed not to use the words "took him away." I'd realized there were other teachers in the staff room listening, and the vice principal had been staring at me for a while over his horn-rimmed glasses, blinking his beady little eyes.

"It wasn't the police, but to some *agency*. Intelligence or National Security or something. It's been days already, but I didn't know about it until just today. I think he's finally finished. What are we gonna do now?"

"Just a minute, Auntie. I can't explain everything right now. Why don't we talk later, alright? I'll give you a call this afternoon after school," I said and hung up.

"Is she a relative of yours, Mr. Kim?" the vice principal asked. "She was looking for you by a different name—Kim something-or-other—at first. In any case, she sounded pretty upset. Did something happen at home?"

"Ah, well, yes. It's nothing serious," I replied vaguely.

I returned to my desk and collapsed in my chair. As I took out a cigarette, my chalk-covered fingers were trembling. I hated the name "Maksu" when I was a child. There was something strange about it, and the neighborhood kids would make up nicknames for me like "Moksu" (carpenter) or "Makgeolli" (rice wine). But I didn't truly begin to hate that name until I was older, after I learned why my father had named me that way. I couldn't bear the fact that he had branded me with a connection to his failed past. In my sophomore year of college, before I enlisted in the army, I went through all the bothersome red tape and finally changed the name myself.

"HOW MUCH DO YOU KNOW ABOUT YOUR FATHER'S PAST, MR. KIM?" THE prosecutor asked.

"His past . . . What past are you referring to?"

"Your father was a communist active in the old South Korean Labor Party. You know at least that much, don't you?"

So that's what this is all about, I thought. I focused on staying alert, to not let my guard down.

"I don't know the details," I said. "But generally. I also know he was in prison for a while after the war. . . ."

I deliberately gave him a little more than what he had asked.

"You seem to know quite a lot," the prosecutor said, looking me in the eye. "So then, Mr. Kim, what do you think of his past activities or his ideas?"

I tried to swallow, but my mouth was dry.

"I was born after the war," I said. "The generation in this country that grew up with a strict anti-communist education. If I were given a choice between the North and the South—though that's not going to happen, so I'm saying *if*—I will obviously choose the South. Why? Because my consciousness, my way of thinking, my lifestyle—everything my life is rooted in was formed under the current system. Most importantly, I'm a schoolteacher who actually gives my students an anti-communist education, aren't I?"

I felt a cold sweat run down my back. There was no way to know how acceptable my answer was to the prosecutor. His face still showed nothing. I looked up at him, my mouth parched.

"By the way . . . what on earth is my father being charged with?"

The prosecutor stopped looking through the file.

"You don't know yet?"

"No. The person who called me yesterday only said it was a violation of the National Security Act and that he'd give me the details when we met in person."

The prosecutor's secretary, who had been writing something, lifted his head slightly and looked at me. I assumed he was the one who had called me at school, talking to me in a hard and officious tone. The prosecutor looked at my face for a moment in silence and then said, curtly:

"Espionage."

I suddenly forgot what I was about to say. The prosecutor, still expressionless, kept his eyes fixed on me, as if he didn't want to miss my reaction to what he'd said.

"A-are you telling me . . . my father's a spy?"

The prosecutor spoke without emotion: "Your father's been charged with espionage. Spying under orders from the North Korean puppet regime to conduct clandestine operations to agitate against the South."

I still couldn't believe my ears. From the moment I had gotten the news from my aunt about my father's arrest, my intuition had been that it had something to do with his past. But it had never occurred to me that he might have committed an actual crime. I had assumed that, at most, he might have said something he shouldn't have while he was drunk at a bar, or something might have come up about his past that required investigation. I didn't know, but perhaps, unconsciously, I'd been admitting the possibility that his subversive ideas and past activities might get him arrested or taken in for a few days' questioning even now. But *espionage*? Like everyone else born and educated in this country, it was a word I had seen or heard used all the time since childhood—in the classroom, on posters and banners, in newspapers—but I had never imagined that it would somehow directly relate to me. Until now, it had remained a word that had no sense of reality to it. But now I could see a newspaper article in the national news section, under the gigantic headline, SPY RING BUSTED! It would feature diagrams with arrows pointing this way and that, pictures of my father's haggard face, and evidence for his spying: coded columns of random numbers, shortwave radio transmitters. It was terrible even to imagine. I could barely open my mouth to speak.

"Th-that's . . . just not possible," I said.

"What makes you say it's not possible?" The prosecutor leaned back in his high-backed swivel chair, his eyes peering at me over the top of his glasses.

"Even if . . . my father had leftist ideas in the past, that was more than thirty years ago . . . and he's not the kind of person capable of such a thing."

"Is that so? Well then, Mr. Kim, what kind of person do you think *could* do such a thing?"

"Well . . . it requires a strong personality and a fierce determination, doesn't it? My father is weak-willed and . . . also pretty much a failure in life. Anyone who knows him will confirm that."

I remembered the last time I saw my father. It was during my winter break. For the first time in months, I had gone to see him in Jongam-dong, where he was living in a single rented room on top of a hill. I'd found him crouching down under the faucet by the kitchen door, his back hunched, washing his underwear by hand. The previous summer, I had hightailed it out of Seoul after finding a position in Gangwon Province at a middle school out in the countryside. My little sister, Hyoseon, had been the only one left to take care of my father in our tiny rented room the size of a rabbit hole. But sometime last fall, Hyoseon became wanted by the police. She couldn't return home, and so there was no one left to cook my father's meals or wash his clothes. I had offered to pay the landlord some money every month to cook and do his laundry, although I didn't really expect her to take good care of him. With my sister gone the place was in shambles—it looked like it had been abandoned. Blankets left on the floor, clothes scattered here and there, empty soju bottles rolling around in the corners. My father was living alone in that dark, filthy room like an old animal wallowing in its own excrement. There was a foul odor in there of something rotting. When I realized the stench was coming from my father, I thought he had started to decompose.

"Earlier, you said your childhood name, Maksu, didn't you?" the prosecutor said. "I mention this because it's what Kim Hakgyu—that is, your father—also said during his questioning. I mean, as proof of his strong ideological convictions. He was so devoted he named his son after Karl Marx."

"I know that story, too," I said, "but . . . don't you think it was just some foolish dream he had when he was young?"

"Dream?"

"You might say it's something he did to make up for his failed life. Don't you think his impulsiveness and self-importance are proof enough that he's not fit for something as daunting as espionage?"

"Mr. Kim," the prosecutor said, a subtle smile on his lips, "that's a very cold and objective analysis of your father you have there."

"It embarrasses me to say this, but . . . from the time I was a child, I've never had any respect for my father. My father never once showed any authority or competence as head of a household. To our eyes he was completely incompetent and destructive."

My face was red. I was filled with an unbearable sense of shame and, at the same time, an anger directed at no one in particular. I realized I had fallen into the wretched position of having to describe all of my father's shortcomings in front of the prosecutor—in my own words—to attest to the fact that my father wasn't cut out to be a spy.

"In any case, the truth will come out in the course of the investigation. But more importantly, Mr. Kim, how about meeting with your father? I'll make arrangements for a special visit."

I looked at the prosecutor, bewildered.

"Actually," he said, "the real reason I asked to see you was to get you to meet with him. He's being detained at the moment in a place where no visitors are permitted. But I can set up a special meeting for the two of you."

"Th-thank you, but . . ."

"I guess you're wondering why I would bother to arrange a special visit like this."

Then the prosecutor summarized for me the incident that related to my father. Recently, an entire North Korean spy network had been exposed and rounded up by the ANSP, the Agency for National Security Planning. The network had been activated by recruiting former members of the old South Korean Labor Party or North Korean partisans, most of them old men now in their sixties or seventies. Using these feeble old men just proved, once again, that the North was an evil regime that would stop at nothing to unify the Korean peninsula under communism. About a decade ago the network had started gathering and reporting intelligence according to plan, and during their arrest, a large amount of irrefutable evidence had been seized—coded number tables, operational money, shortwave radios.

"But . . ." the prosecutor paused. "The problem is with this man, Kim Hakgyu. In every other case, the evidence is conclusive, but for him, there's some ambiguity."

"Ambiguity?" I said. "What do you mean by that, exactly?"

"In other words, there's no evidence. This current group was making use of local networks that are a legacy of the old South Korean Labor Party, and the suspects are all friends of Kim Hakgyu, but there's no concrete evidence. What's more, all the other suspects have singled him out as being the only one among them who has no involvement with this case."

"Then that means my father is clearly innocent, doesn't it?"

"But that's not the problem. The problem is that your father keeps claiming he was also involved."

"H-how could that be?"

"When the agency first detained your father, they considered him at most to be an important witness. He himself seemed not to know what was going on at first. I can't talk about the details of the investigation, but as he began to get a general sense of the situation, your father suddenly started to claim that he was also a participant. He's demanding to be arrested for being involved in espionage."

It was an entirely unbelievable story. If what the prosecutor said was true, then my father was voluntarily giving himself up as a spy. But how could that possibly make any sense? I looked at the prosecutor, confused.

"I'm no legal expert," I said, "but, if the only evidence you have is my father's own confession, that doesn't seem to be enough to establish his guilt."

"That doesn't necessarily apply to anti-communist cases," the prosecutor said. "Just saying 'I'm a communist' is enough to make you guilty. Besides, can you imagine why anyone who's not a spy would claim to be one? Unless he's crazy? Anyway, Mr. Kim, do you understand why I'm making special arrangements for you to make a visit to your father?"

So I should meet my father in person and listen to what he had to say. The prosecutor seemed to think that—whatever the reason for the ungrounded insistence that he was involved in espionage—a father would at least tell the whole story to his son.

"Th-thank you," I said. "I'm sure there was some mistake. Like I said before, my father's not the type of person who would be capable of such a thing."

"That will require further investigation. There's nothing to thank me for. I just want to know the truth."

"When will the visit happen?"

"We'll do it tomorrow morning. Come back here by nine. You'll go to the detention center with me."

I left the prosecutor's office. As I came out of the building, the choking tension in my gut was relieved and I was overcome by a wave of vertigo. A mix of snow and rain was coming down, unseasonable for

February, and I stood there for a moment, looking blankly, right and left, at the dizzying scatter of snowflakes.

"Maksu! Over here. This way!"

Someone was shouting, waving her arms, by the security guard's office. I remembered then that I had told my aunt to wait for me at the coffee shop across the street from the Public Prosecutor's Office building. She must have been standing there in the snow for a long time—her shoulders were wet and her face was blue from the cold.

"You should've been waiting inside the coffee shop," I said. "Why did you come out here?"

"I was burning up inside with worry. How could I just sit in there waiting?" my aunt said nervously. "You had a hard time. Let's find someplace quiet and go inside."

She pulled me along by the arm, glancing everywhere, as if someone were following us. Seeing the degree of her unease and anxiety, I felt inexplicably irritated and angry.

"What are you so afraid of?" I asked. "It's not like anybody's coming after us. We haven't committed any crime."

"No? And why not? Just keeping alive in the country's been a crime. It's shameful."

My aunt was one of my only close relatives. When she was younger, she had been tougher than the average man—no business she didn't try her hand at in the local market—suffering all sorts of ills to raise her three children by herself without their father. Now she was just a pathetic old woman who could no longer hide the signs of age and sickness.

We went up to the second floor of a Chinese place on the street. There was a *yeontan* stove in the middle of the restaurant, but it was still chilly inside. My aunt avoided the people sitting around the stove and pulled me to a corner.

"So what happened? What did the prosecutor say?" she asked as soon as we sat down. "What crime did they lock your father up for?"

Of course, she spoke in an anxious whisper, constantly looking around the room in case people were listening. I briefly conveyed what I had heard from the prosecutor, and the moment I said the word *spy*, she turned pale.

"How could this be happening? *Aigo*, I'm shaking. Your father must have been possessed by some evil spirit."

"It isn't time to despair yet," I told her. "From what I can tell, the prosecutor is determined to see this through properly. . . . Anyway, when I meet Father tomorrow, I'll find out something about what's going on."

"Alright. You go and try to talk some sense into that father of yours. He can't be so stuck on himself he'd do that to ruin his own son's future. All my faith is in you, Maksu."

"Auntie, please don't call me Maksu anymore. You know I changed my name."

"Oh, that's right. Young . . . Youngjin. That's your name. I used to call you by your old name all the time and it's stuck on my tongue. But how can you be so calm, quibbling about your name with all this going on?"

My aunt dabbed at her swollen eyelids with a handkerchief tightly balled in her hand. Her eyes had gotten bloodshot in the interim.

"Your father's got such terrible luck. I feel sorry for him. When he was young he had to be a leftist or something. He could never rest easy at night, and then he even spent time in prison.

"He's been living out in the cold thirty years with that brand on him. I was thinking all that would just be old memories to talk about once you and your sister grew up, but . . . now he's near seventy and living all alone, no one even to do his cooking for him. Who'd know if they came and took him away in the middle of the night? Before he could even shout out for help? What if he just died where he's laying? Who's gonna know?"

My aunt's words carried with them a sense of bitterness and disappointment regarding me, as usual. To her, I was rightfully the bad nephew who'd abandoned his old father to live by himself. Even a fortnight ago, when she'd first delivered news about my father, she had expected me to respond immediately, but I hadn't come up to Seoul then.

"How can you be so harsh and unsympathetic?" she'd said.

After that she had called me again and again to come to Seoul, but I'd kept putting it off with this or that excuse, and now my aunt was finally getting to vent her feelings of disappointment.

"Hate him or love him, but he's still your father, ain't he? You wouldn't even ignore an old next-door neighbor like that. The man who gave you your life and name gets dragged away. There's no word from him in days, and you don't care if he's dead or alive? Hyoseon wouldn't be like that. At least that girl is kind and cares about her father. Even animals recognize their parents and children. How can you be like that?"

Contrary to what my aunt said, I clearly hadn't been indifferent to my father's problems. The truth was that I might have been cultivating that fear myself. Sometimes, alone in my rented room, I would be reading a book, my ear bent to the silence of the night around me, and I would suddenly be plunged into an unbearable sense of fear and despair.

Over the past two years, I had enjoyed peace and quiet in a mountain village too small even to appear on a map. They eked out crops of garlic and pepper on the terraced mountainside, and it was very windy and often covered in windblown dust. The dust was truly terrible there. My toothbrush, hanging in the kitchen of my tiny place, was always coated in black grit and had to be rinsed several times before I could use it to brush my teeth in the morning. When I looked out of the window during class, I could see dust clouds in the distance blowing in over the stream. They would engulf the schoolyard in the span of a single breath. When I came back to the office after class, the first thing I did was use my hand to wipe away the grains of sand that had settled in a thick layer on my desk. Then I went to the sawdust stove in the staff room—a cylindrical stove made of galvanized steel with tiny holes punched in the bottom, allowing the sawdust to slowly trickle down through the holes as in an hourglass. I always lit my cigarettes by sticking them into one of those holes, so after I sucked the smoke, the cigarette would leave an aftertaste, like the persistent powdery smell of sawdust, on the back of my tongue.

I didn't have a special commitment to being a teacher at a rural school. I had half given up on teaching the unruly country children anything in my classes, and to the locals—mostly farmers with sunburned faces—I was nothing more than part of the dull landscape that surrounded them anyway. But what I enjoyed was the boring and redundant tranquility that settled like the dust without your noticing, like the silent trickle of sawdust—like hourglass—sand in the stove. I wanted nothing except that my life not be shaken up by anybody.

The house I had rented was like a poor farmer's house. It had a shabby old-fashioned outhouse with a crumbling slate roof and a ceiling so low you couldn't stand up straight inside. Each time I had to pee squatting like a woman, I would feel a masochistic pleasure, as if I'd been castrated. And yet, somehow, it was all no big deal. There, I was insulated from everything, from the annoyances and clamor of Seoul, from the sting of past memories that I didn't want floating up again. Most of all, it was a place far away from my father.

"In any case, don't worry so much," I told my aunt. "He'll be out soon and he'll be fine. You have to trust that and try to stay calm."

"Well, wouldn't it be nice if I could do that? It's been more than thirty years gone by—what kind of karma is this? All those years living in fear the ground might collapse under him and now, finally, *this* happens. . . ."

My aunt burst into silent tears in the corner of the Chinese restaurant.

It's been more than thirty years gone by. . . . My aunt's hoarse voice was still ringing in my head after we left the restaurant and said goodbye.

In her words was the legacy of fear, of the long years of suffering she was unable to escape, and scars of trauma that could never be erased. She firmly believed that what had happened to my father now was linked to his past of thirty years ago.

Thirty years ago, my aunt had been forced to separate from her husband. Immediately after the Korean War when the order was issued to round up all leftists, my uncle had suddenly disappeared without a trace, and his whereabouts were still unknown. We didn't even know whether he was dead or still alive. The other man she had depended on in the world, her only brother, had lived under a stigma for thirty years.

In the past, my family had lived day by day, each one as precarious as the next. Weighed down by debt, short of food, and late with rent and tuition, we always despaired about tomorrow and yet were somehow always able to put that despair off for another day. But my father had utterly no interest in his family's daily struggle for survival, and so the burden of supporting the four of us, including him, fell entirely on my mother's shoulders. But she never once brought up the issue of money in front of my father.

If for some reason, even unintentionally, she worried about money in front of him, my father's temper flared, and he would go into a rant, as if he'd gone insane. "Money! Money! Money! Don't ever say that word to me. What is money, anyway? Money means nothing to me. I'm not a money-grubber. Not on your life! I, Kim Hakgyu, would rather die than live for money!"

If he didn't want to be a money-grubber, then someone else had to be in his place. I never understood how he couldn't see that simple fact. That someone else was my poor mother. And, of course, the children he had irresponsibly cast into this world, into the wretched underbelly of society, had no choice but to become yet another kind of money-grubber.

Only after I'd grown up did I learn the truth about my father's past: his embracing of communism, his devotion to the leftist movement, his three and a half years in prison. But I could not, for the life of me, imagine that someone like him could possibly have devoted himself, even for a day, to fighting for any cause—any cause at all. Even so, my father went out of his way to defy social norms and institutions. When I was about to enroll in college, he opposed it with an anger so fierce it was hard to believe.

"I want to study literature," I had answered when my father asked me what in the world I was going to do in college.

"Literature?" he thundered. "You punk! You think you need to go to college to study literature? College or not, what kind of literature are you gonna study if you're just reading books? That's for fat asses and their bullshit.

"Literature is something you do while you're sweating at a factory or at a construction site—anywhere you work for a living. That's real literature. Maxim Gorky wrote while he was washing dishes at a restaurant. He's a thousand times better than those writers or professors these days going on about what's literature and what's art. Bastards like that aren't worth the dirt between Gorky's toes. You punk, we can hardly afford one meal a day and instead of stepping up to join the struggle of life you talk about college? What are you gonna do with that rotten consciousness, you crazy bastard? Why don't you just go crawl off somewhere and die?"

At that time, I didn't know who Maxim Gorky was, and I wasn't interested. But I found it quite absurd that phrases like "where you work for a living" or "the struggle of life" would come out of the mouth of someone like my father. Of course, I knew it was unrealistic for me to expect to go to college with my family in those circumstances, but the reason I didn't give up on the idea was because of my mother. From the time I was little, she had always said to me, as if it were a refrain: "Maksu, I wish you'd become a schoolteacher when you grow up. I don't want you to be a rich businessman or a famous celebrity. Just be a good schoolteacher. It won't make you rich or famous, but being a schoolteacher is the best job in the world. Always remember what I said."

My mother believed that the most secure way for me to survive and succeed in society was to become a teacher. That was the kind of wisdom she had gained as she endured a long life of pain and poverty in a society hostile to her, which treated my father as an incompetent. It was also her last hope. The best way to submit and conform to this society would probably have been to become a government employee, but with my mother's experience, she would have thought that working for the government was not only unsafe but, rather, might even be dangerous. In the end, I went to a teachers' college in keeping with her wishes. My literary dreams had yet to be realized, but that actually didn't matter all that much. I had loved to write when I was young because it was a way of escaping my painful reality, and until now, being out here in the country teaching at a no-name middle school was also a way to keep me more than far enough from reality. My mother, who so much looked forward to her son becoming a schoolteacher, had left this world the spring I started college.

That night, I could not sleep easily. I thought about the small mountain village that I had left. I recalled the familiar scenes as I rode the intercity bus: the mill with the rusty tin roof, the shabby town hall with its peeling paint, the sawmill with piles of red sawdust in the yard—all of it buried in the bleakness of the falling sleet and receding into the distance. Seoul had felt unreal to me while I lived in that village, and now it was the village that felt like a distant and unreal place I could never return to. I was still imprisoned in the painful reality of the past. I thought of my sister, whose whereabouts I didn't know. I hadn't heard from her in months. And the last thing keeping me awake was my memories of my mother. She had been tortured for more than ten years by stomach pain. It was so bad that, each time it flared up, she would stagger around the room tearing at her clothes as if she were having a seizure. It would happen several times a day, but she never once went to the hospital and never once took any medicine. The only thing she had for it was baking soda. I didn't know how the chemistry worked, but that strong powder somehow helped temporarily kill the pain of what was destroying the walls of her stomach. When the pain started, my mother would open the lid of the tin and put a spoonful of baking soda in her mouth. I could still vividly remember, even now, my mother's grimacing face, her eyes tightly shut, swallowing the terribly bitter baking soda, and the sound of the tight metal lid of the can opening.

Eventually, that stomach pain was the cause of my mother's death. At the hospital, the doctor said, after viewing her X-rays, that it was already far too late for anything to be done. A simple ulcer had been neglected for so long it had developed into stomach cancer. The doctor said it was almost a miracle that she was still alive. My mother was bedridden for two months before she passed away. Every day during those last two months of my mother's terrible suffering and her desperate struggle for life, my father was continuously drunk as if he had resolved not to be sober even for a single moment. Smelling my father reeking of liquor as he lay asleep after falling down drunk in a corner of our tiny room, hearing the sounds of my mother's groans ever increasing in frequency, I gritted my teeth all night and swore to myself a thousand times that I would never forgive him.

THE DOOR OPENED AND A PRISONER ENTERED ESCORTED BY A GUARD. I almost did not recognize him. It didn't seem possible that the haggard old man in the baggy, ill-fitting blue prisoner's uniform, with his hands cuffed in front of him, was my father. The number 32 was printed on the left side of his chest. It wasn't until the guard practically shoved him in front of the table that he finally noticed me. His stony face twitched with surprise, and after a while, he said, "You . . . what are you doing here?" The prosecutor motioned to the guard to remove the handcuffs. Once they were off, my father sat down.

"How . . . how's your health?" I barely managed to ask.

"Um . . . I'm alright," he said.

I had no idea what I should say next. His cheeks were hollow and the grizzled beard, which hadn't seen a proper shave in weeks, made his face look older and all the more haggard. But most surprising was my father's bearing. He was so calm and dignified that he seemed not to belong in the unsightly prison uniform that was draped over him. Instead of his usual hunched and undisciplined posture, he now sat with his chest out and his back deliberately straight. To me, seeing this image, so different from his usual self, was like watching a performance by a terrible actor.

"Mr. Kim. Your son is very worried," the prosecutor said, breaking the silence. "You're getting up there in years now. Shouldn't you be thinking of your children instead of filling them full of worries?" His voice was soft, as if he were correcting a child, but it did not mask the coercive tone he would have used to interrogate a suspect. Then he said, "Guard, please pretend you didn't see this," and offered my father a cigarette. Getting the guard's cooperation might just have been in keeping with protocol, but on the other hand, it also seemed to be a gesture of kindness and generosity far beyond what my father deserved as a prisoner. But my father didn't show much gratitude as he took the cigarette and put it between his lips.

"I specifically asked your son to come," the prosecutor said. "So why don't you say what you need to say now? Just tell the truth. Lay it all out. Even if it's something you couldn't tell us, you can say it in front of your son, can't you?"

But my father said nothing. He just puffed cigarette smoke into the thick silence.

"Father," I said, speaking first, "how the hell did this happen?"

Only then did he slowly turn to look at me. "It just did."

That was all he said. I was speechless, but I also felt something beyond my control rising up from within me.

"I was told you're charged with espionage, but I think there's been some sort of mistake. If you had to confess for some reason because you were under duress during the interrogation, you can tell me everything now. I know you'd never be involved in anything like that. Something is wrong here. Very wrong."

"*Wrong?* Nothing's wrong. Not a thing."

My father spoke in the same tone of voice. He was unwavering, almost arrogant.

"So are you saying you actually *were* a spy?"

"I was."

"Even when there's no evidence according to the prosecutor?"

"Why would there be no evidence? Everyone they brought in with me is evidence."

"But even they're confirming that you're the only one who wasn't involved. So why are you insisting all on your own?"

"Can't you see they're doing it on purpose? They can see there's a way out for me, so they're trying to save at least one of us."

I was at a loss for words. My father had clearly changed. I had never until now seen him so confident and self-assured. His tone of voice and his eyes were those of a man full of conviction, so much so that he might have been a martyr ready to suffer anything for his cause. But as far as I could tell, this was all ridiculous and laughable. I stood up from my seat. I walked up to my father's chair and took his hand.

"Father, why on earth are you doing this? You can tell them you're innocent—even right now. The prosecutor will ask for leniency in your case. Is it your loyalty to the others that's stopping you? If that's not it, what other possible reason could you have?"

I pleaded with him, holding his hand, but my father kept his mouth shut. Meanwhile, the others—the prosecutor, his secretary, and the guard—were watching us like a cool audience, and I felt terribly ashamed that my father and I were playing out what seemed like a pathetic comedy in front of them.

My father finally opened his mouth to speak.

"You don't know."

"I don't know what?"

"You just don't."

At that I leapt up. I could no longer suppress all the impulses that had welled up in my heart to that moment.

"I don't even want to know what it is. I don't know *what* you believe in but could it really be that important? Don't you think you caused enough pain and suffering for your family? Why should we have to go through it all over again now because of you? For that wonderful ideology of yours? You couldn't possibly have forgotten how Mother lived her whole life and died in misery. Because of what? Why did Hyoseon have to slave away at a factory—and now she has to live on the run? And now you're saying you want her to wear a brand on her back? The daughter of a *spy*? Is that what you want?"

"For you and her . . . I'm sorry."

"You're *sorry*? I don't believe it. You've never once thought about your family. You're an absolute egotist. Even the ideology you said you followed was just some mirage that had no connection with your life. So do whatever you want. Do whatever your convictions and history tell you to do. Go ahead and *be* a spy, be whatever!"

My legs were shaking. I felt so dizzy that I thought I might collapse on the spot. But the thing I couldn't bear was the shame. What kind of disgrace was this? My father sitting there in a blue prisoner's uniform, and the best I could do in front of him was expose myself in such a childish way. Disgusted at myself, I felt an urge to kick open the door and run outside.

"Lepers . . ." my father said, his voice hoarse. "It could mean madmen or just people cursed with leprosy. Either way, they're untouchables. They're outcasts who can't mingle with normal people or healthy people. . . ."

He went on slowly, staring into space, as if he were delivering a soliloquy.

"When the war ended, suddenly there were lots more lepers. Used to be treated worse than animals, and now they roamed in bands out in the countryside and in the cities. Why their numbers suddenly increased like that after the war, I don't know. But one thing's for sure—there were some among them who *chose* to become lepers. When you think about it, I was one of them. . . ."

Then my father paused for a moment. He was still staring off into the distance, and there was a strange unapproachable kind of dignity about him. And for some reason, the longer he did that, the more uneasy I became.

"In the old days we fought for the revolution," my father continued.

"Then the war broke out, and in the end, the Party was defeated, the revolution failed, and the organization fell to pieces. Where did all those people go to and what became of them afterwards? Did they become partisans and all die fighting in the resistance—every last one of them? If we wanted to serve the ideology we believed in, we were supposed to stay here and start another long, long fight to prepare for the revolution while we remained alive. But I couldn't do that. And I couldn't make a lot of money or provide a comfortable life for my family in this system. Couldn't do this, couldn't do that . . . just ended up living the life of a leper."

He paused again and let out a long sigh.

"How much longer have I got to live? I know it's a terrible thing to do to all of you . . . but I made up my mind. Not to die having lived my last days as a leper. That's all I've got to say. . . ."

He didn't open his mouth again, and so the room was left in an oppressively heavy silence.

"S-so what are you saying? You're going to stop being a leper now? By letting yourself be charged with espionage? That's your idea of escaping a leper's life? You think that's the only way to redeem yourself for the past? But what does that even mean? Would it really change anything about your past? Isn't it just some stupid attempt to deny your whole life? I think it's plain insanity! You're just turning into a different kind of leper."

I abruptly stopped my rant. In disbelief, I saw tears flowing down my father's face. He was still staring off into space, his face wrinkled and haggard, awash in silent tears. I couldn't open my mouth again. Instead, I felt something like a lump of sadness about to burst upward through my constricted throat. I collapsed into the chair as if all the strength had left my body.

My father didn't say another word, and I left the room. The prosecutor must have had more questions to ask him. He told me to leave first, and so I had to walk out of the detention center by myself. Before I left, I could have pleaded with the prosecutor to reconsider my father's case, but I thought better of it. My father was serving time in prison for espionage, a crime of which he was innocent, but in the end, I couldn't say that would make him any more miserable than he already was.

As I walked alone toward the front gate, I stopped and turned around. I spent a long time looking at the high walls of uniform gray, the watchtower, and the huge boulders and cold gleam of snowy peaks on Inwangsan in the background. And then I continued walking, but suddenly stopped again. Murmurs and mumbling, groans through clenched teeth, someone screaming at the top of his lungs—all manner of sounds, all mixed together, came roaring out like the crashing of waves. But it was only a momentary hallucination. When I looked back, the massive building was still buried in silence, like a tomb. I slowly walked toward the exit I saw in the distance.

Translated by Heinz Insu Fenkl

THERE'S A LOT OF
SHIT IN NOKCHEON

I

"Next stop Nokcheon! Nokcheon Station! Exit through the left."

Uh, uh, uh . . . Something like a groan leaked from Minu's mouth as he had a bad dream sitting asleep next to Junshik in the hot and crowded train. The worn-out old fans hanging here and there stirred the air, but the car wasn't properly air-conditioned and it was suffocatingly hot inside. Minu slept with his mouth half-open, his head resting uncomfortably against Junshik's shoulder, his face covered in a sheen of greasy sweat.

Is this guy really my brother? Junshik asked himself. A sour smell wafted from Minu's sky-blue shirt, which was soaked in perspiration and probably hadn't been washed in days. His sunburned face was covered in a scraggly beard, but in his dark eyebrows and his thin, refined nose, he seemed to have retained his former looks. He still appeared to be carved from the same mold as their father, who was now buried in the ground. *But was this because they'd met again after so much time had passed?* Junshik wondered.

He found it strange that the more he looked at his brother, the more he seemed to be looking at the face of a complete stranger.

"This stop Nokcheon! Nokcheon Station! Exit through the left door, please."

The train began slowing down. Junshik shook Minu by the shoulder. "*Ah!*" he cried out, opening his eyes wide, startled out of a deep sleep. He looked around for a moment as if he were confused about where he was, and when his eyes met Junshik's, he smiled awkwardly.

"How can you sleep like that?" Junshik said. "We have to get off here."

"Get off here? This is where you live?"

Minu looked out of the window, blinking, as if he couldn't believe what he was seeing. Outside, there wasn't a single light—nothing to see but darkness. But just then the door opened wide and there was no time for Junshik to explain.

After the train had left them with a loud blast of wind, they were the only two people on the platform at Nokcheon Station. It was as if they'd been abandoned, surrounded by darkness in the middle of a desolate field.

"Did we get off at the right stop?" Minu asked, glancing suspiciously around. "When you said you were living in an apartment, I was expecting you'd be in a regular apartment complex."

"It's still under construction. It'll be a proper development soon enough." Junshik took the lead and walked toward the exit.

Minu's suspicion was not unreasonable. Everything around the station was a bleak construction site: pits freshly dug into the earth and buildings going up. Past the mysterious cement structures was a stream flowing with black wastewater from a factory. It had to be crossed to get to the site of the apartment building Junshik had moved in to. From where they stood, it was still out of view.

"Nokcheon. That's one poetic name," Minu said to himself, looking at the sign on top of the station platform. Junshik looked up, too, at the lettering brightly lit up in the darkness.

Nokcheon 鹿川—Deer Creek. Junshik had first started using this station only a week ago, that is, since moving to the neighborhood. Even then he couldn't understand how the place had gotten such a lofty-sounding name, right out of a classical poem. He still didn't have an answer. He had looked all around and come to the conclusion that the only explanation was the pathetic little creek that flowed near the station, but it was long dead and thick with sewage and factory waste-water. Perhaps in some misty past there had been an occasion when a few roe deer had come down from the mountain to drink there, but now that name had a ring of terrible irony that verged on sarcasm.

"Which way do we go?" Minu said. "I don't see a path."

"Just follow me."

Down the stairs from the train platform, they were in the con-struction site not illuminated by a single light. Junshik walked first into the darkness.

"What's this terrible smell around here, anyway?" Minu asked. He looked around, his nostrils flaring.

As soon as they'd entered the construction site, an unbearable stench permeated the hot and humid air. It was like the smell of mas-sive heaps of rotting garbage, sewage, and wastewater all blended to-gether. And there was another thing that couldn't be ignored: the smell of shit.

They couldn't see it now in the dark, but Junshik knew that the area around Nokcheon was entirely covered in shit—and that was no ex-aggeration. Nearby were makeshift eateries and shabby tented food stalls clustered around the train station to provide liquor and food for the workers, in addition to buildings that served as the field offices for the construction sites. But for some reason no one had given any thought to installing proper facilities. If you walked behind the construction sites to get to the train station, you were sure to see piles of human excrement in any dark or secluded spot. The terrible stench was inevitable, but on a sweltering night like this, it was all the more intense.

A light in a distant corner of the construction site cast long shadows of the two men. They didn't look much like brothers.

First of all, they were different heights. Junshik was short and in his mid-thirties, but was already developing a paunch. His arms and his legs were spindly and weak, giving his whole body the appearance of something precariously out of balance. Minu, on the other hand, stood at least a head taller and had a slim, athletic physique.

Junshik looked at Minu, who was walking quietly in the dark. Even now, there were too many things he didn't know about his younger brother. No, it would have been more accurate to say that he knew virtually nothing. But then again, Minu had suddenly reappeared after ten long years.

"He says he's your brother," the waitress had said that afternoon, handing Junshik the phone. The voice had come over the line: "Junshik, it's me. It's been a really long time. . . ." And even then he hadn't completely understood that it was Minu on the other end. It was as if, in the past few years, he'd entirely forgotten that he had a younger brother.

They had been separated since Minu was fourteen, when he ran away from home and went to Seoul. Junshik had seen him only twice since then: once after going home for their father's funeral, and another time—while Junshik was doing his military service—Minu had come to visit him when he was near the Military Demarcation Line along the 38th Parallel. On that occasion, Minu had been wearing the patch of Korea's top university on his chest. Ten years had passed since then. By now he should have been an elite employee of a multinational corporation or at least a high-ranking civil servant. But that day, when Junshik had gotten the phone call and gone to meet him at the café, Minu's appearance had shocked him. He looked like some common day laborer who had just slipped away from a construction site. They had tea together at the café and then went to a restaurant nearby to have some grilled meat and drinks. Even so, Minu didn't tell Junshik anything about himself, only that the small business he'd established during that time had had some problems, leaving him in difficult circumstances.

As they passed between the half-finished buildings, they could finally see the lights of the apartments in the distance across the creek. There, the construction was finished and the buildings were already occupied.

"Is that it?" Minu asked.

They stopped walking for a moment to admire the sight. Stretched out in the darkness, their countless lights blazing, the buildings felt unreal, like a gigantic theatrical backdrop. And among that wilderness of lights, one of them was where Junshik lived.

"Hey, we've finally arrived at our place."

That was the same thing his wife had said only last week when they'd arrived in front of the apartment building with their moving truck loaded with all their possessions. It was true—before finally being able to afford their own place, they had traveled a long, hard road. The apartment they had just bought was located in a remote part of the enormous complex called Sanggye-dong New City, and in a far corner on the first floor of a fifteen-story high-rise. The first-floor corner apartments, as everyone knew, were cheaper than other units with the same number of *pyeong* in the same type of building in similar districts. Those apartments were less expensive and had the lowest investment value. But no matter the value, the most important thing was that, as Junshik's wife had said, they finally had their "real home." After failing the housing lottery nine times, Junshik had felt like he'd finally struck it rich when he picked a good number. From the time of his birth until now, he had become so acclimated to misfortune that he found his sudden good luck hard to believe.

When he'd first come to Seoul and worked as a gofer at the school, he had slept in a tiny room under a staircase. Later, he'd rented a room for thirty thousand won a month in a shabby neighborhood nearby. It was a room where the ceiling leaked like a sieve whenever it rained. Even after he got married, their first nest was a rented room in the basement of someone's house. The ceiling was so low the wardrobe his wife brought with her would not fit, and so he had to saw off the legs, making her as upset as if her own legs had been amputated. After living there two years they'd moved to a slightly better place, this time on the first floor of someone's house. But the second floor of the building next door—whose eaves were practically connected to theirs— was rented by a Protestant church, of all things. Every day they were forced to listen to the noise of hymns and the pastor's sermons with calls for repentance and the cries of "Amen" blasting through the loudspeakers. And because it wasn't properly heated, there wasn't a day when their breastfeeding daughter didn't have a cold; she eventually had to get injections for pneumonia. But now all the heartache of living in the rentals was ancient history. Now Junshik was the proud owner of a twenty-three-*pyeong* apartment with three bedrooms, a small living room, and all the hot water he could ever want gushing from the taps. He could use as much water as he wanted, go around making lots of noise, and there was no one he had to worry about or be considerate of. And not least, of course, he no longer had to worry about the rent going up.

"Why are you home so late?"

He heard his wife's voice even before the door was quite open.

"And you're empty-handed. Did you forget again? How can you be so absent-minded? Did you forget or is it that you don't care? After I told you again this morning . . ."

She showered Junshik with criticism before he could even say anything to explain himself. He had forgotten to buy a goldfish aquarium. When they moved to the new apartment, his wife had set three goals: first, to install an aquarium in the living room, and then to set up first video, then audio equipment. Those three things were what you needed in a living room to not appear worse off than others. They'd moved around living in small rented rooms until then, so they hadn't given much thought to properly setting up their home. But now that they were full-fledged apartment owners, she intended to decorate their place so it looked like the "interiors"—or whatever—that were published in women's magazines. With Junshik's circumstances, it wasn't going to be easy to get a video or audio set right away, but installing an aquarium was a goal easily achieved even now. There were no shops yet in the area around their apartment, so he was going to have to buy one near his workplace and bring it home. The reason he hadn't bought one that day wasn't because he had forgotten his wife's request—it was because he had met Minu.

Instead of answering, Junshik turned to Minu, who was standing behind him, and said, "Come on in."

His wife's eyes went wide when she saw. "Who is this?" she asked. It was an entirely different tone of voice.

"Hello, sister-in-law. Pleased to meet you."

"What? Who are you?" Her expression was both surprised and terribly embarrassed, which was only natural, since Junshik had never once brought a guest home with him since their marriage, and now there was a complete stranger calling her sister-in-law and whatnot.

"This is Minu, my little brother," Junshik said.

"What are you talking about? Little brother?"

"Don't you remember? I told you I had a younger brother and we'd been separated for a long time?"

"Oh . . ." She nodded her head vaguely up and down. But her expression still said she didn't entirely understand what was going on.

No sooner had Minu stepped inside when she grimaced and pinched her nose. It was because of the awful smell coming from his feet. She hated the smell of dirty feet. Minu must not have changed his socks in several days; they were stained in dirt and his big toes were sticking out. But Minu, oblivious, without any sense of honoring their privacy, walked around the apartment opening door after door, and yet it was Junshik and his wife who were flustered and embarrassed. Minu, meanwhile, looked at their sleeping daughter's face—even gave her a kiss—and then joked with Junshik's wife.

"You're more beautiful than I imagined. My brother's a lucky man."

"What a thing to say . . ." She blushed a little, but didn't seem displeased. While Junshik felt happy to see his brother so at ease, the words "more than I imagined" gave him a strange feeling for some reason.

"It's late, so why don't you get some sleep?" Junshik's wife said to Minu. "I'll get the room ready for you."

After she had gone into the bedroom, the two men sat there for a moment in silence. Junshik couldn't help but be deeply moved by the fact that his little brother had sought him out and was now sitting there across from him in his home. There should have been a wealth of stories piled up, waiting to be told, but strangely, in the reality of the moment, there didn't seem to be anything appropriate to say. It seemed the same for Minu.

"It looks like you have a great place here," he said, looking around once again. "How many *pyeong* is it?"

"Twenty-three on paper, but it's really only sixteen or seventeen." Junshik paused for a moment. "It was my dream for so long," he added, "and it's finally come true."

"Isn't this one of those neighborhoods where they had to force the old occupants out so they could put up the new apartments?"

"Yeah. But was that reason enough for me to turn down a place here?"

"I just said that because it came to mind," Minu said. "Anyway, congratulations on your dream coming true, big brother." He smiled.

Junshik thought his brother might have found what he'd said childish, but regardless of what Minu might think, he hadn't been exaggerating one bit. For Junshik, it was the truth. They sat there in silence again until Minu suddenly yawned.

"You must be tired. Why don't you get some sleep?" Junshik said, getting up.

When he went into the bedroom, his wife was lying down facing the wall. He could tell she wasn't in a good mood. He lay down beside her, hoping she was asleep.

"What am I supposed to do when you bring some guest without even telling me?" she said suddenly.

Junshik explained that it wasn't his fault, that Minu had appeared suddenly without notice. He added that Minu was not "some guest" but his little brother.

"But you could at least have given me a call, right?"

He told her that he was sorry, that he hadn't had a moment to call her. When he apologized, she was quiet for a long while, as if she didn't know what more to say, and then she asked him what in the world his brother did for a living to be looking like that.

"That's right. . . . I always thought he was going to be a success," Junshik said. "From the time he was little, everyone talked about how smart he was. He told me he started a business with a friend, but it went under and now it looks like he's having a hard time just making do."

He vacillated about whether or not to tell her that Minu would need to stay with them for a while.

"If he's your brother, how could you have no contact for so long?"

"Because we have different mothers. Way back, when my father was a schoolteacher, he fell in love with one of his colleagues. That's how Minu was born. His mother raised him at first, but she remarried and Minu came to live with us. We were together for a few years after that until my mother passed away, and then his mother came and took him back. We're half brothers, but we have different surnames."

"It sounds like your family was a real headache." She said nothing more.

Junshik couldn't fall asleep. He tossed and turned in the dark, old images floating up from the depths of his memories like frames of a faded film. He was in second grade. One day, when he got home from school, he noticed something strange in the air he had never felt before. His mother should have been working at her stall at the market, but she was sitting at one end of the raised wooden floor staring blankly into space. When her eyes met his she just let out a sigh. Not a word was said. Then he noticed the unfamiliar shoes left on the stepping stone under the floor. They were small shoes—for a child of five or six—shoes that were hard to get at the time. He threw his schoolbag on the floor and opened the door to the bedroom. He was stunned:

inside was his father, who had been gone for several days, and seated in front of him was a stranger: a young boy with big, shining eyes. Junshik turned around, about to shut the door and quickly get out, but he was interrupted by his father's sharp voice.

"You insolent brat! When you see your father, you say hello. Where are you running off to? Come here!"

Junshik walked cautiously into the room.

"This is your little brother. From now on, you take good care of him, understand?"

Junshik just nodded, not speaking, watching the boy out of the corners of his eyes. The boy, pale-skinned and pretty like a girl, was regarding him furtively with eyes full of suspicion. He was wearing shorts and knee socks—it was the first time Junshik had ever seen a boy in knee socks like that, just like a girl. He simply could not believe that this pretty boy, dressed like a spoiled rich kid, could be his brother.

Junshik ran out of the room to his mother, who was still sitting in the same place on the floor.

"That boy in the room," he said. "Is he really my little brother?"

She nodded without a word.

"Why didn't he come out of *you*? Why did *Dad* bring him? Did he find him abandoned under a bridge?"

His mother didn't answer. She just let out a sigh that could have split the earth. Junshik could tell from his mother's behavior that this was some serious secret, but he couldn't ask her anything more. Then he saw a book bag lying in a corner. It was made of leather and looked brand-new. He opened it and found a pencil case, notebooks, and other school supplies, all brand-new.

Just then the boy suddenly ran out of the room after him, screaming, "It's mine! Don't touch it!"

He grabbed the book bag away from Junshik and burst into tears. It seemed that he had been waiting for this opportunity, and when he started wailing, the bedroom door flew open. Their father ran out, grabbed Junshik, and started mercilessly beating him on the head.

"What am I going to do with you, boy? I told you to take good care of your brother. Why did you make him cry? You little punk!"

Junshik lit a cigarette in the dark and put it between his lips. His chest was heavy and sore on one side as if someone had punched him there. His father was in the grave now, but there were still lots of things he wanted to say to him. He was still full of resentment toward his father, who had left the world without giving him a chance to spew out all the things he was holding inside.

"Hey, put out that cigarette!" his wife said in annoyance.

He'd thought she was asleep.

2

Junshik entered the restroom, and when he saw the principal standing in front of a urinal relieving himself, he tried to turn around and sneak back out. But before he quite got out the door, he was caught from behind by the principal's voice.

"Oh, Mr. Hong."

Junshik pretended to be startled, as if he had just noticed the principal, and hastily bowed his head in greeting.

It had been three years since he'd been appointed to the position of a regular teacher, but even now, he felt uncomfortable to have the principal call him "Mr. Hong." Before he'd been promoted to a teaching position at the school, he had been working as a general employee for five years while attending college classes at night. He had pretty much been an errand boy prior to that, and during all that time, the principal had just called him "Hong."

"Are you busy right now, Mr. Hong?"

"Well . . . not really."

"Then let's talk for a moment."

Junshik had to finish calculating his semester grades and compile his attendance report by the end of the day. More immediately urgent was the fact that he had to use the bathroom, but he wasn't able to ask the principal to wait. The principal had already started down the hall without looking to see if he was coming.

To get to the principal's office, Junshik had to pass by the open windows of the teaching staff's common office. He worried that his colleagues might think it odd to see him following behind the principal. But, fortunately, none of the teachers was looking their way.

"So, Mr. Hong, I hear you moved in to an apartment recently? It's a bit tardy, but I wanted to congratulate you."

"Thank you, sir."

"Here, have a seat."

They sat down facing each other on the sofa. The air-conditioning in the room made the air as cool as early fall. Against the wall, a large glass cabinet displayed various trophies and medals. These awards, won by various high school sports teams over the past decade, still gleamed as if they were new. Junshik knew that whenever he had the time, the principal polished them by hand as if keeping them shiny was a hobby of his. The whole athletic field was visible through the large windows, which were all shut. Outside, students were having PE under the scorching summer sun, but it was all silent, like a scene in a film with the sound turned off. It was so quiet in the principal's office that Junshik thought he could hear himself swallowing.

"So, how big is the place?"

"It's small, sir. Twenty-three *pyeong*."

"You're still young. That's plenty big for getting started. As life goes on, you'll eventually be getting a bigger place."

Junshik sat straight, his knees together, waiting for the principal to continue. Clearly, he hadn't brought Junshik to his office to chat about the new apartment. Junshik's heart had already been pounding for a while because of the tension and the anxiety of not knowing, and now his stomach was aching. He suffered from what they called "irritable bowel syndrome" these days, and it tended to get worse when he was anxious.

"Mr. Hong, what's the mood lately among the teaching staff?" the principal suddenly asked in a hushed voice.

"I don't know, sir. I guess . . . it seems pretty good."

"Why so vague? Have you noticed anything? Anyone in particular? Dissatisfied with the school . . . ?"

"No. Nobody like that comes to mind."

Junshik sat on his hands. He had a habit of hiding his hands when he was nervous. When he wore a suit, they would crawl up inside the sleeves of his jacket, but he was in a short-sleeve shirt at the moment, so he kept unconsciously slipping his hands under his buttocks. The discomfort in his bowels was getting extreme, and he was probably unaware of the fact that he was trying to block the pain there.

"What about Mr. Kim? Kim Dongho?"

"He doesn't talk much lately. It looks like he's just devoting himself to his teaching."

"Does it seem like he's still active with the National Teachers' Union?"

"From what I can tell . . . it looks like he hasn't been involved at all since he resigned."

"About the summer school courses . . . because of liberalization or whatever, word came down that we're only to offer them if more than half the students want to enroll. But it all depends on the homeroom teacher. Do it if you want, they say, but what kid wants to come to school and study during summer vacation? And I'm aware that, among the teachers, there are lots who don't like teaching extra classes. But what's the point of staying home doing nothing? Even coming in to teach one thing is to a teacher's benefit. So, Mr. Hong, devote yourself to the success of our summer school courses this year."

The principal looked directly at him, over his glasses. Junshik wanted to avoid that gaze, but he couldn't find another appropriate place to look.

"I think of you differently than the other teachers, Mr. Hong. I trust you more than any of them. What I mean is, you're someone who thinks of this school as your home. Do you understand what I'm saying?"

Junshik understood the principal perfectly. In fact, he had only become a teacher at the school thanks to the principal. Fifteen years earlier, the one who had hired him as a gofer was the deputy headmaster, now the principal, and afterwards it was him, again, who permitted Junshik to take night classes while he was employed in the administration. Of course, Junshik had been working hard during that time, so it wasn't as if the principal was doing him favors for nothing. But it was a fact that, without him, Junshik would not be the person he was today. The principal had just hinted that Junshik shouldn't forget his indebtedness.

"Thank you, sir. I understand."

"Your wife must be happy moving to a brand-new apartment. Tell her I send my best," the principal said with a smile as Junshik left his office. His tone was informal, as if to confirm that he was close to Junshik's family, but Junshik felt only awkwardness to hear him call his wife "Madame" and not "Misook" as he had in the past. He knew, well enough, that the principal was a hypocrite. But he also knew he wasn't particularly more hypocritical than anyone else.

As he left the office Junshik exchanged glances with Yang Guman, who happened to be talking to someone in accounting in the common office. Yang caught on to things much faster than anyone else. He smiled at Junshik as if he had just learned something about him. Junshik felt his cheeks suddenly flush.

After leaving the principal's office and hurrying to the bathroom, Junshik returned to his desk. At the desk across from him, Kim Dongho was looking down, reading a book. For some time now, Kim had seemed constantly sad and hardly ever spoke anymore in the staff office. Now he appeared to be reading only half attentively, his thick eyebrows squirming like caterpillars as if he were consumed by some painful thought. Those dark eyebrows reminded Junshik of his brother, Minu.

It wasn't until that morning, when he was leaving the house, that Junshik was able to tell his wife that Minu was going to stay with them for a while. Knowing her temperament, he'd been afraid of her reaction when she found out. But she must have suspected something even before he told her. As he rushed to get ready for work and was just about to step out the door, she had given him a knowing look and walked into their daughter's room. She meant for him to follow her. When he went into the room, she locked the door.

"Who the hell is this guy?" she asked sharply.

"What do you mean? I already told you—he's my little brother."

"Why did he come to our house?"

"Since when do you need a reason to visit your brother?"

"Alright, you have a point. But do you think he's planning to move in here?"

"Move in?" Junshik said. "What are you talking about?"

"Well, it's the next day, and he doesn't look like he has any intention of leaving!"

"Shhh! He'll hear you! Why are you talking so loud?"

"I don't care. Let him hear."

"He said he needs to stay here for a few days. He asked me yesterday, and I told him it would be alright."

"Without even asking me?"

"I didn't have time to ask you," Junshik said.

"You know you should have called me. It's easy enough for you to invite someone here, but I'm the one who has to prepare the meals and go out of my way to take care of everything. When you go to work, how do you think I'll feel being stuck here alone with him? In this sweltering heat!"

"Well, it's too late. Just be patient for a few days and be nice to him. He's the only brother I have, after all."

"No. I don't care! I don't care, so do whatever you want!"

Junshik got up. It was a good idea to call home in any case. But strangely, though he could hear the ringtone, no one answered. He tried again an hour into the class, but it was the same. Could his wife have gone to the market? But even if that was the case, she was gone for too long and his brother would have been in the house. He couldn't understand why they were both gone.

When he got home, the front door was locked. He rang the doorbell several times without getting a response. He had left without his keys, and standing there, not knowing what to do, he was overcome with confusion and worry. He went down the few steps that led to the custodian's shed and waited, annoyed. A main road passed in front of the building, and beyond it stretched a wasteland still scorching with the heat of the summer sunset. Junshik saw the silhouette of a family walking toward him in the twilight. It was a young couple holding hands with a little girl, and Junshik felt like he was looking at a painting. He envied this happy family. But the feeling was only momentary. How could he have been so blind! It was his own family, but his place had been taken by Minu, who had cleaned himself up and looked very different from the day before. As he watched them approach, Junshik noticed that Minu was wearing one of his navy blue shirts. They were talking about something funny, his wife laughing, her head raised, looking unexpectedly beautiful in the ruddy glow of the setting sun.

It was his daughter who saw him first. "Dad, we saw ducks!" she cried. "Ducks!" She ran to him to share her enthusiasm.

"Sangmi was pestering me so much we took a walk out past Nokcheon Station," his wife explained, looking embarrassed. "It's the countryside out there. Sangmi liked it so much. . . ."

"I called a bunch of times from school, but no one answered. I was so worried! I forgot the aquarium again. . . ."

"What's the big deal?" his wife said as she drew closer, anger suddenly tarnishing her face. "What were you worried about?"

Junshik didn't know what to think about the sudden change in his wife's mood, but at the same time he was happy to see her on such good terms with his brother. All that change in one day.

After dinner, while Junshik watched TV with Minu in the living room, she brought out a small table with two bottles of beer and some snacks. She seemed to have completely forgotten her icy attitude from that morning.

"You have a drink with us, too," Minu politely offered.

"Oh, I'm really not used to drinking . . . but I'll have a drink with you, anyway," she declared, sitting down with them.

Her tone was particularly gentle and kind. Junshik barely recognized the woman he rubbed shoulders with every day. The atmosphere around the table was relaxed. A refreshing breeze came through the open window and even the lights in the building across from them seemed to be peaceful.

"Oh! How can you have such beautiful hands?" his wife exclaimed quietly when she saw Minu's hands holding the glass as she poured his beer.

He did, in fact, have slender, long fingers—the hands of a woman. Obviously embarrassed, he smiled and hid them.

"They're the hands of someone who's never worked in their whole life, aren't they?" he said. "That's why I'm ashamed to show them."

"What do you mean? I like men who have long, thin fingers like yours!"

Junshik considered his own fingers, knowing full well that they were short and stubby. That meant that he did not fall into the category of men loved by his wife—at least as far as fingers were concerned. Talking about one's taste like that was to express an intimate feeling that belongs only to oneself. What did she mean by announcing her preferences like that?

"Finish the story you were telling," his wife said. "So how did she react—the student?"

She approached Minu without looking at Junshik. It must have been a story his brother had started earlier that afternoon.

"She was surprised of course! I asked her to listen to a poem after suddenly blocking the road in the middle of the night. She probably thought I was crazy."

Minu told the story about when he was still a high school student: one night, while he was studying at the library, preparing for the university entrance exam, he suddenly felt like he was suffocating. *What am I doing here?* he thought. *What is the point of studying? What does it mean to live?* He was taken with a sudden, mad impulse to write a poem, and thus inspired, his heart began dictating to him, whispering an uninterrupted series of words. He filled a whole page, but there was no one there to listen to it. He tore the sheet out of his notebook and went outside. A student was approaching. She walked across the street in his direction, where he was standing in the dimly lit alley. He stepped out, blocking her way. "Uh . . . sorry," he said. "I just wrote a poem and I wanted someone to hear it, but there was nobody . . . Would you listen for a moment if I read it to you?"

"So she agreed?"

Junshik noticed that his wife's eyes, fixed on Minu, were shining with a strange glow. He'd never seen her so avidly interested in a story before.

Minu's eyes sparkled. "No. She was scared. She asked if she could listen to it the next day."

"So what happened?"

"'I get it,' I told her. 'Go on! Tomorrow is too late.' She ran off, looking relieved. Like she'd escaped with her life. I walked home all alone, sad that no one would ever hear my poem."

"Oh, what a shame. I would have listened to it," Junshik's wife said. She sighed. "Do you remember it?"

"I forgot most of it," Minu said. "I only remember one of the lines that went something like 'Time paints a shadow of nothingness. . . .'"

"I'd love to hear the rest of this story, but I have to go to bed," Junshik said, interrupting them as he stood up. "I'm really tired. It's the end of semester and we have a lot of work."

"Time paints a shadow of nothingness. . . . That's really a beautiful line," his wife said. She also got up, but it was obviously with some regret.

She threw Junshik a quick glance out of the corner of her eye, but he could see the boredom in her, the unbearable indifference toward him, and it felt to him as if her gaze had pierced his skull.

In the bedroom, she sat in front of her dressing table, her face reflected in the mirror. She seemed absorbed in thought. Of all the things they'd brought with them since their marriage, that dressing table was her most cherished piece of furniture. It was inlaid with mother-of-pearl and was the only thing they had of any value. But it had been much too tall and too garish, out of place in the unworthy little rented rooms they had occupied until then. It was probably in those rooms that they had developed the habit—though Junshik no longer remembered when—of looking at each other in the mirror rather than face-to-face. He had been sensing it for a while now: his wife's eyes, reflected by the mirror, attentively fixed on him.

"It's amazing," she said with a sigh. "I know you're only half brothers, but you still have blood in common. How can you be so different from him?" Their gazes crossed.

"He looks like my father," Junshik said. He was trying to push away an unpleasant emotion he felt quietly rising from the bottom of his heart. "And I look like my mother," he added.

"How old did you say he was?"

"He's two years younger than me."

"But he still looks like a student! And people would already take *you* for a middle-aged man."

"What are you talking about?" Junshik said. "I'm still in the prime of my life!" He turned off the light and stretched his arm out across his wife's back as she lay next to him. She pushed him away in annoyance.

"Oh, I'm hot! Don't bother me!" she said.

She turned away abruptly. He could only contemplate the whiteness of her back through her pajamas. He understood very well what she had meant by pointing out how little he resembled his younger brother, and that stirred an inexplicable, seething fury in him.

It was always the same. Compared to Minu, he'd never had anything in his favor. Junshik's mother had a wide face and a flat nose, with cheekbones prominent like a man's. With her long horse face, she was far from the ideal of beauty or feminine grace. Junshik had inherited all his physical characteristics from her. Compared to his mother, his father was the exact opposite: a very handsome man whose face inspired nothing but sympathy. Junshik's mother had not even completed elementary school, and she was illiterate, while his father was a schoolteacher whose intelligence commanded respect. To put it bluntly, one couldn't speak of a providential bond between his parents. One might even go so far as to claim that the union of a handsome, elegant, and intelligent man like his father with a woman like his mother was a tragedy. Or was the tragedy the custom that led to such a marriage? Couldn't it also have been a great happiness?

His father had abruptly resigned from his post as a schoolteacher in the city of Daegu. As Junshik later learned, it was because of his relationship with one of his colleagues, a teacher who would become Minu's mother. So Junshik's father found himself unemployed, with his wife having to support the whole family. Back then it was no different—when a man who was accustomed to wearing a suit and tie lost his job, he couldn't take just any job afterwards. Men capable of speaking more eloquently than anyone about international affairs— intelligent men who would spend sleepless nights discussing current affairs or the social contradictions inherent in Korean society—could thus be left destitute and unable to afford enough for their family's next meal.

So it was Junshik's mother who took on the responsibility of providing for the needs of daily life: to pay the rent, to buy the charcoal briquettes for heating and cooking, to give her husband his pocket money—and even to make sure that his ramie clothes were always starched properly so he could read his books lying down in summertime. One of her many gifts was the ability to prepare food out of what appeared to be nothing. She could make soup from cabbage leaves she picked off the ground at the market where merchants had thrown them away. Sometimes there would be nothing to eat for breakfast, but if Junshik's father invited someone over that day she would somehow magically have a generous lunch prepared. And there were so many guests!

When they were there, all dressed in their suits and ties like his father, Junshik and his brother would enter the room and bow to them. For some reason, it was Minu, and not Junshik, who invariably captured their attention. Compared to Minu, Junshik's life was like being left out in the cold. Reflecting on it now, Junshik realized that his father's friends probably paid more attention to Minu because they were sympathetic, because he was born from a tragic love affair and was forced to live far away from his birth mother. In any case, Junshik, unlike his younger brother, had never gotten any sympathy from anyone since his childhood. Nor had he ever managed to feel proud of himself.

They said Junshik was someone who had pulled himself up by the bootstraps because he'd come to Seoul alone at the age of sixteen and managed to finish high school by taking night classes while working in a school. And then—after he was hired as an administrative employee—he had finished his college degree once again through night classes and earned his teaching certification.

But every time someone mentioned this, Junshik knew he felt cynical, or something like contempt for himself rather than pride or satisfaction. To put it simply, he had become jaded. His wife was the same. When he was working in administration at the school, she had worked in the same office. But she had graduated from management school and was a regular employee, and she had always looked down on Junshik, whom she'd considered just an errand boy. Even later, after they had somehow gotten married, after Junshik had graduated from night school and become a teacher in charge of technical subjects, her first impression of him hadn't changed at all.

The next morning, Junshik noticed a big change in his wife. She was wearing makeup—pink lipstick and a light touch of mascara on her lashes. Except on the rare occasion of an outing, he couldn't remember ever once seeing her in makeup.

3

"Hey, big brother, you're already getting quite a paunch down there," Minu said with a laugh the next day.

Junshik had just gotten home from teaching, and he was peeling off his undershirt, which was soaked through with sweat. Minu had only been with them for two days, but he already seemed as comfortable as if he were living at home. He'd probably meant the comment as a good-natured joke, but it made Junshik blush, as he'd just been humiliated.

"It's inevitable as you get older when you don't get enough exercise," Junshik said, directing his words at his wife.

But she just gave him a contemptuous once-over. "Why don't you just admit you tend to get fat?"

"Yes, you're so right!" Minu said. "You know, even when we were kids, he already had a little belly. It was plump like a tadpole's."

Damn, Junshik thought. These two are really getting along. He forced himself to smile. "Hey," he said. "I had a distended belly because I wasn't getting enough to eat!"

"Your little brother looks better in just his undershirt," Junshik's wife said to him, smiling toward Minu.

Junshik couldn't help noticing the strange heat in her gaze, but he did his best to ignore that impression. Maybe he was just being hyper-sensitive, but as his wife had just noticed, it was easy to guess that, under his own T-shirt, Minu was concealing an athletic physique. When they were children, Junshik had thought of Minu as a weakling, but now, to his great surprise, his younger brother was solid muscle without an ounce of fat.

"Sangmi, do you want to sing with Uncle?" Minu asked Junshik's daughter.

She immediately climbed up onto his lap as if she'd been waiting for permission. She seemed to have gotten attached to Minu very quickly, without the slightest bit of self-consciousness. Whether it was with children or adults, Minu had always had this surprising gift of instantly gaining trust.

"Throw the pebble—*splash, splash*—don't let big sister know . . ."

They started singing together and his wife joined in. Listening to the three of them, Junshik did not know what to do. It would have been only natural for him to join in, but he simply could not do it. What was it? He felt like a stranger. This moment seemed to belong only to the three of them, and for him to participate would have been immensely difficult. Junshik watched his wife kneeling there, singing the chorus in a soft voice. He was surprised to see that her face was flushed, rosy as the setting sun.

"Dad! Dad! Why aren't you singing? Don't you know this song?"

"Yeah, I do. But I'm going to bed. I'm tired. . . ."

Junshik got up and went to his bedroom without even switching on the light. As he lay down in the dark, he could hear their voices: his wife, Sangmi, and Minu singing together in the living room.

"Throw the pebble—*splash, splash*—don't let big sister know. Let the river flow away, far, far away . . ."

Their singing seemed ever so clear and serene to him. But he could not go into the living room and join in. He tossed and turned, suffering alone in the stifling, dark room. It wasn't so much jealousy he felt, but self-loathing and the bitter disappointment of betrayal. The kind of sadness he felt when he was being punished as a child, when he had to watch from afar as the rest of his family was gathered around the table.

Why couldn't he be out there with them? No matter how much he thought about it, Junshik couldn't keep from clenching his teeth as he lay there, alone and in the dark.

"Would you like to hear a song I loved when I was little?" his wife asked his brother.

The more Junshik tried to fall asleep, the more agitated he became, and that made him even more attentive to the sounds coming from the living room. His wife began to sing.

"When the evening starlight shines on the branches of the elm tree, I miss my old friend . . ."

Her dreamy voice, filled with a secret sadness, echoed peacefully in the darkness of the summer night.

"Oh, that's such a beautiful song," Minu said. "I've never heard it before."

"When I was little, I had tears in my eyes every time I sang this. Funny, isn't it? And now I'm singing it to myself in my mind whenever I feel sad. I imagine an old friend. . . . I don't even have a face or a name, but I imagine he's waiting for me somewhere, just like in the song, and it makes me feel better. . . ."

She had never shared that story with Junshik. She must have been keeping it from him all this time. And he had never heard her, either, speaking in that dreamy voice. He was at his wit's end. Why was she telling this to his brother? Why reveal to him feelings that she'd kept to herself for so long?

When they had been working in the same office at school, she had never shown any interest in Junshik. She was cute, and he slowly became attracted to her, but it seemed to him that she must be dating someone. And since she didn't bother to hide her coldness toward him, he had never dared to try speaking to her. Until one day, when he walked into the office after work and found her sitting by herself, crying. He was embarrassed, and he hadn't known how to react. He couldn't exactly pretend not to see her and just walk out—she was crying so hard—but he also hadn't felt able to ask what was wrong. After crying for a good long time, she was the one who ended up asking him, "Will you buy me a drink tonight?" So that night he shared a drink with her for the first time, and two months later, they were married. And yet, even now, he still did not know the cause of her tears.

Junshik realized he knew very little about his wife, after all. They'd been together for six years now, but he'd never been able to penetrate inside her heart. Why was she giving up her secrets so easily to Minu?

His fury turned from his wife to his brother. Who the hell is this guy, anyway? What is he up to now? What was he doing before he got here? Minu hadn't said much. He'd remained evasive about his past and about the reason why he had to stay with Junshik.

They were no longer singing in the living room. Junshik could only hear two voices talking. Unable to bear it any longer, he opened the door and went to the refrigerator, pretending he was thirsty and getting water. His wife was so wrapped up in her conversation with Minu that she didn't even notice him. He walked over to the small room that Minu occupied. He searched through the clothes that were hanging there, and he felt a wallet in one of the pockets.

Junshik's hands were shaking as he opened it. His heart pounded. He felt like a criminal. But he found nothing special—just an identity card, a few business cards, and some one thousand won bills—nothing that indicated who this man was or where he'd come from. He was about to put the wallet back in its place when he felt something a little stiff. It was a photograph, stuck in the back compartment. A young woman. She must have been about twenty—not beautiful, but cute. On the back of the photo were a few words written in ballpoint:

"The long and steep path you wanted to walk, I would always walk it with you. Mihye."

Junshik quickly put the wallet back, afraid Minu might appear. When he was back in his bedroom, he lay down again in the dark. After a long while, his wife finally came to bed, their daughter in her arms.

"What sort of story could be that interesting?" Junshik asked as she put their daughter down.

"Hey, weren't you asleep?" she said, startled. "I thought you'd gone to bed."

Grinding his teeth alone in the dark, enduring the pain, and this is what it came to. He felt terribly spiteful.

"I think he's so pure and innocent," she said, sitting at her dressing table. "Since I've gotten to know him better."

"Pure? Really?" Junshik turned to his wife's face reflected in the mirror. It was white, covered in cold cream.

"Yes, really," she said. "It's been so long since I've met someone who's still pure like that. It reminds me of the past, right? It makes me realize we've become too dirty. Oh, there was a time when I was pure, too."

Hearing those words made Junshik seethe with anger. *Is purity and innocence what keeps us fed?* he thought. *Does she think I chose this life because I gave up on my ideals?* But he didn't want to get into it at the moment with her. He chuckled. "Sure, he's pure and innocent. How else can he stay here living off of us if he wasn't pure and innocent?" he said.

"What are you saying? He's your brother! And he's so grateful to us for being welcoming to him."

"That's exactly what I'm saying. Being grateful for the hospitality you get—that's real purity and innocence, isn't it?"

She turned and looked Junshik straight in the eye. "Oh, you're so narrow-minded," she said.

4

"There was a man here looking for you," Yang Guman said to Junshik when he had just entered the staff room. "Did he find you? He didn't look like a parent—more like an encyclopedia salesman. Oh, wait—here he is now!"

The man, who appeared to be in his forties, was wearing a striped suit. He walked over to Junshik, his shoulders slumped.

"Are you Mr. Hong Junshik?" he asked in a strangely quiet voice.

When Junshik nodded, he added in a softer and even lower voice, "Could I speak with you for a moment?"

"If it's about ordering books, come another day."

"Books? No, I'm a detective from the police department."

It wasn't the answer Junshik had expected. He noticed that the man's eyes were rheumy, as if he'd slept badly. The skin on his face was dark, with pores so large they looked like they were puncture marks left by a large needle.

"Could we go somewhere a little quieter?"

They went out and crossed the courtyard, which was blisteringly hot in the midday sun, and walked out of the school gate to the café across the street.

"This heat is terrible!" the detective said. "Hey, you, bring us some cold towels!" He rubbed his face with the wet towel that the waitress brought.

Junshik didn't touch his. "Why did you want to see me?" he asked.

"Mr. Hong, you have a brother, don't you?"

"A brother?"

"I already know everything. You have the same father. Your brother's name is Kang Minu. Quite a guy—kicked out of Seoul National University."

Junshik had no idea Minu had been expelled. The detective kept scrutinizing him as if he were watching for some sort of reaction. The man's face was very dark—not just the surface tan from being in the sun, but from deep underneath, enough to make Junshik wonder if there was something wrong with his liver.

"When was the last time you saw your brother?"

"I can't remember—it's been so long . . . We're brothers, sure, but, as you know, we have different surnames. We've been out of touch for a long time without any news from each other. You know, really, we only lived together when we were kids."

Junshik was worried the detective would sense his lie. Feeling the heat rise to his face, he grabbed the cold towel from the table and rubbed his face with it.

"But why are you asking me about my brother?"

"We're looking for him. I'm sorry to be a bother to you, but they say he's one of the worst activists. . . . He took on multiple identities to incite students and workers to riot against the government."

Junshik was dumbfounded. He stared at the detective, his mouth hanging open. He was asked a few more questions about this and that, but Junshik had no new information for him.

"Guys like him give us such a terrible headache! The order for this investigation came down from central admin, so we have to keep coming up with all sorts of reports. You're a teacher. I'm sure you know what I mean."

The detective seemed exhausted. Finally, with a pleading look, he handed Junshik his department business card, which read: "Detective Inspector Gwak Sungu, Intelligence Section."

"Don't hesitate to get in touch if you have any news about your brother or anything else." He said that without seeming to expect anything further of Junshik, as if he were simply speaking out of habit. They left the café and said goodbye to each other. Detective Gwak walked away with his shoulders drooping, exhausted and overwhelmed by the heat. The sight of him was enough to make Junshik want to give him some information just to revive him.

Junshik was still shocked by what he'd just heard, but what he felt most strongly was the unpleasant sense of having been betrayed. Minu hadn't told him a thing.

When he got home after work, Junshik found his brother crouching in the hallway outside the apartment door, busy with something. He was making screens to install in the windows, sweating profusely as he attached the metal netting to the aluminum frames.

"He's so good with his hands," Junshik's wife said, a hint of pride in her voice. "If we had to pay to have it done, it would've cost tens of thousands of won. . . ."

"I've got to do something to earn my keep. And it turns out this isn't so hard, after all," Minu said with a sweaty smile.

Junshik motioned for his wife to follow him to the bedroom.

"Look, Minu's in some sort of trouble. . . ." he said.

"What trouble? What are you talking about?"

He told her about the conversation he'd had with the detective that afternoon, and she listened, but her reaction was the opposite of what he'd expected.

"Wow, so he's important," she said. "I thought he was just one of those typical . . ."

"What do you mean, 'important'? He's a fugitive from justice. A criminal!"

"So what? What does it matter, since what he did was good? Could a normal person do what he did?"

It sounded to Junshik like she was saying that there was no way someone like him could be wanted like that. He was stunned. Was this the same woman who cursed in front of the television every time she saw students protesting, telling him they were immature?

"He must have suffered so much. And how much he must have worried . . . And all the while, living on the run like that, not a single place where he could feel safe."

It was then that Junshik noticed she was wearing a sleeveless dress and more makeup than usual. She looked sensual in a way she had never been before, and it concerned him who this change in her appearance was for.

"You did a great job. It's perfect," she said ecstatically to Minu when he was done with the window screens. "It looks like it was done by a real pro."

Minu actually had finished the screens, installing one in each window with the skill of a true craftsman.

"Oh, you're soaking in sweat! Take off your shirt and I'll get some water to splash over you."

"No, I'm fine," Minu said. "I just need to wash my face."

"No, you have to wash off that sweat. Go ahead, take off that shirt."

She was already in the bathroom, a water bucket in her hand, calling him.

Minu turned to look at Junshik, embarrassed.

"What? Are you ashamed to undress in front of your sister-in-law?" Junshik said.

After what his brother said, Minu peeled off his shirt and went into the bathroom, as if he had no choice.

Junshik went into his bedroom, but even from there, he could clearly hear the sound of the splashing, Minu's cries as he complained about the cold water, and his wife's amused laughter. There was nothing inherently wrong with a sister-in-law pouring water on her brother-in-law's back. Depending on how you looked at it, you could say it was a sweet and innocent scene. Junshik tried hard to see it that way, but he could not contain the emotions seething inside, nor could he stop himself from imagining his wife's pale hands moving up and down the slippery flesh of Minu's muscular back.

When everyone was in bed, he put his arm around his wife, who was lying with her back to him, facing the wall. She coldly pushed his hand away as usual.

"What are you doing?" she hissed. "I'm already dying in this heat!"

But he refused to give up. He forced her to turn over and got on top of her. She resisted stubbornly, and they wrestled silently in the dark for a long time until she finally let go and surrendered. He began to caress her, surprised by the heat of her response. She hadn't been like that in a long time. And as she finished, she moaned breathlessly, unable to stop herself. Junshik covered her mouth, afraid they'd be overheard by his brother, but she didn't even seem to notice. When the frenzied tide had ebbed, she lay there naked, stretched out, exhausted like a snake that had swallowed prey larger than itself, and

Junshik gazed at her, wondering why she had never been so passionate before. Could it be because she'd seen Minu's naked torso that afternoon? That image of him would not go away. Maybe in her head she'd been doing the act with Minu. As he thought this, the very idea that he could be imagining it sent a chill up Junshik's spine.

5

The next day, as soon as Junshik came home, Minu came to apologize.

"I'm sorry I didn't tell you earlier," he said.

Junshik assumed that his wife must have told Minu about the visit from the police detective. He admitted to Minu that he'd been upset, that his lack of frankness was tantamount to a lack of trust. But Minu said that wasn't the case. He'd only wanted to spare Junshik any unnecessary worry.

"But I'm your brother," Junshik said. "You should have told me if it was something like this."

"I'm sorry," Minu said. "But I thought just keeping quiet and leaving would make things less complicated for you and your wife."

"What are you gonna do now?"

"I have to leave soon. I thought about it, and I realized I might be getting you in trouble. . . ."

"What are you talking about?" Junshik's wife interrupted. "What kind of trouble could it be, anyway? We'll be fine, so feel free to stay as long as you like."

"Junshik's a teacher. If things go wrong for me, he could end up being reprimanded. And since the police already paid him a visit, I don't think it's going to be safe for me to stay here."

"But if they knew you were here, they'd already have come after you. You're safe here," Minu's wife said, her face flushing as she looked at Minu. "So stay a little longer if you need to."

Junshik thought she might be dreading Minu's departure. No, he was certain of it. He said to Minu, in a cooler voice:

"How long can you live on the run like this? You're past thirty now—it's not like you're still a college student. You can't just keep running until the world changes. . . . You don't actually believe the world *is* going to change, do you?"

"Whether the world changes or not isn't the important thing," Minu said. "I'm just doing what I believe is right."

"And if you believe it's right, you *have* to do it?"

"There has to be someone in the world who speaks up for what's right."

"You mean like when we were little and Mom lied about our age when she took us on the bus?"

Minu just stared at him as if he didn't understand. He had already forgotten. But Junshik would always remember it.

Their mother had taken the two of them on a bus that day. Junshik was in third grade then, so he was nine and Minu was seven. School-aged children were entitled to a reduced fare, but their mother wanted them to ride for free to save money. So she lied and told the ticket taker that Junshik was six and Minu was five. But she'd subtracted so much from their real ages that there was no way the man was going to be fooled.

"*Ajumma*, stop lying and just pay the fare," he said.

"Lying? What are you saying? They look older because they're tall, but they're only six and five."

"Look, if you're gonna lie, make it believable at least. Who's gonna believe a kid this big is only six? In the old days he would've been old enough to get married!"

Junshik did his best to make his mother's blatant lie believable. He tried to pretend he was like one of those kids whose body grew too quickly, big for his age and a little slow in the head. But the judgment came down very simply from an unexpected source. Minu, who had remained a silent witness until then, suddenly blurted out, "I'm not five. I'm *seven*."

Junshik and his mother were shocked, but so was the ticket taker, who exchanged glances with the bus driver. Junshik still vividly recalled the expression on his mother's face—she looked like she'd just been slapped.

The ticket taker bent down over Minu. "What was it you just said?" he asked. "*How* old did you say you were? Can you tell me?"

Minu looked straight up at Junshik and his mother. She said nothing, but her face gave away the complexity of her emotions and her eyes were pleading with him not to answer.

"Yes," Minu said. And then he went on, as if he were reciting a lesson from a textbook. "I'm seven years old. I'm in first grade at Myeongdeok Elementary School in Daegu." It sounded like he thought he was on the children's radio show *Who's Better than Whom?*

"Yes? Of course!" the ticket taker said, mussing Minu's hair. "You're an honest little boy." He gave Junshik's mother a sharp look. "Aren't you ashamed of yourself, lying in front of a child like this?"

With her charade exposed, their mother had no response except to pay the fare.

"Well, *ajumma*," the ticket taker said as he received the money. "At least you got *one* good son here."

But is it really possible, in this world, to say that one thing is right and another is not? If something is said to be right, then who has the ultimate authority to say it is? Junshik thought, looking into the face of the virtuous son who had turned out to be a criminal on the run.

"You're right, I will have to turn myself in one day," Minu was saying. "But not now—I can't afford to get caught now. It's not just about me, I have to protect my friends, too."

"If they catch you, how long will they put you away?" Junshik's wife asked, her voice full of concern.

"I don't know. I suppose it would be a few years at least."

She sighed quietly. She seemed on the verge of tears, and seeing that made Junshik feel a stab of pain.

"This is terrible, because it's time you got married and settled down," he said. "You *do* have a girlfriend, right?" Junshik looked sidelong at his wife to see her reaction to what he'd said. Maybe it was just his own suspicion, but she seemed shocked. She was trying to keep her expression neutral, but she couldn't hide the fact that she was suddenly blushing.

Minu seemed equally embarrassed. "How did you know that?" he asked.

"The cop told me. I think he said her name is Mihye."

His face red, Minu stared at Junshik in disbelief. "How would they know all that?" he asked.

Junshik watched his wife as she got up without a word and walked into the bedroom, closing the door behind her. When he joined her after a long while, he found her sitting in front of her dressing table, head bowed. He couldn't tell if she was deep in thought or crying. But then, why would she be crying? What was there for her to cry about?

"What are you thinking?" he asked.

She didn't look up. She sat there in that same pose—for how long, he didn't know—until she suddenly turned to face him.

"I think our marriage was a mistake," she said.

6

The dozen or so fish swimming around in the tank looked like they were made out of yellow construction paper. There was a bigger one, with blue spots, hiding among the long aquatic plants, waving its fins. There was also a small mill, with its wheel endlessly turning, spewing bubbles that rose vertically toward the surface.

"Are you here to buy an aquarium?" An old man's bald head suddenly appeared above the miniature seascape.

"Do you take care of the installation yourself?" Junshik asked.

"Is it for your home or someplace like a restaurant entrance?"

"It's for an apartment. In Sanggye-dong."

"I can't go out that far for free. I'd be losing money. . . ."

"What's this one called?"

"That one? Sanctus or something or other . . . I don't really know. We just call 'em tropical fish."

"Can we raise this kind at home?"

"I suppose . . . How big is your apartment?"

"Not very. It's only twenty-three *pyeong*."

"Then I recommend you come over this way and pick a goldfish, instead. The big ones costs five hundred won and the little ones are two hundred. Aquariums go for thirty to sixty thousand. Which one would you like?"

Junshik picked the thirty thousand won model. He bought three medium-sized goldfish at three hundred won apiece and two black ones at two hundred won each. But once he was outside the store with the aquarium on his shoulder, he realized it was going to be harder than he'd thought to carry it all the way home. Sweating profusely, he stood out in the street hailing a taxi, but none would stop for him. An empty cab occasionally did come by, but as soon as the driver noticed the large glass box on Junshik's shoulder, he would speed off. There was no choice but to take the train home.

As usual the train was packed, with hardly room to stand. The other passengers looked at Junshik with annoyance as he forced his way between them with the empty aquarium on his shoulder. He was also carrying the plastic bag full of the goldfish he'd bought. Each time the ceiling fans nodded their heads and wafted the stuffy air around the inside of the car, Junshik's nose was assaulted by the hot, nauseating body odor of the other passengers. He wanted to get to a window and put the aquarium on the luggage rack, but he was hardly able to move. He also had to keep his arm up, holding the plastic bag above everyone to keep it from getting torn. Already, his elbow was throbbing with pain and it felt like his shoulder was being crushed under a lead weight.

A gurgling sound came from his belly. It might have been his IBS acting up again. If he kept living with this level of stress, his whole body was going to fall apart. He looked at the plastic bag. The five fish, in that tiny amount of water, were barely managing to breathe. They were watching him with their bulging eyes, and strangely, to Junshik, it seemed they were full of pity for him. Pity coming from the eyes of a fish? The thought made him burst out laughing.

For what possible reason would I go through all this bother to bring home an aquarium? he asked himself. After all, his wife had seemed to lose interest in it by now. What was he possibly hoping to fix with this aquarium?

"I think our marriage was a mistake." That's what his wife had suddenly blurted out last night. At those words, Junshik had felt as if his heart were collapsing in his chest, but he had done his utmost to hide his feelings.

"What are you talking about?"

"You call this a life? You think what we're doing is living?"

"How do you think we should live?"

"Whatever it is, it's not like this. You can't call what we have an authentic life."

"An 'authentic life'? We're people going on with our lives. How is that not authentic? We all live the same way. Real life isn't like what you read in a novel. Life means having to adapt to reality and being content with that."

"But I feel like I took the wrong path with my life," she said. "It's like I buttoned myself wrong."

"And what do you propose to do about it now?"

"I don't know. I need time to think about it."

Junshik couldn't understand his wife's sudden transformation. Just a few days ago, she'd been preoccupied with buying a new wardrobe to replace the dilapidated old one, whose feet they'd had to amputate the last time they'd moved. She'd only been focusing on the problem of how to set up the apartment: the aquarium, the video, and the hi-fi. Now, suddenly, he was hearing her talk about things she'd never brought up before.

"Everyone needs to tell their own story sometimes," she said.

"What do you mean 'their own story'? What story?"

"Whatever story it is. Stories about their past, when they were children—any kind of story. What matters is that they have someone who listens and understands. I never tried to tell you any of those stories. You never wanted to hear them."

"You just said it. You never tried to tell me. When did I ever say I didn't want to listen to them?"

"I never told you because it's useless talking to you."

The train had just arrived in Nokcheon. The door opened and Junshik was pushed outside. He wanted nothing more than to get a breath of fresh air into his lungs, but all he got was the stifling humidity. His stomach was making strange noises and the pain was beginning to bother him. He needed to put down the aquarium and get to a restroom as quickly as possible, but he knew there was no such thing nearby. He had to endure the distress in his belly, heft the aquarium on his shoulder, carry the plastic bag full of fish, and start walking home. The heavy aquarium was a dilemma now—he felt like he couldn't carry it, but then again, he couldn't just leave it, either.

A long line of garbage trucks was kicking up dust, speeding along the edge of the construction site. They were using garbage as filler to raise a large depression at one corner of the complex. It was barren, dead earth, without a speck of vegetation, and not visible to the eye. But Junshik noticed that a lot of the garbage was plastic and, because of that, it would never decompose but remain there, under the dirt, for thousands—no, tens of thousands—of years. And on top of that, from the lifeless earth, steel-reinforced concrete structures were rising up. He didn't exactly know if they were leveling the site with so much garbage because its elevation just happened to be lower than in other spots. But for Junshik, seeing that quantity of garbage gave him the disappointing feeling of seeing through a façade, as if the magnif-icent background of the drama he'd been watching had turned out to be a set made of threadbare fabric and cheap wooden planks. It seemed ironic to him that the ground that was supporting all those awesome high-rises was actually just a huge sedimentary layer of trash. Now people were living there, planting trees, mowing grass, land-scaping. That was why he and his wife were going to decorate their apartment with an aquarium and put geraniums on their balcony. That was why he was sweating profusely now with this heavy thing on his shoulder.

And yet his wife had told him this was not an authentic life. What *was* life, then? His mind was racing as he struggled to keep the glass box propped up on his shoulder despite the increasing distraction of the pain in his belly. What would the rest of his life be like? Not that he hadn't thought of such things before, but today was the first time that question had come up so urgently. When he thought about it, the trajectory of the rest of his life was pretty obvious. He would probably be teaching for twenty more years at the same school. He would have to go to work every day, give the same lessons, repeat the same thing dozens of times in each class, listen to the same endless complaints from the headmaster, repeat the same instructions and criticisms to the students. Nothing would change. Maybe he could hope to become a head teacher and buy a car or move to a more spacious apartment. But what sort of change was that? What kind of life was it if all he was going to do was grow old like this and then wait around for death to take him?

The truth was that, in the past, he'd dreamed of having such a life. Stable and unexciting, a life in which you knew where you were going to sleep each night, where you didn't have to worry about getting fired from your job. It was all he had wanted, no more and no less. But now that he had finally achieved it, his wife was questioning the meaning of it all, saying it was a lie built on top of a filthy, stinking pile of garbage. As if their twenty-three-*pyeong* apartment, their bathroom with hot water, the aquarium and goldfish in the living room—everything—was just a stage illusion, painted over garbage.

What could he do about it now? *What does she want from me?* he wanted to scream.

His stomach was gurgling again. His lower belly felt like someone was stabbing him with a needle and he was afraid he was going to start leaking at any moment. He couldn't hold it in any longer. But it was still a long time before the sun would go down, and there was no place to squat and relieve himself. The aquarium pressed down more and more oppressively on his shoulder, and Junshik was tempted just to fling it onto the ground. He looked in every direction for someplace that could serve as a toilet until he spotted what looked like a shabby little plastic shed in one corner of the construction site. On the door was a sign that read TOILET, and above that, someone had written DO NOT USE. But circumstances being what they were, Junshik went ahead and put down the aquarium, then pulled the door open. What he saw left him speechless for a moment. There were piles of shit everywhere on the floor, so much there was hardly a place to put his feet. He already knew there was no working sewage system there, but there was so much excrement that it overflowed the tank and was spread all over everything. Junshik was bewildered by all the varieties of shit, some petrified and looking a decade old, others still fresh. He finally stepped inside, found a spot, undid his pants, and sat down. At first he wanted to throw up, but strangely, little by little, he began to feel indifferent to the smell. He began to feel that he was among countless living creatures who were protesting, showing their resistance in the bluntest way possible.

Suddenly, he remembered his mother's face. When he was little, she would do any kind of work to feed her family. She took in sewing at home and she had a spot in the market where she spread out a ground cloth and sold *odeng* and *gimbap*—fish cake and seaweed rolls with rice. All day long at the market, she would clap her hands and call out loudly, in her husky voice, "Get your delicious fresh *odeng* and *gimbap* here! Delicious fresh *odeng* and *gimbap*!"

By afternoon, the market was so crowded there was hardly room to walk. They said the market was "standing room" then, and at those times the tone of his mother's voice was all the more spirited.

"Delicious fresh *odeng* and *gimbap*! Get your delicious fresh *odeng* and *gimbap* here!"

In Junshik's memory, there was no one in the market with a voice as loud as his mother's. Clapping her hands and calling out all day long—whether or not there were passersby—she often had no time to eat or go to the bathroom. In those days, having to use a bathroom in the market was a problem. There was only one public toilet, located behind the market stalls, that was used by all the merchants. That meant there was always a long line.

Junshik's mother, no matter how urgently she needed to use the toilet, could not wait patiently in that line. She found it impossible to stand there, tormented by the thought that she could be selling at least one more seaweed roll. But one day, the result of her impatience had terrible consequences. She had run urgently to the public toilet, only to return to her spot again after seeing the long line. And after returning several times, she simply could not hold it any longer.

"*Aigo!* What to do?" she said. "What am I gonna do?"

Standing in line for the toilet, between all the other people, she stamped her feet and contorted her body, but it was no use. Junshik, watching her, began to feel the same kind of urgency. Even so, his mother gave up and went back to her spot at the market. Junshik didn't understand, at first, why she had gone back to squatting behind the mat where she had laid out all of her goods. She remained there, calm and quiet, and in a moment he smelled something that left no doubt about what she was doing.

"*Aigo!* What's that?" said the mackerel seller, whose spot was just to the right. She crinkled her nose in disgust.

"Someone must have farted," said the bean sprout seller to the left of his mother's spot.

"A fart doesn't stink like that. I think someone took a shit."

"Who would do that? In the middle of the market!"

The two neighboring merchants went on and on, but Junshik's mother remained quiet and expressionless. It was something she was good at—being confident in the most delicate situation while displaying absolute calm. Then she looked peaceful and content once again, her urgency having passed. The mackerel seller kept glancing at her out of the corner of her eye, obviously suspicious, but Junshik's mother wasn't concerned. Even now, Junshik could not forget the impudent and yet serene expression on his mother's face.

Junshik got out of the toilet and lifted the aquarium back onto his shoulder. He had made it this far. He would make it all the way. For him, as it was for his mother, life was far from luxurious or grand or noble. It was a continuous stream of filth and misery and suffering, a never-ending race in which he could not sidestep the hurdles. Sometimes, when he was lucky, he could get a taste of a short vacation or be satisfied with an achievement. But when he thought about it, it seemed to him that those things were just flecks of foam atop a procession of unending waves that would eventually snuff them out forever.

When he was finally home, his wife took the aquarium, but her face was expressionless.

"Why on earth did you bring dead goldfish?" she asked.

She was right. They were all dead. Somehow, the plastic bag had gotten punctured and more than half of the water had leaked out. The fish were belly-up with their eyes still wide-open, staring up at Junshik. Those eyes, full of pity.

7

"Mr. Hong, get in," Yang Guman called out just as Junshik stepped out of the school building. He was holding the car door open. The dean of the first-year teachers was in the driver's seat, and through the rear window, Junshik could see the back of Kim Dongho's thick neck. He climbed in next to him and the car drove off.

"Everyone else already left?" asked the dean.

"Of course! You can miss other things, but not a meal with colleagues. There's a rumor that you were going to give out our holiday bonuses at dinner. I hope it's true."

"Holiday bonuses for the teaching staff? Why, you're paid even during vacation time . . ."

"Oh, you're playing innocent again. How many days do we actually take off from work during school breaks? And we have to sweat it out in the heat to come in and teach extra classes."

"What's the point in staying home doing nothing when you can teach the kids at least one more thing!" Kim suddenly exclaimed. Everyone burst out laughing because he was just repeating the words of the principal.

"Thanks to your dedication, most of our students signed up for the supplementary courses over their summer break," the dean said, after they'd finished their meal at the Japanese restaurant where they had gathered. The ten first-year teachers, all present, were seated in a circle in front of him.

"I'm not saying that because I'm the dean, but in my opinion, we should make those summer courses mandatory if necessary. I know some of you are thinking what good is it if we force them to sit there and study in the heat, but think about it. You let those little beasts loose, and they'll just be up to no good. It's what they do during vacation time that ends up leading them astray. And then think of the headache that makes for you teachers!"

Kim Dongho sucked his teeth. He seemed to be resisting the urge to disagree with the dean. Of course, it was a foregone conclusion. The decision about the summer courses had already been made.

But the dean noticed immediately. "Anyway, I'll keep this short and conclude by thanking you all for your active participation. And this . . ."

He took a wad of crisp paper notes out of his trouser pocket. They were one hundred thousand won checks.

"I talked to the publisher we ordered the summer school textbooks from and put together a little extra for your troubles. I apologize for not having had time to put them in envelopes."

As he drawled on, he handed one of the checks to each of the teachers, who did not all share the same response. Junshik was curious about Kim Dongho's reaction—he was slightly red, fiddling with the check in his hand. After a while, the check had disappeared onto his person somewhere.

As they left the Japanese restaurant, Yang Guman sidled up to Junshik. "Mr. Hong, let's go have a drink," he said in a conspiratorial voice. "I know a place near here. The dean and Kim Dongho are coming, too."

Junshik was already a little drunk from the beers he'd had at the restaurant, but he followed them. For some reason, he felt like getting plastered that night. They walked along a street already lit up on both sides with garish neon signs, though it was still early evening. Yang Guman came to a stop in front of a bar called "The Golden Pond" and led them to the basement entrance.

They went down the staircase, which was dark and damp like the interior of a cave, and entered a small room of six or seven *pyeong* echoing with loud pop music.

"Are you open, or what?" Yang Guman shouted.

The small door in the back rattled open. "Oh! Oh, look who's here." A woman rushed out and took Yang Guman's arm, making a big fuss as if she were delighted to see him.

A fat older woman appeared behind her. "Oh, Mr. Yang!" she said. "It's been such a long time!" Her nasal voice seemed oddly out of place coming from her body. "Why didn't I hear from you all that time? I missed you so much. You didn't happen to get another girlfriend, did you?" she asked, glued to Yang Guman as soon as they were all seated in a back room.

"I have respectable gentlemen with me today, woman. So why don't you say a proper hello?"

"Nice to meet you," she said. "I'm Miss Jang."

"Madam, bring us some beers!" Yang shouted. "And send another girl!"

A young woman, thinner than Miss Jang, soon came with the drinks. She sat between Junshik and the dean, who raised his glass high and declared, "Let's have a toast!"

Junshik emptied his glass in a single gulp. The alcohol burned his throat as it went down and, combining with what he'd already drunk at the Japanese restaurant, it quickly heightened his intoxication. The woman immediately refilled his glass and Junshik emptied it just as quickly. And even that did not quench his thirst.

"Why is our Mr. Hong drinking in such a rush today?"

Yang Guman's hand was under Miss Jang's dress, fondling her breast, and the dean was busily discussing something with Kim Dongho.

"We do not educate only with youthful enthusiasm. Passion and experience are just as important, and the students. . . ."

Kim Dongho just listened without saying anything, his head half bowed. Junshik, staring at Kim's thick eyebrows, suddenly felt like he was suffocating. *What are my wife and brother doing now?* he wondered.

"We need another plate of side dishes," Miss Jang said to Yang Guman. "What shall we get?" She squirmed and giggled as Yang continued to grope her breasts.

"I like mussels," he said.

"Well, that's interesting. I prefer seaweed rolls myself."

Now the two women laughed together. The one who was sitting next to Junshik turned to him. "My favorite is *odeng*," she said.

Junshik's drunkenness took him to another time and place, and he couldn't distinguish the present from his memories. He was on a bus now, with his mother, driving past a market. Through the window he could see the throngs of people, delivery carts, merchants loudly shouting as they jostled each other. His mother, watching the scene, sat up, startled.

"*Aigo!*" she exclaimed. "What am I gonna do? The market's already standing-room!"

She must have imagined, for a moment, that she was still working at her spot. Suddenly, she stood up and started to clap her hands and stomp her feet.

"Get your delicious fresh *odeng* and *gimbap* here!" she cried. "Delicious fresh *odeng* and *gimbap!*"

It was all so sudden that Junshik didn't have time to react. He wasn't the only one who was surprised. The passengers looked at her in bewilderment, but after a moment they began to whisper, tittering and pointing their fingers at her.

"Delicious fresh *odeng* and *gimbap!* Get your delicious fresh *odeng* and *gimbap* here! Good enough to die for!"

And then, just as suddenly, she was quiet. She must have realized she was on the bus and not at her old spot in the market. She blushed and slowly sat back down.

"Strange. She looks perfectly normal, but she's completely out of her mind," said one of the two women sitting just behind Junshik. She spoke so loudly that all the other passengers must have heard. His mother certainly had, but the woman must have thought it didn't matter, since she was crazy.

"Musta been her husband made her like this," the woman said.

"And how would you know?" said the other woman.

"What do seaweed rolls and *odeng* look like? Just like a man's thing, right?"

"Oh, you're so right! He musta had another woman on the side or maybe he just run off . . .'"

"Yeah. Why else would someone who looks perfectly fine like that be screaming about *odeng* and *gimbap* on a bus?"

"*Aigo*, that poor thing."

Junshik emptied his glass. The woman at his side lifted her face to his.

"Oh, why's our principal looking so sad? Did you have some bad news?"

"Hey," he said. "I'm not the principal."

"No? Then vice principal?"

"Look, this gentleman is higher than a principal," Yang Guman said.

It wasn't clear who had originally coined it, but "Principal Wannabe" was the nickname his students and colleagues used for him. The joke was that he had started as an errand boy and was going to make it to principal.

Junshik felt he would suffocate if he didn't release whatever it was that needed to come out of his throat, and to wash away that stifling feeling, he emptied glass after glass.

"Mr. Hong! Mr. Hong! What is it you live for?" Kim Dongho asked, raising his head, red-faced and drunk. Without waiting for a reply, he answered himself. "Me? I've lost my taste for life. No matter how much I think about it, I can't find any joy in living."

"What? No joy in living? Why, this is serious," Yang Guman butted in. "If you already lost your zest for life at your age, it's the end. Understand? The bell's ringing. The day's over."

Junshik saw Kim Dongho's red eyes glaring at Yang Guman. He stared that way, without saying a word, for several seconds. He was clenching his beer glass hard, with the force that he could just as well have used to slap Yang's face. *Go ahead and slap him,* Junshik thought to himself. *Why are you just staring at him like that? Slap him if you've got a pair.*

"What's the matter, Mr. Kim? Did I say something wrong?" Yang Guman's lip curled into an unpleasant smirk.

Kim quickly relaxed his grip on the glass. "Oh, it's nothing," he said. "You're absolutely right. Actually, that's what I was thinking myself."

He turned to Junshik again. "That's why I took up indoor fishing lately. You know about it? You're not fishing in the open air under the sun—it's in the basement of a building. It's the perfect hobby for someone like me who hates seeing the sun."

"You don't like seeing the sun? Well, this is serious. Serious," Yang Guman interjected again. But this time, Kim Dongho said nothing.

"You've got to do something, at least. Otherwise, what's the fun in living?" he said to Junshik. "You know, if you hook the one with the red fins, you win a TV. Keep chasing that bastard and you can't even tell how time is flying. Why don't you come with me sometime?"

"Hey," Yang said, "we're already drinking and the ladies haven't properly introduced themselves. Don't spoil the atmosphere. Who wants to start?"

"Why don't we just pass today? Do we really have to?" Miss Jang said, still clinging to Yang.

"What do you mean 'pass'? The introductions are a special tradition in The Golden Pond, right? Miss Jang, you start. Do a demonstration for us."

"Aren't you sick of seeing mine? Why do you want to see it again?"

"I brought my colleagues today. So why don't you do a proper introduction?" Yang Guman took out two ten thousand won bills from his wallet and placed them on the table.

Jang then stood up without much hesitation. She took off her shoes and climbed onto a chair. Her face expressionless, she removed her blouse and let it drop to her feet like a used tissue. She took off her skirt and tossed it aside, and when she bent over, Junshik could see rolls of flesh jiggling under the sheer black fabric of her underwear. She removed her clothes one layer at a time, as if she were molting, her face blank all the while because it was simply a tedious and boring task for her. She only gave one cursory smile when her eyes met those of the four men who were fixated on her every movement. Kim Dongho, his face bright red, was piercing her body with his stare. The dean looked on as if he were stupefied. The red lights revealed everything—even the patches of cellulite on the woman's flesh. She was big-boned with lots of flab. Her belly sagged, and she looked off-balance because of her pendulous and unattractive breasts. Junshik noticed her large, dark nipples sunk in the two protruding mounds of flesh. They displayed the same indifference and the same insolence as their owner's face as she removed the only scrap of cloth left on her body and began to sing.

"The spring breeze, blowing under the bright pink skirt . . ."

Junshik gulped down the glass in front of him as if he were trying to quench an irresistible thirst. He was holding in the anger and contempt he'd been harboring for a while, and it was becoming less and less bearable because he didn't know who it should be directed at. Suddenly he stood up.

"Delicious fresh *odeng* and *gimbap*! Get your delicious fresh *odeng* and *gimbap* here!"

His colleagues stared at him, flabbergasted, wondering what craziness had gotten into him. Junshik himself didn't understand what had just taken hold of him. He clapped his hands and stamped his feet in rhythm like his mother had done those many years ago.

"He's nuts," said Miss Jang, standing naked on top of the chair, her mood soured.

"Mr. Hong, what's the matter with you? Sit down," said the dean.

But Junshik began to shout even more loudly, walking in circles around the table:

"Delicious fresh *odeng* and *gimbap*! So good they're to die for! *Odeng* and . . ."

Someone suddenly grabbed him from behind. It was Kim Dongho.

"Mr. Hong, you were having such a good time. Why are you spoiling our get-together? You're acting like you've lost your mind. . . ."

Junshik twisted around and shoved him away. Kim lost his balance and fell on the table, dragging the bottles down with him. There was a loud noise of shattering glass and women screaming.

"Yes, I've lost my mind," Junshik said. "I'm crazy! But then what does that make all of you? You call this living? Can you live like this and say you're alive? You pathetic bastards!"

He turned and walked out of the room but then almost immediately went back in again.

"Here, you can split this among yourselves."

As his colleagues looked on, still stunned, he tossed his bonus check and it fluttered to the floor like an autumn leaf.

8

Years ago, without realizing it, Junshik had developed the habit of walking with a slight stoop when he was drunk. It was back in the days when he worked at the high school during the daytime and went to evening classes at the university. He was living in the basement of a house in a tiny rented room. The ceiling was so low he couldn't avoid hitting it when he stood up straight, and so he had to keep his head down. Since then, each time he was drunk, he unconsciously found his way back to that tiny room under the stairs. That's how he was walking now to his apartment, and when he got there he began to pound on the door with all his strength, shouting.

"Hey, open that door! Open uuup!"

His wife's astonished face appeared. "What the hell are you doing? You could at least keep quiet when you come home drunk!"

Despite the alcohol, Junshik noticed that she was wearing makeup again. Her painted face aroused in him a sudden and inexplicable feeling of sympathy. The makeup was evidence that the care she took in her appearance was all in vain. She was pitiful, like an old waitress who continues to paint her face even when nobody looks at her anymore. But he kept his thoughts to himself.

"Look, Jeong Misook," he said, instead. "Let me ask you a question. Why are you wearing makeup at home these past few days?"

"What are you talking about? I just put on some lipstick. . . . And so what if I decide to wear makeup at home? It's only natural. You want to make something of it?"

"Oh, it's natural alright," Junshik said. "So tell me why you never thought to do what feels so natural before! You're wearing makeup every day now, and I want to know the reason. . . ."

She blushed. "First of all, what's it to you whether or not I wear makeup?"

"You want me to answer for you? Why you're wearing makeup now? It's because of Minu, isn't it?"

"What are you saying?" she said. "Are you out of your mind?"

Even in his drunken state, Junshik knew he was going too far. And yet that didn't stop him. He went on and on, his voice growing louder and more strident, though he did not understand why.

"Isn't it true? You want Minu to think you're pretty, don't you?"

"You're drunk, Junshik, but this is too much!" Minu interrupted. He was blushing, too.

"Stay out of this," Junshik said. "This is a problem that concerns the two of us."

"It may be between the two of you, but since my name came up, I'm involved, too. I have a responsibility."

"You see what he's like, Minu? This is what I have to live with! I could die of shame, really!"

"Shame? You're ashamed to live with me?" Junshik said.

"Yes, I'm ashamed! Is there something wrong with what I said? I don't want to hide what's on my mind anymore. . . ."

She couldn't finish what she was saying because Junshik leapt at her. But Minu grabbed him by the arms and Junshik lost his balance.

As he fell to the floor, he accidentally kicked the dressing table. There was a terrible crash, and the whole room seemed to shatter before his eyes. His wife, too—even Minu. It took him a moment to realize he was looking at them reflected in fragments of the broken mirror.

What have I done? he wondered, on the floor, realizing he was alone. The house was strangely quiet. Shards of mirror littered the floor.

The door quietly opened, and his wife entered.

"I'm leaving, Hong Junshik."

"Leaving? Where to?" He quickly got up.

She had woken Sangmi and gotten her dressed. They were standing there together with a suitcase already packed.

"Don't worry about where we're going," she said.

"You're planning to leave here tonight? In the dark?" he said.

"Yes! I can't live in this house anymore!"

He didn't know what to say. He felt so dumbfounded that he couldn't even be angry. "You're taking Sangmi?" he barely managed to say.

"Of course! I have to. You obviously can't go to work and raise her at the same time."

"What the hell's gotten into you? We've been doing so well up until now."

"Doing so well? We were just pretending. Keeping up appearances! I've never really been happy since I married you, Hong Junshik."

"Happy? But what does that mean, anyway?" he replied, feeling defeated. He asked because he felt that he truly did not understand the meaning of that word.

"A human being who lives like a human being is happy."

"Are you saying you aren't living like a human being?"

"That's right. I'm sorry to have to tell you this, but I've lived with you like this against my will, without any benefit to me, without any pleasure. What kind of a life is this?"

What kind of a life is this. He had said almost those same words earlier that night at the bar. It was practically the topic of the evening. But no matter how much screaming and shouting, where was the answer to be found? He felt like he was suffocating, losing his grip, about to lose his sanity.

"So how are we supposed to live?"

"How could I possibly explain in words?"

He couldn't take it anymore. He left the room, kicking the door open with his foot. Minu was standing just outside, his face pale. Junshik grabbed his arm.

"You, fucking bastard! Come here, this is all because of you! It was you who came into my house and made this mess."

"Don't be such a jerk," his wife said. "He hasn't done anything wrong."

"Why not? Who the hell are you?" Junshik said to Minu. "You turned her into this, you bastard."

"Aren't you even ashamed in front of him?" Junshik's wife interrupted, coming between them.

"Ashamed? Me? For what?"

"Your brother dedicated his life to the struggle for justice. What about you? You only think of yourself. You've never raised your voice in protest your whole life! Do you even have a dream or ideals?"

Junshik had no answer. He had hit a wall. For six years they had made a life together, and now he was facing a brick on which he couldn't even leave a fingernail mark. He wanted to cry.

"Listen, Junshik, I'm sorry if she's doing this because of me. But look, you're not going to solve anything by getting carried away like this. Try to understand . . ."

"Understand? Why don't you two try understanding *me*? So I'm a guy who goes on with life not even knowing what living means. No dreams, no ideals, just living like a bug. Depraved and groveling in front of authority—that's the only way I could live. Why do you have to be so moral and ethical? How come you can still be so morally high and mighty?"

Minu remained silent as he listened to his brother's rant. Junshik himself was shocked at what was coming out of his mouth. Except for the lectures he gave when he was teaching—no, not even then—he had never expressed himself so passionately. But now that he had vomited it all up, he felt relieved, even a sense of satisfaction.

"I've always been annoyed by you," Junshik said. "Why are you always so proud? Why is it you're still fighting for justice at your age? Why can't you just be like me and kowtow to people so you can keep your job and feed your family? What have you got that lets you stay on that high horse above everyone else?"

"I'm sorry," Minu said at last, in a low voice. "You have your way of getting through life, I have mine."

"That's right. You said it. I have my way and you have yours. Whatever turns you on. So let's not get into it anymore. Everyone lives as they please."

"Look, Junshik, I never imagined my being here would cause so many problems. I'm so sorry. I'm leaving—right now. So Misook, you try to calm down too and think it over."

"That's not possible. I'm leaving, too," she said, lifting her suitcase. "I can't go on living like this. There's no way."

Go ahead and leave, all of you, Junshik thought. I'll stay here by myself. But he didn't have the courage to say it out loud. His daughter began to cry. Minu was looking embarrassed.

"Look, Junshik, I'm going to talk a little while with sister Misook. . . . Why don't you go out for a bit?"

Junshik let Minu push him out of the apartment. It felt like he was being kicked out of his own house. Standing alone in the parking lot outside, he smoked a cigarette. All the bitterness of the past few days, which he had buried deep in his heart, came bubbling up. From the time they were kids, his brother was always the good guy and he was the villain. He had never liked it, but those roles didn't change. It was still like that now, and it would probably be the same in the end.

In the neighborhood where Junshik grew up, there once was a bread factory. They called it a "factory," but it was just a home business that had a bread machine. The sweet and yeasty smell of baked rolls would waft through the neighborhood making their stomachs growl. The kids would breathe deeply, flaring their nostrils as they walked by so they could inhale as much of the smell as they could into their empty bellies. Every Sunday morning, Junshik's mother would go to work there. She was probably cleaning up the kitchen or doing their backlog of laundry to earn some money. When the family had left the house—wearing their nice Sunday clothes and carrying their bibles under their arms—Junshik would come to the back fence. The house was the last one in a dead-end alley, a place where no one was likely to pass by.

He would wait there a long time until he finally heard a tapping sound against the back fence, followed by a voice whispering, "Junshik. Junshik." He would go right up to the fence then, and from a gap in the slats, a white paper bag full of rolls would emerge. He would quickly grab it, hide it under his clothes, and run back home. His mother would steal several rolls that way, and the next day, she would sell them at the market.

It surprised him that he had never thought of what she was doing as wrong. Neither did his mother since, in her eyes, the supreme virtue was feeding her family. Regardless, Junshik had to become her accomplice in the life-and-death war she waged for their survival. As soon as she gave an order, he had to obey unconditionally and without question. But his little brother was a different species, questioning orders and resisting injustice, even in the most critical moments, so it was dangerous to trust him in this kind of operation, which involved stealing. It was because of him that everything was found out one day. Even so, it was because of her stealing that his mother could offer more new items, like fish cakes and seaweed rolls, to supplement the usual greasy fare she offered her customers.

Before taking them to sell at the market, she kept the rolls in a basket that hung from the ceiling of the kitchen. She stole different varieties with Junshik's help: a kind with red bean, cream, and jelly filling, and a kind with poppy seeds. They all looked so delicious that even glancing at them made Junshik's mouth water. He would swallow a mouthful of saliva, but he could never eat even a single roll because his mother was paying careful attention to her small inventory of stolen goods. Sometimes, however, he managed to sneak one of the rolls out of the basket and lick the crust. He even developed a method for not spoiling them. Hardly a roll escaped his saliva and not one of his mother's customers ever realized it. He never forgot the delicious flavors that spread over his tongue at the time, and since then, he had not once tasted anything as wonderful.

One day, when he was supposed to meet his mother at the crack in the wall, he made a terrible mistake. He was preoccupied playing a game with his friends, and he sent Minu to take his place. It was a fatal error. Minu was stupidly caught by the landlady as he received the rolls. She must have been noticing, for a while, that some of her merchandise was missing. She grabbed Minu by the neck and dragged him home. The young woman, who was originally from Seoul but had fled during the war, began to interrogate him in front of the kitchen entrance.

"You know stealing is bad. You learned that in school, right?"

Minu, white as a sheet, nodded without saying a word.

"You were also taught not to tell lies, right?"

He nodded again.

"So tell me the truth then. Tell me where your mother is hiding the rolls."

Minu's frightened glance went back and forth, in turn, from Junshik to his mother.

"A truthful person goes to Heaven, but liars go to Hell. Do you want to end up in Hell?"

Junshik wanted to close his eyes at that moment. His little brother pointed to the basket hanging from the kitchen ceiling. Everything was exposed in an instant. The owner of the bread factory practically flew up to snatch the basket—and that day it happened to be particularly full.

"My, my, you certainly stole a lot, didn't you?" she declared. "This place might as well be a thieves' den."

His mother just stood there, smiling like an idiot. It was the wrong thing to do because it seemed to provoke the woman's anger. She threw herself at Junshik's mother, grabbing a fistful of her hair.

"You bitch, who are you trying to ruin? I took pity on you because of how old you are, but you've been stealing from me behind my back all this time! And I thought you looked so dumb and honest."

It was Junshik's father who put an end to the confrontation. Witnessing the whole thing from the other room, he let out a strange yell and came running into the kitchen in his bare feet. He grabbed a pair of tongs that were used for charcoal briquettes and began to beat his wife with them, mercilessly. His father's violence must have frightened her, because the owner of the bread factory stepped back, looking panicked. Junshik's mother did nothing to resist the blows. She simply offered her whole body up to the tongs. Junshik's father looked like he had gone mad, but then again, it would have been understandable. How could a gentleman who had lived his whole life with honor and dignity be expected not to lose control of himself in the face of such terrible humiliation?

Minu burst into tears and hung on to his father's arms, begging, "Father, don't beat her. Please stop!" Junshik, at that moment, felt so much hatred toward his brother that he wanted nothing more than to kill him. Maybe the little bastard had planned it all from the start: going along with their thieving, biding his time, just waiting for the right moment to expose them.

Junshik was twelve at the time of the incident. Twelve became twenty-two, and now he was already thirty-four years old. Twenty-two years had passed. But who knew all the hardships he'd endured living those twenty-two years? Not the principal, not his colleagues, certainly not Minu, and not his wife. There was no one who could understand his pain, his loneliness, and his sadness. This world had not once offered him a proper door of opportunity. Sometimes one would seem to appear, and he would yank it open and go through, but it was always like a dog door he had to crawl through, subservient and fearful of intimidation. If there was something he was able to enjoy, it was the reward for all that suffering. But now Minu had come along, and in the same way he had betrayed Junshik and his mother for their stealing, he had laid bare the pathetic foundation of the home that Junshik had created through all his trials and tribulations—Minu had shown that Junshik's personal castle was built on top of a pile of lies and self-delusion. And that was the thing Junshik couldn't bear. It didn't matter what his brother had or hadn't wanted—that was unimportant. What mattered was that everything had started to unravel when he had appeared.

In a corner of the parking lot there was a telephone booth that was brightly lit in the darkness. Junshik walked toward it, his feet moving mechanically. As he got closer, he became so tense and anxious that his heart began to beat violently. He found it hard to breathe. When he finally reached the phone booth he stood for a while staring at it as if he were in a stupor. But it felt as if some force was pushing him, and it wasn't long before he stepped inside. He picked up the receiver and slipped a coin into the slot. His hand shook as he dialed the number.

A drawling voice answered. "Hello? Intelligence Section."

"Detective Gwak, please."

"Please hold."

As he waited, he heard the sound of someone breathing loudly on the line only to realize, after a moment, that he was hearing himself. The receiver felt too heavy in his hand. *Let it go, Junshik,* a voice said from some remote corner of his mind. *It's not too late. Just hang up the phone and it's all over.*

"Hello?"

When he heard the familiar voice, he became so tense the words seemed to stick in his throat, and he could barely manage to speak. And after he'd hung up, he couldn't remember what he had told the detective.

"Don't worry, your wife is staying."

Minu had been standing in front of the apartment entrance, waiting for him. Junshik couldn't say anything to him—he couldn't even look him in the eye. The two of them stood there for a while watching the noisy traffic speeding by along the wide thoroughfare.

"I'm leaving now."

Junshik could see that Minu was carrying the small vinyl bag he had the day he'd arrived. He was about to ask Minu where he was going, but he stopped himself. It was a pointless question.

"I'll walk you to Nokcheon Station," he said.

"You don't have to. You should go in and see your wife."

But Junshik was already walking toward the station. After a few steps, he paused. "I don't know where you're off to," he said, "but how about taking a cab?"

"I'd rather take the train. It's more convenient." Minu looked down at his watch. "The train's still running, isn't it?"

Of course the train was still running. But Junshik couldn't take Minu to the station. Even now, if he could put him in a taxi, Minu would be safe and everything would be back to normal as if nothing had happened. But Junshik could not convince Minu, and they began walking along the same route they had taken together when Minu had first arrived a few days ago.

"What did you say to my wife? What were you two talking about?"

Minu said nothing for a moment. "About love," he said.

"Love?"

"I was telling her how much you must love her."

"How much I love her? How would you know?"

"Of course I know. All I needed to see was how you got all fired up with jealousy." Minu laughed, as if he were joking, baring his white teeth in the darkness.

Junshik didn't know what to say. The hot, humid breeze carried a foul odor. They were almost at Nokcheon Station.

"Do you think we'll be able to see each other again sometime?"

Minu didn't answer. He suddenly stopped walking and looked at Junshik. "I'm so sorry, Junshik," he said. "Will you forgive me?"

"Why are you asking for my forgiveness?"

"I feel like I have to. If you suffered in any way because of me, please forgive me."

Junshik couldn't say anything. He wanted to turn around with Minu and go back, but it was already too late. Nokcheon Station appeared before them. Junshik cautiously scanned the surroundings, his heart beginning to pound.

He could see two men in the distance in front of the station's turnstile. They looked sturdy but were clearly not construction workers. Junshik slowly climbed the stairs, not taking his eyes off them. They had also noticed Junshik and his brother, but they showed no reaction and Minu didn't seem to have noticed anything. Junshik was so nervous his knees were trembling. Even from that distance, one of the men looked familiar with his slightly hunched posture. While he slowly went up the stairs, Junshik was mentally calculating the distance that still separated them.

"Just a moment," Junshik said, grabbing his brother by the arm when they'd almost reached the top of the stairs.

Minu was alerted by the strange tone in Junshik's voice. "What's the matter?" he asked.

"These guys look suspicious. They look like they might be cops. . . ."

"Oh, come on." Minu sounded dismissive, but his body had already stiffened. The two men, noticing their hesitation, began slowly walking toward them.

"Run!" Junshik said. He grabbed Minu's hand, turned, and started to run, pulling his brother behind him.

Minu hesitated at first but then followed. Behind them, they could hear the thudding of their pursuers' footsteps.

They made it down the stairs and rushed headlong into the darkness, the footsteps behind them drawing closer. The sound of Junshik's labored breathing mixed with his brother's. By the time Junshik got his bearings, he realized they had reached the piles of materials at the construction site. He heard a sudden noise behind him—Minu must have tripped over something. Junshik looked over his shoulder to see that the two men were already on top of his brother.

"Ju-Junshik!" Minu called out to him.

But Junshik did not stop. Even while he was running, he kept asking himself, *Why am I running like this? I have no reason to be running from the police. It's not me, but my brother they want.* But those thoughts did nothing to slow him down. Finally, he realized he could no longer hear their footsteps chasing him. He hid on the ground behind a segment of cement pipe and looked behind him. He could make out their vague silhouettes even in the darkness. Minu seemed to put up resistance, but it was only for a moment, and then he gave up and let himself be led away. Junshik watched the whole time, holding his breath.

Even after they had disappeared, Junshik remained there for a long time, unable to get up. There was a terrible stench wafting from somewhere. He felt along the ground and his hand touched something soft. He realized he was crouching in a trench full of shit, and still, he couldn't seem to get up. He felt paralyzed, as if all the energy had drained from his body.

Sitting there, he wondered what had made him run at the sight of the two men at the station. Was it a delayed pang of conscience? Or was it because he didn't want to be suspected of having been the one who called the police?

He lifted his head and looked up at the sky. Even from the trench full of shit, the stars twinkled beautifully, and for no apparent reason, tears began to flow from his eyes. The truth was, he did not feel any guilt. Even if it hadn't been now, his brother would have confronted reality—it was just a matter of time. If Minu was as pure and innocent as his wife seemed to think, then he was just a victim of his own innocence—his naivete.

But then why am I suddenly so sad? Junshik wondered. *Why am I crying now? Why do I feel like there's a hole in my heart, as if I'm the most desperately miserable of all miserable beings?*

He was sobbing now. The tears would not stop, and the more he cried the sadder he became. Despair, deep in his heart, that he could not explain to anyone. A personal despair no one would understand. He stayed like that for a long time, crying loudly like a child, sitting on his haunches in that trench full of shit without a thought of getting up. His face was twisted into a grimace of pain, as if all the sadness in his heart was suddenly being squeezed out. He let himself go, carried by the sadness so long held in his body, shedding tears for the inevitability of nothingness.

A train had just arrived at the station. Passengers disembarked and walked by just a few paces from where Junshik was squatting.

"Why is that guy crying over there?"

"Maybe he's drunk."

"You don't cry like that when you're drunk . . . he musta been in some accident, huh?"

"Don't worry about him. You never know—he might be crazy!"

The people moved away, and he found himself alone again. A long time passed, and then he finally got up, slowly, stiffly. Stinking and covered in shit, he began to walk but found he was staggering like an old wounded soldier or a dog that's just been kicked in the flank. The sobbing in his throat had turned into a kind of hiccup.

What is my wife doing now? he thought. *Is she waiting for me? Has she given up on leaving, like Minu said? How will she greet me later? Could she ever forget all this? What will become of Minu?*

He'll be put away for a long time, away from the rest of the world. But he's not the only one who can't do what he wants in this world. I have to live with constant humiliation, with no dignity, without innocence. He looked into the darkness. He had to go. Back to his twenty-three-*pyeong* nest floating precariously on that enormous pile of garbage in that void in the distance, trampling through all the rubbish, the hate, and abandoned dreams.

Translated by Heinz Insu Fenkl

BURNING PAPER

G RAMMA! GRAMMA! WE'RE IN BIG TROUBLE."

Perhaps it was from squinting all day at the fiery red silk that filled that tiny room, but when Granny set down her needlework and lifted her head, she felt dizzy, and her vision seemed to go blank.

"There's a strange man hanging around out front. He's here to arrest Uncle!"

The sun had climbed over the ledge of the balcony behind the boy, and now it stung her eyes. She could not open them properly. Her grandson was still huffing and puffing after running up from the ground floor, all in one breath, and his face merely shimmered before her in a blur, not immediately in focus.

"What . . . what're you talking about?"

"He asked if I lived in unit 402, and then he said, 'Your father's name is Kim Sungguk, right?' And then he asked, 'Is your uncle's name Kim Sungho?' And then he started asking all sorts of questions about Uncle. Come look, Gramma. You can see him from the balcony."

The boy excitedly pulled her up by the arm and ran ahead to the balcony, peering through the railing. But on the cement-paved street below—too rough to even pull a tricycle over without making noise—there was only the slanted sunlight of the early fall afternoon making her eyes sting. There was no one to be seen.

"You're lyin' to me, aren't you?" Granny said. "Playin' a trick on your old Gramma."

"It's not a lie! It's real! He was just there. He's a detective! For sure, Gramma."

"Nonsense. Why would a detective come here? No one here did anything wrong."

"Another kid told me he saw handcuffs in the man's pocket. Do you know what handcuffs are, Gramma?"

"I think our Shiggi's been watchin' too much TV."

Granny automatically pulled the needlework toward her. Her eyes still smarted from the blinding glare from the street when she'd looked down from the balcony. The afterimages would not go away. *How very odd*, she thought, clicking her tongue to herself. Her heart would not calm down, either. It was still pounding, as if she were suffering from carbon monoxide poisoning from a *yeontan* stove. It felt as if a deep, dark hole had been dug in front of her eyes, and her body was slowly being pulled into it, into a trauma from the distant past, which she had put out of her mind all this time, but her body had never let go.

Just then, the doorbell rang, and the boy clung to her, terrified.

"See, Gramma? It must be him!"

"Who is it?" she called in a choked voice.

There was no answer. The door was unlocked, but the bell just kept ringing, and it was only as she was about to press her eye up against the peephole that it creaked open, and a long, pale face smiled back. It was her sister-in-law.

"Granny, are you alive?" she said. "Did I come at a bad time? Why're you looking at me like you seen a corpse?"

Truth was, she couldn't have been more startled. Though her sister-in-law came to visit two or three times a month, her face—that smile with one side of the mouth drooping—seemed especially frightening today, as if it were not of this earth. ·

"Oh, Sis, are you still messin' with this stuff?" Sister-in-law said, seeing the needlework laid out as she stretched her legs out on the floor.

"A neighbor said it's for her daughter-in-law's wedding dress," Granny replied. "I was workin' on it, since I wasn't doing anything. . . ."

"You don't need to fuss with stuff like this. Think about Sungguk's reputation."

"Sungguk'll throw a fit if he finds out," Granny said. "I've just been getting it dirty from my hands since I can't see anything with these old eyes anymore."

Her oldest son did not like her sewing. She had quit sewing for money, after more than twenty years, when they'd moved in to this apartment. But word got out somehow, and neighbors still often came by with work for her.

"Why don't you do it in the big room?" Sister-in-law said. "You need someplace roomy, with light. What can you even sew in a closet like this? You're gonna end up sticking a needle through your finger."

In truth, Granny also sometimes felt that the small room she occupied was dark and stuffy like the inside of a coffin. It had a small window facing west and was always in shadow. She shared the room with her younger son, Sungho. The cramped apartment of only thirteen *pyeong* was divided into a two-by-three-meter room, a kitchen, and a living room. Finally, there was this tiny makeshift room—the one she lived in. After bringing in an old wardrobe and a desk for Sungho, who was a university student, there wasn't enough space in there to roll over in her sleep.

Granny hardly ever used the big room after her daughter-in-law had left home. She felt comfortable in that room, with bright sunlight spilling in through the wide balcony door, but she would not let herself sit in there during the day when Sungguk was away at work. She did not want to enter that room without its owner there and see all the household items like the makeup bureau or wardrobe that had been touched by her daughter-in-law.

"You brat. Why do you hide every time you see me?" Sister-in-law reached out her hand to the boy. "Now, come to your grand-auntie. We might be once removed, but your grand-auntie's still a grandma."

The boy just clutched the hem of Granny's skirt and would not budge. He was not a shy child, but for some reason, he disliked and feared his grand-aunt.

Sister-in-law opened her purse. "See this?" she said. "Our Shiggi . . . let your grand-auntie give you a hug. Come on—I'll give you this money."

The boy finally inched forward. But even as he took the money, he scrunched his face as if he were swallowing bitter medicine in his grand-aunt's embrace. When she kissed him on the cheek with an audible smacking sound, the boy let out a strange wail and ran out of the room, excitedly clutching his money, the suspicious man from earlier entirely forgotten.

After listening to the reverberating cries of the boy recede, Sister-in-law spoke. "Still no news, eh?"

"What news would there be?" Granny asked.

"I just don't get young people these days. How can she sleep at night after abandoning a child like that? What could be worth it?" Sister-in-law clicked her tongue audibly.

Granny's daughter-in-law was someone Sungguk had brought

home, saying he'd met her during his yearlong stint out in the countryside. They seemed to have met at some restaurant in Busan, where he used to order lunch. When she showed up, she already had a big belly. Granny was shocked, but on the bright side, she considered it a blessing to have gained a daughter-in-law with such little fuss in their poor state, and since the girl was already showing, Granny hoped that maybe she would give birth to a healthy boy. So she had accepted the situation without any complaints.

Because her daughter-in-law had come with just the clothes on her back, there were no gifts or dowry to give or receive. Granny just let the couple have the big room and a set of blankets she had been saving, and then started sharing the other room with Sungho. But perhaps her daughter-in-law wasn't the kind of woman to be satisfied being just a housewife—she'd left home before the baby was done nursing, and there hadn't been any news from her since.

"Maybe he's wise for his age . . . he never asks about his mother. . . ." Granny mused.

When there was no response, she turned to look at her sister-in-law and saw that she was asleep. She sat with her chin resting on one knee and mouth half-open, already looking unconscious. Granny clicked her tongue.

"Just wait," Sister-in-law mumbled through half-parted lips, as if she were talking in her sleep. "How can you nag me like this when I'm at someone else's home? Have you no shame?"

Her voice was tinged with the honest annoyance of someone speaking to family.

"What was that about?" Granny asked her sister-in-law, who had suddenly taken away her needle and thread as she was blinking her blurry eyes, struggling to thread the needle. "What were they nagging you for?"

"Food. They're hungry ghosts that follow me around everywhere. I can't stand it anymore." Sister-in-law wetted the end of the thread with saliva. She spoke as if she were talking about her own ill-mannered children.

"No matter how much they eat, it's never enough," she said. "So what am I supposed to do? When I pick up a rice paddle, a gaggle of 'em come rushing over. I can't even tell you how much of a bother it is."

It was two or three years ago that Sister-in-law had started having strange symptoms. She said that she saw the ghosts of dead people. She said that she could see them just as clearly as living people, and that some even spoke to her. Then she started nodding off at any time, anywhere, day or night, sitting like a broody hen or lying down. She would even nod off while walking down the street, talking nonsense in her sleep. She said that was when the spirits would communicate with her.

According to her, there were so many ghosts that they were sitting crowded together on the stovetop when she opened her kitchen door in the morning. There were ghosts waiting in the bathroom, too; and when she left the house, the ghosts would surround her and tag along, heedless of getting kicked. She said they crowded around her head at night, making it difficult to get any sleep. And she wasn't the only one who found all this unbearable. Because she would talk in her sleep or get annoyed—as if an infant were demanding to be breastfed—even her own children avoided sleeping in the same room with her.

Sister-in-law had done week-long fasts at a prayer center and tried staying at a sanatorium, but there was no improvement. She was even admitted to a mental hospital for several days, but the doctors couldn't identify the illness. Her children even called in a renowned shaman—for an exorcism—but when the shaman stepped inside the room and saw Sister-in-law lying in her sickbed, all she had to say was, "I can't perform the ritual." When they asked why, she said, "How can I heal a shaman who's greater than me?" and ran off, as if she'd been chased away. What was strange was that over time, Sister-in-law, who had been so miserable, gradually started to deal with her visions quite naturally. She had frequent debilitating bouts of narcolepsy, perhaps from her body being fatigued, but she was now at ease with the ghosts as much as she was with living people.

"That's right, how could I forget?" Sister-in-law said. "This isn't the time. Sis, I came today because there's something I need to tell you."

"What is it?"

"First, you have to promise to believe what I say. If you don't, I'm not gonna tell you."

"That's ridiculous. How am I gonna know whether to believe it or not if I don't hear it first?" Granny said.

Her sister-in-law would not willingly begin the story; her attitude was odd today even as her eyes were shining with excitement. Granny's heart trembled with an ominous feeling. Sister-in-law had the eerie look of an old shaman in thick makeup, her face dazzled by light from the bright fabric of her clothes. It gave Granny the chills, and it felt as though some terrifying story was about to come from that mouth.

"Last night, I saw Brother for the first time in a long while," Sister-in-law said after a long silence. She spoke as if she were reading a fortune, in a voice so low it could easily have been missed.

Before Granny even realized what it meant, her vision turned dark, and her hands shook as she clutched her needlework. "Did you say your brother?"

"Do I have another one? My brother, that's your . . ."

"I don't understand what you're saying."

"Brother came to visit me, last night. He came as a ghost. He said it's already been more than thirty years since he died."

"That's nonsense!"

"He said he hasn't had a single warm bowl of rice in over thirty years and got by with just spoonfuls of offerings from strangers' memorials."

Granny tried her best to continue with the needlework, but her hands kept shaking and she just kept poking at thin air. She wanted to give her sister-in-law a piece of her mind, but she couldn't open her mouth.

Sister-in-law kept on, slowly, without emotion or inflection. "'Tell your sister-in-law to please leave a bowl of rice out with a spoon in it. I'm beggin' you,' is what he said. I couldn't just keep this to myself. Sis, we should have a memorial ceremony right away."

"Memorial? What memorial? Don't talk nonsense." Granny's mouth was so dry she barely managed to respond. She suspected that maybe her sister-in-law had made the story up. Previously, she had suggested several times that they change the official status of Granny's husband from "missing person" to "deceased" and hold a memorial. Granny had rejected it each time.

"Sis, please. I'm beggin' you," Sister-in-law said. "I promised Brother last night I would talk to you and have the ceremony."

"You saw nothing. Why can't you just get it through your head that the things you see aren't real?"

Hearing that coldhearted answer, her sister-in-law just looked at her, stumped.

Granny suddenly felt a sharp stabbing pain. It must have been the last remaining molar she had all the way back in the right side of her mouth. After the ones on the left side fell out last spring, she'd made do, chewing on the right side, but now even that side had started to hurt. As the teeth began to decay and crumble away, one after the other, the pain would return just as she was about to forget about it. As each tooth fell out, the pain would also miraculously disappear, only for a new pain to begin.

"Brother said that, too. . . ." Sister-in-law said after a long pause. Her voice was rough and hoarse, as if she were someone else, as she continued. "In all the world, there's probably no one as cold and heartless as your sister-in-law. Even if she didn't have much, couldn't she put even just a single bowl of rice out on a little dog-legged table as an offering? Doesn't she know that a family that mistreats a spirit is doomed to ruin?"

Though Sister-in-law was speaking words that Granny's husband was supposed to have said, Granny was certain that she was spewing something else that had been buried somewhere deep inside her own heart. That coarse manner of speech was just like when her sister-in-law was a pimply sixteen-year-old girl picking fights with her over nothing, when Granny was a new bride.

When Granny didn't respond, Sister-in-law continued.

"Forget about the mother for now . . . what's wrong with the boy? He's all grown up now. He should at least be wondering what happened to his father, whether he's dead or alive."

"Don't you talk badly about Sungguk," Granny said. "It's *my* decision. They haven't done nothin' wrong. I'm the one who told them not to hold memorials for their father, a long time ago."

"Of course." Sister-in-law changed her tone and added, more softly, "Sungguk is such an honest and deeply devoted son.

"So I told him, 'Brother, what you're saying isn't fair. There's no one in the whole world like Sis and Sungguk. To this day, Sis thinks you're alive somewhere. She never would've forbidden the ceremony if she knew you were no longer of this world. She holds memorial ceremonies without fail for Father and Mother, who passed away long ago.'"

"Don't even say a word about this," Granny said. "They might hear you."

"I just can't understand why you're being so stubborn. Didn't we see him when he was being loaded onto the truck in front of Daegu Prison? And later we heard the rumor that everyone on that truck was found dead, buried in the same hole."

"*Who* did we see? The crowd shouting and shoving each other in front of that prison, looking for their husbands and sons? Were we even in our right minds then? There was a man with a long face and pointy chin, so I called out 'Sungguk's Father!' but he didn't even turn around. I still don't know if it was him or not."

"You still don't believe me," Sister-in-Law said. "When Brother came to visit me last night, he was wearing green army pants and a white shirt. I'm sure that's what he was wearing the last time. The pants didn't have a belt, and his shirt was stained black from grime or dried blood."

"Will you please just shut your mouth!" Granny shouted without realizing it. She pushed her needlework aside and slumped against the wall. Her tooth ached mercilessly as if she were biting down on a needle.

"No matter what you say to me, I deserve it and more," Sister-in-law said, sobbing, as if she were talking to herself. "You can even call me the bitch who killed her own brother." With her handkerchief, she dabbed at the bags under her eyes—shiny from tears or sweat.

Granny clicked her tongue, wondering how she could still have tears left, at her age. In good times and bad, they'd lived by relying on each other. After struggling for so long, when her sister-in-law was just getting to the point where she could barely make enough to feed herself, she'd lost her mind and now lived surrounded by ghosts, night and day. Granny felt bad for her, but there were still times when she would upset her like this.

Was it in spring, the year before the war? Her sister-in-law got married, and the groom just had to be a policeman, of all things. When Granny's in-laws passed away, she'd left Andong—her birthplace—and followed her husband to Daegu, where they rented a room by the Bangchun Dike, in Daebong-dong. She was free from having to take care of the in-laws for the first time, but her husband was never home. Instead, his sister from back home came up to work at a sock factory and stayed with them.

But she didn't go to work at the factory, as she'd said. Sister-in-law was always out and about as if she were possessed. Every morning, she took two hours to wash her face and her thick hair and only left the house after a big production: sitting in front of the mirror, powdering her face, putting on lipstick, and wiping it all off—only to put it on all over again. It turned out that the person she was secretly meeting—and dolled up for—was that policeman. Though he was short, with slits for eyes, his shoulders were broad, and there was something manly about him.

There was nothing wrong with him being a policeman. In those days there was absolutely no harm in having a policeman around. It was only after they were married that Granny found out that her husband—whom she'd thought of only as being well-educated—was wanted by the police for his ideological beliefs.

To Granny, her husband appeared to be an ordinary and rather soft-hearted man. After joining an organization called the National Guidance League, he no longer had to run from the police. She was, therefore, grateful to her sister-in-law's husband, more than anyone. It was because he was the one who had suggested the National Guidance League and helped her husband join.

"You didn't do nothin' wrong," Granny said. "It was just his fate."

"Of course I did. I committed more sins than I can pay for, even in the next world. Brother being hauled away was my fault for meeting the wrong husband, and it's me who's responsible for the sins against poor Sungho."

"That's nonsense. Why would you drag *Sungho* into this?"

"If only I had never met that damned con man. . . ."

"Stop it!" Granny closed her eyes. Her head was spinning, and she felt nauseated, as if the tiny room was a boat being tossed about in a storm.

"Sis, I'm begging you," Sister-in-law said. "Let's at least throw him a ceremony at a temple near here. Think how happy Brother would be if we just burned some paper and prayed for his spirit to move on."

"If you've said what you came to say, go home," Granny said flatly, putting down her needlework. "It's time for Sungguk to come home from work, so I won't keep you."

Sister-in-law just stared, her expression shocked, at a loss for words. When she finally got up, her face seemed older and wearier.

Just as she was about to open the door and leave, Granny said to her, "My Sungho looks just like his dad. No matter what anyone says, he's the spitting image of his father. Don't you forget that." As she spoke, she realized her voice was trembling. But what she'd said was not a lie.

Sungho had always had a lean face and a pointy chin, but lately— no, since returning from the army—his cheekbones had grown even more prominent, making him look even thinner. His face was completely different from that of his brother. When Sungguk, the older one, closed his mouth tightly, his jawbone protruded as if he had chestnuts in his mouth, looking rather like her, but the younger one's face had been long and slender since he was a child. She used to tell the older one, all the time, "Sungho looks just like your father. If you want to know what your father looks like, just look at your little brother. They say the acorn doesn't fall far from the tree, but still, how can they look that much alike?" It seemed Sungho was becoming more like his father with each passing year as he grew. It was more than surprising, and it became a source of concern for her.

"The one seeing things isn't me. It's you," Sister-in-law said as she walked out the door. "How long do you plan to go on living like this, Sis? Fooling your children and even yourself."

But Granny just sat there, leaning against the wall. She heard a child crying somewhere. She focused her ears on that sound, wondering if it might be her grandson, and the toothache grew sharper. The tip of that pain, she realized, was touching another pain hiding deep within her body. When she suddenly realized what it was, she was mortified. The tooth had reawakened a certain memory of a pain that had been numbed and covered by thick calluses over the course of three decades.

On that night, more than thirty years ago, she had also been suffering from a toothache. For the several chaotic days at the start of the war, with rumors of the imminent approach of the North Korean People's Army, her tooth had ached terribly. It had begun when she became pregnant with her first child, and it grew worse over time. But because pain medication was hard to get, she had no choice but to wait for it to pass on its own. Even now, she thought she could feel it as vividly as being poked with a hot needle from back in time. It had happened while she was dealing with this pain, sitting on the edge of their cramped living room. She heard suspicious footsteps beyond the outer wall, and then someone started banging hard on the plywood gate. Her husband got up, his face pale with fear, and stood by the attic door. Once there was news of war, he had been hounded by fear again. He hid up in the attic whenever there was even a hint of someone approaching the house. Toward the back of the dark and cramped space, there was a small window just big enough for a grown man to squeeze through, allowing him to crawl onto the neighbor's roof. "Brother, are you home? It's me." She heard the familiar voice over the plywood wall, which was painted black with tar, and her husband listening from the attic surely heard it, too. She opened the gate, and in the darkness, she saw the familiar figure of a squat man with broad shoulders. He asked in a whisper, "Brother's home, isn't he?" Before she could even answer, she saw the outlines of several other men standing against the wall by the gate, and she heard the attic door open again. But she just stood there, her entire body shaking as if she were having a seizure; she could not even think to yell out. As the shadowy forms from the darkness grew to immense proportions and pressed down on her, she could only watch as if she were in a night terror, paralyzed.

"Gramma! Gramma . . ."

There was the loud sound of footsteps coming up the stairs, then the boy came running in through the door.

"That man is coming! He's coming to our house, now! With Daddy . . ."

After Sister-in-law left, she must have been sitting absentmindedly without realizing the time. The room was already dark.

"See? I told you," the boy rambled on excitedly, gesturing with his hands. "I told you he was a cop. Daddy was coming home, and the

man asked if his name was Kim Sungguk, and then he said, 'I'm so-
and-so,' and he flashed a badge from his pocket. A real police badge!"
Suddenly, he stopped.

They heard two pairs of footsteps coming up the stairs and stopping in front of the door. The door opened. Sungguk's face appeared,
and behind him stood a stranger.

"Pardon the intrusion. You're Sungho's mother, correct?"

"W-who is this?" Granny asked her son. She had to use both hands,
and yet she could barely support herself up on her knees, from which
all the strength had fled.

"So . . . he's uh . . ." Sungguk stammered, his face pale.

The man answered in a booming voice, "I'm from the department,
ma'am."

"By 'department,' you mean 'police department'?" Granny said.
"What's happened . . . there's nothing here to concern the police."

"It's nothing to be concerned about. I just came to share some information. Is this Sungho's room? May I go in?"

The man opened the door and went in without waiting for an answer. He looked around, both hands in his pants pockets, then went
over to Sungho's desk, pulled out a random book, and half-heartedly
flipped through the pages, saying, "Our type can't understand difficult books like this."

"I don't know what brought you here," Granny said, "but our
Sungho is a truly kind boy. His only hobby is reading books. Ever
since he was young, even when he came home after getting beat up,
he could never hurt someone else."

"These days, even being too kind can cause trouble," the man said.
"Reading too many books can be trouble, too. Now, Mister Kim, could
we talk for a bit?"

Sungguk took the man into the big room and locked the door,

then came back out and called Granny into the kitchen, his voice hushed.

"Mother, you know that bottle of imported liquor? Please, fix us a tray with that. Slice up some fruit, too."

"What in the world is going on?" Granny asked. "Did Sungho cause some kind of trouble?"

"Don't worry. It's nothing important."

"If it's nothing important, why would a detective show up at our house?"

"Just relax, Mother." Sungguk's face seemed drained of blood.

She stood leaning against the kitchen sink for a long time, her mind blank, not knowing what to do; even her hands would not move. Only the pain of her tooth grew even more intense, making it seem as if everything she could think or feel was hanging on it—not the pain of just a single tooth, but her entire body turned into one great mass of pain.

She suddenly recalled the pitch-black sky that had come crashing down on her head that summer night more than thirty years ago. As her husband was being taken away, held by the arms of the men who had accompanied her brother-in-law, she was suffering unbearable pain and could not think of what to do. He had surrendered himself to those men without resistance, as if he had already anticipated the outcome.

"He should be out safely, soon. It's just a protective measure," her brother-in-law had said. "Don't worry—trust me." It was a polite tone he had never used before.

She'd remained squatting on the ground just outside the living room, with both hands supporting her chin. If her sister-in-law hadn't some-how found out about it and tried to intervene, she would just have sent her husband off like that, as if he were going out with friends for a bit. But Sister-in-law rushed straight to him and clung to his pant leg. "No, you can't!" she cried. "You can't take my brother away." "What's with this? You don't know what you're talking about, woman." "What don't I know? I already know *everything*. You can't take him. If you want to, kill me first." Sister-in-law prostrated herself on the ground and screamed, and even as she was being dragged along, she would not let go of her husband's pant leg. "Oh, no! What will I do? I deserve to die. My brother's gonna die because of this stupid wench meeting the wrong husband. . . . What am I gonna do. . . ." Even when they finally kicked her sister-in-law free, wailing and screaming on the ground, she herself could only tremble, squatting there outside the living room. All she felt was the maddening pain of that tooth—it was as if all her other senses had gone dead. It was truly strange that, faced with such a calamity, she should have forgotten about the pain. Perhaps she had wanted to escape that fear. Perhaps she preferred clinging to that pain in order to escape her unbelievable reality.

It was over an hour later that the door to the big room opened. Both men had red faces, and the stranger was still chewing a piece of dried squid even as he laced up his shoes.

"I'll leave it in your hands, then, Sungguk. And thanks for the drinks."

"Turns out we went to the same high school," Sungguk said to her as he took the man's outstretched hand. Perhaps it was the liquor, but his face looked better than earlier. "Let's meet up from time to time. Maybe grab a beer outside."

"Why would you want to meet up with me again?" the man said. "The less you see of people like me, the better."

The two of them laughed in exactly the same tone, but as soon as the man left, Granny saw the smile go stiff on Sungguk's face. "Crazy fool," he said.

She couldn't tell whether he was talking about the detective who had just left, or his younger brother, but her heart sank again.

"Gramma, he's gone. I saw him leave."

"And your uncle? You don't see Uncle yet, right?"

"Why is a little kid like you wandering outside this late?" Sungguk said. "Stay inside!"

The startled boy clung to his grandmother.

"It's not the child's fault," Granny said. "I told him to wait outside. In case Sungho came home, clueless. I don't understand what's going on."

"I told you, there's nothing for *you* to worry about." Sungguk clammed up then.

Granny freed herself from the boy clinging to her skirt hem and stepped outside the apartment. It was already dark and empty on the street. She paced in front of the apartment building and looked toward the darkness that was even thicker in the direction of the main road.

Before that day, Sungguk had never once raised his voice at home. He was a man of few words and did not express his inner thoughts easily, and even though she had given birth to him, she often felt awkward and uneasy with him. He had been malnourished from the time he was a child, and he had known only hardship. When he was rejected from the military academy after barely finishing high school, he'd voluntarily given up on college. Then he had become a civil servant and—though he still seemed to be on the bottom rung—he'd managed to secure this subsidized apartment on his own and enrolled his younger brother in university.

Even after his wife left home, nothing much had changed. He always came home from work on time, except twice a week when he had the night shift, and in the mornings, he always left home early to catch the 7:10 train. He also never skipped his calisthenics before breakfast, and she often watched him get out of bed to exercise in the morning. Maybe it was because he hadn't eaten properly while he was growing up, but when she saw him swing his long, skinny arms exposed by his tank top, or when he did handstands, his face red and his eyes bulging, she felt nervous, as if she were watching a balloon that was about to burst.

"What are you doing out here?"

Granny looked back in surprise. It was Sungho. He had appeared out of nowhere and was smiling innocently.

"I've been waiting for you," Granny said. "What've you been up to, outside the house? A detective came by."

"Really? Is he still here?"

"Your brother liquored him up and sent him away. Watch yourself when you go in. He's upset."

"I'm impressed. I thought he was a square."

"You've been drinkin', haven't you?"

"Yes, but I'm completely sober."

Now she noticed he was carrying something like a ramen box on his shoulder. He walked a bit unsteadily, as if it were heavy.

"What are you carryin' around this late at night, like someone out to burgle a house?" Granny asked.

"Burgle? Ha ha. No, these are books."

When Sungho went inside, Sungguk was standing there, just inside the door, waiting for him. Even as he struggled to take off his shoes, Sungho still refused to put down the box he carried on his shoulder. Sungguk watched in silence, with arms crossed, as his younger brother staggered trying to kick off his shoes. He grabbed the box from Sungho and threw it onto the living room floor.

"Open it!" Sungguk said.

As if unable to resist his older brother's sharp command, Sungho obeyed and opened the box. Granny saw what was inside—not books but flyers, freshly printed with text that seemed to leap frantically off the page with a life of its own.

Sungguk pulled out one of the flyers from the stack and read it carefully. "Are you out of your mind?" he said.

"Please, you have to understand. . . ."

"Understand? You want me to understand someone going around printing things like this without any concern for the consequences?"

"It's not like they're bombs or something. They're just words and ideas."

"You think only bombs can hurt people? If this was a bomb, you could just fall on it and blow yourself up, but this will hurt lots more people."

"I won't let it hurt you, so don't worry."

"What did you say?"

"I don't like saying this, but if this is something harmful, I'm ready to sacrifice myself to make sure it doesn't hurt others."

"So, you're telling me that, if the situation requires, you're willing to die for the ideas printed on this paper?"

"If death is the only option, depending on the circumstances, I could die. Yes."

"Go to hell, you fraud."

"What?"

"Listen close. I despise bastards like you the most, understand? The ones that are all talk. Ones who *say* they would do anything. Ones who spew out all sorts of noble talk, all the while making life hell for their parents, siblings, and children. Ones who *say* they would die for something—they're the ones who are ready to kill others for that something. We have a word for your kind—Reds."

"Be careful what you say, Brother!"

"What, do you think Reds are a different species? You and I are both children of a Red, you idiot. At least you can carry on his legacy."

"Hey, that's enough. You want to be struck dead by lightning? Who's a Red?"

"You think I don't know, Mom? I know everything. Why do you think I was even rejected by the military academy? Do you know why I never get promoted? It's all because of our great father. That great father who was willing to toss his wife and children aside like they were worn-out shoes. All for his beliefs and his ideology."

"I don't know what you heard," Granny said, "but that . . . that's not true. Your father abandoning his wife and kids . . . Heaven will punish you for that kind of talk."

"Then why hasn't he shown up? He's still listed as missing. Where is he? He didn't go missing during the war like others did—though maybe that might have been better—and he was alive until at least Sungho was born. But I've never once seen Father's face. There's not a thing about Father left in my memory. Exactly how, where, and for what cause did he fight?"

Granny's vision went dark as if she'd taken a hard blow to the head. Something had flipped inside, and her entire body trembled with vertigo. She had to say something, but her parched mouth would not open, and if it did, she was sinking into a pit of despair about what might come out of it.

IT WAS A TURBULENT TIME DURING THE TAIL END OF THE LIBERAL Party's reign. One day, her sister-in-law came to her all excited, saying that her brother was alive. Not only alive, but they could even meet him. She did not believe her sister-in-law at first. Since her husband had been dragged away like that and turned missing, Sister-in-law often

said such things. She had been to a fortune teller who said that he was
alive, for sure; a certain Daoist master said that he'd taken a new wife
and was living somewhere else; there was all sorts of talk. But this
time was different. Sister-in-law said that a man had come to find her
with a message from her husband. That he was hiding somewhere
nearby, and since he was in no condition to come in person, she should
come to meet him on a certain day, at such and such a time, and she
should bring two hundred thousand *hwan*. Of course, she must keep
it a secret from everyone else. Whatever had made her believe in such
a tall tale . . . she went to meet that man with her sister-in-law, taking
the two hundred thousand *hwan*. She had barely managed to come up
with it, and she carried it in her bosom wrapped in newspapers and
bound carefully again in cloth.

Since then, no matter how hard she tried, all she could recall about
him were his slightly fierce eyes and the occasional hint of a northern
accent. He was a stoic man, and his face was one of those you could
not easily remember. They followed him to the outskirts of Daegu, to
the entrance of Donghwa Temple. It was early winter and cold. The
man said Sister-in-law had to wait at a restaurant nearby and only she
could go on. She thought it was a bit strange, but the man was cautious
about being seen by others, as if he had something to hide, and that's
what might have made her go with him without being suspicious.

The pine forest made terrible noises in the night wind. She tripped
on stones many times trying not to lose the man, whose teeth chat-
tered audibly as he walked ahead not looking back even once. She followed him into the forest, where there was no sign of people, hardly able
to control the fear creeping up her throat. "Where is he! Where . . ."
she shouted, and the man stopped in his tracks. Then, in the dark, she
saw the shadow of another man slowly rising up. "Thank you for making
the difficult journey," he said. It was not her husband's voice. She felt

like something was gagging her, and she could not move an inch, as if her legs had frozen stiff. The men took the money away from her, easily. "The world needs good people like you, so people like us can survive . . . don't think too harshly of us." When they overcame her struggles and bent her over at the waist, she finally started to scream. A large hand covered her mouth, and she heard the sound of her clothes being roughly torn. "What's with the struggle? We just want to have some fun." The man's hot breath stabbed at her face. "How fortunate. You're a widow, from what I hear." All the while, the wind was wailing, twisting the pines. She thought she was dying. She thought her breathing would stop and that she would be released from all of this.

"YOU GOT IT ALL WRONG. YOUR FATHER IS ABSOLUTELY NOT THAT KIND of person," Granny barely managed to say. "Your mother's been waiting all these years for your father, hoping that he must be alive somewhere, somehow."

"I don't have a father. Even if that person called 'Father' walks through that door alive, I'd have nothing to do with him. After I failed at the academy, dropped out of college, and became an office clerk—no, even before then—I buried Father with my own hands."

"Well, how admirable."

Sungho—who had been sitting with his head stuck between his knees as if his neck was broken—suddenly popped his head up. His eyes, glaring at his older brother, were as sharp as metal spikes.

"I see *you're* the one who could kill anything. You're someone who can—for the academy, for a promotion—kill anything. Even Father."

"What's that, you punk?" Sungguk thundered. He clenched his brother's collar.

"That's right," Sungho shot back. "Do you think that someone who could kill his own father couldn't kill a piece of shit like you? Here. Die by my hands."

Though she knew she had to break them up, Granny's whole body trembled as if she'd had a stroke. Then she realized what she had been most afraid of all these years. She suddenly looked at her grandson. He sat tucked up against a wall with eyes closed and hands pressed up against his ears.

"Boys!" It burst from her mouth, abruptly, and only after yelling did she realize that the thing that had exploded from her was the thing that had been fighting to escape from deep inside her bunched-up innards, twisting and stretching itself unbearably.

Her sons stared at her, wide-eyed.

"Fight!" she said. "Use your fists and your teeth. Why should only one of you die? Fight till you, and me, and everyone's, dead! There's no such thing as mothers, fathers, or brothers. Why are you just standing there, you little punks? Are you out of strength already? Did you run out of hate? Fight, I said. . . ."

Granny did not fully realize what she was saying. It felt as if she were just sitting there absentmindedly while something like an animal's howl escaped from deep inside her, on its own. And when it had all come out, she felt spent, completely empty inside. The room was oddly quiet. Suddenly, her younger son, Sungho, began to sob, his shoulders seeming to crumble, then rise again. Granny sat there, calmly, as if she were listening to her own crying. Sungguk, the older son, smacked his lips and lit a cigarette, and as if that were some sort of signal, Sungho suddenly stood up and stormed out the door, still in tears. Granny sat, not moving an inch, until the door slammed shut behind her son, and it was quiet again.

The boy approached her, sobbing. "Where's Uncle going, Gramma?"

"Shiggi, carry this outside with Gramma," she said in a calm voice.

The boy sensed something, and he followed her willingly, dragging the box outside after him. But the box was too heavy for an old woman and a six-year-old child to carry. They had to pause many times as they came down the four flights of stairs.

The night was pitch-black, and a wind raked across the square in front of the apartment. She did not see her sons anywhere. She was thinking about the empty yard behind the apartment building. It needed to be as out of the way as possible. Her tooth still hurt, but—perhaps because her old, worn-out gums had grown numb—it felt like even the pain had dulled, and the half-uprooted molar that had come loose wiggled every time her tongue touched it. When they got to the empty lot behind the apartment building, where dry weeds poked at her ankles, she opened the box and dumped out all the paper inside. Then, holding a few sheets to use as tinder, she lit a match.

The flames rose quickly. The papers started to turn black around the edges; the black letters printed clearly on the white paper seemed to scream as their bodies twisted in the flames, but in the end they all disappeared. She did not know what those words said or meant, but there was a relief, as if she had finally gotten around to doing something she had been meaning to do for a long time.

As she was being violated by the men that night, her only wish had been to die. It made her despondent, the fact that this abhorrent life could be so resilient, that it could not end itself, even in such a horrific moment. Then she thought of her husband and, strangely, she could feel the heat of his body all too vividly. She was burying her face in his back. He was pedaling a bicycle, and she was sitting behind, her arms wrapped around his waist. After he joined the National Guidance League, they were finally able to have a stable married life for the first time. Her husband found a job at the finance cooperative, and he even bought a bicycle to commute on. One night, she rode it for the first time. Despite her protests, her husband easily picked her up by the waist, put her on the back, and set out for Bangchun Dike. Once they were up there, she held on, tight. She could not have felt more secure, hugging him like that, her arms wrapped around him. He was whistling, and the sun was setting in the direction where Suseong Creek flowed. Even with her eyes closed, the sunset filled her vision.

Even after the men left, she remained there, lying in her tattered body. Her husband's warmth, which had been on her cheek, had also departed. Leaving her body to be clawed by the wind as it passed, she lay there. "Sungguk's dad . . ." she called out to her husband in a low voice. She knew that she was alone again. The following year, she gave birth to Sungho.

The flame danced in the wind as it pushed the burning papers upward into the air. With only their white edges remaining, the papers were sucked up into the sky where they finally disintegrated and scattered in the wind.

Higher. Climb higher and higher. She realized that she was talking to herself. When they made offerings to the gods back home, they used to burn paper like this. They prayed for the well-being of the souls of the dead, or for wishes, and they said the more completely the paper burned and the higher it went up, the better. *The one seeing things that aren't there isn't me—it's you, Sis. How long do you intend to go on living, fooling your children, and even yourself?* Her sister-in-law's voice rang in her ears. It felt like the scales that had covered her eyes all these ages had suddenly fallen off. *Yes, I need to come clean about everything. I am going to sit with Sungguk and Sungho and tell them about their fathers.* She was hardening her resolve that she must not hide or disguise the truth—no longer.

"Shiggi, pull out this tooth for Gramma."

She opened her mouth wide before the boy. He grimaced and shook his head.

"It's because Gramma's in pain. You don't want Gramma to hurt, do you?"

She guided the boy's hand and had him grab the loose tooth between two fingers. He hesitated, his brows furrowed, and then he closed his eyes. She swallowed a scream as he yanked the tooth out.

As the boy stared down at it in disbelief, not knowing how dirty it was, she snatched the tooth out of his palm. It looked wicked, rotted black down to the root. But the pain did not subside immediately. She tossed it into the flame, that part of her body that still felt like a small bundle of pain.

"Gramma, are you crying? Does it hurt?"

She dabbed her eyes with the hem of her skirt. "I'm not crying. It's the smoke," she said. "When you're old like Gramma, you can't even cry anymore."

She continued to add papers to the fire.

"Shiggi, you make a wish, too, if you've got one. If you make a wish now, it will all come true."

Whether he understood or not, the boy was staring silently into the flames, his face deeply contemplative. Could he be praying for his mother to return? The eyes of the child, who held his mouth tightly closed, were burning with the light from the flames, and she suppressed the urge to hug him.

Translated by Yoosup Chang & Heinz Insu Fenkl

A LAMP IN THE SKY

I

It was the year I turned eight, late in the winter when the piles of snow were starting to melt and turn to slush. That day I was taking the private school entrance exam, standing there, stamping my freezing feet, waiting my turn in front of the classroom. The school was notoriously difficult to get into; it was for the richest people in the city, and I still remember the shiny hardwood floor of the hallway was cold as ice. The reason I'd applied to that school was purely due to my mother's greed. There was a public school near the house where we rented a room back then; it was practically on the other side of the wall, but my mother had to drag me all the way to *this* school that was more than half an hour's walk. The moment I stepped inside, I realized it was a place I was not meant to be. I understood at a glance that the kids there were of a different species than me. And most of all, even at that age, I could see how it just didn't look right—my mother standing there stuck between the other parents. To put it bluntly, this wasn't the kind of school where the parents were going to welcome a woman who sold drinks at a market stall.

Finally, it was my turn. With my mother holding my hand, I entered the classroom where the test was given. Five or six teachers were sitting in front of a window facing me. One of them told my mother to please wait there. Mom stayed standing by the door, and I walked up to the teachers by myself. They asked for my name and age first. I answered them in a loud and confident voice, the way I'd practiced over and over.

—What's your father's name?

They all wore nice suits and ties; one woman teacher wore glasses. It was the first time in my life so many adults were looking at me.

—Your father's name? Don't you know your father's name?

They repeated their question but I still wasn't able to answer. I actually didn't know my father's name—no one had ever asked me before and I'd never been told. My mother, still by the door, answered for me in an urgent voice:

—She doesn't have a father.

—Is he deceased?

—No . . . that is . . . how can I tell you about all the hardships we two had to live through . . .

—That won't be necessary, the older, dignified teacher, said, cutting her off. Then he asked me:

—Is salt bitter or sweet?

I was confused, squinting at the bright light that came through the window in front of me.

—Quickly, please. Is the taste of salt bitter or sweet?

The voice, still so soft and calm, urged me to answer. My feet were going numb and I thought I was going to go blind from the dazzling sunlight that streamed through the window behind their backs.

—It's b-bitter!

That's all that came to me after a long pause. But even as I spat out those words, I knew I'd given the wrong answer. My mother shouted from where she was standing by the door:

—No, you little brat! Bitter salt?! Salt is *salty*! Answer again! Now! Tell them salt is *salty*!

But for some reason, I couldn't open my mouth. My mother's face was twisted in despair.

—What are you waiting for? Answer, quick! Tell them: Teacher, salt isn't bitter, it's salty. . . . Like that! Answer like that!

—Enough. We're done here. You can go out with your daughter, said a calm, young voice, straight out of the light.

But my mother didn't give up.

—Please, sirs and ladies, ask one more time. She'll answer right this time. Please give this poor little girl who grew up without a father another chance. . . .

—We're done, ma'am. You can take her out now, please.

—You stupid bitch! Answer, quick! What does salt taste like?

I couldn't speak. For some reason I couldn't open my mouth. I couldn't move a muscle, as if my whole body had turned to stone.

Those unfamiliar faces in the dazzling sunlight, that suffocating silence, my mother's twisted face—the memory of that terrible moment remained etched in my mind for a long time. Even now, after twenty years, I realize I'm still not able to get away from that question. Even now, I'm being assaulted by questions that can't be answered.

Now you're asking me *who I am*. But unfortunately, I don't know the answer to that question. I know only one thing for certain: the fact that you're forcing me to be something other than myself.

"HEY, WHAT'S THE MATTER? YOU HAVING A DREAM?"

Shinhye woke up suddenly, terrified. The creased face of the police chief, with his patchy beard, was thrust right up against her nose, and it was only then that she realized she had dozed off for a moment, curled up on the narrow sofa in the corner of the police station. Still, she couldn't quite tell if this was a nightmare or reality, and her heart was hammering like a drum. She shivered and turned her body to look out the window. The blinding headlights of a car illuminated the glass as it parked in front of the building. She could hear the stuttering of the engine.

"Get ready!" said the chief. "They came from the central station to get you."

She saw from the wall clock that it was already six a.m.

Her teeth were chattering. Her whole body shook in the grip of the icy cold, and Shinhye thought she must be trapped in yet another bad dream—a nightmare that was reality itself, one from which she could never wake. It made her desperate.

"Look, I'll give you a little advice up front," said the chief. "You're gonna have to be truthful and let everything out when you're at the main station. You'll suffer less, too, that way. Understand?"

"What is it you keep saying I have to let out? I already told you I don't *have* anything else!"

"Are you gonna keep acting this way? I'm telling you all this for your own good!"

Before the chief had even finished speaking, the door swung wide-open, letting in a blast of cold air. A man in his mid-thirties, wearing a gray jacket, entered the room. He raised his hand absentmindedly to salute the chief before rushing directly to the stove, his body shuddering from the cold.

"Inspector Nam! It's good of you to run down here so early in the morning. You're still on duty today?"

"Don't even ask!" Nam said. "It's been three days since I got to stretch my legs and get some sleep! And the heater went out again in that piece of crap car—it's a refrigerator now. *Aigo*, I just want to beat this, get another day over with as soon as possible. Better off being a monk in some temple somewhere . . ."

As he spoke, he suddenly noticed Shinhye.

"Is it you?" he said.

His eyes quickly scanned her head to toe. Shinhye, not knowing how to respond, just nodded. He gestured with his hand. It meant she should come closer. Shinhye hesitated before she went to him.

"How old are you?" he asked.

". . . Twenty-three."

"You're older than you look. What university you from?"

"Sir, I'm not guilty of anything . . . I just work at the café here and sell coffee. I haven't done anything wrong."

The inspector's face was thin and pale, almost white. A blue vein protruding at his temple made him look angry, and at first glance, he looked more like a rural middle school teacher than a police inspector. For a while he simply stared at her without a word. In front of those piercing eyes that seemed to stick to her body, Shinhye felt embarrassed and confused. She didn't know what to do.

"You're saying you work at Café Yonggung. You ever see me there?"

"I don't remember."

"Well, I remember seeing *you*. I never forget a woman's face." His own face seemed to be lit by a faint smile for some reason. "Come on," he said. "Let's get going. We don't have much time."

"No. I don't . . ."

When he pulled her by the arm, she held tight to the armrest of the sofa and wouldn't let go. She was suddenly like a child seized by a blind fear. "I haven't committed any crime," she said. "Why do you need to drag me all the way to the central station for questioning? I'm not going."

A hard expression came over Nam's face, as if he were saying *You'd better*, and suddenly he grabbed her in a bear hug. It was almost playful—she struggled with all her might, kicking her feet, but the more she fought, the more tightly he wrapped his arms around her. She bit him. He screamed and rolled up his sleeve. Teeth marks were clearly visible.

But instead of being angry, he looked at her, his eyes amused.

"Getting cute with me?"

It seemed like he was searching for something on his belt. Shinhye heard the snap of metal and felt a ring of ice tighten around her thin wrist. Strangely, the cold and eerie touch of the steel on her flesh made her lose any will to resist. She had never once imagined the chill of handcuffs could reach all the way into her bones. That specific sensation seemed more real to her than the unbelievable situation she was in.

Shinhye jerked her arm free of the inspector's grip as soon as they were outside. "Let me go," she said. "I'll get in on my own."

Parked in front of the building in the cold morning fog was a Jeep covered in mud and dust. He pushed Shinhye into the passenger seat, got in, and immediately started the engine.

"Angry? If you'd listened earlier, I wouldn't have put you in cuffs. If you behave, I'll take them off in a little while."

He looked at her and smiled. The inside of the vehicle was bitter cold, the windows white with frost. Outside, the station chief approached.

"Inspector Nam, I'll join you later. I need a little shut-eye first. I was up all night questioning her."

"It seems you've been working hard, Chief. Who knows? Maybe it's a big fish you caught after all this time."

"Well, whether it's big or not—we'll have to wait and see."

The chief's eyes met Shinhye's for a moment. He seemed to want to say something to her, but at that moment, the car pulled away. With both hands shackled and wedged between her knees, defeated, Shinhye was jostled about as she looked out of the window at the receding early morning street.

They drove past the café where she worked, the street still dark. The electronics store, the newspaper depot, the Gohang bathhouse, and the Ant Mini Supermarket appeared in the shadows—amidst them was the familiar acrylic sign that read "Café Yonggung."

Just then, a young woman emerged cautiously from the Manhojang Inn across the street. Shinhye leaned her face against the glass, wondering if she might know her. She was probably a café employee like Shinhye, or a bar girl, leaving after a short night sleeping with the young mine workers. Inspector Nam swerved the car, honking the horn, pretending to sideswipe her. As the woman turned her head in surprise, her pale face, tired and sagging, freshly washed and cleaned of makeup, appeared momentarily in the car's headlights, then disappeared. Along the bottom of the bank wall, what the drunks had vomited up had turned to slush. A mine worker, still drunk, staggered like a ghost out into the middle of the street. He stopped abruptly and made an obscene gesture at the car.

"Son of a bitch," the inspector said under his breath as he continued on his way.

Ding, ding, ding!

The bell at the rail crossing rang, and with a loud commotion, a train passed by, every window lit up. Realizing it was the express to Seoul, Shinhye felt a dull pain rising from deep in her heart. It had only been a month since she'd left and yet it felt like whole seasons had passed since then. Suddenly, she felt a nostalgia so intense she thought it would tear her heart.

....

WHEN SHE GOT OFF THE TRAIN, A GLOOMY AFTERGLOW STILL RE-
mained of the winter evening, but the unfamiliar mining town that
wound along the ravine seemed to be trapped in a darkness as dense
as a blanket of carbon paper. It must have been the coal dust covering
everything in sight: the coal heaps at the station depot, the muddy and
black earth mixed of coal and snow, the miserable shacks clinging to
the foot of the barren mountain like a series of identical scabs, everything sunk into the darkest dark as if it had been smeared in black oil
pastels. In the pit of that blackness, the lights of the cafés, bars, and
inns seemed out of place; their neon lights lit up seductively, compet-
ing with each other in the background of this gloaming. Shinhye
gazed at all of this for a long time, clinging to the rusty iron railing on
the slope leading from the station down to the streets. Those who got
off the train with her hurried by and scattered in the dark. But she
didn't have the courage to go down with them. It had been nearly four
hours since she had boarded the train, four hours of being gripped by
doubt and anxiety, and now that she had arrived at her destination,
she was paralyzed. *Why did I come all the way here?* she thought. *What
could I possibly do here? Maybe I made an irreversible mistake. . . .*

Suddenly, a truck came from the station behind her at a terrifying
speed, honking its horn. As she turned around to look, something wet
and thick hit her face. The truck passed her, leaving behind the laughter and shouts of the young men on board.

"Hey, we're coming tonight! Clean up your honeypot and wait
for us!"

Shinhye opened her bag and found the toilet paper she had bought
from the peddler on the train. She wiped herself again and again. But
how odd—at that moment, what she felt was not just disgust but a
strange thrill. With her face covered in the sticky saliva of a man she

didn't even know, she'd suddenly felt as if she belonged in this unfamiliar place. *All right, let's give it a try,* she said to herself, shuddering. *I'm not backing down now. Didn't this strange and evil land just welcome me in the most fitting way?*

"HOW LONG WILL IT TAKE?" SHINHYE ASKED.

Inspector Nam had both hands on the steering wheel. Outside town, the road was no longer paved and the melted snow had refrozen into a mix of gravel and ice.

"It's only around twenty kilometers," he said. "But since the road isn't good it'll take at least half an hour."

"I meant the interrogation," Shinhye said. "I haven't caused any problems since I've been here, so I'll be released quickly, right?"

There was no answer. Shinhye looked at her watch. But it was dead. Maybe it was the battery, but no matter how many times she shook it, the needle-thin hand wouldn't move.

"The reason I came here . . . really, I just came to earn some money. You must suspect me because I'm a college student, and I'm working as a café waitress. But that's the only reason I'm here. I needed money and I couldn't find another job."

Still no response. The sun had not come up yet. Rattling like a cart, the old Jeep sped along the white road that stretched like a tunnel into the dark.

The twists and turns of the dark road, its frozen surface, and the low-lying stream shimmered drearily in the headlights. On the hillside, the frightening shapes of trees were illuminated before their bodies stretched out, buried again in the darkness. All of it seemed unreal to Shinhye, like frames of a black-and-white movie flickering momentarily on an old projection screen.

"You like music?"

Inspector Nam put on a cassette. A soft pop song came on. "The Saddest Thing" by Melanie Safka. It was a song she'd loved in high school. Who would have imagined she would be listening to it now in handcuffs?

The inspector was smacking his lips as if he were keeping time with the music. *What sort of man is he?* Shinhye wondered. He probably wouldn't be any different from the other men who came to the café, who spewed obscene jokes and tried to grab her arm whenever they got a chance. This thought relieved her for some reason.

"Can I ask you a question?" she said.

Nam glanced over at Shinhye, still keeping time with his lips. They were red and glistening—enough to make her feel uncomfortable.

"How did you know about me?"

"Why do you ask?"

"Someone reported me, right? Who was it?"

He didn't answer. Shinhye knew it was a dumb question. Even if he had known, he would never have told her. The plump face of Miss Seol, who worked at the café with her, suddenly came to mind. *Had she even gone out tonight? Does she know I've been taken by the police?*

MISS SEOL HAD WORKED AT THE CAFÉ FOR MORE THAN THREE YEARS. She was three years younger than Shinhye, just twenty, but given all the things she had endured, Shinhye considered her a far more experienced senior. She said she came from Suncheon in South Jeolla Province and that her original name was Kim Boksun, but she'd changed it herself to Seol Yeonga. Her new surname was "Seol," she said; "It means 'snow,'" and she had laughed out loud.

"How did you get here?" she asked Shinhye one night. "You really don't look like the kind of person who ends up in a place like this."

After their shift at the café, they would sleep in the tiny closet-sized room attached to the kitchen, and Seol would tell Shinhye about all the hardships she had suffered in her life.

"Is there some certain kind of person who comes here?" Shinhye asked.

"Of course! Don't let my looks fool you—I know how to read people. And from what I see, I can tell you're someone who's educated. Just from the way you talk."

Shinhye felt like she'd just been jabbed in an old wound. The factory workers she once lived with had told her the same thing. No matter how much she tried to be like them, renting the same rooms, wearing the same clothes, eating the same instant noodles together, they'd never accepted her. They always thought of her as being different from them.

"So you're, what do they call it? A student activist?"

When Shinhye told her about her own past, Seol was immediately full of longing and admiration.

"I knew it. From the moment I saw you, I knew you were special."

"I'm not a student activist. I'm nothing. It's just—you told me everything about yourself, and I couldn't just keep my mouth shut about me. But I'm not the kind of person you think I am."

"I know what you're saying," Seol said. "Don't worry, I won't tell anyone. I know at least that much. It's such a scary world these days and saying the wrong thing can get you in big trouble."

Shinhye did not believe it was possible for Seol to have denounced her. If someone had backstabbed her, she suspected it was the madam of Café Yonggung. The one-month contract Shinhye had signed with her was up in three days, and she was due to collect her salary of four hundred thousand won. But if she was arrested by the police, the madam wouldn't have to pay her. Shinhye blamed herself for being so distrustful, but she couldn't shake off her suspicion.

The madam always wore bright and elegant traditional dresses when she sat at the counter guarding the entrance to the café. She glossed her plump lips with deep red lipstick and greeted each customer in a high-pitched nasal voice, with a sensual smile, playing the coquette. The men were helpless when she made eyes at them with that voice. She reminded Shinhye of a queen bee surrounded by a swarm of drones who brought her pollen. The madam's attachment to men and money was truly pathological. According to Seol, she'd been the second wife of a rich mine owner and had inherited the café from him. Even now, there wasn't a single man of any influence in town whom the madam wasn't involved with in some way.

When the call had come from the police station last night, it was almost midnight. It was after business hours and there were no customers in the café. Shinhye and Seol were cleaning up together. There were two other employees, but they had gone out on deliveries and hadn't yet returned.

It was the madam who answered the phone. For a delivery the conversation usually didn't last more than a few words, but for some reason this call took a bit longer, and the madam only answered "Yes, yes," or "I understand."

"Miss Han," she said when she hung up. "You're going to have to go out and deliver some coffee. They're working late at the police station tonight and they just ordered three cups." Like all the other girls, Shinhye worked there under a different name.

"But it's almost midnight," Shinhye said. "Didn't you say there wouldn't be any tickets after eleven?"

"What am I supposed to do? I can't afford to displease these people if I want to stay in business."

Seol, who was mopping the floor, looked up, worried.

"Shinhye, I can go for you."

"No, not you," the madam said. "They want Miss Han."

"*Me*? Why do they want *me*?"

"How would *I* know? Maybe somebody thinks you're pretty."

That was when Shinhye first sensed something was a little off. There was nobody at the police station who knew her. The station was at a three-way intersection on the far end of the street, and unless there was a special reason, the people there didn't come in very often. It was less than a five-minute walk from the police station to Café Yonggung, but there must have been a dozen other cafés along the way.

Shinhye was about to leave with the thermos bundled up in a cloth. The madam was watching, her arms crossed. "You're going dressed like *that*?" she said.

Shinhye wore jeans and a thin gray sweater—not enough for the cold outside—but it was a bother to put on extra clothes, so when she had a delivery, she would just go out in what she had on.

"Why? What's wrong with these clothes? This is how I always go out."

"Never mind. Just go."

The madam had looked a bit upset, but with the thermos bundle in hand, Shinhye pushed open the café door and left without trepidation. Though it was late at night, three officers were at their posts at the police station. Shinhye served them the coffee and stood waiting for them to finish their cups, but she could sense something odd about their behavior. They just sat there, rigid, ignoring their coffee and taking quick sideways glances at her from time to time.

"Could you drink a little faster, please?"

"Why are you rushing us?" said the officer with two leaves on his epaulets.

"I have to hurry back. To close up."

"You won't need to go back tonight."

"Oh?" Shinhye said. "Why?"

"You're going to have a little chat with us."

"About what?"

"We're very interested in you."

"Oh, that's scary," Shinhye said. "I get so scared when a policeman says he's interested in me. Even if I haven't committed a crime." She was just playing along, since what he said was like the usual flirtation of the men when she delivered coffee, and yet she couldn't hide the tremor in her voice.

"Haven't committed a crime?" the officer said. "Hey, there's no point in playing innocent. We already know everything."

"What . . . do you mean?"

"Jeong Shinhye, the show's over! You can quit the charade now." It was the chief, the other man, who had been silently watching until then, speaking for the first time. "Why are you acting so surprised? You want to pretend your name isn't Jeong Shinhye?"

Without even being aware of it, Shinhye covered her burning cheeks with her hands. She tried to remain as calm as possible. "Yes, that's right," she said. "That's my real name. But have I done anything wrong? Is it a crime to change your name to work in a café?"

"Are you going to play this drama to the end, Jeong Shinhye? Do you think we don't know you were kicked out of college for organizing a demonstration? Who sent you to this little coal town? What are you doing here?"

Shinhye couldn't even think of what to say in response. Strangely, she had long anticipated this moment when she would be caught, and now that it had arrived, she felt helpless and full of resignation.

THE JEEP STOPPED SUDDENLY.

"I need to take care of something. Be right back," Inspector Nam said, getting out. When he returned a few moments later, his head and shoulders were dripping wet. The snow had been falling for a while.

He climbed back in the Jeep, but he didn't seem to have any interest in continuing the drive. He lit a cigarette instead, took a few puffs, and started coughing.

"Shit!" he said. "I can't even smoke with this damned cold!" He snubbed the tip of the cigarette and put it out. The cassette had run out and, for a moment, there was a strained silence in the vehicle.

"Why aren't we going?"

"Let's take a little break. It's snowing . . . pretty, isn't it?"

Shinhye didn't know what to say.

"I like it when it snows," the inspector said, his voice suddenly mellow. "It reminds me of my first love, in college, a long time ago in Seoul."

"You went to college in Seoul?"

She only asked because it seemed to her that he was expecting her to.

Inspector Nam spoke slowly and deliberately in a low voice. "I was in technical school for two years. I had to do my military service after that. Came out on my first leave and my girlfriend had already left me. She tried to hide her tracks, but I found out she married some guy from a rich family. An only son. After I was discharged, I dropped out and studied for the civil service exam. Failed seven times and ended up in the police force."

She wondered, uneasily, why he was taking his time to tell her all this. He was silent for a moment, then he turned and grabbed her hands.

"What are you doing?"

"No reason to be scared," he said, smiling. "I'm just removing the cuffs. I told you I'd take them off if you were nice."

He undid them and took off his jacket.

"Here, put this on."

"No thanks, I'm fine."

"Put it on. You're shaking. It doesn't look like much, but it's duck down. It'll warm you up right away."

He draped it over her shoulders. Shinhye didn't know how to interpret that gesture, but she already felt her body getting warm under the jacket.

"It's curious," Nam said.

"What?"

"You really don't look like a student activist."

"Why? Did you think activists had horns or something?"

"It's not like that. But, you know, the kind of girl who's aggressive like a guy, makes you lose your appetite to look at them."

"That's not true. Those girls can be sweet and kind just like any other female student. And I'm not an activist. If I was really an activist I wouldn't be doing what I do now."

Nam was silent. Maybe he just wasn't listening to her. Shinhye noticed that he was watching her with a feverish look in his eyes. After a while, he said, still staring at her:

"You have experience with men. Am I right?" His voice was soft and too quiet.

"I . . . wouldn't know about that."

The snow was hitting the windshield and dispersing, the wipers endlessly beating left and right, pushing it aside. But it came back immediately to pile up on the windshield. Suddenly Nam stretched out his hand and touched her face.

"To me, it looks like you enjoy men. I have a good eye. You're not fooling me."

"What are you doing? Let's just get going!"

Shinhye pushed his hand away.

"Working at the café, you must've offered up your body a few times," Nam said. "I have to figure out why you came out here and hid your identity. You're going to suffer. But I could take care of you. I'm not heartless. If we meet under different circumstances, it could be beautiful. You know what I'm saying? I'm telling you this because I like you."

She knew exactly what he was saying. Despite the shiver running up her back, she took off the jacket he had put over her shoulders.

"You've got the wrong person. I haven't done anything wrong, so you can investigate me however you want. Just take me to the central police station."

Nam's face seemed to harden for a moment, as if he'd been insulted.

"You don't like me?"

"What's to like or dislike? I don't even know you. . . ."

He stared at Shinhye silently for a moment. Suddenly a horn sounded in front of the Jeep. It was a plow coming toward them, clearing snow from the road.

"You think you're really something special, huh? Now I see you're one special bitch."

Shinhye hugged herself. Looking at her, Nam's eyes shone with a frightening animosity. He abruptly switched on the ignition.

2

When I first started college, I joined a literary circle. Then I switched to a reading circle. Was it an underground organization? We didn't meet in basements, but we weren't recognized by the university, either. We met once a week in a room that a former student rented in Yaksu-dong. Her name was Cha Gwanghi, born in Gwangju. She was four years older than the rest of us. She dropped out in the middle of her studies and was staying at home. It's not a lie! I can tell you everything about her—without hiding anything.

The books I was reading then were *The Economic History of the Western World, Historical Awareness of Times of Division*, Rosa Luxemburg, and *Pedagogy of the Oppressed*. No, not "depressed" but "oppressed." They're not radical books, just basic texts. But they woke me up, like I had cold water splashed on my face.

How can I put it? Until then my life was like wandering around in a hazy, gray fog, and suddenly I could see there was a clear order to things.

We called her Gwanghi-hyeong, as if she were an older brother. Her room had a truly unique feeling to it. More than anything else, I think

I was fascinated by the atmosphere in that room. Because from the time I was little, I always lived with my mother in a single rented room, so I never had a room of my own. In Gwanghi-hyeong's room there were thick black curtains, bouquets of dried flowers, and a mask from the Hahoe mask dance. Above the desk, there were two photos tacked to the wall. One was an African child with a swollen belly, but so skinny you could count every single rib. The other was Mother Teresa. How can I put it? This was a room that mixed polar opposites: beauty and ugliness, peace and pain. Next to the photos it said:

—Fly. Give everything up and fly away!

I wanted to know what that meant.

Gwanghi-hyeong replied with a mysterious smile,

—It's exactly what it says. I want to be a bird.

Anyway, I liked her. I was fascinated by how she would hold a cigarette in her long, slender fingers. I was tempted to start smoking myself.

Gwanghi-hyeong suffered from terrible neuralgia. Some days it was so bad she couldn't get up, and the rumor among ourselves—though I don't know who started it—was that she'd been tortured by the army in 1980 during the Gwangju Uprising. There was also the story that the man she loved was killed in May that year. But she never mentioned any of that herself. Except one time.

There was a picture frame she always kept turned the other way on the corner of her desk. One day when I turned the frame around, I saw it was a photo of a young man. When I asked why she kept the picture turned away, she told me it was too painful for her to look at his face. She was smiling, but there were tears welling up in her eyes. I guess that man was her boyfriend.

Gwanghi-hyeong wasn't really an activist. But she was more sensitive and romantic than other people. She would recite poems by Kim Su-yeong and Shin Dong-yeop. Once, in the middle of a heated discussion about what we'd read, she cried out:

—The bird fights its way out of the egg. The egg is the world. Who would be born must destroy a world. The bird flies to God. The God's name is Abraxas.

It was also one of my favorite passages from *Demian*, the well-known novel by Hermann Hesse. But a girl named Sooim said, with a serious look:

—Gwanghi-hyeong, are you still stuck on such juvenile and sentimental ideas?

Gwanghi blushed. Obviously, Sooim had hit a soft spot. She replied with a silly smile:

—You're right. I'm still too sentimental.

Then, Sooim said, without even a change in her expression:

—If we're flying somewhere, it's not to some Abraxas. It's to the people, isn't it?

I really hated her then.

Where is Gwanghi-hyeong now? The next fall, she committed suicide. I don't know why. No one who knew her could explain why she had to take her own life. In any case Gwanghi-hyeong never became a bird or got to fly anywhere—to Abraxas or the people. She just fell.

THE CENTRAL POLICE STATION WAS A LARGE CONCRETE BUILDING THAT loomed over the small shabby street where it was located. Inspector Nam got out of the Jeep, grabbed Shinhye by the arm, and took her straight up to the second floor. At the top of the stairs was a room with a black plaque that read, INTELLIGENCE SECTION.

Despite the very early hour, several men were standing around the stove. No sooner had Shinhye followed Nam into the room when they walked over and examined her, eyeing her up and down with great interest.

"You're finally here! We couldn't wait to see what this bitch looked like."

"Look at her! That face!"

"Yeah, gotta be pretty to get to the men in these parts."

Shinhye reminded herself that she had to be brave. She kept her mouth closed and her eyes wide-open so as not to crumble under their scrutiny. But her eyes burned from the strain, and she felt like she was about to burst into tears.

A man in his mid-fifties sat at the desk in the middle of the room. He looked dignified in his dress uniform, and he wore glasses.

"Do you have any idea where you are?" he thundered, glaring at Shinhye. "To come crawling in without being afraid?"

He must have been the highest-ranking person in the room because Inspector Nam had immediately saluted him when they arrived.

"I only came here to earn some money," Shinhye answered, looking him straight in the eye. "Isn't this still the Republic of Korea, where people have the freedom to change their residence?"

She told herself it was better to seem assertive from the outset rather than humble and intimidated, like someone who might be guilty of something. She was totally mistaken.

"Come here!"

One of the men, leaning against the desk, gestured to her with a finger. He was looking at her oddly. Clearly, he was addressing her, but his eyes were directed elsewhere. She hesitantly walked over to him, and he abruptly slapped her hard across the cheek.

"You will never answer like that again! Understood?"

His tone was entirely matter-of-fact, as if nothing had happened just then. It felt like her cheek was on fire, but the slap had been so unexpected she didn't even have time to cry out.

"Are you a communist or a socialist?" he asked. Then he repeated the question. He still seemed to be watching something a few inches off to the side of her face, but Shinhye realized he was looking at her.

"W-What do you mean?"

"Just answer the question, bitch! Are you a communist or a socialist?"

Shinhye's cheek still burned, and his sideways-looking eyes confused her.

"Look, we already know everything. So just tell us the truth." This time it was the man in the uniform who was sitting behind the desk.

In contrast to the other man, his voice was gentle. Shinhye wanted to ask why they were asking her questions if they already knew everything, but she kept silent for fear that they would hit her again. Maybe they actually did know something about her. She realized she didn't exactly know the distinction between communism and socialism. And that was precisely why she had the absurd fear that she could be one or the other.

"I'm not a socialist or a communist," she answered after a long time. Her voice lacked confidence.

"Of course, that's what you'd say. Who ever saw a Red that admitted to being one, eh?" the wall-eyed man said with a snort. "But it won't be long before we make that mouth of yours tell the truth. So get yourself ready."

Shinhye knew she had to remain calm, but her body was not able to hide the fact that she was afraid. *Please*, she thought, desperately, if this shaking would just stop, she could defeat this fear and be courageous.

"How you're treated here depends entirely on how you behave. So be nice and cooperate with us. Understand?" the uniformed man behind the desk said to her calmly.

"Detective Kim, you get started with the questioning. Get tough on her if she doesn't cooperate."

A tall man in his mid-thirties stood up and told her to follow him. She was somewhat relieved—he didn't look mean.

He led her into the next room. It was a small space and the only furniture was four or five metal desks, a few chairs, and a rusty stove. The walls were bare, except for the slogan, LET'S ROOT OUT THE LEFTIST COMMIES IN DEFENSE OF DEMOCRACY! A dangling fluorescent lamp lit up the emptiness. Kim picked up a metal chair, put it in front of a desk, and told Shinhye to sit down. He pulled a chair out for himself, sat down. He opened a drawer, took out an unopened pack of Sol cigarettes. He ripped open the pack, lit one for himself, then abruptly offered Shinhye one, too.

"I don't smoke."

"Don't waste our time being modest. Smoke when we say you can smoke. It's okay."

"I don't smoke. Really."

"I hear all female students in Seoul smoke these days. Is that true? You came all the way here disguised as a café waitress, you must at least know how to smoke!"

"Not all female students smoke. And I didn't disguise myself as a café waitress. I *am* a waitress."

"A *real* waitress?" he snickered. He opened the desk drawer, took out a ballpoint pen and some paper, and pushed them in front of her.

"Start by writing down all the details of your life. Don't try to hide anything."

"I already wrote all that last night at the police station."

"Just shut up and do as you're told."

First, she wrote down her name and those of her family members, and then she listed her education, occupation, friends, possessions, property, monthly income, her interests and hobbies. For occupation, she hesitated for a moment between student and waitress, then ended up writing "café employee." The detective took the paper and read it carefully.

"Why don't you own any real estate?" he asked.

"Because I don't have a house."

"You must have put down a *jeonse* payment somewhere."

"I don't have that much money. I have to rent by the month."

"You say that you don't have a father and your mother runs a business. What is it?"

"She sells fish. She doesn't have a store. She gets her fish at the fish auction at dawn and rents a spot on the ground in front of someone else's store at the market."

"So your mother suffered like that to sacrifice herself to pay for your college. And instead of studying what you're supposed to, you went off to this stuff?"

Shinhye had nothing to say. At the mention of her mother, she felt unable to respond to any accusation.

"You're wanted by the police, and so you're lying low, aren't you? It's no use trying to hide anything. I'll be checking everything with the computer in Seoul."

"No, I'm not wanted. Like I wrote before, I was disciplined by the university, but there's nothing else. I'm clean."

"And why were you disciplined at school?

". . . They said I organized an illegal assembly."

"So you incited a student demonstration. When was that, exactly?"

"It was fall, two years ago? It would have been October of 1984.

But it wasn't a demonstration. It was just us getting together for a meeting to discuss problems at the school."

THAT FALL, THE WHOLE CAMPUS WAS ABUZZ WITH ACTIVITY PREPARing for the annual Fall Festival. Banners and posters hung between the golden ginkgo trees. And at the entrance to the subway, the students, even while having their bags searched by the police, went diligently to their classes or busied themselves looking for a partner for the festival like well-trained elementary school kids. Everything looked normal on the surface.

The semester exam was after the festival, and when the exams and her papers were done, it was time for Shinhye to graduate. She was turning twenty-two in a few months and would become an elementary school teacher.

Of course, her mother looked forward to Shinhye's graduation more than anyone. She behaved as if Shinhye were already halfway a teacher, believing that she was no longer handling fish slices at a market but the mother of a respectable educator. It wasn't an unreasonable attitude. Her whole life she had endured all manner of suffering, sacrificing everything with her hopes riding on her daughter's success, waiting, and now, finally, she could see those hopes becoming reality.

But Shinhye didn't want to accept all of this for some reason. She was caught up in a sense of impatience, feeling that she was being pushed toward something she hadn't wanted. Deep down, perhaps she wanted the same things her mother wanted, but her own desire had to be even stronger, and as the reality approached, she had become uneasy. It was probably this overwhelming anxiety that had prompted her to run away.

Sooim was the first to speak out. "Isn't it kind of pointless to end our college careers like this?" she said. "It seems like we don't even know how to get angry anymore. What will it be like when we're teachers? After finishing school like this, what's going to happen when we go out to our teaching assignments? Are you just going to be a loyal slave of the educational system?"

It was at the reading circle meeting where the friends who had studied together had gathered.

"You're right! We can't just stay like this," Shinhye said. "Someone has to stand up and rekindle the cold hearts of students! If no one else will do it, then it's up to us."

"When did you become such a radical, Shinhye?"

Sooim's remark made everyone laugh. In fact, among the friends, Shinhye had always been the skeptical and passive one until then. Someone quietly raised a question.

"But what could we possibly do?"

"We could at least organize a rally calling for democratization on campus."

"But what's the use of having a rally? What would that even accomplish these days?"

"It's important now, even if we just end up throwing rocks," Sooim said. "We can talk to students all we want about how to resist this fascist regime or defend the rights of people, but they won't get it. We have to start with something they can actually touch that shows them they have the power to act. What are students most unhappy with right now? Isn't it the dean? The undemocratic way he runs the university? All the female students are sick of being treated like they're still high school girls. So the most effective thing would be to gather those complaints and push for democratization in the school."

No one could disagree. Holding an assembly to demand democratization seemed an unimaginable challenge in the current political climate.

But when they thought about having to do, themselves, what no one had been able to do until then, Shinhye found herself shaking with excitement as if she were plotting a revolution. Even a long time afterwards, she still did not understand the nature of that excitement, that self-destructive impulse that welled up in her chest at that moment.

They began to discuss how to set up an assembly right away. The first hurdle was getting permission from the school authorities because, without it, their assembly would be broken up before they could even get started. Shinhye volunteered to take care of it. Professor Song, the dean of students, was also a well-known poet, and he liked Shinhye and had paid her special attention ever since she'd published some poems in the student newspapers.

She went to ask him for permission to hold a meeting. She said it was to survey the students about the Fall Festival.

"Do you really need to have an assembly for that?"

Ever the fashionable poet, black beret on his head and pipe in his mouth, he looked at her with suspicion.

"It's because the students all have different opinions. We'll only need an hour."

Shinhye smiled, playing a student passionate about literature—a lover of poetry and an admirer of poets—but inwardly, she felt guilty.

"All right, but only an hour. And you know you're absolutely not to discuss any other topic, right?"

The assembly was initially a great success. More than three hundred students gathered in the student union cafeteria and a heated discussion ensued.

And then it was as if a dam had broken. All the frustrations and dissatisfactions that had been bottled up until then came pouring out: undemocratic management of the school, the self-serving arbitrariness of the dean, the problem of teaching assignments after graduation, and numerous other issues. A pale Professor Song had come rushing to Shinhye, who was moderating the meeting.

"How could you trick me like this? I trusted you."

Soon, his face red in front of the booing and hissing students, it seemed he had no choice but to step down. He had been anxiously fretting in the back of the room behind the students, but as the meeting approached its third hour and they were finally beginning to demand the dean's resignation, he had ended up coming up to the podium looking like he was about to cry.

"Shinhye, please consider my situation. Do you really need to watch me resign?"

His hands were shaking as he adjusted his glasses. It was the first time Shinhye had seen another human being so consumed by fear. Seeing this fifty-year-old professor-poet in such stark terror shook her resolve. She put together a few demands and quickly brought the discussion to an end. But then, after the assembly, she had to listen to Sooim's sharp reprimand.

"You're so frustrating! We had a great opportunity, and you ruined it to save that professor's reputation! In a fight, there's no pity for the enemy!"

"But Professor Song isn't our enemy!"

"You can't even tell who the enemy is, can you? They're all the same—puppets pulled by the strings of the fascist regime. We'll never change anything if we sympathize with them or try to understand them."

The assembly was over, but there was never a response to the demands, only the indefinite suspension of the five student organizers.

One of them was reinstated after writing a letter of apology. As for the ones who refused to apologize—they had no choice but to take their punishment. Shinhye and Sooim were among those four.

"IF YOU ORGANIZED A DEMONSTRATION, WHY DIDN'T THE UNIVERSITY just cut you loose?" Detective Kim said, blowing his cigarette smoke into Shinhye's face. "What's this indefinite suspension business?"

"The indefinite suspension was an unfair punishment. We didn't shout any political slogans. We were only discussing campus issues with the dean's permission."

"You were suspended two years ago. What have you been doing since then?"

"Nothing . . . I was home by myself, studying."

"So you've just been staying at home this whole time?"

He narrowed his eyes and gave her a sharp look. She hesitated with her answer. If she said one wrong thing she could get strung up by her ankles. But, then again, she couldn't afford to hide something and have it found out.

"No. Actually, I left home and worked for about a year."

"Doing what? And where? Did you get a job at a factory under an assumed name?"

"Not a job . . . I went to night school. A few months. Six months, actually."

"Where?"

"I was in the Guro District at first, but they watched us too closely, so I moved to Seongnam."

Detective Kim suddenly stood up. The door opened and two men entered the room. One of them—the one in his fifties—Shinhye had seen that morning in the other room. The other man wore a beige uniform. He was thin and had his graying hair neatly combed back. Detective Kim quickly saluted him.

"You said your name is Jeong Shinhye?" the man in the beige uniform asked.

The way he blinked his small eyes behind his glasses made Shinhye uneasy, and she answered in a timid voice.

He didn't say anything else to her. Instead, he asked the man in the suit who was standing next to him, "Did you feed her? If you're gonna interrogate her, at least give her something to eat." Then he left the room. The man in the suit followed him out but then immediately returned.

"Did you get anything?" he asked Detective Kim.

"It's not going to be easy to get this girl to talk. She's not the type who'll listen if we just use words."

"That's because you're too nice! Anyway, we have to feed her, so bring her out."

Shinhye staggered momentarily as she stood up. She had been sitting for several hours, and her knees felt like they'd turned to stone. It seemed her morning interrogation had ended more easily than she'd imagined. She let out an involuntary sigh of relief. But there was no assurance that it would continue that way. Nor did she even know, at the moment, how much longer it would go—or even if she would be released safely.

When she entered the other room, Detective Kim already had the phone in his hand.

"Hey, what do you want to eat?" he asked.

She hadn't eaten anything since her arrest, but she didn't feel hungry at all.

"I don't have much of an appetite."

"Don't give me that crap. Will it be *gomtang* or *doenjang jjigae*?"

She ordered the *gomtang*, beef soup, and was just standing there, vacantly, when someone tapped her on the shoulder. It was Inspector Nam, the one who had brought her there.

"Drink this. You'll feel better."

He handed her a disposable cup full of coffee.

"Inspector Nam, always such a gentleman!" Kim exclaimed, looking toward them.

She sipped the coffee while sitting in a chair in the corner of the room. Her hands were shaking so much they could hardly bear the weight of the paper cup. She knew Nam had been watching her this whole time. When she turned her head to look at him, he bared his teeth in a silent laugh. She was so startled that, in her trembling hands, the coffee she was bringing to her lips spilled onto her clothes.

3

—Girl, you're ruining your life!

That's what my mother shouted when she learned I was suspended. Seeing the despair on her face, I couldn't ignore what a terrible blow it must have been.

I couldn't get my mother to understand what I'd done. No, to be honest, I couldn't understand it, either. Did I have such strong convictions that I'd become a leader like that? And even if I did, was that worth so much to me that I was willing to crush the hopes and dreams my mother had clung to her whole life?

The funny thing is that I didn't feel the slightest bit proud of what I'd done. And I didn't feel any regret, either. Even if I *had* felt regret, what would be the point? That water had already been spilled.

But my mother believed that the water could be put back somehow, that I had to be readmitted at any cost, resume my studies, graduate, and be a schoolteacher. That was her dream, one she would never give up—even if the sky split in two!

One day she forcibly dragged me back to the university. She said if I apologized for my wrongdoing, they would forgive me. I tried to tell her it was no use, but she's so stubborn I couldn't change her mind.

Returning to campus for the first time in the months since I'd been kicked out—with my mother dragging me back against my will—imagine the humiliation! I kept my head bowed because I was afraid I might be recognized. But I had no choice. I went where my mother took me. She was holding my hand tight, thinking I might run away at any moment, and she took me to the dean's office—to Professor Song.

—Go in! Get in there and apologize—with your own two lips. Say your crime was unforgivable, but beg him to forgive you!

She spoke in a low voice with such a determined look on her face. I couldn't refuse.

—But Mom, please . . .

—Hurry! You knock on the door, or I'll knock myself!

Finally, I knocked and walked into the office. Professor Song was wearing his beret as usual. A pale purple smoke rose from the pipe in his hand.

—You! I was hoping I'd never have to lay eyes on you again.

He didn't even ask me to sit down.

—I haven't had a decent night's sleep since what happened. I keep thinking about it in the middle of the night, and I can't get to sleep. I keep telling myself—everything I've done up until now as a poet, as an educator—that I've wasted my life.

I had nothing to say.

—I've lived fifty years, and there was always one thing I was certain about: that the most important thing in the world is *trust*. The one thing we should never, *ever* betray as human beings. But after what happened, everything's gone to pieces.

—I'm sorry, Professor. Please forgive me.

—Do you really want to come back to school?

—Yes.

—Under two conditions. If you accept them, the school can reinstate you.

—What are they?

—One: give us the names of all your student activist friends and tell us what they do. We have no ulterior motives here except to prevent anything like that from happening again. As for the other condition . . .

I just looked at him, speechless.

—You will write an article for the student paper, in which you'll admit publicly that you regret everything and that your views have changed. You *are* a good writer, after all. I think if you compose it in the form of a letter to the dean, it'll be much more compelling for both the students and the faculty.

He went on:

—You know, it was your mother who persuaded the faculty to agree to readmit you under these conditions. She came to see *me*, of course, but she also went to the dean of the university—all the way to his house—and begged him to take you back. Everything is thanks to her. Don't you ever forget your mother's devotion.

My mother was crouching in a corner down the hall, and as soon as I got out of Professor Song's office, she ran up to me and grabbed my hand.

—How did it go? Did he say they'd forgive you? You can re-register next semester, right?

I told my mother I needed to go to the bathroom. I could see the bright yellow forsythia outside the bathroom window, and an indescribable anger and sadness welled up in me. Then I saw my mother standing there a ways off at the corner of the building, waiting, endlessly waiting, for me. That's when I decided I had to get away from there. I had to leave my mother. So I went out the other door of the bathroom and left campus by myself. For the first time in my life, I left my mother's side. I ran away.

Where did I go after I ran away? Once I was out in the street, I realized I had nowhere. I hadn't planned anything. I didn't even have change in my pocket. I couldn't think of anywhere to go, so I went to Sooim's.

She was already working at that time. I wanted to work in the factory with her, but it wasn't easy because the surveillance for undercover workers was getting stricter. Sooim told me I shouldn't feel obligated to work in the factory and said I should give night classes instead.

I started teaching a class somewhere in the Guro industrial district but had to stop because of the police crackdown. Then I moved to Seongnam, in the outskirts, where I started night classes for workers in the basement of a church.

Sooim lectured to me. That we should try to think and feel like the workers, that it wasn't us teaching them but learning from them. It wasn't just that we had to be *like* them, but we had to become *one* with them and be reborn.

I really tried to do what she said.

The problem was, no matter how much I lived with the workers, I couldn't get rid of the skepticism and doubts that constantly rose up in me. I did my best to share their sufferings, their thoughts, their anger. But no matter how much I tried, I was myself—I could never be them. The more I tried to be like them, the more I felt like I wasn't being honest. I felt like I wasn't me, but some silly clown onstage in a play I didn't know anything about. I couldn't become them, and I wasn't myself anymore—no matter how much I tried to deny that, I couldn't. And I couldn't stop feeling guilty because of that.

The truth is, if you consider we were born and grew up in the same circumstances, I wasn't any different from the workers. Then or now. If anything, I just had more education. And my hands were pale and soft from having only held a pen. But why couldn't I be like them? Why couldn't I think like them? Was it because I was selfish and my head was already corrupted beyond redemption with petty bourgeois ideas?

I really envied my friends like Sooim, who worked so hard with their unshakable faith, who never had any doubts. I could clearly see it wasn't hypocrisy or wanting to be a hero that motivated them. But if their convictions were true, what about the truth that I couldn't get over my own doubts? I was constantly tormented by that question.

I just wanted to go on living like I had been. I wanted to go to movies, listen to music, buy something nice to eat once in a while. But I couldn't do any of that if I stayed with them. The things I wanted to do seemed immoral and always made me feel ashamed.

I wanted to believe that I was doing the right thing. That what I was doing was something everyone should be doing, that if I could improve the lives of the people of my country even a little bit by doing this, it was enough.

But my mind and will were too weak to go on with that kind of faith alone. I couldn't endure. No—inside me there was another self that kept saying I should escape.

Then, one day—it must have been about six months after I left home—Sooim paid me a surprise visit to my dorm room. She was wanted by the police after she'd organized a strike at the factory, so she had to impose on me and stay for a while until she found another hiding place.

That day, just by coincidence, some students from the night class also came by and they started a discussion with Sooim about working conditions. But for some reason, I couldn't participate in that discussion. "Organization," "working class," "class contradiction," "liberation of the worker"—all of the terms they used, which I'd also often used until then, sounded strange to me. They sounded like a foreign language and made me feel uncomfortable. I was overcome by the thought that maybe I was somewhere I shouldn't be, where I didn't fit in, in a place where I didn't belong.

I was sitting alone behind them like an outsider who had nothing to do with them. Suddenly, I had a craving for pizza. It was inexplicable to me. They were having a heated debate about the harsh reality of labor, how workers, with all their blood and sweat couldn't even earn the bare minimum to live like a human being—and I was thinking of pizza! But once that thought had entered my mind, I was helpless. To this day I think there must be something wrong with my head or my stomach.

I slipped out without their noticing. I started walking down the main street looking for a pizza place. But I was in the industrial area, and there was no pizza place no matter how far I walked. As time passed, I felt like I was choking. My craving was like an unbearable thirst. I could see it all vividly before my eyes, as if I could just reach out and touch it: the cheese covering the hot dough, the slices of ham, the onions.

I couldn't find a pizzeria, no matter how far I walked, so I ended up taking the bus to Seoul. The traffic was bad that day, so it took almost an hour before I was able to get to a pizza place somewhere in Jongno. But how do you think I felt walking out of that place after ordering and eating a pizza all by myself?

It wasn't fullness, like I'd just filled my belly with something I wanted to eat—it was an intense feeling of shame and guilt. I was disgusted with myself.

My punishment came all too soon. When I got back to my dorm room, I instantly knew that something had happened. It was a shambles. My roommate, Sunok, was sitting there all by herself, in a daze.

—They took Sooim! Thirty minutes ago. The police surprised us . . . we didn't have time to run.

Sunok was shaking. I stood there motionless for a long time, as if I'd been struck by lightning. All I could think of was the fact that I was eating pizza while it all happened. That's when Sunok asked me:

—Where the hell were you?

I couldn't answer. It would have been easier for me to tell her I'd just murdered someone or even that I'd just returned from reporting Sooim to the police. I would have felt less guilty. How could I tell her that I'd sneaked out alone to eat pizza? I couldn't have said that even if someone tore my mouth open.

The next day, I called my mother. She came to the night school, and it ended up with her dragging me back home.

SHINHYE TURNED TO LOOK EVERY TIME THE DOOR OPENED. IT WAS strange. For a long time now, she had been possessed with the feeling that someone who knew her was going to walk through that door and take her out of there. She knew it was childish, unrealistic, and too hopeful, but even so, she couldn't keep her eyes off the door.

She was barely able to eat her lunch. She left more than half of the *gomtang* they'd delivered from the restaurant. But for some reason, the interrogation didn't resume, and she had no choice but to wait for a long time alone in the corner of the office.

"I can't do this fucking job anymore."

It was late afternoon when Detective Kim finally appeared, his face red, angry about something. He threw a stack of thick black files on the desk and glared at Shinhye.

"Who did you come with?" he asked.

"Who? What do you mean?"

"Hey, it doesn't matter how ballsy you might be, you certainly did not come down here to a little coal town in Gangwon-do all by yourself. So tell me—right now—who came with you?"

"You really have the wrong person. I only came here to earn some money, like other girls."

"To earn money? Do you even know who you're dealing with?"

He grabbed one of the files and slammed it down on her head. The cigarette butts and ashes in the ashtray scattered all over. Shinhye scrambled to clean up the mess, as if it had been her own fault.

"It's true," she said. "I need a lot of money to pay my registration fee for next semester."

"Registration fee? *What* registration fee? You said you were suspended indefinitely."

"I still have to register even if I'm suspended. If you don't register, they automatically expel you."

Shinhye hadn't given up on registration even after she was suspended. It might have been very naive of her. Among her friends who had been suspended from school, Sooim immediately gave up on registration and accepted expulsion on her own. The rest of them, in the hopes of being readmitted, had registered for a semester or two afterwards before dropping out.

"Indefinite suspension is the same as being expelled," Sooim said. "So it's stupid to think they might reinstate you. Until the fascist administration unconditionally surrenders, there won't *be* any readmittance unless you go crawling on your knees and agree to be their dog. Why should we hand over the money we earned with our blood?"

"But that's exactly what the administration wants, isn't it—automatic expulsion for failing to register?" Shinhye objected. "If we don't want to walk into the trap they dug for us, wouldn't it be better for us to register until the bitter end to show that our punishment was unfair?"

"That's just semantics! Our legitimacy has nothing to do with whether or not they let us back in."

Shinhye knew Sooim was right. But she couldn't give up on registration. It wasn't because she wanted to cling to the futile hope of returning to school, it was because of her mother, who could not give up on that dream. She did not have the right to abandon that dream—it belonged to her mother, who had sacrificed her whole life for her daughter's sake.

"So you wanted to pay the registration fees, like you said. But why be a café waitress in a coal town?"

"I heard you could make a lot of money in a month."

"What else?"

"It's true that I was interested in a coal mining town. But it was just curiosity."

"Just *curiosity*? You came all the way out here because you were *curious*? What, are you a comedian now?"

From the look in his bloodshot eyes, Shinhye expected him to punch her then, and she realized she had been mistaken. For a moment, she had thought even detectives who had to do this kind of work would be ordinary human beings capable of listening to other people and empathizing with their stories.

"What're you looking at? I'll pluck your eyes out, you arrogant bitch!"

Detective Kim curved his finger into a hook and thrust it at her face. "I'm sorry. But, honestly, I came here with pure intentions."

What she said sounded a bit ridiculous, even to her.

"*Pure?* Now I'm gonna die laughing! So a girl with pure intentions like you has nothing better to do than come down to a coal town to sell her snatch?"

"I told you already, it was to earn money for registration. And I never did anything like what you're saying. You can ask the madam and other waitresses at Café Yonggung. They'll tell you."

"You think I'm some kind of pushover? A thoroughly committed student activist like you comes down here to serve coffee so she can pay her registration fees? You actually expect me to believe a lie like that?"

"I asked myself a lot of questions, too. Like, if there was no other way. You say I'm thoroughly committed, but if I did this, it was because I wasn't committed enough."

The detective looked at her blankly, as if he had no idea what she was talking about. Suddenly he mashed out the cigarette he'd been smoking.

"You really are something else, huh? Turning the conversation this way and that way so you can weasel out of this? You think I'm a pushover because I'm just a little country detective? I won't put up with that shit. It's gonna take some disciplining to bring you back to your senses. Get up!"

He stood up first and approached her, and in spite of herself, Shinhye's legs began to shake.

"I really don't understand why you're all treating me like this. I really haven't done anything . . ."

In his hand, he was suddenly holding a stick. It was grimy from lots of use. *Is he going to hit me with that?* Shinhye gave him a pleading look.

"Hey, Detective Kim! You can stop now." The policeman in the suit she had met that morning had entered the room. "Send her up to the anti-communist section. They're taking over now."

Shinhye stifled a sigh of relief. She had at least avoided a beating for now. But immediately, she wondered, *Why are they sending me to the anti-communist section?*

"Shit! It's always the same! As soon as I get started, they interrupt me! My whole morning was for nothing!"

Detective Kim continued his grumbling as he walked Shinhye out the door. The anti-communist section was on the third floor. When they entered, there was a man sitting at a desk in the middle of the small office, and standing next to him was a large man in a shiny black leather jacket. When he turned to look at them, Shinhye's heart began to pound again. Each time she met a new face here, she felt a new uneasiness and fear.

"Sit over here."

The inspector, who remained seated at his desk, motioned Shinhye to a chair next to him. His attitude toward her was gentler than she'd expected. She noticed a large nameplate, inscribed in mother-of-pearl, on the desk in front of him: SHIN——, CHIEF INSPECTOR, ANTI-COMMUNIST SECTION.

"Having a rough time?"

"No, sir." Shinhye bowed her head. His voice was so soft that she felt a heat in her throat as if she were about to burst into tears.

"Maybe you're under the impression that you can continue to hold out even in here, but that would be a mistake. Waste our time and you're the one who loses."

Shinhye raised her head. But the chief went on with his gentle voice and expression.

"We had information that agitators infiltrated this area to spread propaganda among the coal miners, so we started an investigation. Until now, we were looking for a man. We never would have imagined it would be a girl like you working at a café. But now you've been found out, so it would be in your best interest just to lay everything out."

Shinhye couldn't tell whether what he'd said was true or false, whether it really was the case or was just part of the interrogation.

"Even if what you say is true, it's not me," she said. "I really don't know anything."

A hint of annoyance passed across his face. The inspector stared at her for a moment, without a word, as if he were trying to control his anger. But then he softened, as if he had forgiven her. He turned and pointed to the man in the leather jacket standing next to him.

"From now on, he's the one who's going to question you. He's very good but can be rather impatient. So you'll cooperate with the investigation, all right?"

She replied, "Yes," confused. The inspector patted her head, just like a schoolteacher, and stood up.

"Detective Cheon," Detective Kim said before he left, "this bitch is a lot tougher than she looks. She's going to need a little handling before you start questioning her."

The man called Detective Cheon did not respond. When the two of them were alone in the room, he lit a cigarette.

What time was it? Automatically, she glanced at her wristwatch. The needles were indicating precisely the hour of some other day when it had died without her knowing. She saw a black-rimmed circular clock on the far wall. It was five thirty. She had been there for nearly ten hours.

Out of nowhere, her mother's face appeared before her. *How would she feel if she knew I came all the way out to this little coal mining town in Gangwon-do? That I got arrested by the police?* She felt a sharp pain in her heart as if someone had stabbed her with a knife.

AFTER GIVING THE NIGHT CLASSES, SHE'D RETURNED HOME TO HER mother, and she'd been confined in that tiny house on the hillside in Seongbuk-dong for several months.

Those months of doing nothing had been hard to bear. Moisture oozing down the walls of their single rented room, constant headaches from smelling the toxic fumes of the coal briquettes, the suffocating view outside the window of the countless flat little houses, and all those little noises that seemed to hover around her that would suddenly lump together and come crashing over her—amidst all of that she lived day by day, doing nothing. It was like a period of complete inaction. Her ability to think seemed to have atrophied, and she could barely read a line in a book. Her only productive activity was to change the coal briquettes twice a day.

There were whole days that went by without her saying a word. Of course, she had no one to talk to, but it was also because talking scared her. Sometimes, afraid she would become mute, she would talk to herself out loud.

"*Jeong* Shinhye, what are you doing now?" "I'm not doing anything." "Then what will you do in the future?" "I don't know. What is there that I could do?"

Since her return, her mother watched her constantly, afraid she would run away again. Shinhye found it all hard to endure. At some point she realized she had to leave again. To continue living like this was too stifling. She was in terrible pain every time she met her mother's gaze. Every night, when she saw her mother return from work at the market exhausted, on the verge of collapse, she felt an unbearable guilt.

Every night, her mother moaned from the pain in her knees and shoulders, and yet every morning she would get up at dawn to go to the auction and buy the fish for that day at the market. She watched her mother's suffering, that hopeless life, and she would think of leaving. And sometimes she would reproach herself: *Don't I have a conscience—or the least bit of sympathy?* But the more she witnessed her mother's pain, the more she felt that she could not realistically help, and that itself was an unbearable pain.

She finally resolved to do something, anything. Even if it meant betraying her mother again. She had an excuse. She had a real reason to leave home in order to earn money: the registration fee was due in two months. Her mother said they would somehow manage by going into debt as they had done before, but Shinhye objected, saying that she couldn't be a burden to her mother forever. A few days before Christmas, she went downtown, and just by chance, she noticed an employment agency sign on Jongno Street. She went in, blindly, and that was how she had met the madam of Café Yonggung, who was there to get girls.

"COME OVER HERE."

Detective Cheon had finally decided to open his mouth. She sat in front of his desk as she was told.

On the whitewashed wall facing her, she noticed the Korean flag, a photograph of the president framed in glass, and slogans like STRIVE FOR SOCIAL JUSTICE, SUPPORT NATIONAL DEVELOPMENT, A SOCIETY OF DEMOCRACY & PROSPERITY. So many words that seemed an ironic and cruel joke to her eyes.

"Hey, like he said, I'm an impatient man. So let's not test my patience, alright? I'm still stuck here at work because of you."

His face was rough and dark, his lips were thick, and his eyes bulged slightly. In short, he had the plain and crude features of someone who—if she had met them elsewhere—would have struck Shinhye as a stubborn farmer. He opened his desk drawer and took out an interrogation form.

"Start by telling me about the organization you belong to."

"The organization? There isn't one. I don't know anything about an organization. I've never belonged to one."

"Then who ordered you to come here?"

"No one ordered me. Who would be giving me orders?"

"Is that how it's gonna be?"

An invisible smile seemed to flit across his face. It was a leisurely expression, as if he already knew everything there was to know, as if there was no reason to rush anything

"You must be in communication with someone, right? You know, like reporting what it's like to be living in a coal mining town? You talk about it with friends, don't you?"

"I just came here to earn some money. I'm already ashamed to be working as a café waitress, so why would I tell anyone?"

"Look, let me give you some friendly advice. When I ask you nicely, you answer me politely. You heard what the chief said—I'm a very impatient man."

His eyes seemed to bulge even more when he opened them wide to intimidate her. Shinhye suddenly came up with a nickname that suited his face and even said it to herself silently. And for a moment, she had the pleasure of savoring a little revenge.

"What's the matter? Am I not making sense?"

His goldfish eyes bulged even more. Shinhye suddenly thought all of this must be a joke, that the detective and she were both engaged in something utterly pointless and unrelated to themselves. It felt ridiculous to see a man so excited for no reason, who was threatening to gobble her up with a frightening expression on his face.

"Bitch, are you making fun of me!"

Perhaps she had let a smile slip from her lips. He stood up, eyes even wider, his face trembling, like someone who had just suffered a terrible affront. His huge hand flew at Shinhye's face, and before she could even draw a breath, he slammed her head against the metal desktop again and again. Everything was spinning, confusion, sparks exploding before her eyes. She wanted to beg for her life, but he didn't give her time to say a word.

He lifted Shinhye's head again and slapped her, hard.

She fell to the floor this time. "*Oh!* Mommy!" she cried.

Her ears were ringing, and when he yanked her back up to her feet it grew so loud and high-pitched she couldn't even hear her own sobs. Now he stiffened his hand and sliced it down on the back of her neck in a karate chop.

The sound in her ears grew louder and louder, as if her ears themselves had turned into bells. Her body was a limp rag, and she was helpless but to go where he dragged her. Each time he hit her, it was the fear of the next blow, more than the pain, that terrified her, and she screamed every time. Her ears were ringing so loudly now her whole head was just a huge bell that someone was striking nonstop, and with each blow her entire body shook with enormous force.

Suddenly it was quiet. It was as if the clapper had broken. All the commotion stopped. Shinhye was curled up on her knees. Without thinking, she had crawled under the desk. Like a frightened animal, she pulled her legs up against her stomach, covered her head with both hands, and tensed her muscles. The last strains of the bell echoed in her ears. She was still conscious, sobbing so hard it must have been pitiful.

"Come out of there!"

Detective Cheon bent down and motioned to her. She complied and crawled out from under the desk. In a calmer voice, he told her to sit down. Shinhye's legs were wobbling, her temples still pounding, as if struck by a hammer.

He casually lit a cigarette, exhaled a puff of smoke, and said:

"You know a guy named Kim Gwangbae, don't you?"

4

My breasts started to grow when I was only in fifth grade. I guess I just developed faster than the other girls, but all I felt was terrible guilt. In gym class, I had such a prominent chest you could make out my breasts through my running shirt. I was so embarrassed and ashamed I didn't want to go to school on days when we had PE. Sometimes I'd pretend to be sick and stay in the classroom by myself.

If my changing body scared me, it was because of my mother's influence. She was sure that women with large breasts were only treated like cheap sluts by men. She never let me wear anything that might show off my breasts—like T-shirts. So even in summer, I had to wear clothes that buttoned all the way up to my neck, and even those had to be drab and colorless.

Being pretty enough to attract attention, playing with boys, dressing in a feminine way—I believed all of that was sinful. If my skirt was even a little disheveled when I sat down, if my knees or thighs were exposed, my mother would get upset and scream:

—Girl, you're ruining your life!

That was what she would say whenever she was mad at me. She'd been a bar girl when she was young, and so she was sick with the fear that I would repeat her fate, having to raise an illegitimate child without a father.

Running away down here to this coal mining town and working at a café, I sometimes remembered my mother's words. And I wondered if I hadn't, on my own, somehow found the path my mother was so afraid of, the path of that cursed fate.

When I first decided to take this job, I thought it was all about selling laughs and flirting, but I was so naive! It wasn't until I got here that I realized that a mining town café waitress also has to be a bar girl and a prostitute.

They say that down here a woman is more effective than ten policemen for maintaining law and order. Because women are the only outlet for the frustrations and desires of the oppressed miners exhausted from hard labor. There were at least twenty cafés in town, and with five girls employed at each of them, that made around a hundred girls. And since there were another hundred or so women working in the bars and the little hotels, that made nearly two hundred girls to service the miners. At Café Yonggung there were five girls, including myself, who came down here to do that kind of work.

Do you know what a "ticket" is? Here, instead of serving customers in the café, we usually go out on deliveries. Not just to offices but to restaurants and bars and even hotel rooms. I had to deliver coffee whenever a phone order came in. Of course, we take coffee, but we also have to spend some time with the client. That's what we call "taking a ticket." A "ticket" has a fixed price of five thousand won. Men aren't just buying coffee but also the time of the girl who delivers it. For us, it's about flirting with the men and listening to their silly jokes, or sometimes, when they drink, we'd sing or keep time with chopsticks.

But a "ticket" was selling our time, not our bodies. That was different, and it was after the café closed. For that, we would take the ticket during the day, and after we came to an agreement, we would meet in a hotel room that night. The other girls at Café Yonggung did it almost every night. They came to this mining town to make money, and they were working hard to achieve that goal. They were basically just being faithful to the role created for them in this town. If you told a girl that prostitution was the most degrading form of capitalism because it was about commodifying her body, she would have just snorted, "So what?"

But I couldn't go out at night like they did. There were lots of men who asked me when I went out on deliveries during the day. Some men tried to seduce me secretly, and there were others who tried to bargain like they were buying something at the market, but I used all my skills to protect myself. For what reason? Did virginity mean so much to me? Or was it that I didn't need the money desperately enough to sell myself?

Once, I asked Seol how she felt after sleeping with a man—if she had any feelings.

—Feelings? What do you mean, *feelings*?

She answered with a question, as if she were mocking me. But then she had a blank look for a moment, like she was thinking about it.

She said that at first she was miserable and cried a lot, having to live like that, but now she must have gotten used to it because it didn't bother her anymore. She even added:

—Sometimes, when I meet a decent guy, I really have a good time. Then I think I must have been born for this.

What she said shocked me. Until then, I thought that women who sold their bodies did it out of desperation. It never occurred to me that a woman could have fun doing it.

When Seol asked me if I'd never had an experience like hers, I told her that I'd never slept with a man before. Her mouth hung open in disbelief, and she said:

—What! You're still a virgin? At your age?

She was staring at me as if the fact that I was a virgin made me belong to a different species than her. And yet I took no pride in that fact in front of her. I was ashamed of not having any experience with men and even embarrassed that I was stubbornly guarding my virginity even after coming out here. I knew I was bothering the other waitresses. Sometimes they would even talk loud enough to make sure I could hear them.

—So there's a gilded bitch in this coal town? Bring her out so we can have a look.

They said I had come to sell my body to earn money just like them. So what made me so special that I refused to sleep with men? What gives you the right to protect your virginity?

I had nothing to say. Just like at the night school last month, I was different from everyone else. What is virginity, anyway? It can't be touched. It can't be seen. But it clearly separated me from them.

To keep it, to believe that it was necessary to protect. Maybe it was just my vanity? Just like my not canceling my registration at the university. Wasn't it also a shackle that bound me? More and more, I suffered from these doubts.

SHINHYE WAS LOOKING AT A COLOR PHOTO, A PORTRAIT OF PRESIDENT Chun Doo-Hwan, hanging on the wall opposite. The face in the frame stared at her with such eerie coldness it made her shudder. Bald, the corners of his lips downturned, he always looked anxious about something. Looking at him, Shinhye remembered the nicknames people called him because of that physiognomy, nicknames full of contempt and ridicule: "Octopus" and "Rock Head." But there was absolutely nothing to ridicule about that face now. It represented frightening authority, as cold as the barrel of a gun, and she realized, for the first time, exactly how much she should fear it.

"Kim Gwang . . . *who* did you say?"

It wasn't that she didn't know that name, it was rather that she hoped she could hide her surprise.

"Kim Gwangbae. Do you know him or not?"

"Yes, I know him."

"What's your relationship with him?"

"What do you mean? He's just a customer at the café."

"Listen, bitch, you don't get it, do you? Answer me straight! Or do I have to smack you some more before we go on?"

He growled, raising his head as if to strike her, and seeing his eyes open wide again, Shinhye immediately submitted.

"I'm sorry, I was wrong . . ."

"Alright. So you know this guy, then? Kim Gwangbae . . . now tell me everything you know about him."

Shinhye felt her heart pounding again. She was certain he had ulterior motives for suddenly bringing up Kim Gwangbae.

"He's a miner. He works at a small coal mine in Gohang."

"What else?"

He waited for her to answer, still staring into her face.

"And . . . I think I heard he was one of the leaders of the 1980 uprising in the mines."

"Who did you hear that from?"

"It's something everybody knows, so I don't really remember who I heard it from."

....

IT WAS ABOUT A WEEK AFTER SHE STARTED WORKING AT THE CAFÉ that Shinhye met Kim Gwangbae for the first time. That night, a man abruptly pushed open the door of the café. In the middle of her habitual "Welcome," she had been startled into silence. The man who walked in was black from head to toe. It was only after regaining her composure that she realized he was a miner covered in coal dust. Nearly all the young men who frequented the café were miners, and anyone who came from working underground in one of the shafts would look like that, but this was the first time in her life Shinhye had seen such a thing. The man was out of place amidst the garish lights of the café, a frightening image, as if he had just risen out of the earth from the cursed underworld.

"What the hell is this?" said the madam. "You want to come in here in that state?"

"What's the matter? Is something wrong? I was passing by and I wanted to come inside to see my friends. To have a drink with my miner brothers."

He grinned at the madam, who blocked his way. His whole body was black except for his eyes, which had a strange gleam, and he was so drunk he staggered precariously on his feet.

"You have to change before you come in here. Look at yourself!"

"*This?* I'm wearing my suit. My *mourning* suit! How could I not wear it when another one of my brothers departed to the other world today? This is how we miners dress for mourning."

It was only then that Shinhye remembered what she had heard that afternoon: an accident at the mine. Customers had told her that the ceiling of a shaft had collapsed, killing a miner on the spot. Two others had been taken to the hospital with injuries. And yet, despite the accident, nothing had changed. The miners finished their shifts as usual, and afterwards they looked for a bar or a café where they could go to watch soap operas on TV while laughing over silly jokes with the girls.

"Hey, my brothers! What are you doing here? How can you have coffee on a day like today? We need to celebrate with a real drink! One of our comrades just left Hell to go to Heaven by the grace of God! We have to celebrate! I'll buy a round! Hey, madam, a glass of whiskey for all my comrades here!"

He was loud and drunk, slurring his speech.

"Brothers my ass!" someone spat. It was one of the young miners sitting in front of the TV with the others.

"Hey, Kim Gwangbae! Stop acting like a fucking idiot. If you're drunk just quietly get your ass to bed and sleep it off."

Kim Gwangbae's expression was twisted and hard. It was less an expression of anger than pain from a wound that had reopened. Shinhye was sure a fight would break out, but instead, Kim Gwangbae broke out in a wide smile, baring his white teeth.

"Come on, guys, let's just have a drink! I'm buying . . ." he said, approaching the men.

The young man immediately pushed him away.

"What? You think we're gonna go nuts because we can't afford to bum our own drinks? You got no business with us, so get lost."

Kim Gwangbae was still smiling even as he let the much younger man push him this way and that all the way to the door.

"Come on, my brothers, let's have a drink together, alright? This human being, Kim Gwangbae, just wants to buy you a drink!" he cried out, as if he were pleading with them.

Shinhye couldn't understand why he was being so submissive, like a stupid clown who keeps trying to be funny even when he knows he's despised.

"He's like this sometimes. He's a strange one," Seol told Shinhye after he'd been kicked out. Then she said, her voice low so no one could overhear: "You know, the miners rioted around here a few years ago. I heard about it when I started here. It was a huge uprising."

Shinhye knew about the uprising in that region in the spring of 1980. She had read in the newspapers that even the women in the miners' families had joined in the riots, that they had ransacked the home of the corrupt union president, kidnapped and assaulted his wife, and that the whole city had descended into anarchy in a pitched battle with the police. It had taken three days to crush the uprising, which had shocked everyone with its suddenness and violence and ended with the arrest of many workers.

"You know, they say Kim Gwangbae was one of the leaders," Seol said.

"No, how could that be?"

"It's true. There's nobody around here who doesn't know about it."

Even after what Seol told her, Shinhye still had her doubts: First of all, she couldn't believe that the leader of such an uprising could continue to work as a miner in the same place. Then, his strange behavior earlier was hardly in keeping with someone who could be a leader. And what was the reason for his submissiveness and the blatant contempt from the other miners?

In any case, it was after this incident that Shinhye became interested in Kim Gwangbae. She wanted to know more about him and, if possible, just to talk to him.

"SO ONCE YOU KNEW ABOUT HIS PAST, YOU DELIBERATELY APPROACHED him, is that it?" Detective Cheon asked.

"I didn't really approach him. I was just interested in him."

Before she could even finish what she was saying, he grabbed a fistful of her hair, and she screamed in pain. It felt like he was tearing all of it out—it hurt so much she couldn't close her mouth.

"You fucking *bitch!* Are you playing with me? I told you again and again. You answer me when I ask you nicely if you want me to treat you the same. I treat you like a human being and you answer me like one. I'll tell you one more time. When I ask you for one thing, you show your cooperation by giving me two, alright? If you think I'm gonna go easy on you because you're some female comrade, then you're the loser here."

He added another stern warning:

"I'm crueler to women."

"What is it you want me to say?"

"Just answer my questions truthfully. Don't get me mad for nothing. You decided to get closer to Kim Gwangbae because he was a leader in 1980. Otherwise, he would have been of no interest to you. Am I right?"

"*Yes.*"

"So you admit that you deliberately approached Kim Gwangbae because you already knew who he was?"

Shinhye felt she was slowly approaching an invisible trap. But unfortunately, she did not know how to avoid it. She told herself she had to come to her senses, but the longer it went on, the more it seemed like a dream in her head. Could it be that her body was already exhausted from his beating? As inappropriate as it was, she was beginning to nod off.

"Is what I'm saying correct?"

". . . Yes, that's correct."

"So why are you twisting your words around and making a nice guy like me angry? Tell me now—how and when you approached Kim Gwangbae—without leaving anything out."

HE RETURNED TO THE CAFÉ A FEW DAYS LATER. SOMEONE HAD JUST walked in. Seol poked Shinhye in the ribs and said:

"It's him—the one who caused the ruckus the other time!"

Shinhye didn't recognize him at first. He looked like a different person. Unlike the last time, when he'd been entirely black and covered in coal dust, he was clean and well-dressed. He was sitting in a corner alone, gazing vacantly at the large poster hanging on the opposite wall. An image of a half-naked blonde foreigner on a beach: a young woman always there in the same place, exposing herself for free to the people in the café, her naked body tanned golden and well-proportioned, wearing a smile made more seductive by her squint and her slightly protruding tongue. Shinhye served Kim Gwangbae a cup of green tea and sat down in front of him.

"It's really cold out, isn't it?"

"I was freezing my balls off."

Those were the first words they exchanged. He lifted his eyes slightly and looked at her.

"I haven't seen you before."

"I've seen *you* before," Shinhye said. "The day you were in your mourning suit."

He frowned. "Mourning suit," he repeated. Then he grinned silently. It was a strange expression, as if he were laughing at himself, his lips quivering without really being able to smile.

"Can I buy you a cup of tea?" she asked.

He looked bewildered. "You're offering to buy me tea? The sun's gonna rise in the west! What's the world coming to? Till now it's always the girl who asked me to buy *her* a drink. This is the first time a girl wants to buy *me* one. Do you like me? You want to go out on a date with me?"

"Sure, why not?"

But then she remembered that asking a café girl to go out on a date had a particular meaning. It meant to sleep together at a hotel. Of course, lots of girls were paid for it, but regardless of how much money was offered, the girls didn't go out on dates with men they didn't like. According to Seol, that was the last bit of pride and self-respect a woman could hold on to in this world.

"When?" he said. "How about tonight?"

"No, not *that* kind of date. I mean a *real* date."

"A *real* date?"

He stared at her as if he didn't understand what she was saying, and then, all of a sudden, he blushed. He looked at her for an awkward moment, silently, his face red. She saw the doubt and suspicion in his eyes: Was this girl making fun of him?

"You're not a spy, are you?"

She burst out laughing.

"HEY! OPEN YOUR EYES!"

Shinhye opened her eyes at the sound of the detective's voice. She must have fallen asleep for a few seconds. She didn't know how much she had said. Since dawn she'd only been able to sleep for an hour on the sofa in the police station. She found it hard to believe that she could have nodded off under these circumstances.

"So you seduced him, is that it? And he fell for it?"

She had to think hard about his question—*And he fell for it?*—as if it were a problem written on a blackboard. But she didn't immediately understand what it meant. *Why is he asking me that?* Sleep crept up on her from behind like a shadow touching her shoulder.

"I don't understand what you mean."

"When you tried to seduce him, asking him for a date, how did Kim Gwangbae respond?"

Concentrate! She heard a faint alarm go off somewhere in her head as she struggled to keep her eyes open.

"I didn't seduce him."

"Bitch! Haven't you understood anything yet? With your own mouth! You just confessed that you offered to go out on a date with him!"

"I didn't seduce him. I was saying I was interested in getting to know him."

"It's the same thing, bitch! Even one single lie out of you and I won't forgive you. I can find out everything by asking Kim Gwangbae himself."

Shinhye wondered if he'd already been arrested. From the way the detective spoke, it seemed not yet. But even while she was thinking that, she was again overcome by sleep. She strained to open her eyes. The detective's head was bowed as he busily wrote on the interrogation form. She suddenly noticed a poisonous red pimple on his forehead. It was probably very annoying and painful. She was both surprised and comforted that, in her current predicament, she was still aware of that kind of detail.

"You want to sleep?"

Detective Cheon looked at her with a mocking smile. She nodded without being aware of it.

"Just answer my questions truthfully and I'll let you sleep. You must have met with Kim Gwangbae a lot after that? What did you talk about at those meetings?"

"I did see him a lot. Because he came to the café regularly. But . . ."

THE NEXT DAY, KIM GWANGBAE APPEARED AT THE CAFÉ AGAIN. HE was wearing a suit and tie and looked like he had just had a haircut. Shinhye sat down across from him.

"What's going on? Before you were in your mourning suit but today it looks like you're getting married."

He blushed. He sat for a long time, embarrassed and tense, without saying a word. He didn't look at Shinhye but at the poster of the foreign blonde on the wall behind her.

"What's your name?" he asked.

"I go by Miss Han here, but my real name is Jeong Shinhye."

He fell silent again then said:

"Why don't you ask me *my* name?"

"I know your name. The truth is I heard lots of stories about you."

"What stories?"

"Lots! I heard about how you suffered in 1980 and . . ."

Before she even finished, she realized it was a mistake to bring up that incident. Kim Gwangbae's expression had hardened noticeably. In a choking voice, he asked her:

"What the hell do you want out of me?"

"Nothing. I just want to get to know you a little . . . talk to you . . ." She tried to smile, but the more she did, the more his face seemed to stiffen. He suddenly stood up from his seat.

"I don't know what you want to hear, but I have nothing to tell you. So go look somewhere else."

....

SHINHYE SUDDENLY CAME TO HER SENSES, ALARMED. DETECTIVE
Cheon, his eyes still bulging, was looking right at her.

"Excuse me," she said, "but I didn't hear what you were saying."

"I asked you if you had sex with Kim Gwangbae."

"Nothing like that ever happened."

"You're sure? I'm going to confirm this with Kim Gwangbae, and
if it turns out you're telling even one lie, you'd better be prepared . . ."

"I'm not lying."

Detective Cheon began writing something diligently on the paper.
Like a schoolboy practicing his penmanship, he would periodically
look over what he had written, shake his head in disapproval, crumple
up the page, throw it away, and start over. Shinhye had no way of
knowing what he could be making up to put on record. *What the hell
did I say to him? Have I told him things I shouldn't have?* She searched her
memory but found nothing specific. At least while he was brandishing
his ballpoint pen, she could have a moment's respite. But sleep silently
encroached on her again, and succumbing to its temptation she felt
an almost perfect contentment. *Just leave me alone like this,* she thought
in the comfort of that brief and precious silence. *Just leave me alone so I
can sleep.* The urge was so intense she wouldn't have objected if they
had framed her and sentenced her to life in prison for being a North
Korean spy.

"Here, read it. It's your statement so far."

She opened her eyes to the detective's voice. He had spread a few
sheets of paper in front of her.

"Read this and sign it with your thumbprint. Then you can go
down and sleep."

The handwriting was so bad she had trouble making out what it
said. But what made it hard to understand wasn't just the handwriting,

it was that she was half asleep and unable to fully comprehend the content of those crammed pages. No, it wasn't even a matter of understanding the content—it was all just a bother. The only thing she wanted at that moment was to sleep. She dipped her thumb in the inkpad and pressed the red print on the spot the detective pointed out.

"I could've kept you awake all night, but I'm quitting now out of special consideration for you. Understand?"

He stood up and yawned, his mouth open wide. At that moment his face was completely different—he was just a good-natured normal man, worn out and tired. But then, as soon as he closed his mouth, his face was hard and expressionless once again.

The clock on the opposite wall indicated it was already past midnight.

"Follow me."

Shinhye staggered momentarily as she stood up. Her shoulders and legs felt as if they were being pricked with needles. Detective Cheon took her down to the office on the first floor. It was much larger than the other room, full of people, and noisy. There was a steel-barred holding cell in one corner. It was divided into two sections: one for men, the other for women. As Shinhye walked past the men's section, where they all sat hunched over, they lifted their heads and eyed her up and down. Their faces were oily and grimy from not having washed in days. Only their eyes shone vividly. Detective Cheon opened the barred door of the women's section and shoved her inside.

A woman in her thirties, her hair in tangles, began to move around as if she'd just woken up. She looked up at Shinhye.

"Miss, where are we?"

Her breath reeked of alcohol. Her eyes were unfocused under puffy lids. She was still drunk.

"We're at the police station," Shinhye said.

"Police station? But what am I doing at the police station?"

Shinhye didn't answer. All she wanted was to be left alone to sleep for a while.

"Those bastards! They put me in here! Evil bastards! Cowards! I'll get you back for this!"

The woman wouldn't stop cursing. Shinhye was shivering because the floor was so cold. If only she could sink her whole body into a hot bath, that would be the ultimate luxury.

"Tell me, miss, why are *you* here?" the woman asked.

Shinhye found her annoying, but she forced herself to answer:

"I don't know. I don't know why I'm here."

"You, too? Then you're just like me!" She laughed. "Where do you work? A bar? Café?"

"Do I look like I work in a bar or café?"

"Of course! I've been kicking around this place for years. I could tell at a glance."

Shinhye grabbed a dirty blanket she saw and wrapped herself in it. It stank, but she decided to endure the smell because it was preferable to the cold. During the interrogation she could barely stay awake, but now that she was locked in the cell, she found it hard to sleep. She heard the woman muttering beside her. Shinhye thought of what she'd said, how she'd immediately taken her for a café waitress. And yet here she was, accused of being a fake café waitress, a labor organizer in disguise. *Which is the real me?* she thought, and in the next moment, a cold shiver ran through her body as she remembered what she had said to the detective about Kim Gwangbae, putting her thumbprint on the statement. *Why didn't I check the statement before signing it? How did I end up like this? Until now I lived without knowing who I really was, and now I let them make up whatever they want and give them my thumbprint.* Eyes tightly closed, head pressed to the floor, she groaned, choking with unbearable shame.

5

I couldn't feel any connection with the miners who frequented the café. Not the slightest interest or compassion for people who labored in the lowest rung of society. Maybe it was different for my friends like Sooim. How do you get them to realize their own power to participate in history? What can you do so their joy and sadness, anger and collective resistance, lead to something? If I were Sooim I might have been stuck on such problems, but I wasn't that sort of person. The miners, in my eyes, were just men I had to interact with while I did my job. Everyone I met as a café waitress was pretty much the same: shallow, snobbish, and shamelessly vulgar. They were men who came to the café only to joke around and think about calling us out to a hotel at night.

Every time I dealt with them, what came back to me was the memory of the spit on my face that day I had first arrived. Even after all that time, I still couldn't shake off that cold and repulsive feeling. Any customer could be the one who had spat on me that day, or they were all an anonymous crowd who could do that to me at any time. And then, one man in that crowd—Kim Gwangbae—had stepped out in front of me.

He came to the café every day without fail after that. When he worked the day shift, he came in the evening, and when he worked the swing shift or the night shift, he would come sit in the café all day doing nothing. But whenever he came, he tried his best to pretend he didn't know me. If I tried to get close and talk to him, he would give me a cold look and avoid me.

On the other hand, he got along with Seol. He was friendly and respectful, buying her tea and laughing with her as if he wanted me to see. But even so, I knew he was always thinking of me. He pretended to be indifferent, but when I ignored him back, I could see he was angry and upset. It was written all over his face. It was childish, adolescent behavior, and it was pitiful, but it also amused me for some reason. Maybe I was just secretly enjoying that subtle tug-of-war.

The problem was Seol. After a while, she had begun to fall for him.

—He's much nicer than I thought! He seems to have a kind and gentle side. . . . I guess appearances can fool you. You can't tell from just the outside.

I sensed that Seol had more than just a crush on him. From the time she was young, she'd been wandering around here and there living off her body and enduring all manner of hardships, but in the end, she was just a lonely and tired little girl who couldn't help but crumble at the slightest sign of interest and affection. I wanted to tell her to beware of him, that the affection and kindness he showed her weren't sincere. But I couldn't.

One day, I went across the street to deliver coffee at the Manhojang Hotel. When I walked into the room that had placed the order, I was stunned to see Kim Gwangbae sitting in there by himself. I struggled to hide my shock and served the coffee for him, just like I did for any other customer. But when I handed him the cup, he grabbed my wrist instead.

—Go out with me today.

His voice quavered, and it was so loud it sounded like some incomprehensible scream.

—What are you doing? Let me go!

I screamed, too, and pulled my wrist free.

—You said you wanted to go out with me.

—I didn't mean it that way.

—Then what *did* you mean? Are you playing with me? This is the only way I know. I paid the ticket, so I'll just add a tip, alright?

—You've got the wrong person. I guess I was wrong about you. I'm leaving.

I got up in a hurry. I was afraid he'd hold me back by force. But, to my surprise, he just sat there with his head bowed until I got out of that hotel room.

Back at the café, I was full of remorse. It was all my fault! Why did I have to behave like that with him in the first place? Because he was a failed leader in the workers' movement? But what did that have to do with me?

—Guess who I was out with! Seol said to me early the next morning after spending the night out.

—It was with *him*, Kim Gwangbae!

—Really?

I didn't take my eyes off the magazine I was reading because I didn't want her to notice that my face was suddenly red, and I tried to sound indifferent, but there was a tremor in my voice. Why would she make me blush and my voice tremble?

—Do you know what he said? He asked me if I'd consider moving in with him. The nerve!

—So, what did you tell him?

—I told him not to look down on me, huh?

I really didn't understand it. Each word in Seol's excited chattering was like a sharp stab to my heart. I didn't know if I was just jealous, or angry at being betrayed, or sad for Seol, who didn't know anything.

After that day, Seol had more outcalls at night, and the customer was always Kim Gwangbae. They used a hotel room at first, but then she started going to his house. Every day, she seemed to fall more and more in love with him. Sometimes she seemed anxious and worried for no reason, other times she was playful because she was so happy. She worried me.

I knew the illusion she held on to would soon shatter and leave her nothing but pain and bitter disappointment, and I wasn't wrong. A few days ago—I guess it was the night before I was arrested—I saw Kim Gwangbae again. He didn't come to the café—he phoned, and the place I went to for the delivery was a restaurant. When I arrived, I heard a woman singing inside and the clatter of chopsticks keeping time. I walked to the back of the restaurant to a tiny room in the corner, and I saw a man sitting with a barmaid. I was just about to walk into that room, but I stopped. It was Kim Gwangbae.

The room was thick with cigarette smoke and reeked of grilled pork. The woman was dressed in traditional *hanbok* and sat close by his side. She wore thick makeup, but even under all that powder, she couldn't hide the fact that she was over thirty.

—Ah! You're here! Come on in.

His face was already red from the alcohol and his eyes seemed slack. I realized he had called specifically for me, and he'd bought two tickets. I had no choice but to go in. I sat across from them, unwrapped the thermos, and started making coffee. The whole while, they were cuddling, playing with each other. He slid his hand inside her dress over her breasts, and with each movement, she squirmed and giggled. I did all I could not to look at what they were doing, but I couldn't block out the sounds.

—Hey, come over here. I'll take care of both of you, he said, looking up, his eyes out of focus.

Then, making sure I could see, he held the woman's face and kissed her as she burst out laughing. I silently wrapped the thermos back up in its cloth. Then I got up and said to him:

—Mr. Kim, you're uglier and more despicable than I thought. I have a piece of advice for you. Don't ever touch Miss Seol again. A man like you is beneath her.

And I ran out of that room. But that wasn't the end of it. Not long after that, he appeared at the café, staggering drunk.

—Hey, what did you say to me? I'm ugly and despicable?

He was screaming at the top of his lungs like the day I first saw him.

—Yes! I'm ugly and despicable! I'm human garbage worth less than a bug! You—you're a college student from Seoul, a labor activist! So why'd you wag your tail at someone like me? You want to go out with me? You really want to date me? Are you making fun of me? You think Kim Gwangbae's the kind of man you can make fun of? You think you're too good for me? Well, exactly how good *are* you?

I couldn't say anything in response. Everyone was staring at me, and I didn't know what to do with them looking at me like that. And I saw Seol there, her shocked and dismayed expression. Our eyes met, and then she abruptly pushed open the door of the café and ran out. I wanted to follow her, but for some reason I was stuck in that spot, helpless and petrified, as if I'd turned to stone.

"SO, DID YOU GET SOME SLEEP LAST NIGHT?"

Detective Cheon had just raised his head. He was at his desk, busily writing something.

"Yes."

"Pretty uncomfortable in the holding room, huh?"

"It was manageable."

"Wait there a moment."

He spoke to Shinhye matter-of-factly, as if she had come to see someone. She sat, absently looking out the window fogged with grime. The green awning that covered the lower half of the window was also pale with dust. It was hard to see outside; she could hear only an occasional car and other noises from the street. Suddenly she wondered if she would ever be able to go outside again. There was just a single window in-between, but the outside world and this place seemed so distant from each other.

"So, I reread your statement from last night."

Detective Cheon finally turned to face her. Shinhye saw that he was holding in his hands the statement she had stamped with her red thumbprint the night before.

"This isn't adequate. You say you approached Kim Gwangbae and formed a group to raise consciousness among the miners. But all of the specific details are missing."

"Is that what it says?"

Cheon looked momentarily annoyed by her question.

"That's the statement you gave with your own mouth and signed last night."

"I never said anything like that! I did not approach Kim Gwangbae to raise the consciousness of miners! I never even dreamed of anything like that. I must have been so sleepy last night that I signed without even knowing what it said."

Her heart was pounding harder and harder as she spoke. Detective Cheon just silently stared at her. At first, he looked like he couldn't believe what she had just said, but then his face paled, as if she had insulted him.

"Now I see you're not just some ordinary bitch."

He angrily tore up the statement and waved it in front of Shinhye's eyes.

"This is worthless. Bitch like you needs to be taught a lesson first."

Seeing his rigid expression, Shinhye felt goose bumps all over her body.

"Come with me," he said curtly, standing up. She followed him into the next room. It was tiny, with only one small window and no furniture except a few metal chairs. The door opened and another detective walked in.

"Listen, bitch, Kim Gwangbae already sang. Why are you dragging this out?" the new man said in a coarse Gyeongsang dialect.

"Then let me see him. If you have us confront each other, you'll get the truth, right?"

"This bitch still looks like she's got some energy left. You wanna leave here as a corpse, or what?"

Shinhye realized their viciousness and brutality weren't just an act they put on to intimidate her. She could tell from their tone of voice and their eyes that they truly hated her enough to want to kill her. And yet she couldn't understand why they would hate her so much. As far as she knew, she hadn't done anything to deserve such hatred.

"Sit down," Detective Cheon said.

Just as she was about to sit down to obey, the other detective suddenly slammed his fist into her head.

"Who told you you could sit there? On your knees!"

She got out of the chair and knelt on the floor, head bowed. Her legs were shaking.

"I've seen a lot of bitches like you."

Detective Cheon's leather shoes jiggled in front of her nose.

"Still wet behind the ears and you think you know everything there's to know about the world. Just flapping your mouth like a communist. Do you know why we call communists 'Reds'? It's because they're just like you. Every time they open their mouths, what comes out is a fresh, red lie. That's why we call them Reds."

"I'm not a Red."

"Well, like you say, maybe you're not, but . . ."

He bent down and lifted her chin with his hand.

"Do you know what you'll be when you get out of here? You'll be a Red for real. No question about it. Wanna bet?"

She thought he was probably right. It had happened to people she had known. A lot of them, after being arrested and serving time in prison, had become hardened like steel, even more determined leaders. But Sooim had always called her an incurable skeptic—could the same thing happen to someone like her?

"This is your last chance. Are you gonna tell us everything nicely or what?"

"What do you keep wanting me to tell . . . I'm really frustrated, too."

"So you wanna hold out to the bitter end? Fine."

Detective Cheon made her get up from the floor and sit in the chair again. He pulled her hands behind her back, cuffed them, and ordered her to tilt her head up. The other detective leaned his weight on her, bending her head back and down. She saw the dim light of an old fluorescent and then nothing: they had covered her face with a handkerchief. Until then, she had not understood what they were going to do to her. It was only a thin piece of cloth that covered her face, but it seemed to cut her off from the whole world, and suddenly she was overcome with the fear that she was just a corpse.

What am I trying to protect by enduring this fear and pain? she thought. But sadly, she had nothing to protect. She had just fallen into a trap without even knowing why. Perhaps if she had come with a purpose, as these two men suspected of her, if she had actually done such work, she might have found it easier to resist. *If I only had a reason to lay my life on the line,* she thought.

Suddenly something cold poured down her face, and by the time she realized what they were doing, she was already overcome by a suffocating pain. They held her hair in one hand, her chin in the other, and jerked it from side to side. With each motion the water rushed into her nostrils. She couldn't breathe. She heard the oscillation of Detective Cheon's voice.

"You know where you are? Right under the nose of the 38th parallel! A bitch like you dies in here—we drag you up there and bury you, and that's the end of it."

"Why bother goin' up there?" said the man with the Gyeongsang dialect. "We got abandoned mines all over the place. Just stick her in one of them and cover her up and no one will know till Judgment Day."

Her nostrils filled with water again. It came in waves. One would recede and then another would come crashing in.

"Mommy!"

It was as if her body were sinking forever, but there was no bottom. She felt a terrible dizziness that reminded her of being seasick, and when she shook it off and came back to herself, she suddenly felt a wetness on her thighs. She heard a voice in Gyeongsang dialect:

"What? The whore just pissed herself!"

She collapsed onto the floor. Her face pressed against the cold cement, the lower part of her body soaked. But she felt no embarrassment or shame, just a simple relief because the torture had stopped.

Just then the door opened and someone entered. Stretched out on the floor, Shinhye saw his shoes come toward her.

"What the *hell* are you two doing?"

It was the chief of the anti-communist section she'd met when she first arrived. He started scolding them as if he were furious.

"What is this? Give her a change of clothes! Are you gonna leave her like this?"

The one who spoke in dialect left the room grumbling to himself, displeased with something. Shinhye remained on the floor, not moving. She didn't have the strength to get up and her clothes were ruined. She even had trouble breathing. After a long while, the man returned with a baggy pair of men's pants and underwear still in its packaging, as if he had just bought it at a store. A belt was still looped through the pants; it must have been worn by someone, but she was in no condition to figure out who. The chief opened the door to an empty room and told her to go in there and change. She staggered to her feet and took the clothes in her arms, amazed that she could still walk on her own. The pants didn't fit, and when she tightened the belt as far as she could, it looked ridiculous, like she was wearing a canvas sack. When she returned, she found only the chief seated behind the desk waiting for her. She did not see the other two men—they were gone.

"You know, I have a daughter your age," the chief said. "She's a college student in Chuncheon. Parents are all the same. Wouldn't it break your mother's heart if she knew you were suffering like this?" His voice was full of sympathy.

Shinhye thought it might just be a clever interrogation trick, but she didn't care. Even if it was hypocrisy or calculation, she was grateful to be treated like a human being. Her throat tightened and tears welled up in her eyes. And then she broke down and began to cry. She could not stop crying.

"Go ahead," the chief said. "Cry as much as you want. It'll make you feel better."

After a long while, he gave her a wad of toilet paper from a roll. She used it to wipe her tears and blow her nose.

"I know you're suffering, but believe me, it's hard for us, too. Who would enjoy this kind of work? So . . ." He slid a piece of paper in front of her. ". . . wouldn't it be better to put an end to this suffering for both of us? Instead of complicating such a simple matter, why don't we just hurry up and get this over with?"

Still sniffling like a child, Shinhye began reading the typed statement, but she barely managed to get through a few paragraphs before she was again seized with dizziness.

The typewritten words began to flicker then squirm like individual insects that joined into a frantic swarm. *I, the undersigned, a student on indefinite suspension for organizing an illegal assembly during my fourth year at XX University in Seoul . . . in solidarity with the workers to overthrow the government . . . with the goal of raising political consciousness among the mining community . . . approached Kim Gwangbae . . .*

"Just print your name and sign here, and it'll all be over. Then you can get out of this place right now. It's simple."

"But how can I confess to things I didn't do?"

"Look, I can't just let you go. This has already been reported to the top. We have our own reputation to protect. So just cooperate and we can resolve this with a little warning. . . . You get what I'm saying?"

"But this isn't true."

"You're still not getting it. You want to quibble over what's true and what's not? Then we'll have to start all over again, from the beginning. It wouldn't do you any good, and we're getting tired of this!"

"I'm sorry, but I just can't."

"I'm telling you—this is nothing. It's just a formality to let you go. Don't you understand?"

When she didn't reply, his expression hardened for a moment, and when he spoke again, it was clear that he was trying hard to control himself.

"You really are as stubborn as they said. But you don't have to resolve this right now. I'm giving you one last chance, so go back to your cell and think it over. Understood?"

When they took her back, the cold and dirty floor had never felt more comfortable. She immediately collapsed onto it.

But lying there, she couldn't sleep for some reason. She shivered repeatedly with chills, and every part of her entire aching body seemed to be on fire. And yet she remained painfully fixated on the idea that she had to forget everything and get to sleep. Even as she nodded off and began to dream, she kept telling herself that she had to get to sleep. Familiar faces appeared in the blurry mirror of her consciousness, looking at her, talking to her, and she couldn't tell if it was in a dream or in reality.

"Shinhye, don't give in to the darkness. We're still inside the tunnel of history."

It was Sooim talking. *But what the hell was in that tunnel?* Shinhye wondered. *When was there ever a time when we weren't in the tunnel of history? My whole life I've been walking inside a dark tunnel of pain, a tunnel that never ends, with a dim light in the distance, not even knowing if that light is real or just an illusion.* She saw her mother's face and the faces of friends she'd met at the evening classes when she worked at the factory in Seongnam. And then the faces of the many people she knew, even the faces of people she had entirely forgotten. Gradually, she fell asleep.

6

—Let's fly, let everything go and fly away.

I still remember those words posted on the wall of the room Gwanghi-hyeong was renting on top of the hill in Yaksu-dong. It wasn't until long after she died that I realized their meaning.

Her death was a huge shock to all of us. We couldn't help but feel betrayed when someone who had studied with us, who had been such a big influence, so easily took her own life. But more than anything, the world we had learned about and believed in together had suddenly shattered. We were left in total chaos. Sooim said it was because of that that she couldn't forgive her.

Why Gwanghi-hyeong killed herself will forever be a mystery to me. But I felt those words she left behind penetrate deeper and deeper into my heart as time passed. Wasn't it freedom she wanted more than anything else? She said she wanted to become a bird, to throw off everything that was holding her down, to be truly free and nothing else. But could a human being ever be truly free? And what does it mean, anyway, to become free from all the shackles of reality?

I don't know, but I think that, for a long time, I also dreamed of that freedom, just like Gwanghi-hyeong. So many shackles around weak and delicate ankles, but I couldn't find the strength to shake them off of myself, the ones that were holding me back.

I couldn't keep going to school, and yet I couldn't just quit and become a source of heartache for my mother. I couldn't throw myself headlong into a faith in the progress of history. I was going around in circles, between my struggle and my skepticism, and I didn't have the inner strength to do anything about it. But even if I did have that strength, the problem was still there.

The question was, what did I really want? Where is there freedom without desire? Unfortunately, I didn't know what it was I truly desired, and so I was stuck in a laughable self-contradiction of constantly wanting to be free without even knowing what it was I wanted to do. What do I want to become? No, what am I now, in the present? Who am I?

Everyone treated "me" as someone other than myself. My mother, my friends like Sooim, my professors. But I couldn't accept the "me" they were all pressuring me to be. I don't know, but maybe my coming to this mining town was because of my need to get away from them. But now you also want me to be what I am not. You're all trying to turn me into the activist that I could never be in real life. How ridiculous, right?

"JEONG SHINHYE, ARE YOU ASLEEP?"

Shinhye struggled to open her eyes. She saw the vaguest silhouette of a man's backlit face. Even after she realized it was Inspector Nam, it took her a moment to recover her senses.

"I'm sorry to wake you, but you'll have to get up and come with me."

She looked at the clock—it was just past two a.m. He led the way up the stairs and down the desolate hallway and took her once again into the room labeled ANTI-COMMUNIST SECTION.

The chief was alone at his desk, eating ramen. As Shinhye stood, waiting for him to finish, her stomach gurgled shamelessly. Inspector Nam sat by the stove. He didn't speak, but from the harsh sound of his breathing, it was clear that he was drunk.

"So, Jeong Shinhye, have you thought it over?" the chief asked, wiping his gleaming lips. "You know, we can't even go home because of you. If you'd just cooperate a little, we'd all be fine. Why do you have to be so stubborn?" He wiped his oily face, blew his nose, and threw the tissue into the empty noodle bowl. Then, with a satisfied expression, he looked at Shinhye.

"Look, you were stubborn. You preserved your self-respect. It's time to end it now! Do you think you're the only one who's suffering? We're suffering too! We all know how this works, so what's the point of dragging it out any longer? Sign this!"

He pushed the statement at her again.

"I'm sorry, but I can't admit to things I didn't do."

The chief stared at her in silence for a moment, his face twisted. Suddenly he spat, "You fucking bitch!

"You're really impossible, aren't you? It's the first time I've seen a vile thing like you plugged up both front and back. I told you you'd regret it! Inspector Nam! Get her out of here. Get it over with by tonight! Where do you want to do it? Room 305 is pretty quiet, isn't it?"

Shinhye stood up, her legs shaking. Fear, by now, had become a kind of routine. She followed Inspector Nam upstairs to the third floor, down to the end of a dark and narrow windowless corridor, and arrived at the corner room. Perhaps because it was so early in the morning, there wasn't a soul to be seen there. Everything seemed strangely silent.

"You and me meeting like this is really unfortunate—a tragedy," Inspector Nam said as they entered the room. "I told you when I first saw you, didn't I? If we'd met under different circumstances, it could have been so beautiful."

He was looking at her with a faint smile. His breath smelled of alcohol, but his face was pale.

"Me, I'm not like the others," he said. "Tonight you and I are going to finish it, right here. Understand?" He left her standing while he got himself a chair and sat down.

"Do you know why they sent me out here to the boonies?"

He kept his eyes fixed on her as he answered himself.

"Back in Seoul I killed a man while I was questioning him. Just bad luck."

Shinhye thought he must be lying, but she also knew he could just as well be telling the truth.

"Look, I don't really want to tell you this stuff. But even if I kill you, all I'd get is a dressing-down."

"Are you planning to kill me?"

"Why? Is that what you want?"

"No, I want to live."

He gave her another faint smile.

"Nobody wants to be a murderer, but accidents at work do happen. After all, some people are born lucky, but others have terrible fates. Me, I think of our meeting as fate, and I'd rather not make it a bad one. So I'll tell you one more time. This is really your last chance. Are you going to sign the statement or not?"

"I'm sorry, but I can't admit to things I haven't done."

"Is that it?"

There was a strange light in his eyes.

"Alright then. I don't know what kind of uppity bitch you are, but this'll be hard for me."

He stood up and suddenly undid Shinhye's belt. Her borrowed pants were so baggy she was afraid they'd slide off when the belt came out. She was confused about what he was about to do. She thought for a moment that he was going to beat her with the belt, but instead he took it and hung it from a nail in the wall.

"Do you know why I'm hanging this here?" he asked, looking Shinhye in the eye. "You don't know, but you might need it later. If it comes to the point that you can't take any more, you may want to hang yourself with it."

The belt dangling there reminded her of a gallows she had seen in a movie. And even while she believed the inspector's horrible threat was just another thing meant to intimidate her, she felt the chill of terror course through her body all the same.

"How many times did you sell yourself since you got here?"

He pulled the chair back and sat down in front of her.

"I never sold my body."

"Is that the truth?"

"Yes."

"Then was there a time you slept with a guy for free? If you were seducing miners to raise their consciousness, you must have used your body, right?"

"I never did that."

"Not even once? With Kim Gwangbae?"

"No, I've never done such a thing."

"Then are you telling me you're a virgin? Really?"

She bit her lip and said nothing more.

"Well then! I'll have to confirm it for myself. Lift up your shirt."

When Shinhye didn't immediately understand what he wanted, he raised his voice.

"Fucking bitch, didn't you hear me? I said lift up your shirt!"

She wanted to protest but couldn't get her mouth to open. Her body had become petrified with a new kind of fear she had not known until then.

"Listen to me, or this is gonna be hell for you! It's after two in the morning. Nobody's coming into this room. I can do whatever the fuck I want to you, and no one's around to blink an eye. Understand? So if you don't want to get fucked up, you'd better do what I say!"

As if she were controlled by an irresistible force, Shinhye lifted her T-shirt and undershirt with a shaking hand to reveal her bare skin. With her other hand she held on to the waistband of her pants, which were hanging loosely on her hips with the belt gone, afraid they might slip down. The inspector stood up and went behind her. It felt as if his hand brushed against her back, and in the blink of an eye Shinhye's bra, unhooked, fell to her feet.

"Keep your shirt up. Don't move!"

He sat down again and regarded her body with the frank eye of a surgeon, and after a moment, her shame seemed to disappear. What remained was a bottomless pit of terror.

"You've got great tits," he said with a sigh.

His Adam's apple moved up and down, and Shinhye could hear him swallowing his saliva. He walked to a metal cabinet mounted on the wall where there was a small transistor radio on top. He took a few moments to adjust the dial this way and that, and a sweet, soft pop song began to play, seeming to come from another world.

"You—you look so much like my first love. I couldn't believe it when I saw you."

Still holding her T-shirt up, Shinhye's hands were shaking. Heat seemed to radiate from the inspector's eyes, and he followed the rhythm of the song on the radio, his lips popping *ba-bam ba-bam* to the beat.

"Why are you doing this?" she said.

Suddenly, his hands were on her breasts.

A pleading sound came from her mouth but her body was paralyzed, unable to move. He moved his hands slowly, and his eyes seemed to get heavier and heavier as if he were drowsing in some sort of fantasy.

Memories can make the past shine again like a jewel. And so we dedicate this nostalgic pop song, "Unchained Melody," to make this night a memorable one for you . . .

"Stop it! Please . . ."

"Be quiet," he whispered into her ear, his voice hoarse. His breath was like an animal panting. "You're just saying that. You're actually enjoying it, aren't you?"

She thought that maybe none of this was real. Rather, like when she was having a nightmare when she was little, if she earnestly repeated, "This is a dream, this is a dream," she would awaken from it enfolded in her mother's familiar smell. Her need to believe this was so intense she thought she might be going mad.

"Looks to me like you lied when you said you're a virgin," Nam whispered again, pressing his face close to hers. "I can tell by looking at your breasts. I'm an expert when it comes to women. You have lots of experience with men, don't you?"

To overcome her fear, Shinhye tried to muster all the hate in her heart, but he was too loathsome, and she found herself choking with dread as she drew back and saw his bloodshot eyes below her chin.

"Take your pants off," he ordered in a rough whisper. "You can scream, but it's useless. It would be better for you just to do as I say or this'll end up being a lot worse than it has to be."

It occurred to her that he might be purposely torturing himself.

He must have been fully aware that he was about to commit an unforgivable crime.

"You want me to strip you myself?" he said, grabbing the waistband of her pants. She collapsed, but in the next instant he had a fistful of her hair and pulled her back up to her feet.

"So will you take them off? Or do I have to do it?"

She lowered her pants with her own hands. But even after they had fallen to her feet, he wordlessly gestured with a finger. It meant she should take off her panties, too. A young man's soft voice still came over the radio. *"The first time ever I saw your face, I thought the sun rose in your eyes . . ." Have you ever felt that way, dear listeners? It's "The First Time Ever I Saw Your Face," the theme song from* Play Misty for Me, *a movie that shows how great love is, but how it can feel like a gift from the stars and the moon, but how it can also be the most frightening thing in the world.*

The cold enveloped her nakedness, raising goose bumps over her entire body. Whatever it was he wanted, she wanted to avoid the thing she feared most. And not even knowing what that was, what she wanted most of all was to avoid it.

"Get up here," Nam said, pointing at the desk.

Strangely, now that she had taken off all her clothes, she found herself unable to resist. She climbed onto the desk like an animal obeying a command. Her legs shook. Standing on top of the desk, she saw a red cross. It was pitch-black outside the window, and the red light of the cross stood out as if it had been carved into the darkness.

Why did that cross suddenly appear before my eyes? What does it mean at this moment? Is it there to relieve my suffering? Is it just a lit-up sign made of wood or steel—what sort of salvation or providence could it be?

Shinhye shuddered as she thought this to herself. Even then, she could not find a single word of prayer. Instead, the cold and doubting person she was had to suffer a terror and despair beyond what she could endure.

She was intensely aware of the fact that there was no possible rescue. This covering of flesh, wrapped around her, thick and heavy like armor. If God was punishing her now, maybe it was for not believing in anything, not even knowing her own desires, never having truly loved anyone other than herself. . . .

God, forgive me, she prayed, silently looking at the cross. *If all of this is for the sins I have committed, please forgive me. Please make it stop.*

"Sit down," the inspector said. He was sitting in the chair looking up at her.

She obeyed, sitting hunched over, trying to cover her nakedness as best she could with her hands. But he would not allow it.

"Put your hands on your head."

His eyes gleamed as he devoured every part of her body. Shinhye knew she could never erase that face, every tiny nuance of expression, from her memory. She felt as if she was suffocating with despair and shame, but all she could do was close her eyes.

"Spread your legs," he said in the same dry monotone. "Wider."

God, forgive me, forgive me. She clung to that short prayer as if it could, by some miracle, save her now.

"You think I'm a pervert, don't you? Tell me. Right?"

"N-no . . ."

"It's alright. You can tell me the truth, because I really am."

His hand dug into her groin, and she doubled over, screaming. He silenced her harshly.

"You make another sound, and I'll shove my hand up your cunt and rip out your uterus. You won't be able to get married or have children."

To Shinhye, his words were no longer just a threat. She imagined he was capable of doing anything. What truly scared her was that she had no way of knowing what he would do next.

She bit her lip to hold back a scream. Nam's hand stroked her leg, which was bristling with goose bumps, and gradually slipped up toward her belly. She wished that every cell in her body capable of sensation would go numb.

"Are you really a virgin?"

His gleaming lips came closer. The smell from his mouth was disgusting, and as she tried to endure the nausea he pushed his hand between her legs. She arched her back, screaming.

"Stop it. I'm just checking if you're really a virgin or not."

She shut her eyes as his fingers wriggled between her legs. From her lips leaked an animal moan that did not seem to come from her. *God, forgive me. Please forgive me . . .* She repeated those words in her mind as if they could miraculously rescue her from all her suffering.

"Hey, want me to show you something nice?" Nam stood up and began to unbuckle his belt. Shinhye shook her head vigorously.

"Come on, look at it." His voice was hoarse. It sounded like it was coming out of a deep cave. Shinhye kept her face averted, her eyes shut so tight it hurt. He grabbed her chin and turned her face toward him.

"Open your eyes," he said. "Open them!"

His strong fingers dug into her chin, and she felt a stabbing pain as if her neck would break. Her eyes opened involuntarily.

"So, what do you think?"

She saw his gleaming eyes and the whiteness of his teeth—undeniably the face of an animal. He forcibly twisted her head so she was facing his open fly. She desperately tried not to look, but she closed her eyes too late. The image was indelible, like a cut that would never heal, and she would not be able to erase it until the day she died.

"So how does it feel? First time you've seen one, huh? Take a good look." He was still clutching her chin in one hand. He was clearly enjoying himself now. With his other hand, he pressed downward on her head. His penis, released from his pants, was right in front of her eyes. A thick animal smell assaulted her nostrils. She made a retching noise and vomited.

"Fucking bitch!"

He pushed her head back, but even released from his grasp, she couldn't help the dry heaves that came up her throat.

"I'll do whatever you want," she said. "I'll write a statement. Just please stop."

"You should have done that before. It's too late now."

"Please—I'm begging you. Just listen to what I'm saying. I'm not that. I'm not the kind of girl you all think I am. Something went terribly wrong here. I'm not a subversive. I'm not even an activist. It would be great to have that kind of courage or conviction. But I'm not strong like that. I'm weak . . . and afraid. And suspicious . . ."

She began to blurt out anything that came to mind—anything to escape the suffocating agony and terror.

"I'm an ignoramus," the inspector said. "I have no idea what you're talking about." His eyes burned with a terrible fire, as if some immeasurable rage was about to explode from inside.

"Bitch! What are you so worried about, anyway? Why are you making everything so hard and complicated? I hate girls like you. You make it look like all the problems in the world are on your shoulders, you make easy things hard for no reason, you bitch about stuff and make innocent people suffer. . . . People like you need to disappear to make the world a better place to live. You understand? Today I'm gonna show you what the world is really like and what life is all about!"

He pushed her roughly onto her back on the desk. She could see him taking off his pants. Overcome by fear and anger, she could no longer plead with him. She wanted to say something, but no sound would come out, as if something was blocking her throat.

He pressed his weight down on top of her body. She desperately tried to resist, but she realized it would be impossible. "You'll be the ruin of us, you bitch!" Her mother's face appeared before her eyes. She tried to recall all the faces she knew and desperately called out their names one by one in her mind. But she was too far away from them, she was too far from the world.

She felt something with her hand. A large glass ashtray. She lifted it and slammed it down on his skull with all her might.

"*Ah!*"

The inspector screamed, straightening up, his hands holding his head. She slammed the ashtray into him again. She quickly sat up, jumped off the desk, and ran for the door. Cursing, with blood streaming down his forehead, Nam tried to catch her. But it took a moment for him to pull up his pants, and in that time Shinhye was just barely able to turn the handle and open the door. She found herself in the empty hallway lit only by fluorescent lights. She cried out for help in the cold, barren space but what actually came out of her mouth was a barely audible moan, almost an animal whimper. She ran down the hall, the inspector following right behind her. She tumbled down the stairs, rounded a corner, collapsed onto the cold cement floor. She had collided with someone. She saw a young police officer in a blue uniform looking down at her in amazement, and then she lost consciousness.

7

I lied when I said I wasn't guilty of anything. It's only now that I realize what my crimes were, so I will confess them now.

First of all, I was wrong to believe that I was innocent. My ignorance in not knowing the source of the problem—that foolishness itself was a crime. The problem was within myself.

I never once got outside of myself until now. Even while I pretended to educate the workers at night school, I never felt the slightest sympathy for the pain of the common people, for the persecuted, for the abandoned, or for my neighbors, or my brothers and sisters. I did not know how to feel their pain as my pain, their anger as my anger. I knew the contradictions and the evils of society, but I didn't throw myself into a fight against them. I didn't feel passionate enough to throw myself headlong into anything.

Even the love I felt for my mother wasn't genuine. From the time I was a child, I lived with the idea that I had to be a good daughter to her, that I could somehow make up for her pain and self-sacrifice by studying hard. But even then, one part of me constantly wanted to escape from her. I closed off my heart to even the smallest things, like a flower blooming on the side of the road.

I still existed, though, and felt in the first-person singular. I lived on a distant island in a prison, far away from my friends, my neighbors, society, and even my mother. Even while I kept screaming to the world to save me, I never once thought of trying to swim to the outside.

Only now do I finally realize my wrongdoing, my unforgivable crimes. The crime of not ever being able to let go of myself, the crime of never once trying to find hope on my own, the crime of never extending my hand to others and never letting others reach out to me, the crime of never having shed a tear for anyone other than myself.

Forgive me for these crimes.

WHEN SHE WALKED OUT OF THE POLICE STATION, THE FIRST THING Shinhye saw was the white snow blanketing everything. She had been locked up inside for three days and nights, and during that time the snow had poured down and covered the whole world in white. For a moment she couldn't even properly open her eyes. The heavy piles of snow on the roof of the post office and the farming cooperative across the street shone lucidly under the bright winter sun, and in the corner of the police station courtyard, someone had made a big snowman with a comical expression. It was something you could see anywhere in Korea: the winter landscape of any village in which people lived, a scene so peaceful it put your mind and body at ease.

Shinhye began to walk cautiously down the icy, snow-covered street. It was strange to feel her feet touching the ground. She walked slowly, one foot in front of the other, forcing her knees, which felt like they were about to collapse.

"It would be better for you not to say anything when you're outside," the chief had told her before her release. "Of course, you're not the type to be that stupid. So forget everything that happened last night—completely. Is that understood? Nothing happened."

Nothing happened, Shinhye kept saying to herself. And it seemed like nothing actually *had* happened. The winter sky was so clear it chilled the eye, and on the snow-covered road, children were shouting, having a snowball fight. An old woman riding on the back of a bicycle gave someone a toothy smile. Whatever she had suffered during that time seemed like a lie—and the world outside hadn't changed at all, not even a scratch.

"His behavior toward women has always been a bit of a problem. He's been a little twisted ever since his wife ran off with her dance instructor. So just forget what happened."

She had regained consciousness early that morning on a sofa in the corner of the office. The faces of the chief and a few strangers were watching her. Someone had haphazardly put some clothes on her naked body.

"In any case, you've been through a lot," the chief said. "You've probably had an opportunity to learn a lot, too. We don't want to meet again like this in the future, right? Take care of yourself, and if we should meet each other again, let's hope it's with a smile."

He had extended his hand to her, and it seemed she could still feel the lingering warmth of his palm. She couldn't think of a single thing to say; she was just relieved to finally be released.

"Can you make it alone?" he asked. "We can take you to Gohang if you like."

"No, you don't have to."

She still didn't understand why they had let her go so easily. As of that morning, they had stopped trying to get her to sign a confession. It had all ended abruptly, as if a curtain had come down on the play. Just as it had been absurd at the beginning, the end seemed like a lie. In the end, they had held her three days and three nights, using all manner of violence and intimidation, only to get nothing from her. She had held out until the end. And yet that fact gave her not a speck of pride or comfort.

At the intersection, Shinhye paused a moment, not knowing which way to go. No one paid any attention to her. She realized that on the outside there was nothing to distinguish her from the people passing by. It was reassuring at first, but then it also made her feel an unbearable sadness and sense of injustice.

She couldn't tell where the pain was—her entire body ached. But what was broken was more psychological than physical. She was baffled that nothing seemed to be wrong with her. She should have lost her mind, collapsed in tears, had a nervous breakdown, and yet not only did she seem fine, she was unbearably hungry. Now that she thought about it, she realized she had eaten almost nothing in the past day. She was thinking there was nothing left of her self. Nothing to dream about, nothing to protect. All that was left was a disgusting shell of a body. But that body was feeling an intense hunger that she could not endure. Instinctively, she went into one of the restaurants on the street.

She sat down and ordered a bowl of *gomtang*. But as the first spoonful of hot liquid entered her mouth she gagged. She tried everything, but she couldn't keep from throwing up. It felt like her entire past life was coming up her throat, and when she had nothing left to throw up, the tears began to flow. With her face buried in her arms, she started loudly sobbing, and when the first tears had burst, she could not stop crying. She could hear the other customers whispering behind her back.

"*Aigo*, she wasted that whole dish . . ."

"Is she just a girl or a grown woman? Why do you suppose she's crying like that?"

"She must be sick, or maybe . . ."

Shinhye abruptly turned to them and shouted, "What are you doing?! Who do you think you are? What do you even know about me? Why are you saying stuff about someone who doesn't concern you? What's the *matter* with you?"

They just stared at her silently, looking alarmed at her insane outburst. She left the restaurant right away. Perhaps it was because she had cried and screamed to her heart's content, but she felt suddenly exhausted and despondent as if she were empty inside.

She took the bus to Gohang because she had to go back. The bus passed in front of the police station again, and, in the brief interval when it made a short stop, Shinhye looked through the window at the station building across the street. The sentry, his shoulders slightly hunched, guarded the police station. Beside him, a man in his forties in a gray jacket was talking and laughing with an old man who looked like a farmer. As she watched the white mist from their breaths mixing in the cold air, Shinhye suddenly realized who the man in the gray jacket was. Her entire body froze. It was Detective Cheon. Her shock was not due to the memory of the tortures he had subjected her to. It was because the man she now saw before her eyes looked like a good person: simple and kind, scratching the back of his head, his face deeply wrinkled with genuine, good-natured laughter. She could neither believe nor understand it. "Oh, God!" The sound came from her mouth like a cry of pain without her even knowing.

She arrived in Gohang after it was completely dark. The main street had not changed at all. The narrower streets, tangled like fish guts, still stank. It was still dirty and noisy. She crossed the small bridge over the silent black stream and entered the alley of cafés and bars, which began to look beautiful with the evening, like an old prostitute. Drunken men were fighting with their jackets off, a dog with mud dripping from its fur was rummaging through a trash bin, and a Yoon Sooil song called "Apartment" was playing on a radio somewhere. Yonggung Café had the same cracked acrylic sign, the same narrow and steep stairs, the same musty smell. When she opened the door and entered the café, she heard the same familiar nasal voice.

"Welcome! Oh, my . . ."

Behind the counter, the madam's face froze, her mouth still open. Shinhye spoke with as little emotion as possible.

"How are you?"

"W-what's going on? The police . . . let you go?"

"What's going on? You're talking like you were hoping they'd never let me out."

"What are you saying? You have no idea how much I worried. . . . Anyway, I'm glad you came out safe. Come sit here where it's warm."

Shinhye sat there and looked around the café as if she were a customer. She did not see Seol, but two waitresses she didn't know were standing around, bored, watching television. Nothing else had changed. On the opposite wall, the naked foreign woman was still there in the frame, her tongue still half-protruding, regarding Shinhye through her narrowed lids. Oddly, Shinhye felt a kind of closeness with her.

"How you must have suffered, Miss Han. It's such a relief that you got out like this." The madam gracefully lifted the tail of the traditional skirt she wore and sat down facing her.

"I'm not Miss Han. My name is Jeong Shinhye. You know that, right?"

"What gave you the impression that I know anything about you? Maybe you thought I did, but I don't know anything at all."

"It doesn't matter either way. I just came for my money. Give me what I earned working here."

"Why such a hurry? Don't worry about the money. Would you like something hot to drink?"

"No. Just give me my money. I have to leave."

"Where to? Seoul?"

The madam stared at her silently for a while, waiting for her to answer. Then she got up and walked over to the counter. When she returned after a moment, she was holding a white envelope.

"You were short three days because you got arrested, but there's a full month's pay in here," she said, as if she were being generous.

The envelope contained four one hundred thousand won checks. Shinhye had come to this remote coal town for this money; it was the tuition money that could postpone her withdrawal from the university, and it was her only compensation for what she had just endured. But strangely, she felt nothing at all. No regret. No sorrow. No despair. She folded the envelope, put it in her pants pocket, and stood up.

"Alright. I'm leaving now."

"You don't need to go up to your room. Your bag is down here."

The madam pulled out a familiar brown vinyl bag from under the cash register. The inside of the bag was a mess as if someone had searched it. Maybe it was the police. But all of that was irrelevant now. While she had the bag open, confirming its contents, the madam watched her, arms folded, her face hard and cold.

"Well, I hope you make a lot of money," Shinhye said.

She picked up her bag and went toward the door.

"Shinhye, I'm so sorry!"

To her surprise, it was Seol waiting for her as she came outside the café. The tip of her nose was red from the cold.

"It's all my fault, Shinhye! I thought Kim Gwangbae was cheating on me. . . . I hated him and I hated you. . . . But I still don't know how I could have done that to you. I deserve to die."

"You mean you're the one who reported me to the police?"

Shinhye couldn't believe what Seol said. But she was nodding her head, her face twisted with anguish. Her eyes welled up, and then ugly tears were running down her cheeks like wax on a candle.

"You're never going to forgive me, are you?" Seol said.

"I was just going to go see Kim Gwangbae. Is that alright?"

Seol's eyes were suddenly full of suspicion and fear, almost crossed as they focused intently on Shinhye's face.

"Don't worry," Shinhye said. "I won't talk about any of this. Can you tell me where he lives?"

"It'll be hard to find on your own," Seol said. "I'll take you there."

She led the way. Neither of them said a word as they walked along the narrow, winding path. When they crossed the stream, they could see a group of little shacks at the foot of the mountain. The houses of the mine workers. Shinhye stared up for a long time at the scene of those identical shacks lined up like so many rows of matchboxes in the darkness.

"Is it there?"

Seol nodded. "Do you see the lamppost over there? It's the next house, number 209. Alright, I'm going back now."

But she didn't move. Shinhye started up the steep slope that led to the miners' shacks. After a few steps, she turned around and saw that Seol was still standing there in the same spot looking at her.

"Shinhye!" Seol called out abruptly. "We decided to live together. Over New Year's we're going to his hometown so I can meet his family."

Shinhye just nodded silently with a faint smile. Only then, reassured, did Seol smile back like a child.

The snow piled on the ground had frozen, making it very slippery underfoot.

Shinhye walked past houses, some without a gate or a fence, every one of them shabby and miserable, and arrived at one lit by the cyclopean eye of a streetlamp. On the door patched with pieces of plywood, she saw the number 209 written in black paint.

A beam of light leaked through a gap in the door. Shinhye stood there for a long time. What had made her come to this place even she herself did not exactly know. What she did know was the fact that it was some irresistible urge from inside herself.

She finally shook the flimsy wooden door, but there was no response. She tried knocking, hard. An unfamiliar passion stirred inside her—she was almost shaking with excitement. Again she asked herself why she had come here. But whatever the reason, the important thing was to meet Kim Gwangbae right away. She had been obsessed by this need since she had left Yonggung Café—no, since she had been released from the police station. She pulled on the door handle. She thought it would be locked, but it opened wide, almost coming off its hinges.

What she saw first was the kitchen. She noticed a battered pot left on the stove with a few strands of ramen dried up inside, a half-collapsed cupboard, and various small dishes covered in dust. "Anybody home?" There were holes in the paper panels of the door leading to the bedroom. She opened it. The light was on but the room was empty. A tattered and faded army blanket covered the broken glass of the window, and she could see clothes dangling from the wall as if they had hanged themselves.

Shinhye stood there for a moment, overcome. She had no idea what she should do now. The impulse that had driven her here had been so strong that she felt a violent confusion. She thought Kim

Gwangbae could not have gone far because he'd left the lights on in the empty house, but there was no way to know when he would be back. Outside, she noticed a red light shining in the darkness at the far end of the neighborhood. A lamp for the dead. Someone in one of the miners' houses had departed from this world. It might even be someone she knew who had died. Kim Gwangbae was sure to be in that house. Shinhye began to walk up the steep path toward the light. Two men who seemed to be mourners were just then coming out of the house, still hunched over.

"Just a moment . . ." Shinhye said.

They looked her up and down suspiciously.

"You're coming out of this house of mourning?"

"Yes. . . . What do you want?"

"Do you know if Mr. Kim Gwangbae happens to be there?"

"And how might you know him, miss?"

She was relieved—they seemed to know who he was. One of them was grinning.

"You're his girlfriend, maybe?"

"Excuse me, but could you call him, please?"

"Wait a minute then."

The man went back into the house, and it was a long time before Kim Gwangbae emerged, approaching her slowly, as if he couldn't believe what he was seeing.

"All the way up here . . . What's going on?"

"Would you let me sleep here tonight?" she asked.

His expression froze in shock. He stared at her face in silence and began walking.

"He was an old miner. He spent his whole life working in the mine and he died last night. Left three kids behind . . . A few years ago, his wife took out a loan and ran a small business. Then she got swindled and ran away. He had to raise his kids alone, like a widower. He was diagnosed with black lung but kept working in the mine, bragging all the time about how he wasn't gonna die—no, not him. Last night he was drunk and a train hit him as he was walking home on the railroad tracks. There's not gonna be a penny of compensation. He ended up dying like a dog."

He walked in front of her and the sound of his voice resonated from his back. Shinhye felt the cold of the night on her skin. Stars scattered here and there twinkled in the inky sky as the wind tore the clouds.

"So, why did you come all the way up here?" he asked.

In the dim light of his bedroom he looked older and more tired than when she had seen him last. The room reeked of sweat mixed with a man's body odor. But as she thrust her feet under the filthy blanket, she was surprised to find that the floor was warm.

"I asked you earlier," she said. "To let me sleep here tonight."

Still leaning against the wall, he examined her with eyes full of suspicion, and when their eyes met, he looked down awkwardly as if he were the one in someone else's house.

"I thought I'd never see you again. . . ."

A smile twisted his face. Almost a spasm that made him look like he was laughing at his familiar self.

"That's why I came to find you."

Shinhye smiled, still looking at him. She felt a sharp pain as her parched lips stretched too tight.

"Did you hear what happened to me?"

"Yes, I know you were arrested."

Shinhye couldn't think of anything more to say. He kept pulling on the tip of one of his socks. There was a small hole worn through there, but it wasn't out of embarrassment—just an unconscious habit that made him keep doing it.

"You aren't asking me one thing about what happened at the police station," Shinhye said. "You could at least offer sympathy for what they did to me. I was worried they might arrest you and make you suffer, too, all because of me!"

He finally raised his head.

"Why did those people put me away? You don't seem to know about it, but I'm not an important person. The police know that better than anyone."

That same faint, bitter smile appeared again on his face.

"You were wrong about me from the start," he said. "I don't know if you thought I was a victim of the system, oppressed because I was part of the workers' movement. Or maybe someone who was preparing for a new fight in the future. But I'm not that type. The truth is the opposite. Years ago, when the riots broke out here, I denounced my coworkers. When I was arrested by the police, I told them everything they wanted to know. I sold them all out—all my friends. I'm a filthy, despicable human being because even after all that, I was an informant for the police. That's what I am."

He let out a hopeless sigh. As he pulled at his sock, Shinhye noticed that his thumbnail looked dead—it was completely black.

"The truth is," he said, "I was at the police station, too."

He went on, though it took some effort. "Yesterday morning the detectives came by to take me in. I understood the situation as soon as I got there. At first, they worked on you because they thought they could get something out of you, but since they got nothing and they couldn't just let you go, they tried to make up a story. They asked me to write a statement saying you tried to recruit me."

"So what did you do?"

"I told them I couldn't do that. People may say I'm just a snitch, but I said I wouldn't do it for anything. I told them they could kill me . . . do anything they wanted . . ."

Maybe it was from the heat that warmed her body, but suddenly Shinhye was overcome by sadness, and it felt as if all the strength had drained from her body.

Kim looked at her and said, as if to justify himself:

"They said I was a *fraktsiya*—a spy for the cops—but I never gave them what they wanted. That's the truth."

"Come closer," Shinhye said.

He looked wary and anxious for a moment, but then he got up and awkwardly sat down next to her. His fingers careful, like a child touching something for the first time, he brushed Shinhye's hair and stroked her face. His hand was rough and his fingers calloused, but they softened as if they had thawed.

"What happened to you?" Shinhye asked, gently touching his thumb where the nail was black.

"It's nothing. Just . . . crushed by a support beam at work."

Without a word, she kissed each of his fingers one by one.

"Why don't you leave this place?"

"Why don't I leave?" he said, as if he were talking to himself. There was guarded silence for a moment.

"Well . . . for what reason? I don't know. Maybe out of pride."

He fell silent again, and after a long while he continued slowly and with difficulty:

"People would laugh to hear me talk about pride. Everybody here thinks of me as an idiot. To my fellow miners I'm just a coward and a dirty traitor. As for the police and the bosses who used me—they treat me worse than a dog. And since they don't exactly have it wrong, there's nothing I can do about what they think of me. When the police arrested me back in 1980 during the incident, I was scared—terrified. They made me into something despicable, more lowly than the lowest vermin. I really believed I was worthless. That's why I had no choice but to do whatever they told me."

His voice quavered. Shinhye had rested her head on his shoulder, and she thought she could feel the trembling through her own body. It reminded her of the unbearable suffering buried in her own heart.

"But no matter how much they spit on me and despise me, I'm not leaving this place. No, I *can't* leave. I can't leave here branded as a rat. Not until I've proved to them that I'm not that kind of person. That is the unshakable pride of this man named Kim Gwangbae. You don't understand me, do you?"

"Yes, I understand."

Shinhye slowly stood up. She undid the buttons on her blouse one by one as he watched her every move.

"Take me," Shinhye said.

Her mouth was so dry she spoke with a parched voice.

"Hurry! Don't you understand?"

He approached her slowly, his face hard and contorted. As if he feared that her body would suddenly disappear from before his eyes. She hugged his head. She could smell the faintly fishy scent of the oil that permeated his hair. She was overcome by unbearable pain and sadness, and to resist that terrible pain, she held tightly on to his neck.

SHE HEARD THE SOUND OF A TRAIN SHAKING THE DARKNESS AS IT passed. Her eyes open in the dark, Shinhye listened to the sound as it pressed unceasingly down on her chest. How much time had passed? She got up quietly. A faint light entered through the gap where the blanket hung over the window, revealing the face of Kim Gwangbae soundly asleep, snoring. So as not to wake him, she groped around in the dark to put on her clothes, then grabbed her bag and left the house. She did not look back once as she made her way down the steep path.

It was dawn. Now the darkness was sloughing off a layer at a time, and a corner of the sky had already appeared in the distance, gleaming blue like the back of a fish. Shinhye stopped to look at a single star above her, twinkling in the middle of the sky, holding its place and shining brightly, indifferent to the fact that it would soon be erased by the light of day.

Who could have lit that single unquenchable lamp burning so high above the hill?

Her head tilted back, Shinhye looked at that star for a long time. She had never in her life felt a star so close. Even while she had suffered those terrible things at the police station, and while she'd been with Kim Gwangbae, even at that very moment, the Earth still turned in its orbit, and, high up in space, the lonely star was shining in its place.

In the next moment Shinhye felt a chill, as if she were doused in ice, and felt something from deep inside pierce the confusion in her soul. *This star is there in the sky, and I am here, standing. No one—nothing— can take the place of that star. In my heart, too, is a star that no power in the world can take away. Yes, here I am, alive!* An overwhelming desire to live filled her heart. Suddenly the star seemed to fly right in front of her eyes and explode there, and she found herself bursting into tears for a reason she could not fathom.

The lamp was still hanging in front of the house of the dead, and a fire was burning outside. She went there, as if drawn unconsciously to its warm light. Five or six people stood around the fire, keeping warm, and when she approached, they stepped aside to make room for her. Just like them, she stood in silence, watching the rising flames. The light of the crackling fire dyed their faces red. The firelight flickered, illuminating each face, one after the other, a different expression, a different color. Countless embers floated up and faded into the winter sky. Shinhye suddenly reached into her bag and got the envelope the madam had given her the previous night. She did not know why.

"Could you please give this to the family?"

She handed the envelope to the man who looked the oldest.

"But . . . what is this, miss?"

"It's just money . . . for condolences."

He took the envelope, examined it tentatively, front and back, and looked at Shinhye.

"There's no name on this. Who are you, miss? Did you know Mr. Choi?"

"I . . . someone sent me . . . I . . ."

She turned and hurriedly left without finishing what she had to say. It sounded like someone might be calling out to her, but she didn't look back.

The hoarse whistle of a train pierced the darkness. It would be the 3:05 to Seoul, and she knew that if she hurried, she could catch it. With only her vinyl bag in hand, exactly like the day she'd arrived in the coal town, Shinhye ran toward the station.

Translated by Heinz Insu Fenkl